Praise for
The Christmas Spirits on Tradd Street

"If you prefer your holiday tales with bit of a ghost story, look no further than *The Christmas Spirits on Tradd Street*. It's perfect for fans of *A Christmas Carol* and *Hamilton*, blending a tale of spectral rumors and American Revolutionary history."　　　　　　　　　　*—Entertainment Weekly*

"What a treat to open up a new Tradd Street book by Karen White and disappear into her witty, wonderful, and haunted world. . . . No one does ghosts better than Karen White, and this is one of Tradd Street's best."　　　　　　*—New York Times* bestselling author M. J. Rose

"While this is the sixth in White's Tradd Street series, it can be read on its own, but make time after the holidays to binge read the previous five for more adventures with these characters. . . . A cliff-hanger ending and promise of another book will please avid fans."　　　*—Library Journal*

"This is a fun-filled, festive, and witty read—a welcome, suspenseful story at a busy time of year!"　　　　　　　　　*—Connecticut Post*

"Full of history and details of the American Revolution; White continues her streak of entertaining, well-paced, and expertly told stories of the town of Charleston."　　　　　　　　　　*—The Nerd Daily*

"Overall, an entertaining read. The Christmas theme is very secondary in the book, making it a good read for any time of the year."　　　　　　　　　　　　　　　*—Girly Book Club*

"This page-turner is a little bit spooky and a whole lot of fun."　　　　　　　　　　　　　　*—Grand Strand*

"Series fans will enjoy spending the holidays with Melanie Trenholm. The plot threads move pieces of this long-running saga forward, and the ending suggests that there's more to come."   —*Booklist*

"Christmas spirits from the past come alive in this festive supernatural tale. . . . Adventure meets mystery in this seasonal page-turner."
—*Woman's World*

THE
CHRISTMAS SPIRITS
ON TRADD STREET

KAREN WHITE

Berkley

New York

BERKLEY
An imprint of Penguin Random House LLC
penguinrandomhouse.com

Copyright © 2019 by Harley House Books, LLC
Readers Guide copyright © 2019 by Penguin Random House LLC
Excerpt from *The Last Night in London* copyright © 2020 by Harley House Books, LLC
Penguin Random House supports copyright. Copyright fuels creativity, encourages diverse
voices, promotes free speech, and creates a vibrant culture. Thank you for buying an authorized
edition of this book and for complying with copyright laws by not reproducing, scanning, or
distributing any part of it in any form without permission. You are supporting writers and
allowing Penguin Random House to continue to publish books for every reader.

BERKLEY and the BERKLEY & B colophon are registered trademarks of
Penguin Random House LLC.

ISBN: 9780399584985

The Library of Congress has catalogued the Berkley hardcover edition of this book as follows:

Names: White, Karen (Karen S.), author.
Title: The Christmas spirits on Tradd street / Karen White.
Description: First edition. | New York : Berkley, 2019. | Series: Tradd street ; 6
Identifiers: LCCN 2019005554 | ISBN 9780451475244 (hardcover) |
ISBN 9780698193017 (ebook)
Subjects: LCSH: Christmas stories. | BISAC: FICTION / Contemporary Women. |
FICTION / Ghost. | GSAFD: Ghost stories. | Suspense fiction.
Classification: LCC PS3623.H5776 C49 2019 | DDC 813/.6--dc23
LC record available at https://lccn.loc.gov/2019005554

Berkley hardcover edition / October 2019
Berkley trade paperback edition / October 2020

Printed in the United States of America
1 3 5 7 9 10 8 6 4 2

Cover art by Andrew Haines
Cover design by Sarah Oberrender

To the real Rich Kobylt, who allows me
to use his name, and who actually wears a belt.

Acknowledgments

I am full of gratitude for my editor, Cindy Hwang, and the other amazing people at Penguin Random House whose enthusiasm and dedication to all the steps in getting my books into readers' hands are so very much appreciated. I couldn't do this without you!

As always, thanks to my first readers, Susan Crandall and Wendy Wax, for gallantly reading every word I write and for constantly challenging me to be a better writer. Thank you for your friendship.

And a huge thank-you to James Del Greco, RN, MSN, for allowing me to use your name for one of my favorite new characters in this book. You won a raffle and were so kind to let me use my imagination to sculpt your character into one I'm sure my readers will love as much as I do. Note to readers: All aspects of the character (except physical description) are completely fictional and simply a figment of the author's imagination.

Last, but certainly not least, thanks to my readers who have fallen in love with Melanie and Jack and the rest of the characters who populate the Tradd Street series. The series was originally supposed to be only two books, but you have inspired me to make it seven. Yes, there will be one more! Sign up for my newsletter at karen-white.com so you'll get the scoop first.

THE
CHRISTMAS SPIRITS
ON TRADD STREET

CHAPTER 1

Smoky silhouettes of church spires stamped against the bruised skies of a Charleston morning give testament to the reason why it's called the Holy City. The steepled skyline at dawn is a familiar sight for early risers who enjoy a respite from the heat and humidity in summer, or appreciate the beauty of the sunrise through the Cooper River Bridge, or like hearing the chirps and calls of the thousands of birds and insects that populate our corner of the world.

Others, like me, awaken early only to shorten the night, to quiet the secret stirrings of the restless dead who wander during the darkest hours between sunset and sunrise.

I lay on my side, Jack's arm resting protectively around my waist, my own arm thrown around the soft fur of General Lee's belly. His snoring and my husband's soft breathing were the only sounds in the old house, despite its being currently inhabited by two adults, three dogs, a teenage girl, and twenty-month-old twins. I never counted the myriad spirits who passed peacefully down the house's lofty corridors. Over the past several years I'd extricated the not-so-nice ones and made my peace with the others, who were content to simply exist alongside us.

That's what had awakened me. The quiet. No, that wasn't right. It was more the absence of sound. Like the held breath between the pull of a trigger and the propulsion of the bullet.

Being careful not to awaken Jack or General Lee, I slowly disentangled myself from the bedsheets, watching as General Lee assumed my former position next to Jack. Jack barely stirred and I considered for a moment whether I should be insulted. I picked up my iPhone and shut off the alarm, which was set for five a.m.—noting it was four forty-six—then crossed the room to my old-fashioned alarm clock, which I kept just in case. Jack had made me get rid of the additional two I'd once had stationed around the room. He'd accused me of trying to wake the dead each morning. As if I had to try.

Since I was a little girl, the spirits of the dearly departed had been trying to talk to me, to involve me in their unfinished business. I'd found ways—most often involving singing an ABBA song—to drown out their voices with some success, but every once in a while, one voice was louder than the others. Usually because a spirit was shouting in my ear or shoving me down the stairs, making it impossible to ignore regardless of how much I wanted to.

I stumbled into my bathroom using the flashlight on my phone, silently cursing my half sister, Jayne, and my best friend, Dr. Sophie Wallen-Arasi, for being the cause of my predawn ramblings. They had taken it upon themselves to get me fit and healthy after the birth of the twins, JJ (for Jack Junior) and Sarah. This involved feeding me food I wouldn't give my dog—although I'd tried and he'd turned up his nose and walked away—and forcing me to go for a run most mornings.

Although I was more a jogger than a runner, the exercise required lots of energy that shouldn't be provided by powdered doughnuts—according to Sophie—and made me sweat more than I thought necessary, especially in the humid summer months, when bending down to tie my shoes caused perspiration to drip down my face and neck.

Barely awake, I pulled on the running pants that Nola had given me for my last birthday, telling me that they had the dual purposes of being fashionable *and* functional, sucking everything in and making one's backside look as if it belonged to a lifelong runner. I tried to tell Jayne and Sophie that these wonder pants made the actual running part un-necessary, but they'd simply stared at me without blinking before re-turning to their conversation regarding lowering their times for the next Bridge Run, scheduled for the spring.

I tiptoed back into the bedroom, noticing as I pulled down the hem of my T-shirt that it was on inside out, and paused by the bed to look at my husband of less than two years. My chest did the little contracting thing it had been doing since I'd first met bestselling true-crime-history author Jack Trenholm. I'd thought then that he was too handsome, too charming, too opinionated, and way too annoying to be anything to me other than someone to be admired from afar or at least kept at arm's dis-tance. Luckily for me, he'd disagreed.

My gaze traveled to the video baby monitor we kept on the bedside table. Sarah slept neatly on her side, her stuffed bunny—a gift from Sophie—tucked under her arm, her other stuffed animals arranged around the crib in a specific order that only Sarah—and I—understood. I'd had to explain to Jack that the animals had been arranged by fur patterns and colors, going from lightest to darkest. I'm sure I did the same thing when I was a child, because, I'd explained, it was important to make order of the world.

In the adjacent crib, Sarah's twin, JJ, slept on his back with his arms and legs flung out at various angles, his stuffed animals and his favorite whisk—even I couldn't explain his attachment to this particular kitchen utensil—tossed in disarray around his small body. My fingers twitched, and I had to internally recite the words to "Dancing Queen" backward to keep me from entering the nursery and lining up the toys in the bed and tucking my little son in a corner of the crib with a blanket over him.

It was a skill I'd learned at Jayne's insistence. She was a professional nanny, which meant—I suppose—that she knew best, and she insisted that my need for order was borderline OCD and not necessarily the best influence for the children. There was absolutely nothing wrong with my need for order, as it had helped me survive a childhood with an alcoholic father and an absent mother, but I loved my children too much to dismiss Jayne's concerns completely.

I would not, however, retire my labeling gun and had taken proactive measures by keeping it hidden so it wouldn't "disappear" as my last two had.

As I stared at my sweet babies on the monitor, my heart constricted again, leaving me breathless for a moment as I considered how very fortunate I was to have found Jack—or, as he insisted, to have been found by him—and then to have these two beautiful children. An added and welcome bonus to the equation was Jack's sixteen-year-old daughter, Nola, whom I loved as if she were my own child despite her insistence on removing my three main food groups—sugar, carbs, and chocolate— from the kitchen.

"Good morning, beautiful," Jack mumbled, two sleepy dark blue eyes staring up at me. General Lee emitted a snuffling snore. "Going to work?"

Before I was married, I'd always risen before dawn to be the first person in the offices of Henderson House Realty on Broad Street. But now I had a reason to stay in bed, and he was lying there looking so much more appealing than a run through the streets of Charleston. Of course, spending the night in the dungeon at the Old Exchange building was also more appealing than a run, but still.

"Not yet. Meeting Jayne for a run." I stood by the bed and leaned down to place a kiss on Jack's lips, lingering long enough to see if he would give any indication that he wanted me to crawl back in. Instead his eyes closed again as he moved General Lee closer to his chest, giving me an odd pang of jealousy.

I quietly closed the bedroom door and paused in the upstairs hallway, listening. Even the ticking of the old grandfather clock seemed muffled, the sound suffocated by something unseen. Something waiting. The night-lights that lined the hallway—a leftover from when Jayne lived with us and a concession to her crippling fear of the dark and the things that hid within—gave me a clear view of Nola's closed bedroom door.

She'd been sleeping in the guest room, as I'd decided right after the twins' first birthday party in March that her bedroom needed to be redecorated. I felt a tug of guilt as I walked past it to the stairs, remembering the shadowy figure I'd seen in Nola's bedroom window in a photograph taken by one of Sophie's preservation students, Meghan

Black. She was excavating the recently discovered cistern in the rear garden and had taken the photograph and shown it to Jack and me. We'd both seen the shadowy figure of a man in old-fashioned clothing holding what looked to be a piece of jewelry. But I'd been the only one to notice the face in Nola's window.

Having recently dealt with a particularly nasty and vengeful spirit at Jayne's house on South Battery, I hadn't found the strength yet to grapple with another. Despite promises to be open and honest with each other, I hadn't told Jack, bargaining with myself that I'd bring it up just as soon as I thought I could mentally prepare myself. That had been eight months ago, and all I'd done was move Nola into the guest room and then interview a succession of decorators.

I stifled a yawn. *Just one more week,* I thought. One more week of working every possible hour trying to make my sales quota at Henderson House Realty, trying to put myself on the leaderboard once more. It was important not just for the sense of pride and accomplishment it gave me, but also because we needed the money.

Then I'd have enough energy and brain cells to be able to figure out who these new spirits were and to make them go away. Preferably without a fight. Then I'd tell Jack what I'd seen and that I'd already taken care of the problem so he wouldn't have to be worried. He had enough on his plate already, working with a new publisher on a book about my family and how Jayne had come to own her house on South Battery.

I entered the kitchen, my stomach rumbling as I reached behind the granola and quinoa boxes in the pantry for my secret stash of doughnuts. But instead of grasping the familiar brown paper bag, I found myself pulling out a box of nutrition bars—no doubt as tasty as the cardboard in which they were packaged. Taped to the front was a note in Nola's handwriting:

Try these instead! They've got chocolate and 9 grams of protein!

Happy visions of running upstairs and pulling Nola from her bed earlier than she'd probably been awake since infancy were the only reason I didn't break down and weep. The grandfather clock chimed, telling me I was already late, so I gave one last-minute look to see if I could spot my doughnut bag, then left the house through the back door without eating anything. If I passed out from starvation halfway through my run, Nola might feel sorry enough for me to bring a doughnut.

I stopped on the back steps, suddenly aware that the silence had followed me outside. No birds chirped; no insects hummed. No sounds of street traffic crept into the formerly lush garden that my father had painstakingly restored from the original Loutrel Briggs plans. When an ancient cistern had been discovered after the heavy spring rains had swallowed up a large section of the garden, Sophie had swooped in and declared it an archaeological dig and surrounded it with yellow caution tape. Several months later, we were still staring at a hole behind our house. And I was still feeling the presence of an entity that continued to elude me but that haunted my peripheral vision. A shadow that disappeared every time I turned a corner, the scent of rot the only hint that it had been there at all.

Walking backward to avoid turning my back on the gaping hole, I made my way to the front of the house, tripping only twice on the uneven flagstones that were as much a part of Charleston's South of Broad neighborhood as were wrought-iron gates and palmetto bugs.

"There you are!" shouted a voice from across the street. "I thought you were standing me up."

I squinted at the figure standing on the curb, regretting not putting in my contacts. I really didn't need them all the time, and not wearing them when I ran saved me from seeing my reflection without makeup in the bathroom mirror this early in the morning.

"Good morning, Jayne," I grumbled, making sure she was aware of how unhappy I was to be going for a run. Especially when I had a much better alternative waiting for me in my bedroom.

I was already starting to perspire at the thought of the four-mile jog in front of me. Despite its being early November, and although we'd been teased by Mother Nature with days chilly enough that we'd had to pull out our wool sweaters, the mercury had taken another surprise leap, and both the temperature and the dew point had risen, as if summer was returning to torture us for a bit.

Even though Jayne had already jogged several blocks in the heat and humidity from her house on South Battery, she was barely sweating and her breath came slowly and evenly. We'd only recently discovered each other, our shared mother having been led to believe that her second daughter, born eight years after me, had died at birth. Jayne and I had grown close in the ensuing months, our bonding most likely accelerated by the fact that we shared the ability to communicate with the dead, a trait inherited from our mother.

"Which way do you want to go this morning?" she said, jogging in place and looking way too perky.

"Is back inside an option?"

She laughed as if I'd been joking, then began to jog toward East Bay.

I struggled to catch up, pulling alongside her as she ran down the middle of the street. Dodging traffic this time of day was easier than risking a turned ankle on the ancient uneven sidewalks. "Will Detective Riley be joining us this morning?" I panted.

Her cheeks flushed, and I was sure it wasn't from exertion. "I don't know. I haven't spoken to him in a week."

"Did you have a fight?"

"You could say that." Her emotions seemed to fuel her steps, and she sprinted ahead. Only when she realized she'd left me behind did she slow down so I could catch up.

"What . . . happened?" I was finding it hard to breathe and talk at the same time, but I needed to know. I'd introduced Jayne to Detective Thomas Riley, and they'd been a couple ever since Jayne, our mother, and I had sent to the light several unsettled spirits who'd been inhabiting her house earlier in the year.

"I told him I wanted to go public with my abilities to help people communicate with loved ones. He said it was a bad idea because there are a lot of crazies out there who'd be knocking on my door."

I looked at her askance. "Funny, he didn't . . . seem to . . . have such qualms . . . when he asked me about some of his . . . unsolved cases."

I'd recently considered working with Detective Riley on a case involving a coed who'd gone missing from her College of Charleston dorm room in 1997.

"That's because you're working incognito. I want to advertise. And Mother said she'd be happy to work alongside me. She thinks you should also go public and work with us." She sprinted ahead again, but this time I was sure it was because she didn't want me to respond. Not that I could have since my lungs were nearly bursting.

I doggedly pursued her, turning left on East Bay and almost catching up as we neared Queen Street, dodging the fermenting restaurant garbage waiting for pickup on the sidewalk. My feet dragged, the humidity seeming to make my legs heavier, and my breath came in choking gasps. My stomach rumbled and I quickly did a mental recalculation of my route. In an effort at self-preservation, I took a left on Hasell, not even wondering how long it would take Jayne to notice I was missing. With my destination in mind, I jogged toward King Street and took a right, my steps much lighter now as I headed toward my just reward.

Catching the green light on Calhoun, I nearly sprinted across the street toward Glazed Gourmet Donuts, almost expecting Jayne to show up just as I reached the door and yank me away. Instead I was merely greeted by the heavenly scent of freshly made doughnuts and the delicious smell of coffee gently embracing me and inviting me inside. I stood in the entryway for a moment, inhaling deeply, until I heard a cough from behind me.

I turned to apologize for blocking the doorway but stopped with my mouth halfway open. Not because the tall, dark-haired man standing behind me was a contender for *People* magazine's Sexiest Man Alive, or because he was smiling at me with more than just casual interest, his dark brown eyes lit with some inner amusement. Nor was it because he wore tight-fitting running clothes that accentuated his muscled chest and that he breathed slightly faster than the average pedestrian—although, like Jayne, he appeared to be barely perspiring. I stared at him because I'd seen him before. Not just that morning, not just in the doughnut shop, but around town several times in the past few weeks as

I jogged down the streets of Charleston or ran errands or traveled to various house showings in the city.

It hadn't struck me as odd until right at that moment, when we were standing only inches apart. Charleston was a small city, and it was inevitable that I'd run into the same person occasionally. But not every day. I blinked once, wondering what else about him captivated my attention, and realized what it was just as the door opened behind the man and Jayne appeared, looking flustered and not a little bit annoyed.

"I knew I'd find you here," she said, walking past the man to stand in front of me and no doubt try to intimidate me. Which was hard to do considering we were the exact same height.

I looked at the man again. "Are you related to Marc Longo?" I asked, half hoping he'd say no. Marc was my cousin Rebecca's husband, and Jack's nemesis after having stolen Jack's book idea. We were still trying to recover from the financial and professional setback it had caused Jack. Marc was also a boil on the behind of our collective well-being, as he was currently trying to get us to allow in our house on Tradd Street the filming of the movie based on the novel he'd stolen from Jack. Because he was that kind of insufferable jerk. The fact that I'd once dated him didn't endear him to Jack, either.

"I am," he said, a shadow briefly settling behind his eyes. He held out a slim hand to me. "I'm Anthony Longo, Marc's younger brother. And you're Melanie Middleton."

"Melanie Trenholm now," I corrected. I hesitated for a moment before placing my hand in his.

He grinned. "Don't worry. The only things my older brother and I share are our last name and our parents."

Turning to Jayne, he said, "And you two beautiful women must be related. Twins?"

I almost smiled at the compliment but didn't. Because I was certain he already knew exactly who we were to each other. Being in the same family wasn't the only thing Anthony Longo shared with his brother.

Jayne lifted her hand to shake. Her lips worked to form words, and before I could clamp my hand over her mouth, she said, "You have very dark hair. It's brown." She blinked rapidly before dropping her hand. "I mean . . . yes, you have hair. Well, it's nice to meet you." Her face flushed a dark red. Turning to me, she said, "I'm going to get us some coffee and doughnuts."

"Sorry," I said, watching her departing back. "My sister, Jayne, hasn't had a lot of experience with the opposite sex. She seems to get tongue-tied when dealing with attractive men."

He laughed, a deep, chest-rumbling sound. "I accept the compliment, then."

I took a step back, as much to put distance between us as to allow a couple to enter the shop. I was reserving judgment, wanting to hate him on sight, but there was something likable about him. He was charming, like Marc, but without the smarmy self-love that Marc exuded from every pore. I met Anthony's forthright gaze. "Have you been following me?"

His eyes widened, and I wondered if I'd taken him by surprise with my candor or if he was just pretending. Instead of answering, he said, "Why don't we sit so we can chat?" He held out his hand toward an open table, and I led the way.

We sat just as Jayne approached with a bag and two coffees. Anthony immediately stood and took the coffees from her while Jayne clutched the doughnut bag close to her. "You don't eat doughnuts?" she said to Anthony, then quickly shook her head. "I mean, you don't have doughnuts."

He grinned warmly and I wanted to kick him to tell him being attractive and charming wasn't going to help matters.

"I've got a delicious protein shake waiting for me at home, so I'm good, thanks."

"She won't share," Jayne forced out, clutching the bag even tighter. We were going to have to work harder on social interactions with men. I'd thought that her relationship with Thomas Riley was a good sign that she'd been cured of acute awkwardness, but I'd been wrong. It apparently was on a man-to-man basis.

Anthony's smile faded slightly as he glanced at me, as if needing reassurance that Jayne wouldn't bite.

"She's probably referring to me. I don't share my doughnuts, and if anyone tries to take one, he will lose a finger." I didn't smile, trying to show him that I wasn't joking.

I took a sip from my coffee while eyeing the bag expectantly, but Jayne kept it clenched closely to her chest, no doubt planning to hold the doughnuts for ransom until I finished the run. "So," I said, "why have you been stalking me?"

Anthony quirked an eyebrow. "Stalking? Hardly. More like looking for an opportunity to approach you that wouldn't be noticed by any of your friends, family, or coworkers. It's very hard to do. You're a moving target."

I glanced around, glad we were in a public place and that Jayne was with me. Alarm bells were starting to go off inside my head, the same ones that rang out when Sophie or my handyman, Rich Kobylt, asked to talk to me. It was usually something bad—like wood-boring beetles in the dining room floor—and always something I didn't want to hear, such as the cost of the repair.

"So why did you want to see me?" I asked.

"I'd like to make a deal with you."

"A deal?" Jayne repeated.

Anthony leaned forward. "You may or may not be aware that I own Magnolia Ridge Plantation—or, as it's known now, Gallen Hall. It was formerly owned by the Vanderhorst family—the same family who once owned your house on Tradd Street. It was purchased at auction by my grandfather back in the twenties, sold shortly afterward, and then bought by Marc a few years ago. My grandfather was the man found buried beneath your fountain, if you recall."

Like I could forget. I kept still, trying not to remember the menacing ghost of Joseph Longo, or how his body came to be buried in my garden along with that of former owner Louisa Vanderhorst. "Okay," I said, not sure where this was heading but fairly certain I didn't want to go there.

"You may also recall that Marc and I started a winery venture together a few years ago, using the land around the plantation."

"Vaguely." The alarm bells were getting louder now. Jack had recently read to me—somewhat gleefully—an article in the *Post and Courier* about a Longo family member accusing Marc of swindling and threatening legal action.

"Yes, well, my dear brother knew the land wasn't good for a vineyard—a fact he kept from me when he told me from the goodness of his heart he was going to allow me to buy out his share and give me a good deal." His hands formed themselves into fists. "A good deal on worthless land."

"That wasn't very nice," Jayne said, her tone similar to the one she used when settling disputes between the twins. And Jack and me. She was a nanny, after all.

"You could say that," Anthony said, giving Jayne an appreciative grin. She blushed, then resumed her deliberate breathing.

"So what does that have to do with me? He's married to my cousin, but we're not close."

"I know. Which is why I was thinking we needed to talk." He leaned very close. "It seems we both have a bone to pick with my brother."

"We do? If you're referring to Jack's career, he just signed a new two-book deal and is hard at work on the new book. Marc gave us a setback, but that's behind us."

"Is it? I thought Marc wanted to film his movie in your house."

"He does. And I believe Jack told him where he could file that idea."

Anthony smiled smugly. "I'm sure he did. I've never had the pleasure of meeting your husband, but I've heard Marc rant about him often enough to know they're not friends."

Jayne coughed.

"You could say that," I said. "Which is really why we're putting all of that in the past and moving forward."

"Yes, well, too bad Marc didn't get that memo."

The alarm bells were now clanging so loudly I was sure everyone in the restaurant could hear. "What do you mean?"

He leaned in a little closer. "Marc has lots of . . . connections. Has a lot of influence, even in the publishing world. Jack's new contract might not be as ironclad as you'd like to think."

"That's ridiculous," I hissed. "He's signed it and received the advance. He's working on the book now and his publisher has big plans for it."

Anthony shook his head slowly. "Doesn't matter to Marc. He has . . . ways to get what he wants."

"And what does he want?"

"Your house."

"My house? We're not selling. Ever. We've gone through quite a lot for that house." I thought of the ghost of Louisa Vanderhorst, who watched over us, the scent of roses alerting us of her presence. Of old Nevin Vanderhorst, who'd left the house to me in his will, knowing long before I did that the house and I were meant to be together for as long as I lived. Or, as Jack had said at our wedding in the back garden, perhaps even longer.

Anthony smiled, but it wasn't friendly. "Tell me, Melanie. Would you be financially solvent if it weren't for Jack's income? I'm sure he's getting royalties from his earlier books, but without a new book, sales of his older books peter out, don't they?"

I thought of how we'd had to borrow money from Nola, who had made a few lucrative sales of music she'd written, to keep the house. It was a loan, and we were still working on paying it back.

I started to say no, but Jayne kicked me under the table. "It's none of your business," she said, speaking slowly as if to make sure the right words came out.

"Right," I agreed. "It's none of your business." I stood, and Jayne stood, too.

Anthony slid his chair back and stood as well, blocking our way to the door. "What if I said I could help you outmaneuver Marc and make a lot of money at the same time?"

"What do you mean?"

"Marc found something that's convinced him that there is something valuable hidden in the mausoleum at the Gallen Hall cemetery. He can't get access, though."

"Why?" I asked, although with the mention of the mausoleum, I was afraid I knew why.

His voice very quiet, he said, "I know that you can speak to the dead."

Jayne inhaled quickly, but I kept my eyes on Anthony. "I don't know where you heard that. . . ."

"Rebecca, of course. I know she has premonitions in her dreams—she's even told me of a few she had about me. But she said your powers are much stronger, that you can actually talk to the dead."

"Well, she's mistaken." I slid my chair up to the table so I could inch my way around Anthony to access the door and saw Jayne do the same thing. "I've got to go. Sorry I can't help you."

We'd made it only a few feet before he said, "I heard about that cistern in your back garden—how several grad students assigned to the excavation refuse to return to the site. I was curious, so I did some digging. Do you know where the bricks came from?"

A chill pricked at the base of my neck as I recalled the apparition of the man in the photograph standing by the edge of the gaping hole and holding what appeared to be a piece of jewelry. And the menacing aura that had pervaded my house and yard ever since the cistern was discovered. "No," I said, my voice wavering only a little. "And I don't care."

We'd made it to the door when Anthony called out to us, "They're from an older mausoleum in the Gallen Hall cemetery. I thought you'd want to know. Just in case."

I turned to face him. "Just in case what?"

"Just in case you find something . . . unexpected in your cistern."

Jayne pushed the door open, then propelled me into the warm morning air with a gentle shove to my back. I turned around to see whether Anthony would follow us out and found myself staring at the glass door of the shop. Except instead of seeing my own reflection, I saw the clear specter of a gentleman in what appeared to be an old-fashioned cravat and jacket staring back at me with black, empty sockets.

CHAPTER 2

I had just finished drying my hair in the bathroom when Jack walked in, his pajama pants riding low on his slim hips, his defined abs under smooth skin making me almost drop the blow-dryer. His dark hair stuck up in a tousled fashion that I'm sure models had to work at, his beard stubble making him the perfect dictionary picture for the definition of *devastating.*

He turned on the shower and slid off his pants, his gaze in the mirror's reflection never leaving mine as he walked up behind me. Lifting my hair, he pressed a warm kiss to the back of my neck. "Could this gorgeous creature really be my wife?"

It took me a moment to find my voice. "You like my dress?" It wasn't what I'd planned on saying, but Jayne had apparently rubbed off on me.

"Mmm," he said, burying his nose in my hair as his hands skimmed over the red fabric that clung to my hips. "I like what's in it the best."

I gasped as his teeth found my earlobe. "You better not be practicing dialogue for your book."

He continued nibbling at the delicate skin of my ear. "I do like to re-create dialogue as authentically as possible." He used his hands to

I nodded, my gaze slipping down to his lips, both because I couldn't meet his eyes and because his lips were so much more interesting than the conversation. "So we wouldn't need the money Marc's throwing in our faces for us to agree to film his movie here."

"Not right now. That could change, of course, but I'd rather have all the unpleasant ghosts you've gotten rid of come back to rattle their chains than agree to that."

My eyes shot back to meet his. "Don't say that out loud. You never know who might be listening."

Cocking his head to the side just like JJ did when watching Sarah babble at shadowy corners, Jack said, "Is there something you're not telling me?"

"Maybe."

He quirked an eyebrow. *Just one more week,* I thought to myself. Just one more week of domestic peace and contentment. One more week to get my life in order before I would attempt to discover what was lurking in my backyard. And who, or what, had taken up residence in Nola's bedroom.

"'Maybe'?" Jack repeated.

"I can't tell you about your Christmas present. Or am I not allowed to keep it a secret?"

He kissed me softly on the lips. "You can try. But I have ways of finding out all of your secrets."

"Do you, now?" I asked.

His phone, left on the counter, beeped. He glanced at it expectantly before turning back to me, but not before I'd seen the shadow of disappointment cloud his eyes.

"Who was it?" I asked, although what I really needed to know was who it *wasn't*. Right before we'd discovered that Marc had stolen Jack's book idea and had already signed a huge publishing deal, Jack's agent and editor had stopped returning his phone calls. For the second time that day, alarm bells began clanging inside my head.

He paused for a moment before answering. "It was my mother. I'll call her back."

"Were you expecting someone el—" I began, my words swallowed by his kiss.

"Let's find out if this dress is waterproof." His words were muffled against my neck as he dragged me into the shower, my senses perilously close to abandoning me completely, but still clinging to me enough to make me wonder what he was avoiding telling me.

Women's voices came from inside my mother's Legare Street house as I pushed open the front door. The house had belonged to her family for generations, our ownership interrupted for a few years by a Texas junk-yard millionaire following my parents' divorce. My formerly estranged mother, retired opera diva Ginette Prioleau, and Sophie were still work-ing hard to erase the "creative touches" inflicted on the house by the previous owner, but at least the house was now back in the family. My mother had remarried my father on the same day I'd married Jack, and my parents now appeared to be living in marital bliss in the home in which I was born and had lived for the first six years of my life.

I followed the voices to the front parlor, where the glorious floor-to-ceiling stained glass window sparkled in the morning sunshine. A few years before, Jack and I had discovered the secret hidden in the glass that led us to unraveling an old family mystery, but now all I could see was the beauty of the window and the way it seemed to draw me into the parlor. Or maybe it was because of the sudden drop in temperature or the slight scent of Vanilla Musk.

There were about fifteen women seated in the parlor on the sofas and chairs, the furniture recently having been rescued from the leopard and zebra prints it had been forced to wear by the former occupants and now re-covered in historically accurate (and contemporarily expensive) dam-ask and silk upholstery in shades of cream and pale blue.

I knew I'd find Veronica Farrell in the group even before I caught sight of her red hair. The presence of her dead sister's perfume had al-ready alerted me that she'd be there, although I was surprised to find her at the Ashley Hall Christmas Progressive Dinner fund-raiser meeting.

Her daughter, Lindsey, was a close friend and classmate of Nola's, but ever since I'd flat-out refused to help her communicate with her deceased sister, Adrienne—and then been more or less threatened by her husband, Michael, to let it be—I hadn't seen her. Even at school functions, we always seemed to be on opposite sides of the room, although I could never be sure by whose design.

"Mellie," my mother said, her trim figure floating toward me in a sea of blue silk chiffon, looking much younger than her sixty-six years. She and Jack were the only two people allowed to call me Mellie. It had once grated on my nerves, which was why Jack had adopted it, but now I found it endearing. She kissed me on the cheek as my mother-in-law, the perpetually elegant owner of Trenholm Antiques, Amelia Trenholm, stood and greeted me with a warm smile.

The two women had been friends since childhood, both attending Ashley Hall, so it made sense that they'd be on the committee. What didn't make sense was the way they had each taken hold of one of my arms as if they were afraid I might escape. I smelled cinnamon and coffee, and I wondered if they were trying to keep me from bolting toward the refreshments set up on a Chippendale mahogany sideboard.

All gazes were fixed on me as my mother began to speak. "Ladies, may I please have your attention? Now that my daughter is here, I thought we'd go ahead and get started with a major announcement."

I gently tried to pull away, but the two women held me tight. I wondered if escaping would be worth the scene and the comments I'd hear for years.

My mother continued. "Melanie's dear friend Dr. Sophie Wallen-Arasi, a professor of historic preservation at the college, couldn't be with us today, but she has graciously volunteered both herself and her expertise, along with my daughter Melanie, to be in charge of the wreath-making workshop this year."

She paused for the surprised gasps from the audience, mine being the loudest.

Mother continued. "She has also agreed to spearhead the decorations for the host homes for the dinner, promising to ensure that all materials and methods for both the wreaths and the decorations will be authentic and period-specific to the Revolutionary War era, which is our theme for the progressive dinner this year. As you all know, the workshop was a major fund-raiser last year, and with these two talented ladies at the helm, we expect to double our proceeds."

I turned to my mother to express my true feelings regarding historic wreath making but my words were drowned out by the round of applause. I'd never suspected that such slender and well-coiffed women could make that kind of noise.

The arrival of another latecomer turned everyone's heads. My cousin Rebecca Longo wore her signature pink—pink dress, pink shoes, and pink eyeglasses frames. I was pretty sure she didn't have a prescription inside the frames but was using them merely as a fashion statement. In her arms, and dressed in a coordinating pink dress, was her dog, Pucci. Pucci and General Lee had had a short-lived yet torrid affair that had resulted in a litter of puppies, two of which—Porgy and Bess—now belonged to Nola. They technically belonged to Jack and me, since they were a wedding gift, but when Nola was home they devoted their lives to following her around as if she'd bathed in beef broth and they never let her out of their sight. They even went into a mini mourning period each day when Nola left for school.

"Sorry I'm late," Rebecca announced. "I had to cook three filets mignons before I found a temperature Pucci would eat. I'm exhausted and it's barely ten o'clock!" With a heavy sigh she gracefully took a seat on one of the new sofas, smiling brightly at the women around her.

"Any alumnae could sign up for the committee," Amelia said quietly, anticipating my question.

I sent a weak smile in Rebecca's direction and she beamed back at me. I found some satisfaction in the pallor of her skin, caused by the sun shooting orange light through the stained glass and transforming Rebecca's blond hair to rust.

My mother turned to me. "Why don't you get seated so we can start going over the subcommittees and deciding who will head the entire fund-raiser?"

"I nominate Sophie," I said through gritted teeth.

"Sadly, she never attended Ashley Hall," my mother said, pushing me toward a settee.

I was already in front of it before I realized the other occupant was Veronica Farrell, and it was too late to change directions and find another seat without appearing rude. I liked Veronica and wouldn't have minded sitting next to her. It was the spectral form of her sister standing behind her that made me want to sit anywhere except that corner of the room.

Amelia began walking around the room handing out sign-up forms. "Please write your name on the top of the page if you're interested in being in charge of the fund-raiser. Then, at the bottom, please put your name beneath your three top choices of committees that you would like to participate in, and add an asterisk if you'd like to be the committee head. We already have two fabulous committee heads for wreath decorating, but I'm sure they would appreciate your help. And we expect everyone to sign up for at least two—even if you're the chair of one." Amelia smiled at me, her eyes focused on the middle of my forehead, as if she was afraid to meet my eyes and acknowledge that she'd been a part of my railroading. I was sure it was all my mother's machinations, but I held Amelia guilty by association.

Veronica leaned over to me. "I'm going to sign up to be the decorating committee chair, so if you sign up for that committee, I'll make sure you have the easier tasks. I know how busy you are." She smiled and I smiled back, hoping she wasn't being nice to me because she wasn't done asking for my help.

"Thanks," I said.

A strong whiff of Vanilla Musk wafted over us. Veronica's head jerked up, so I knew she smelled it, too. I quickly looked down at the paper in my lap, pretending to study it.

"She's here, isn't she?" Veronica whispered. "Whenever I smell her perfume, I know she's near."

"Who's here?" I asked, trying to sound uninterested.

Veronica simply stared at me, a look of reproach in her eyes. After a moment, she said, "You probably already know this, but your sister,

Jayne, has been talking with Detective Riley to help with the reopened investigation into Adrienne's murder. As a mother and a sister, I'm sure you understand why I'm doing this. I can't accept not knowing what happened—not if there are other avenues out there to solving this crime." She smiled softly. "I just wanted to tell you that because I didn't want any awkwardness between us. Our daughters are good friends, and we'll be seeing a lot of each other. I'd like us to be friends, too."

"I'd like that, too," I said, sensing the presence moving away, and resisted a huge sigh of relief. "So," I said, eager to change the subject, "I guess I'll sign up for the decorating committee, then. Although wouldn't you think being in charge of the wreath-decorating workshop is punishment enough?"

Her laugh came out as a snort, bringing back memories of working together on a history project in college. I remembered I'd liked that about her, the fact that she could have such an ungracious laugh, but one that other people couldn't help but smile at because it showed real joy and happiness. I remembered, too, envying her that laugh, because at that point in my life I hadn't had a lot of reasons to laugh.

I tried to focus on the rest of the meeting, wondering how soon I would be free to mastermind a devious plot to get back at Sophie for volunteering me for the workshop. My mind wandered as I considered putting laminate over the wood floors in my dining room. Or giving her a litter of puppies.

My mother's voice interrupted my reverie. "Anyone else want to volunteer to host one of the dinner courses?" She looked pointedly at me, but I pretended I hadn't heard the question. She knew how a lot of activity in the house could sometimes cause the spirits to become restless. And there were two spirits I wasn't eager to awaken.

Veronica raised her hand. "My house is a Victorian on Queen Street. I'd be happy to open it up for one of the courses."

Amelia made a note on her clipboard, smiling her approval at Veronica. "Thank you. That gives us five houses. We just need one more house to host the main course. Perhaps one of the grander and restored homes.

It would sell more tickets, and the more tickets we sell, the more money for Ashley Hall."

There were murmurs of assent, and I could feel more than one set of eyes on me. I concentrated on recrossing my legs and straightening my skirt, trying not to be obvious as I scanned the side tables for where the coffee cake might be hidden, having already checked on the sideboard and seen only coffee cups and the tall coffee server. Veronica's half-eaten piece sat on the coffee table in front of us, and it took all of my willpower to resist reaching over with my fingers and popping it in my mouth.

Rebecca stood. "Marc and I would like to donate twenty thousand dollars to the fund-raiser." She smiled broadly as she turned to accept the applause, her gaze finally settling on me. I began to feel sick. "With just one condition."

She waited for a prolonged and very uncomfortable moment while my stomach roiled.

Without moving her gaze from mine, she said, "We will donate the money provided that the Trenholms will agree to host one of the courses. Not to put the burden all on Melanie, I promise to help her with the decorating."

There was another surprisingly loud round of applause amid murmurings about Rebecca's generosity and how such an offer would be impossible to refuse. I didn't know what I found more horrifying—the idea of pink garlands festooning my beautiful Adams mantels and a pink-frosted Christmas tree in the front parlor window for all the neighbors to see, or the idea of all the agitated spirits shaken awake.

"I . . ." I began, then stopped, realizing how futile protesting would be.

"Thank you, Melanie," my mother said, leading another round of applause, which sounded more and more like nails being hammered into a coffin.

She turned back to the room. "I believe that concludes our meeting, ladies. Please make sure I have all the committee forms, and please be checking your e-mail for the name of our new fund-raising chairperson and which committees you've been assigned to. Thank you all for coming."

As the other women began to gather their things and say good-bye while thanking Rebecca as if she'd just found a cure for cancer, I stayed where I was, torn between strangling my cousin and faking my death and moving to another country. Because where there was Rebecca being generous and kind, there were ulterior motives.

"You okay?" Veronica asked softly.

I sent her a grateful glance. "I will be. Just as soon as I find a way to make my cousin disappear."

She grinned wryly. "Yeah, I could probably help you with that. What's with all that pink?" She picked up her plate, and I watched as she crumpled the remainder of her cake into a napkin. Veronica continued. "I'm getting bad vibes about her decorating skills. Want me to volunteer to help?"

I nodded enthusiastically. "Please. Maybe I can hold her down while you put normal Christmas decorations that don't resemble cotton candy around the house."

She snorted, then abruptly stopped as Rebecca approached, her expression managing to appear chagrined. "Will you excuse us for a moment, Veronica? I need to speak with my cousin."

With a little smile, Veronica left, offering a reassuring pat on my shoulder.

Rebecca slid onto the sofa in the spot vacated by Veronica. "I'm sorry, Melanie. I really am. But you've got that big, beautiful house just aching to be shown off. It's a historic icon—just ask Sophie. People will be buying tickets just to see inside."

I pulled back. "You're trying to get film people inside the house, aren't you? You just can't take no for an answer, can you?"

She looked deflated, unprepared for me to expect the worst from her. But she'd never shown me reason not to.

"I'm sorry, Melanie. I really am. But Marc's on my case about getting the movie filmed inside your house. He's obsessed! I figured if we could get some of the film people in the house to take pictures, they can re-create it in a set. And then we'll all be happy."

"Really, Rebecca? You think that would make Marc happy?"

Her shoulders sank. "I had to try. You know what he's like."

I frowned. "I met your brother-in-law. Anthony. He told me something very interesting."

She looked at me warily. "Yes?"

"He said that Marc wants our house." I leaned forward, resisting the impulse to press my index finger into her chest. "Please make sure he knows, in no uncertain terms, that I'd rather burn my house down to the ground than see him take possession of it."

Pucci whimpered, and Rebecca held the little dog's head against her chest. "I'm sure you don't mean that. Marc is my husband, remember."

"Oh, that's not something I'd forget."

I thought she'd jump up and leave in a huff, but she stayed where she was, an expression that I'd come to recognize on her face. A signal that she had something unpleasant to tell me.

"I had a dream," she said.

I almost stood and left right then. All of my life, avoidance had been my modus operandi. But ever since my marriage to Jack, I'd been trying to change. To be a more mature version of myself by facing unpleasant things instead of pretending they didn't exist. I still failed as many times as I succeeded, but Jack said that as long as I tried, it wasn't a complete loss. I took a deep breath. "And?"

"It was about Jack. He's in danger."

She had my full attention. "From what?"

"I'm not sure. There's another man—no one I recognized. And he was . . ." She stopped.

"And he was what?"

"He was burying Jack alive."

CHAPTER 3

I'd halfway opened the bottom drawer of my desk, my mouth already salivating at the thought of the leftover doughnut from Glazed still nestled all soft and sugary in its bag. I'd resisted it for a day and a half and knew I had to eat it now because it couldn't be expected to stay fresh forever.

At the sound of my phone beeping my hand jerked, bumping hard against the solid wood of my desk. I hit the intercom button. "Yes, Jolly—what is it?"

The receptionist's voice was hushed. "Someone is here to see you, but he doesn't have an appointment. I told him that you have a showing in half an hour and to make an appointment when you'd have more time, but he was very insistent." The disapproving tone brought my attention away from the sweet-smelling bag and back to the intercom.

"Did he say what he wanted?"

"Just that you were old friends and he'd explain when he saw you."

I sat up straighter. "What's his name?"

"Marc Longo. Should I send him back?"

I slammed my desk drawer. *Marc?* He was the last person I expected or wanted to see, and I briefly considered stealthily opening one of the windows in my office and escaping into the parking lot. But that's what the old Melanie would have done. The Melanie who used to hide from her problems and avoided confrontation at all cost. I was the new, grown-up version of Melanie who didn't do things like that anymore. Most of the time.

I picked up my cell phone to call Jack to come over but changed my mind. He was working on a book that meant a lot to his career, and I didn't want to distract him. It was the same reason, I kept telling myself, why I hadn't told him about the face in Nola's window. Or about Rebecca's dream. It had nothing to do with my insecurities and fears of abandonment, despite all of Jack's reassurances that he loved me and was with me for keeps, even if I was prone to distractions of the paranormal kind. Old habits, I'd found, are like a favorite pair of worn-out old shoes; you just can't toss them out. You allow them to linger in your closet until you're tempted into walking around in them again because you crave the comfortable and familiar.

"Thank you, Jolly. Send him back."

I stood, straightening my skirt and trying out several relaxed and non-posed poses. I was awkwardly perched on the edge of my desk when Marc walked into my office, but I was spared greeting him by the avalanche of my phone, agenda, and desk lamp cascading to the floor because of an accidental tug of the cord by the leg I nonchalantly tried to cross.

"Let me help you," he said, crouching down to pick up the lamp, which had miraculously survived the tumble.

"Just leave it," I said. "Really. I'd rather you just tell me why you're here and then go."

He placed the lamp in the middle of my desk, the shade completely askew, and he grinned at me when he caught me noticing. I clenched my hands into fists so I wouldn't reach over and right it, and somehow managed not to start singing ABBA songs backward.

"Is that how you talk to all your clients, Melanie?"

"Well, you're not a client so it doesn't count."

He sat down in one of the chairs where legitimate clients usually sat and smiled. The resemblance to his brother was apparent: the same coloring and build, the same sexy smile. Except where I'd detected warmth behind Anthony's eyes, Marc's were like cold, lifeless stones. All his attention and devotion were directed inward. I couldn't remember if they'd been like that when I'd dated him or if this was something new. Being married to Rebecca could do that to anyone, I supposed.

He stretched his long legs in front of him and crossed his Italian-loafer-clad feet at the ankles. "Oh, but I could be."

Having given up on a casual lean on my desk, I returned to my chair. "I doubt it." I made a big show of avoiding looking at the crooked lampshade and instead glanced at my watch. "I'm afraid I have an appointment—"

As if I hadn't spoken, he said, "I'd like to buy a house. A nice, big, old one south of Broad. And I'm willing to pay a lot more than what it's worth."

I suddenly recalled what Anthony had said about Marc wanting my house, and frigidity spread from the base of my neck to my toes. I squared my shoulders, preparing to do battle. "If you're referring to our house on Tradd Street, I'm afraid it's off the market and I don't anticipate it being available for purchase for at least another hundred years or so."

He propped his elbows on the arms of the chair and steepled his fingers. Tilting his head slightly, he said, "When we were dating, I don't remember you being quite so . . . unwilling."

He'd emphasized the last word, making it seem sordid, and I felt my cheeks redden. His smile widened, his strike intentional. I stood. "Seeing as how we have nothing else to discuss, I'd like you to leave. I've got a lot of work—"

Marc cut me off. "Did Jack tell you his editor was let go?"

"What?" I groaned inwardly, wishing I hadn't allowed him to take me by surprise.

"Ah, I see he hasn't mentioned it. Happened last week. Not to repeat hearsay, but the rumors had something to do with being too friendly with an intern. A relation of mine, actually—what a small world, right? And now other victims are crawling out of the woodwork, eager to add to the growing pile of accusations. With the current social climate regarding workplace harassment, the publisher had no choice but to let him go." He grinned again. "Regardless of whether it was warranted. High-profile companies just can't take the chance, now, can they?"

I shivered, either from the chill that wouldn't dissipate or from the way he looked when he said the accuser was related to him. Something Anthony said pinged at my brain. *Marc has lots of connections. Has a lot of influence, even in the publishing world.* I tried very hard to keep my voice even. "I'm sure the reason Jack hasn't mentioned it is because it has no impact on him or his work. There are lots of really good editors at his publishing house. I'm sure with such a valuable asset as Jack is to them, they'll make sure they match him up to someone who's a good fit."

Marc sat up, a look of mock concern on his face. "I'm not sure if you're aware, but when an editor who has been the single and loudest championing voice for a particular author or book is suddenly let go, the author is, effectively, orphaned. Sure, Jack will be assigned to a new editor. But it just won't be the same, will it? Not unless the new editor shares the same passion and enthusiasm for the book as the previous editor. And that, my dear Melanie, rarely—if ever—happens."

I walked to the door and held it open so my intent was obvious. "I'm sure Jack and his project will be fine. Sorry I can't help you."

"Ah, Melanie. Still so naïve." He stood but didn't move, instead taking his time examining the contents of the top of my desk.

My voice shook a little when I spoke. "I'm not naïve. I know Jack is a very talented author, with a solid track record, and his new publisher knows this. His new book idea is brilliant and will succeed with whatever editor he's assigned to. He's got a fabulous agent who believes in him and has his back. So stop making these stupid threats and go away. We're not selling our house, nor will your movie be filmed there. And there is nothing you can say or do that will make us change our minds. You think your big donation to the Ashley Hall fund-raiser might give you a loophole to get stills or shots or whatever it is filmmakers do, but I will fight you every step of the way. And you won't get a single scene shot anywhere near my home."

When he didn't move, I jiggled the doorknob to remind him that he was just leaving.

He wasn't smiling anymore. "I'm being nice now because you and I have a history. But this courtesy has a limited time span." He walked slowly toward me, and stopped so that he was definitely invading my personal space. I didn't step back. "I'm not a patient man, Melanie. And I always get what I want. One way or another."

"You didn't get the Confederate diamonds," I said, referring to the treasure hidden in the house by a former Vanderhorst owner at the end of the Civil War. Jack and I had found them before Marc could, much to Marc's ire. I hadn't meant to antagonize him, but I couldn't stop myself. His smugness on top of what he'd done to Jack—to *us*—was too much for me to let it slide.

His nostrils flared. "You can make this easy, or you can make this hard. Either way, my wife and I will be moving into Fifty-five Tradd Street in the very near future, and we will happily open our doors to a film crew who are champing at the bit to begin filming what I'm sure will be a huge blockbuster hit." He leaned closer so I could see hazel flecks in his eyes. "And you can tell your historic-house-hugging professor friend that I have all sorts of ideas of what I'd like to do in the house once it's mine and that there will be nothing she can do to stop me. Just know that it will involve the removal of most of the interior walls and all of those tacky wedding-cake moldings."

Of all the things Marc said, that hurt me the most. My back still ached when I thought about how I'd hand sanded the wood floors, banister, and spindles. My head hurt as I recalled how much money I'd spent on replacing the roof, and the time and focus it had taken Sophie to repair the antique silk Chinese wallpaper in the foyer. Most of all, I couldn't forget the beautiful garden my father had brought back from ruin, or the memory of walking with Nola down the grand staircase on my wedding day and then carrying the twins up to their nursery on their first day home from the hospital. What Marc was suggesting was pure desecration. Considering I'd never wanted the house in the first place, I was stunned at the ache in my heart at just the thought of Marc and Rebecca moving in and ruining *my* house.

I leaned forward so that our noses were almost touching. "Over my dead body," I hissed.

Something flickered in his eyes before he stepped back, a crooked grin splitting his face. "That could be arranged."

A small frisson of fear erupted inside of me, but I refused to look away or even blink. Marc Longo was a bully, and I wouldn't be cowed by him. "Get out," I said through my teeth. "And don't even think you or your film crew will get past the front gate."

He walked out into the hallway, then turned around to face me. "I made another rather generous donation to Ashley Hall and promised them that I'd have movie professionals document the progressive dinner so they can use it for promotion. I think you'll have a hard time telling them no. But that's really just to annoy you and Jack. Sure, I'll be able to get some great interior shots of the house, but I think I'll wait until my name is on the deed before I make plans for the real filming to begin." He scratched his chin as if deep in thought. "I'm thinking Emma Stone—she'd have to dye her hair again, of course—would be the perfect actress to play Rebecca, don't you?"

Something pinged again at the back of my brain, and my anger slipped away, replaced again by something that felt a lot like fear. I just needed to make sure he didn't see it. "Why do you want it so badly, Marc? There are plenty of other beautiful historic houses much grander than mine for sale. What is it about my house?"

He paused for a moment. "Simple, really. It belongs to Jack. And you. But not for long." He raised his eyebrows before turning on his heel and walking away.

I watched him until he disappeared around a bend in the corridor, a sense of unease settling in the pit of my stomach. Marc was a businessman. Everything he did had to be a means to make money or get ahead in some way. Marc had originally purchased the Vanderhorst plantation because he'd thought the Confederate diamonds had been hidden there. And then he'd lied to his own brother about turning it into a winery to extricate himself from a bad investment. He'd even professed his love for me just to access the house I'd inherited so he'd be in a good position to search for the diamonds.

There was something else about my house on Tradd Street besides jealousy that made Marc Longo want it. I just needed to figure out what it was before it was too late. I returned to my desk and sat down, knowing whom I needed to talk to. My finger was poised over the intercom button when Jolly tapped on the doorframe, her dragonfly earrings swinging. I could tell by the look on her face that she'd heard every word.

"He is not a nice man," she said, a deep crease between her brows. "He has a black karma cloud that hovers around him, but I think you have to be a psychic like me to see it." She gave me a sympathetic stare.

"I'm sure." Jolly was convinced she had psychic abilities and had begun taking classes to learn how to use them. So far, she'd had more misses than hits and had arrived at the firm conclusion that I had no abilities of my own. I was more than happy to have her continue to believe that.

"Would you like me to call Jack for you?" Her green eyes were wide with concern.

He probably was the first person I should call, but I couldn't. Not yet. If it was true that he'd lost his editor and hadn't told me, he had enough to worry about. "No. But I do need you to find a number for me. For Anthony Longo."

Jolly raised her eyebrows in question.

"Yes, Marc's brother. I believe he's local. I seem to recall Marc once telling me that his younger brother owned a house downtown. Hopefully he has a landline."

"Would you like me to put the call through if I can get him on the line?"

I shook my head. "No. Just get me the number. Please."

She nodded, then left my office, and I reached over to straighten the lampshade because I couldn't take it anymore. My iPhone buzzed and I looked down at the screen and saw a text from Rebecca.

I dreamed of a man in old-fashioned clothes with empty sockets for eyes. He said he was coming for you. And Jack.

I quickly hit CLEAR before leaning back in my chair and closing my eyes, wondering how, once again, my formerly orderly world had suddenly become everything but, and why the restless dead never seemed to want to leave me alone.

CHAPTER 4

When I walked in the front door after work, the smell of Mrs. Houlihan's Christmas cookies baking in the oven wafted from the kitchen, drawing me to the room like a cat to catnip. Or a dog to, well, baking cookies, since General Lee, Porgy, and Bess were all camped out in front of the kitchen door, gazing at the solid wood surface as if just the weight of their stares might open it.

It was still November, but Mrs. Houlihan insisted on stuffing the freezers with sugary holiday treats way in advance of any Christmas company we might have. I personally thought she did it to torment me, especially because only she and Jack had the keys to the large freezer in the carriage house and it was always locked. I knew because I checked. Daily.

I joined the dogs in their vigil, holding my breath to listen for any signs of movement from the other side of the door. I'd recently been banned from the kitchen while my housekeeper, Mrs. Houlihan—inherited along with General Lee and the house—did her Christmas baking, following the infamous cookie-cutting incident in which I was showing the children how to use cute winter shapes on the rolled-out cookie dough. I'd been eating all the leftover dough to make cleanup easier, ensuring the children didn't see me because Jayne said raw dough wasn't good for them. I'd eaten raw dough my entire life without issue, so I was sure Jayne's ban hadn't included me.

Mrs. Houlihan had been upset when she discovered she didn't have enough dough for a second batch and gave me a warning, not seeming to care that I was hungry or sugar deprived—or that I paid her salary. When her stash of red and green M&M'S, which were supposed to be the snowmen's buttons, mysteriously disappeared, she threatened to quit if I didn't leave, and I had no choice but to exit the kitchen in defeat. Even the twins had watched my departure with what looked like disappointment in their eyes.

Pressing my ear against the door, I could hear Mrs. Houlihan bustling about inside. With a sigh, I turned to the dogs. "Sorry. We'll have to wait until she leaves, and then I promise to sneak us something to sample."

"I heard that!" Mrs. Houlihan called out from the other side of the door. "Just be aware that one of my pies and three dozen of the cookies were made from recipes Dr. Wallen-Arasi gave me with all vegan, gluten-free, and sugar-free ingredients. And I'm not going to tell you which ones they are."

I found my mouth puckering with the memory of some of Sophie's culinary recommendations and gave an involuntary shudder. I squatted to scratch behind three sets of furry ears. "Don't worry. I promise to stop by Woof Gang Bakery tomorrow and bring you home something tasty."

They resumed their vigil as I carefully hung up my coat in the small cloak closet. It took me longer than it should have because no one had buttoned and zipped up their coats or hung them all in the same direction, so I had to fix them. I made a mental note to bring it up with Nola and Jack during dinner. I was halfway to the stairs to head up to the nursery when I heard JJ's squealing laughter followed by Jack's deep-chested chuckle coming from behind me. I followed the sound toward Jack's closed office door, then carefully opened it before thrusting my head into the opening.

Jack's computer screen was dark, and he was lying faceup on the rug in front of his desk, JJ sitting on top of his chest. They both wore cowboy hats, Jack's stuck under his head on the floor, and Jack was bouncing his son up and down in a good imitation of the movement of a horse. All my insides melted as I watched them, wondering what I'd done to be so lucky. Not once during my own difficult childhood had I imagined this life. But now that it was mine, I clung to it with both hands like a squirrel in a hurricane might cling to a palmetto trunk.

My gaze slid to the corner of the room where Sarah sat in a shaft of sunlight, waving her hands and babbling as if in conversation. Which she was, I realized, although I couldn't see anyone. But I could smell the faint scent of roses, the telltale indicator that Louisa Vanderhorst, former resident of the house and planter of the Louisa roses in our garden, was nearby. Although she was a gentle maternal spirit, and one who only periodically visited, I felt a small shock of alarm. Because Louisa stopped by only when she felt we needed her protection.

I turned back to a now hatless Jack, who'd sat up and placed JJ in his lap. "Where's Jayne?" I asked, bending down to kiss Jack on the lips, then loudly blow a raspberry on JJ's cheek before swooping up Sarah into my arms. She smiled at me, her blue eyes bright and sparkling as she kissed my nose, then turned to wave her pudgy fingers at the empty corner.

"I sent her home." Jack didn't meet my eyes as he stood, intently focusing on lifting JJ onto his shoulders.

"You sent her home? But I thought you said you needed as many writing hours as you could get to turn your book in by the deadline."

"Did I?" he asked, starting to trot around the room, JJ's giggles bursting from his tiny chest like bubbles.

I almost allowed myself to let it go. Not to let harsh realities intrude on this sweet family moment. To pretend that I didn't know that my husband had heard bad news and had chosen not to share it with me. But if there was ever a moment when I needed to be the new Melanie I was intent on becoming, this had to be it.

"Jack," I began, ready to tell him about my conversation with

Anthony, my run-in with Marc, and Rebecca's dreams—and maybe even the unwanted visitors I'd seen in the house.

"Mellie," Jack said at the same time, preempting me. Despite my good intentions, I was completely happy to let him go first. I smiled encouragingly at him, trying not to be obvious that I was holding my breath.

"My editor was let go. Patrick took a huge chance on me and was my main advocate at the publishing house, so it's a little devastating. They've assigned me to one of the newer editors—a young woman not much older than Nola, I think. Her name is Desmarae." He grinned, but it was a poorly executed replica of his usual smile. "Not that being so young is necessarily a bad thing, but she admitted when we spoke on the phone that she'd not only never read any of my books, but she also had no idea who I was when they assigned her to me."

My heart burned at the indignation. "Then I guess she's been living under a rock." Forcing a bright smile, I said, "You still have your awesome agent, who believes in you almost as much as I do."

He didn't even try to force a smile this time. "Desmarae did say she loved my author photo on the back of my last book."

I remembered that picture. It was what had convinced me to go out with him. I tried not to think of another woman looking at the picture and having the same thoughts I did. I cleared my throat. "So you still have a contract and a book deadline."

"Affirmative," he said, jostling JJ on his shoulders and making our son squeal with delight.

"Then why would you let Jayne go home early? So you could wallow in self-doubt?"

He stared back at me for a long moment. "Yeah, probably." He slid JJ from his shoulders and handed him to me.

"I'm going to feed and bathe the children and get them ready for bed while you write. Do not leave this room until you have finished at least three more pages. I'll have a little surprise waiting for you when you're done." I gave him our special look to show him just what kind of a surprise I had in mind, hoping, as I said it, that it wasn't Nola's turn to host her study group at our house that night.

Not that it would matter, I thought as Jack's face became serious and he returned to his desk chair.

"I can always try. It will probably all be crap because my brain's not in it right now, but writing is rewriting, as my ex-editor used to say." He jiggled the wireless mouse on his desk, and his computer screen came to life. He read the lines on the screen, his brows squeezed together in concentration.

With a child in each arm, I began to back out of the room, apparently already forgotten.

"What were you about to say—before, when I interrupted you?" Jack kept his fingers poised over his keyboard but turned around to face me.

"Nothing important." I smiled, and he began typing. I could still hear the clacking of his fingers on the keyboard as I began to nudge the door behind us with my foot.

Without slowing down the pace, he said, "And I haven't forgotten what you said about a surprise if I write three more pages. I'm going to hold you to it."

I smiled at the back of his head, feeling an odd mixture of relief and guilt grab me in a choke hold. I started to take a step toward him, to tell him everything, to be the Melanie I'd promised myself I was capable of. But each click on his keyboard was like a tap on the nails in the coffin of my resolve, convincing me that the best choice at that moment was to let him work.

I stood in the doorway for a long moment, battling with my conscience, but then JJ began to squirm and Sarah rubbed her eyes. Looking at Jack's head bowed over his keyboard, I said, "I love you."

He continued typing without looking up, already lost in his own world. I put the children down, then gently closed the study door.

General Lee walked docilely on his leash beside me while Porgy and Bess, on a separate double leash, both seemed determined to head in opposite directions. If they weren't so innocent-looking, I would have suspected them of trying to kill me. Behind us, Jayne pushed the double running stroller with JJ and Sarah buckled inside and bundled up against the sudden drop in temperature, unperturbed by the bumps and jars of the uneven sidewalk as we headed down Tradd Street toward East Bay and my meeting with Anthony Longo.

"Remind me again why you need an entourage for this meeting?" Jayne asked.

I kept my gaze focused ahead of us. "For moral support."

"And it has nothing to do with the reflection of that guy in the doughnut shop window."

I jerked my head around to stare at her and immediately tripped over one of the dogs. When I'd righted myself, I said, "You saw him?"

"Of course, Melanie. I see dead people, too, remember?"

"Right," I said, a surprising jab of jealousy invading my psyche. Although I'd always hated my "gift," it had always belonged to me and me alone. It had separated me from the proverbial crowd. And now, suddenly and unexpectedly, I was supposed to share it. It was as if I'd been downgraded to less than special. Which wasn't how I really felt at all. Really.

"I mean," Jayne continued, "it would seem that whoever or whatever that was in the window is somehow connected to Anthony, right? Except I've seen the same spirit at the cistern in your backyard." Our eyes met as we both stopped.

I shivered, and I wasn't sure it was due to the cold wind. "Anthony said that bricks from a mausoleum at the Vanderhorst plantation cemetery were used in the cistern."

"It could be a coincidence," she said.

Our eyes met again. "Except there's no such thing as coincidence," we said in unison, echoing Jack's favorite saying. And he'd yet to be proved wrong.

A wild barking came from a pretty Victorian behind a Philip Simmons gate, making General Lee pull at his leash, nearly separating my shoulder from its socket. I had no choice but to follow him to the gate, where a small white terrier mix with teddy bear ears and a sweet face was jumping up to greet General Lee.

"This is Cindy Lou Who," Jayne explained, bending down to offer a scratch behind a small furry ear through the fence railing. She straightened to allow General Lee to take her place in ecstatically greeting his canine friend. "I always walk the children past this house, and Cindy Lou Who always rushes over to the gate to say hello. I think she has a thing for General Lee."

"I think the feeling's mutual," I said. "I don't think I've seen her before. Should I tell her that he's already fathered puppies from another relationship?"

"Her family just moved here from California. I've met the mom—Robin. Very nice lady. I let her know that General Lee wasn't fixed yet but that you'd take care of it very soon so the two of them could play on the same side of the fence."

I pulled on General Lee's leash, feeling terrible at the looks of anguish he and Cindy Lou Who gave each other as they were separated. "I know—you're right. I'll get it taken care of. That would be a terrible way to welcome new neighbors to the street."

We continued walking down Tradd, each block a nod to a different architectural period, the houses ranging from brick-fronted Colonials to Greek Revivals and double-piazza single houses. Growing up in Charleston, I'd never noticed the veritable treasure trove of historic houses that made up the landscape of my childhood. I'd been too preoccupied with ignoring the spirits who beckoned me from each doorway and window, in every alley, and behind every tree. It had taken years to learn how to block them out so I could traverse the brick streets of my hometown. But now, with Jayne and me together, our light shone too brightly, a lighthouse beacon to the restless dead in a sea of perpetual night.

Since my sister and I had found each other, there were several things I'd learned about her. Like me, she loved all things with sugar, small children and dogs, and the sound of St. Michael's bells. Her favorite color was blue, always worn when she felt she needed confidence; she was very shy around men, especially good-looking ones, disliked onions, and preferred wearing flats to heels. We both could see dead people, but whereas I could pretend not to see them, Jayne, eight years younger than I, and not as jaded, sometimes found it difficult to ignore them.

Growing up, she'd found ways to mentally block them, but now that we were together, she was finding it more difficult.

I watched as Jayne stopped in front of a Neoclassical Revival (according to Sophie) where two young boys, about eight and ten, sat on the porch steps. The children looked real except for the sickly yellow pallor of their skin and the fact that the steps they were sitting on no longer existed.

"Come on, Jayne. There's nothing we can do without a full intervention, and that's just not going to happen."

"But they're children."

"I know," I said firmly, my resolve as much for her as it was for me. "But if you start paying attention to every spirit you see, more will follow, and they'll never leave you alone. In your waking or sleeping hours. So let them be."

She began backing away from them, turning away only after they vanished, a plaintive wailing disappearing with them. We were silent as we walked past the house whose new owners had sold the Philip Simmons gate for scrap metal, prompting Sophie to cross the street to the other side whenever she walked past it. I'd thought I'd seen her spit on the ground in front of the modern gate a few times.

When we reached East Bay, we turned right toward Battery Park and the gazebo. The day had turned blustery, whipping the Cooper River into white-frothed tips like a mad chef with too much meringue. I spotted a pirate ship with a hole blasted in its side slowly sinking beneath the waves, and when I glanced at Jayne, I knew she'd seen it, too.

We needed to come up with a way to block the proverbial target with the arrow pointing at us for all restless spirits to follow. Maybe I could buy her another ABBA CD so she'd learn all the lyrics and we could shout them together in a mutual effort to discourage hangers-on. I'd already gifted her with several CDs, but Jayne had a way of accidentally stepping on them or misplacing them. I made a mental note to ask Nola for help in downloading a playlist for Jayne to listen to on her phone so there would be nothing to step on and break. Or lose. It was the least I could do.

Jayne spotted Anthony leaning on the railing of the gazebo at the same time I did. "He's wearing clothes," she said. "I mean, he's here, and he has on a warm jacket."

I rolled my eyes. "Remember you're here for moral support, so please don't say anything unless you have to, and only after you've rehearsed it several times in your head. All right?"

She nodded as Anthony smiled, then walked down the steps to greet us. "Good morning, ladies. I was only expecting Melanie, but I have to admit that seeing Jayne, too, has made my day."

I wanted to roll my eyes again, but there was real warmth in his eyes as he looked at my sister. Jayne's cheeks reddened, not entirely due to the wind, and she quickly bent over the stroller to make sure the children were still bundled like little fat sausages.

Anthony shoved his bare hands into the pockets of his jacket. "I have to admit I was surprised to hear from you so soon."

"Yes, well, I surprised myself. But your brother paid me a little visit to not only make an offer on my house, but also to threaten me if I didn't comply. I remembered what you'd said about him having influence everywhere, and I realized that I needed to be proactive."

"Good move," he said, distracted by a metal whisk hitting him in the shin.

"Sorry," Jayne said, quickly picked it up, wiped it off with a cleansing cloth she'd conveniently attached to the stroller's handle, and gave it back to JJ. "Whisk," she said, as if that explained everything.

Anthony leaned forward and made a face at the children, and they both giggled. "Is his name 'Whisk'?" he asked JJ.

"Whisk," JJ repeated, throwing it at Anthony, who quickly intercepted the kitchen utensil before it beaned him.

He handed it back to JJ, then stepped out of throwing range. "When I was a little boy, I had a special attachment to a yellow bath sponge." His face sobered. "Until Marc cut it into shreds and soaked the pieces in black paint."

"That explains a lot," Jayne said slowly, and I wondered how long she'd had to practice in her head before speaking out loud.

"So, what do we do now?" I said, directing my attention toward Anthony.

"I need you to come out to the Vanderhorst plantation. To help me gain access to the mausoleum. If there's a treasure buried there, we need to find it before Marc does."

"But doesn't the property belong to you, and Marc's digging would be trespassing?"

He looked uncomfortable. "Marc doesn't always ask first. He just does. To be honest, I'm a little afraid to tell him no, regardless of how clear it is he's in the wrong. But there are certain . . . elements that are barring both of us entry to the mausoleum. Which is why I need your help. I was hoping we could set up an appointment to meet there as soon as possible."

I shivered inside my heavy sweater. "Why couldn't you just tell me this on the phone?"

"Because I can't be completely sure Marc hasn't found some way to intercept my calls and texts."

Remembering my encounter with Marc in my office, I couldn't say Anthony's concerns were without merit. I started to tell him more details about Marc's visit when I noticed what looked like black smoke forming behind him inside the gazebo. "Is there a fire . . . ?" I began. Jayne grabbed my arm, stopping me as she noticed the billowing dark cloud.

I didn't smell anything burning, and despite the strong wind, the black shape didn't waver, its edges appearing to pulsate with radiant heat. Aware that we were staring at something behind him, Anthony turned around just as the plume of dark smoke began to take on an almost human form, a dense shadow with distinct arms and legs and a head, its sex undeterminable.

Anthony took a step up the stairs toward it, his hands clenched in fists as if ready to do battle. "Don't!" I shouted, but I was too late. His head jerked backward, and then an unseen punch to his midriff had him buckled over. He turned to escape down the stairs, but something was holding him back. His feet slipped on the top step of the gazebo, his arms flailing as he tried to stay upright. I moved toward him with my arms raised to push him back as Jayne shoved the stroller out of harm's way.

I thought I imagined a low laugh that sounded like distant thunder right before the weight of Anthony's body hit me, crumpling us both to the ground. My head hit the packed earth and for a moment I saw stars behind my eyelids, the air deserting my lungs. When I'd found my breath, I opened my eyes to find Anthony's face only inches above mine, his look of surprise mirroring my own, the dogs barking hysterically.

"So," drawled a familiar voice above us. "Did my invitation to the party get lost in the mail?"

I blinked and saw Jack peering down at us with a bemused expression, the tattered remains of the smoky cloud dissolving in the air above him, leaving behind only the foul stench of rotting flesh.

CHAPTER 5

I quietly closed the door of the nursery after helping Jayne put the children down for their naps, pausing with my ear to the door just in case JJ was faking being asleep. Amelia said that at the same age, Jack would wait until the door was closed before wreaking havoc in his bedroom, which had once included removing all of the stuffing from his mattress and shoving little balls of it into the heating vents in the floor.

"He's asleep, Melanie," Jayne whispered. "We can go. Besides, you have the video monitor. But you won't need it."

I gave her a leveling stare. "He's still Jack's son." I pressed my ear against the door one last time, then felt my sister tug on my arm.

"How's your head?" she asked.

"Just a little bump. Mrs. Houlihan gave me an aspirin. And a cookie. I'm feeling much better now." I rubbed my head.

She was silent for a moment as she looked at me. "Did you tell Jack everything?"

"Mostly. I told him why I was there to meet Anthony and about my conversation with Marc."

"And the figure in Nola's bedroom?

I studied a spot on the wallpaper. "Sophie said this is all hand painted. Did you know that?"

"Melanie." Jayne's voice was full of warning. "You need to tell him everything. And if you don't, then I might have to. I don't like the energy I feel when I pass by Nola's bedroom. We need to take care of it soon, and Jack will have to know."

"I know, and I agree," I said, realizing her hand was still on my arm. "I'm just trying to figure out where to begin. And I really don't want to bother Jack with any of it until I know something for sure. The spirits are not showing themselves to me, like they don't want to talk to me."

"Or they don't know they're dead," Jayne suggested.

"Or that. At least I know Louisa is here, protecting the children while I try to sort everything out. I promise to tell Jack everything when we're ready to deal with it, all right? He's got a lot on his mind right now."

I ignored her sideways glance as she kept her hand gripped firmly in the crook of my elbow, leading me down the stairs and in the direction of the parlor. "I think he'd rather know than be caught by surprise. Like finding you flat on your back in front of the gazebo in Battery Park with another man sprawled on top of you."

I couldn't argue with her logic, but I was distracted by the firm tug on my arm. "Where are we going?" I asked, suddenly aware that I was being led for a reason.

"Both of your parents are here, and Nola and Jack are with them in the parlor. They'd like to have a little chat." Despite my digging in my heels at the mention of an apparent audience waiting to talk with me, she'd managed to pull me into the doorway of the parlor, where everyone had gathered, drinking coffee and tea and snacking on a plate of what looked like Mrs. Houlihan's holiday fudge. Each piece was decorated with green marshmallow-covered Frosted Flakes and tiny cinnamon drops to make them look like holly. They were my favorite, and Mrs. Houlihan had been keeping them under lock and key. I headed in their direction, but Jayne pulled me back.

"Hello, Mellie." My mother smiled and stood, followed by my father and then Nola. Even the three dogs, previously asleep in front of the fire, stood and faced me.

I eyed them all suspiciously, my gaze settling on Jack as he approached. "Is this an intervention?"

"Funny you should use that word." Jack stopped in front of me and smiled. It wasn't one of his devastating ones, which I was used to. This was the smile of a man about to have teeth pulled. Without anesthesia.

"Why is it funny?" I hedged, looking for a way to snag a piece of fudge en route to my escape.

Jack seemed to be speaking from behind gritted teeth. "Because only someone who thinks they might need one would ever assume that a gathering of loved ones might be an intervention."

"Well, no one's died, so I know it's not a funeral," I said, crossing my arms.

"Mellie. Sweetheart," he said, placing his arm around my shoulders and pulling me toward him. I tried to retain my indignation, but the scent of him, that "Jackness" that I couldn't name but could always identify, made me almost lose track of why I was supposed to feel indignant.

"Mmm," I mumbled into the soft cashmere arm of his sweater, enjoying the feel and smell of him but keeping my body rigid.

"How old are you?"

I jerked back. "Excuse me? Are you about to make some dig about how you're younger than I am?"

"I would never," he said solemnly. "It's just that while you were upstairs, we've been having a conversation where we all agree that you're old enough to know who to trust. And that would be everyone in this room."

"I have no idea what you're—" He stopped me with a firm kiss on the mouth that erased my next words.

"Get a room," Nola grumbled.

He grinned his Jack grin. "Glad that still works. As I was saying, you should have told me and the rest of us about your meeting with Marc and your decision to meet with Anthony. We're all in this together, remember? We're a family. We love you. We love this house and every-one connected to it. Well, most of them. Your problems are our prob-lems. And we solve them together."

"But with your deadline, you don't need any distractions—"

He put his finger on my lips, stopping me. "You, your safety, and our happiness are never a distraction."

"Mellie, dear," my mother said. "Your father and I divorced all those years ago because we didn't communicate and because we each thought we knew what was best for the other. And look where that led us."

I stepped away from Jack so I could gather my thoughts. It was hard to think with him standing so close. "I understand your concern. I do. And I thank you. But I decided to do it myself not because I don't trust you. It's because I thought I could handle it on my own. Maybe I was wro . . ." I couldn't finish the word. I tried again. "Maybe I moved a little too fast and maybe I should have waited before agreeing to meet with Anthony. And I did tell Jayne," I said in a small voice.

"Right before we left, before I could get reinforcements," Jayne added with look of admonishment.

I stepped over to the couch and sat down. "Well, I'm still not con-vinced that I can't handle it. I was just a little blindsided by . . ." My gaze slid to my father. "By an unexpected visitor."

One of the reasons for my parents' divorce had been my father's un-willingness to accept or try to understand something he couldn't see. In the years since our reconciliation, he'd learned to tolerate the unex-plained events that seemed to follow my mother and me, but he'd never accepted them. While no longer openly hostile to the improbable idea that speaking with the dead might be a viable thing, he simply turned his head the other way so he didn't need to confront it, like an ostrich with its head stuck in the sand: If he couldn't see it, then it must not be there.

"Mellie," my mother said with a warning in her voice. "You should still have told us about Marc's threats. You could have put yourself in danger. Remember, we're always stronger together."

I knew she was referring not only to the members of our new family unit currently surrounding me, all of them responsible in part for the happiness, the house, and the family who lived within its ancient walls, but also to the mantra we'd used before and since Jayne came to us to bind our strength together to fight angry spirits. Although being together made our beacon brighter, it also made us much, much stronger.

I watched as Nola snuck a piece of fudge from the side table next to her and shoved it in her mouth. I frowned at her, but she looked up at the ceiling—something she'd probably learned from my father.

"I realize that now," I said slowly. I'd been independent of all family connections for so long that it was still hard for me to believe I wasn't expected to do it all on my own. Maybe, deep down, I missed that part of the old Melanie. Despite some of her quirks, which I was trying very hard to bury, my independent nature wasn't going to go down without a fight. Perhaps I didn't want it to. Perhaps I only wanted to temper it, to meld the old Melanie into the new to create a stronger me who was fiercely independent but also needed the love and support of others. I apparently didn't have a clue as to how to make that happen.

I chewed on my lip as I thought for a moment. "So, I guess this means I'm supposed to bring someone with me to the mausoleum at the Vanderhorst plantation cemetery? Although I don't see—"

"I'll go!" Nola stuck her hand up as if she were in a classroom.

"I believe you have school." Jack sent his daughter a stern glance before directing his attention back to me. "Obviously, if a Longo is involved, I need to go with you. They're like sand fleas—you don't realize they're about to swarm and bite until it's too late."

I threw up my hands. "See? Another distraction from your writing! Exactly what I was trying to avoid."

"I'll go with you," Jayne offered. "If Mother could watch the children, of course. It's probably not a good thing if the three of us go together."

I wasn't sure which part of her comment made me more uncomfortable—the fact that she understood already the complexities of our abilities or the fact that she'd moved from "Ginette" to "Mother." It wasn't that I'd expected her to ask for my permission, but for more than forty years, I'd believed myself to be the only person in the universe authorized to call her Mother.

"Or you can stay here with the children and Mother will come with me. Just like old times." I felt everyone looking at me.

My father cleared his throat. "Jayne said the last time Ginny encountered unpleasant spirits, it took her nearly a month to fully recover. So if Jayne wants to go with Melanie, then I'll go, too. For protection. Jayne's kind of new to all this."

I jerked my head in his direction. "Who are you, and what have you done with my father?"

He had the decency to appear abashed. "While Jayne and I have been working in the garden, we've had some long and interesting chats. I still think there has to be some scientific explanation for everything, but Jayne has made me understand that if it's real to her, then I should give her and you and Ginny the benefit of the doubt and go along with it. At least until I can offer an explanation."

I saw a serene smile of mutual appreciation pass between Jayne and my mother, leaving me with the familiar feeling of being picked last for a team in gym class. The new Melanie was grateful that my parents and sister now had a close relationship despite having been separated for most of Jayne's life. But the old Melanie felt the hurt and abandonment smoldering like a banked fire, sparking bits of burning ash into the room.

I smelled chocolate and turned to find Nola holding out the dish of fudge to me. I smiled gratefully and took a piece, more relieved than I cared to admit that I wasn't the only person who recognized the weirdness of what had just happened. I took a bite and chewed, glad for the excuse not to have to speak immediately.

"Then it's settled," my mother said. "You'll let us know when you're meeting after you speak with Anthony Longo?"

Before I could tell her I needed to consider my options, the doorbell rang. The dogs began their alarm barking, alerting us that a threat from potential marauders had invaded the piazza. It was never clear what sort of protection the dogs might offer other than ferocious licking around the ankle area, but they were serious about their role as our protection detail.

"I'll get it," Jack said, touching my shoulder on the way to the front door.

We heard the door open and then: "Jack—it's been ages!" Rebecca's voice carried through to the parlor as those remaining let out a collective groan.

"Rebecca, so good to see you. Feels like yesterday that we saw you last. You and Marc are like a stain we can't rub out completely."

"Oh, Jack," she said, standing on her tiptoes to air-kiss his cheek. "Always the joker."

"Am I?" he asked, his tone one of mock innocence.

I hurried after Jack so I could stop him before he said something so direct that she might actually get it, and then I'd have to spend hours making her feel better. My mother would insist, since Rebecca, by some horrendous twist of fate, was a cousin. A distant one, I kept reminding myself, but still a cousin.

She turned her attention to me, a crease between her brows. "Did you tell Jack about my dreams?"

I quickly shook my head and was lifting my index finger to my neck in a close approximation of slicing it to make her stop, but Jack turned too quickly and saw it.

"Really, Mellie? There's more to what you haven't told me?"

Before I could think of an appropriate response, Rebecca said, "Oh, come on, Melanie. Surely your marriage is strong enough that you can tell each other everything—even the bad things. Right?"

"Apparently not," Jack said.

"Of course," I said simultaneously.

Jack met my gaze, his eyebrows raised expectantly.

Rebecca cleared her throat. "I had two dreams: one where a man without eyes and wearing old-fashioned clothes was after you and Melanie, and the other was of an unidentifiable person—I think it was a man—trying to bury you alive."

"I see," he said slowly. "Well, then, thanks for letting me know that

I should avoid strange men and open graves. Just wish I'd heard it from my wife."

To my relief, Sophie appeared from behind Rebecca carrying a large box stuffed to the brim with piney-smelling greenery. Her face was covered but I knew it was her from the bright blue braids of hair that crisscrossed her scalp like she'd been attacked by a runaway sewing machine.

Blowing a pine bough away from her mouth, she said, "There are a bunch more boxes in the back of Veronica's SUV if someone could help bring it all in."

"I'll get it," Jack said. He took the box from Sophie, setting it down in the vestibule before turning his most charming smile on me. "We'll talk about this later."

I started to say something that might sound like an apology, but I was distracted by the small bag that Rebecca clutched in her pink-gloved hand. "What's in there?" I asked.

"Contraband." Sophie stepped in front of us, her hands on her hips. "I've already explained several times that all the decorations in the progressive dinner homes have to be authentic—as in what people would find in houses during the Revolutionary War period."

Rebecca looked outraged. "That's only because the colonists didn't have bedazzling guns back in the day!" She held aloft what looked like a small laser gun with a dangling electric cord. "But if they did, I'm sure all of their pineapples and mobcaps would have been bedazzled."

Sophie took a step toward Rebecca. "If you don't put that thing away, it won't be fruit and caps getting bedazzled!"

"Stop," I shouted, grabbing the gun from Rebecca's hand. "I'm sure we can speak rationally about this later. Right now, let's get everything inside to see what we have and decide where it's going to go, all right?"

An icy wind blew through the door, even colder than the chilly November day, and I looked up to see Veronica and Jack entering the vestibule, followed by Veronica's husband, Michael. I smelled Vanilla Musk perfume before I saw the blob of light hovering behind them, announcing a familiar presence.

I greeted the newcomers, hoping Michael would leave as soon as he'd deposited the bags he'd brought into the house. Ever since our uncomfortable confrontation in which he'd told me in no uncertain terms that I was to have nothing to do with helping his wife in her quest to find out what had happened to her sister more than twenty years before, I hadn't spoken two words to him. I hoped he was as eager to avoid me as I was to avoid him.

I turned toward Veronica and smiled. "Glad to see you're wearing black and white, as I have a feeling we might need to play referee with Rebecca and Sophie." I picked up several bags containing dried oranges and cloves and brought them to the dining room table to be artfully displayed by someone besides myself, hoping by the time I'd returned, Michael would be gone.

"Hello, Melanie." Michael's voice was close to my ear, making me drop one of the bags on the smooth dark wood of the table, spilling oranges, which began to roll. I was on the opposite side of the table and couldn't reach them before they fell off the edge, my view blocked by the ginormous centerpiece of flowers and greens from the garden that Mrs. Houlihan changed almost daily. I stood frozen, waiting for the sound of the oranges splatting on the floor.

When all I heard was the sound of General Lee licking himself under the table, I walked slowly to the other side and was brought up short by the sight of six plump oranges lined up in a neat row like soldiers, perched precariously at the table's edge.

"How did you do that?" Michael asked, his voice a little higher than usual.

I searched the room for Adrienne, Veronica's spectral sister, wondering why she was hiding from me. But I knew she was there. I could smell her perfume as if it had just been sprayed in the air in front of me.

I met his gaze. "Magic," I said.

He didn't smile. "I don't believe in magic."

"I don't think you need to believe in magic to see it."

He picked up one of the oranges to examine it, perhaps hoping to find a squared bottom. Without looking at me, he said, "I'm glad

Veronica has found something to occupy herself with other than the pointless search for her sister's murderer. I hope you remember what I said before—about how important it is to me that you don't get involved with Veronica's little . . . obsession. It will go away a lot faster if it's not validated."

I tried to keep my temper in check. "I don't find the desire to solve her sister's murder an 'obsession.' I think it's a reasonable quest. As for me helping her, she hasn't asked."

He was still holding the orange as his gaze shot back to meet mine. "And if she does? I know she wants you to channel—or whatever it is you say you do to speak with dead people—Adrienne. Would you say yes?"

"I've never claimed to communicate with the dead." This, at least, was true. Denial was my best friend when it came to my special "gift." "But I'd like to think I could help Veronica in other ways to deal with her grief, and if she asks, I'd say yes."

Very carefully and deliberately, he put the orange down in the middle of the table. He held his hands out, palms up, his face a mask of desperation. "I don't know what to do, Melanie. Veronica talks about nothing else, like she believes finding out who killed Adrienne will make her come back. I really fear for Veronica's mental health." He closed his eyes for a long moment. "Please, Melanie. Don't get involved. You won't be helping her, and you might actually be hurting her. Veronica needs to move on with her life, and this is just holding her back." He stopped speaking for a moment, but I could tell he had more to say; he just wasn't sure how much or if he should continue at all.

Finally, he said, "It's affecting Lindsey in a negative way. She can barely sleep at night and her grades at school are slipping." He pursed his lips. "It's ruining our marriage."

I folded my arms across my chest. "I'm sorry, Michael. I really am. But all I can do is promise not to encourage her. I can't do any more than that."

"Then you'll probably regret it. I'm sure Nola wouldn't be thrilled if Lindsey were forbidden from seeing her. Or if your talents were advertised in a public way."

His mouth twitched as he held back either anger or tears; I couldn't tell which. His voice was very quiet when he spoke. "I want our lives back, and I see you as a potential interference to that happening. Please, Melanie. Please don't encourage her."

"I won't. But assuming I could help, don't you want to know the truth of what happened?"

He shrugged. "We already do—Adrienne's boyfriend killed her and his fraternity brothers helped give him an alibi and cover it up so he got away with it. Veronica thinks this necklace she found means someone else was involved, but I think it's just wishful thinking. Even Detective Riley can't find any connection." Michael shook his head. "I wish we'd never found that stupid necklace."

I began leading him from the dining room. "Yes, well, maybe this will run its course. Anyway, I'm sure we'll be busy with the decorating tonight, so no time to speak of murder or supposed evidence, all right? We'll be happy to drive Veronica home, so no need to stick around."

A solid thud from behind me made me spin around in time to see an orange plop to the ground at Michael's feet, a red splotch covering the spot where the fruit must have collided with his jaw.

His eyes were wide as he looked from me to the orange, then quickly turned to examine the room, as if expecting to see someone else.

"Sorry about that," I said. "They're supposed to be dried. A fresh one must have slipped into the box." I pretended that that was the only thing weird about the flying fruit.

"How did you do that?" he asked, holding the orange and looking around the room.

"Magic," I said with a lot of force, as if that might make him believe it. With a smile, I left the room, Michael's footsteps hurrying after me, the scent of Adrienne's perfume following close behind.

CHAPTER 6

M y father picked up General Lee before reluctantly placing him inside my car and then sliding in next to him in the backseat. "Is this really necessary?" he asked, moving closer to the dog and giving him a firm scratch behind his ears.

"Yes," Jayne said, buckling her seat belt next to me. "There are plenty of dogs looking for homes, and we don't want to be part of the problem. Porgy and Bess are going in for their procedures next week, so this is good practice for all of us."

By the time I pulled out onto the street, General Lee was panting heavily, his eyes wide with anxiety. I glanced accusingly in the rearview mirror at my father. "Did you tell him where we were going?"

"I might have mentioned it. Seemed like a man-to-man talk was necessary."

I rolled my eyes. We were on the way to the mausoleum to meet Anthony, and since we were passing the veterinary clinic, Jayne had made an appointment to have General Lee neutered. When I'd inherited him, having never had a dog before and knowing nothing about dogs, I'd had no idea how old he was or that all of his equipment was intact until Porgy and Bess came along. Both Nola and Jayne had been badgering me ever since to get him "taken care of," but every time I'd asked him about it, he'd seemed less than enthusiastic. The night before, Nola had made a special dessert in General Lee's honor consisting of mixed nuts rolled into sugarless and vegan cookie dough and rounded into the shape of small balls. They were delicious. But maybe I was just desperate for a cookie.

I turned up the heat in the car, then opened a rear window a bit so General Lee could stick out his head, one of his favorite activities. But he ignored the beckoning window, remaining stoic and looking straight ahead like a soldier heading into battle.

When we dropped him off, I gave him a kiss on top of his head, then waited as the nurse led him away. I called after him, "Remember, sweet boy, that we have a playdate with Cindy Lou Who when this is all over!"

General Lee looked back once and gave a low *woof* before moving in front of the nurse toward the door, his tail and head held high. I was embarrassed to find I had tears in my eyes and quickly wiped them away before I returned to the car.

We headed south on Highway 17 over the Ashley River Bridge toward Highway 61. Although it wasn't as scenic as the Ravenel Bridge over the Cooper, which allowed drivers to admire the skyline of the Holy City and the spires of the many churches that gave Charleston its nickname, I almost enjoyed the views of the Ashley and the marshes more. Most likely because I heard Sophie's disparaging voice every time I spotted a cruise ship in the Port of Charleston as I crossed the Ravenel Bridge.

There was still a lot of mumbling among residents about the height of the cruise ships that docked there, overwhelming the historic buildings that crouched in their shadows like rabbits sighting a hawk. Sophie's voice had taken up residence in my brain as my conscience, it seemed, as I also heard it when I searched for mass-produced wallpaper to replace the hand-painted strips in the dining room, or used an electric sander to take off stubborn paint on the nursery door.

As we turned off Highway 17, Jayne pointed at a billboard advertising visits to the USS *Yorktown*, docked at Patriots Point in Mt. Pleasant.

"Oh, look—an aircraft carrier," Jayne said, tapping on the window. "Since Mother said she's free all day to watch the children, maybe another day the three of us could . . ."

I looked at her in horror. I'd made the mistake of once joining Nola's class on a tour of the ship, embarrassing myself by having to leave only fifteen minutes after boarding. I should have assumed that many of the men who'd served on the ship over its long history might never have left and might have been waiting all this time for someone to talk to.

Before I'd been politely escorted off the ship, Nola told me that I'd been singing ABBA's "Take a Chance on Me" so loudly that no one could hear the tour guide. I hadn't remembered that part, my attention focused on the crush of wounded men calling my name and moving toward me, and the sight of one man in uniform smiling, half of his face missing, telling me his name was John and he needed to get home to see his girl, Dolores. I remembered gasping for air, and breathing in the stench of unwashed bodies and fresh blood, and hearing my name being repeated over and over.

"No." I shook my head to emphasize the word. I didn't look at her, hoping my abrupt answer would be all she needed.

My father leaned forward from the backseat. "Probably not a good idea, Jayne. I mean, besides a cemetery or hospital, I'd pick an old aircraft carrier that's seen wartime as being a pretty busy hotbed of paranormal activity, if such a thing existed. According to our conversations, that would make sense, right?"

Jayne sent him a warm smile. "You're absolutely right. Thanks."

I stole a peek at my father just to make sure this wasn't a joke. I was happy he was finally beginning to listen to someone on a subject that had always been taboo with us. And I was even happier that Jayne had been completely accepted by him. But, like a tiny splinter stuck beneath the skin, his ease with listening to Jayne and trying to see her point of view bothered me. A small annoyance that could easily be brushed aside. Or left to fester. Or, my favorite, ignored long enough that it went away on its own. I deliberately focused my attention on the passing landscape to distract myself from recalling all the times that strategy had failed dismally.

Autumn in the Lowcountry is not so much about the variable temperatures or the fact that we sometimes get four seasons in the space of a single week. Instead, the change of seasons is marked by a gradual shift in light and the leaching of colors from the tall sea grass and trees. Only the live oaks and southern magnolias clung to their greens, while all else faded to hazy golds and browns. New England's claim to fame for its beautiful fall foliage was rightfully earned, but fall in the Lowcountry wore its own jeweled crown. It was one of the growing reasons why I loved calling this place my home. I'd probably love it a lot more if it wasn't so full of restless spirits, but at least the scenery was nice.

Jayne read the directions Anthony had given me, although they'd been so simple I hadn't really needed to write them down. Drive about ten miles on 61, then take a right on an unmarked road, then turn at the red arrow on a wooden marker.

I missed the arrow the first time and had to make a U-turn. We bumped along an unpaved road for a short distance before coming to a large wooden sign nailed to an ancient tree, and I was glad Sophie wasn't there to see it. The blue paint had faded, but the large lettering was easy to read. GALLEN HALL PLANTATION.

Jayne looked at me. "Gallen Hall? I thought the Vanderhorst plantation was called Magnolia Ridge."

"It's actually the same place—just a different name. It's a convoluted story, so I'll tell you later—but I'm glad Anthony thought to mention it so I wouldn't be driving all over looking for the wrong plantation. Apparently, things change slowly in South Carolina, because most people around here still refer to it as Magnolia Ridge even though the name change happened two hundred years ago. If I'd driven around asking for Gallen Hall, we might still be looking."

We both turned back to the sign. Beneath the plantation's name were the edges of black letters that were visible over deep and repeated gashes in the wood that appeared to have been made with a sharp stick. Or a knife. Clearly, someone was trying to obliterate whatever had been written there. I wondered if it had something to do with the failed winery. I could imagine that kind of treachery between brothers might lend itself to the force and violence needed for that kind of damage.

We passed through an open iron gate set between brick pillars, each with a concrete pineapple perched on top. According to Sophie, it was the symbol of hospitality in Charleston, hence the two dozen pineapples she'd ordered for my house for the progressive dinner. I'd told her that I hated pineapple and had given her a few specific suggestions as to what she could do with the leftovers after the tour. She hadn't been amused.

As I drove down the long road edged with old-growth trees, my father leaned forward, peering through the windshield from the backseat. "So, this used to belong to the same Vanderhorsts who owned your house."

I nodded. "Although it had passed out of the family by the time Nevin Vanderhorst left Fifty-five Tradd Street to me." We all jerked as I swerved to miss a large rock in the middle of the road. "Joseph Longo owned it for a short time in the twenties, and more recently Marc Longo purchased the plantation, believing the Confederate diamonds were hidden here, and when he discovered that they weren't, he tried to buy my house, believing—correctly, as it turned out—that they were there. Not that we allowed him to find them first."

My father sat back in his seat. "Almost makes you feel sorry for the guy."

"No, it doesn't," Jayne and I said in unison.

"Especially because he's still not done trying to own my house," I added. "But as our lovely librarian, Yvonne Craig at the Historical Society Library, has said, he'll get what's coming to him. Her only wish is that we're all there to witness it."

Almost under his breath, my father said, "Vanderhorst. Vanderhorst." He tapped his fingers against the leather back of my seat.

"What is it, Dad?" I asked.

"I know I recently read something about the Vanderhorsts. Yvonne's been helping me find old plans and articles in the archives about the gardens at our house and yours, so I've been reading a lot about the

Vanderhorsts." He scratched his head. "Something you said about the diamonds is ringing a bell." He was silent for a moment, and when I glanced in the rearview mirror he was pursing his lips. He continued. "I remember making a copy of the article for you and sticking it somewhere, and then I promptly forgot all about it. I was distracted by a sketch I'd found of the parterre garden from our house on Legare and got all excited."

I shared a glance with Jayne. "Yes, well, we found all the diamonds in the grandfather clock, remember? Still, I'd be interested in seeing the article. I've been working on a scrapbook for Nola, and I think a copy of it might have a place in the section on what our lives were like before she joined us. I don't have a lot of material for when she was a baby and little girl, so I thought miscellanea of Jack and me and our lives before she came to live with us might be fun for her. I mean, the whole mystery of the Confederate diamonds is how Jack and I met."

"I'll look for it," he said. "And we can ask Yvonne. She has a memory like an elephant's."

Yvonne was probably in her eighties but looked and acted like someone two decades younger. She had a terrible crush on Jack, with whom she'd been working for years on his book research, but I forgave her because I understood all too well how irresistible Jack's charms were. It's one of the reasons he had three children, none of them planned.

We came to an intersection and I stopped the car. A directional sign lay faceup, dirty and stained from the elements, half of a wooden stake still in the ground, its top half jagged and splintered where it had been decapitated. The letters on the sign were barely legible: GALLEN HALL WINERY.

"Anthony said the cemetery and mausoleum were near the house, so I'm guessing it must be this way." I drove in the opposite direction of the defunct winery. I assumed we were heading in the direction of the Ashley River, as most river plantations had direct access to the river for shipping crops and for basic travel. I'd learned all that and more, apparently by osmosis, from hanging around Sophie. I'd even found myself using terms like *curtilage* and *fenestration* and wondering out loud if a particular paint color was historically accurate for a specific neighborhood when discussing a real estate listing.

The tall pines fell away, revealing an alley of magnolias, a leftover from the founding Vanderhorsts. I knew they weren't the original trees, the life span of a magnolia being only eighty to one hundred and twenty years, although some were reported to be at least ten times older than that. But these were at least one hundred years old, their dark trunks thick and winding, giving the appearance of open hands with fingers holding bowls of wayward branches with shiny leaves. I imagined it was glorious to travel through the alley when the magnolias were in bloom in the spring. Yet a heavy feeling of dread that seemed to saturate the air as we drew closer made me hope that I wouldn't be coming back.

"You feel that?" Jayne asked quietly.

I nodded, the hair on the back of my neck pricking at my skin like sharp fingernails. A large house loomed at the end of the alley, and directly to the left of it, separated by an enormous live oak surrounded by benches in its generous shade, lay the cemetery. An elaborate and rusted iron fence with a closed gate would have informed any visitor what it was, but I knew because of the cluster of people in fashions from past centuries that were pressed against the inside of the gate, looking directly at us.

I started singing a loud rendition of "Knowing Me, Knowing You" while Jayne did her best to recall enough of the lyrics to sing along with me as we both tried to drown out the sound of multiple voices speaking at once.

"Stop," my father shouted from the backseat. "What are you doing?"

I slammed on the brakes, jerking us all forward in our seat belts. "Sorry," I said, keeping my face averted from the cemetery so they'd take the hint that we didn't want to talk. "I thought before we went inside I'd tell you what Sophie told me about the house."

"I thought you already did." I met my father's annoyed gaze in the rearview mirror.

I swallowed, relieved to hear the voices receding but needing more time to get them to stop before I was prepared to get out of the car. "Yes, but not about the architecture." I gave him a shaky smile. "As you can probably tell, it's not Greek Revival. The original house was built by a bachelor and was a simple farmhouse. By the time his grandson inherited the property in the early half of the nineteenth century and got married, the plantation was much more profitable. It was his wife who insisted on something grander, in accordance with their place in society, and she wanted what was all the rage in England at the time, and that was Italianate."

I wasn't exactly sure what features were required to make it fit in the Italianate category, but I was going only on what Sophie told me and that it looked nothing like Tara in *Gone with the Wind*. I just needed a reason not to have to continue on the road, mostly due to the British soldier in full redcoat uniform who was at that moment standing in the middle of the alley and pointing his musket directly at us.

A quick intake of breath let me know that Jayne saw him, too, but my father appeared unaware of the soldier or his gun as he continued speaking. "Was she the one who changed the name of the plantation from Magnolia Ridge to Gallen Hall?"

"No," I said, the tremor in my voice almost imperceptible. "That was done around the time of the British occupation of Charleston during the Revolution, not that long after the first house was built. But all of the older maps and even some of the new ones still refer to it as Vanderhorst–Magnolia Ridge Plantation. I wonder if it bothered the subsequent owners that people still referred to it that way—as if the Vanderhorsts had never left."

"Maybe they haven't," Jayne said, half under her breath.

I gave her a sharp glance, noticing how she was sitting up straight, her gaze focused on the road ahead of us.

I continued. "Sophie wasn't able to find out the reason for the name change but thinks it might have had something to do with a family rivalry the Vanderhorsts had with the Draytons. The Draytons' Magnolia Plantation was established around the same time, but the Vanderhorsts wanted the name for their own plantation, so they just added the word *Ridge* to differentiate. Someone eventually saw reason and changed the name to avoid confusion. To make sure that everyone knew which plantation they were visiting, the Vanderhorsts added real peacocks to the lawn, where they flourished until the Civil War."

As I stared out the windshield, the specter of the soldier began to shimmer as waves of light rose from the ground like steam, before he disappeared completely.

"What happened to the peacocks?" Jayne's voice was stronger than mine had been, but I could still detect a slight quaver.

"They ate them." We exchanged a glance. "It was during the war and everybody was starving." I frowned as the sun glinted off of what could have been a part of a musket that was no longer there. "On a happier note, according to Sophie, a peacock symbol has been used on everything that ever originated from the plantation since the name change, including rice barrels and all of the furniture. I bet it was one of the first uses of a logo."

"Can we keep going?" my father asked impatiently. "I'm speaking at the gardening club at our meeting tonight, and I'd like to be able to go over my notes first."

"Of course," I said, reluctantly putting my foot on the gas again and moving forward down the lane. The full house had just come into view when we heard the sound of a siren behind us. I moved my car to the side for the unmarked car with the flashing dashboard light to pass, blowing up dirt onto my car before it came to a squealing stop in the circular drive right at the front steps of the house. Not sure what I was supposed to do, I followed, parking my car behind it.

Detective Riley, wearing dark sunglasses and a jacket and tie, stepped out of the driver's-side door and looked back at us with an obvious frown. Jayne tensed beside me. "He's tall. His shirt is blue."

My father had already stepped out of our car and was walking toward the man with an outstretched hand and smiling with familiarity. I grabbed my sister's shoulder and shook it gently. "Come on, Jayne. Get it together. We've been practicing, remember? It's Detective Riley. Thomas. We know him. You've been on dates with him. He's a nice guy."

I watched as she swallowed, nodding. "I can do this."

"Yes," I said, opening my door. "You can. Unless you want to pretend you're a dumbstruck teenager meeting Elvis for the first time."

We walked together toward the detective, who greeted us both with a perfunctory nod, reminding me that Jayne said they'd had a fight. "So good to see you, Thomas," I said with a smile, unused to his brusque greeting. "Why are you here?"

His gaze moved to Jayne and then back to me. "I was about to ask you the same question."

Jayne spoke up before I could. "We're meeting with Anthony Longo." Her words were slow and deliberate, but at least they were coherent.

His frown deepened. "Well, I'm afraid he's not here."

"He's not? Because we have an appointment." I paused. "And how would you know he's not here?"

"Because he's in the hospital. Someone tried to run him off the road on the Crosstown. He'll be okay, but his car is totaled."

"Thank goodness," I said, the skin of my neck prickling even more. "What happened?"

He was silent for a moment, as if deciding how much he could say. "It's not clear, although witnesses say it appeared to be a single-car accident. He wasn't exactly . . . coherent. Kept talking about someone hiding in his backseat and causing him to wreck. And then he said he was meeting someone out here at the winery and that he was afraid the same person might be here to harm them. I thought I should check it out. Imagine my surprise to find it's you."

While we'd been talking, my father had begun heading toward the cemetery, walking with a limp I knew he didn't have.

"Dad? Where are you going?"

He continued walking toward the cemetery gate as if he hadn't heard me.

Jayne began moving toward him. "Dad?" she called, but I was too worried about him to be annoyed at her use of the word Dad. "What's wrong?"

As he approached the gate, it swung open with a loud squeal of rust and old iron.

"Stop!" I yelled, the temperature plummeting.

He stopped, then slowly turned around, but it wasn't him. Not really. It was the same salt-and-pepper hair, the same strong jaw and crooked nose from having been broken several times in bar fights before he'd gotten sober. But it wasn't my father. Whoever it was had distorted his features, making them run together like ink in rain.

I stopped ten feet in front of him, the scent of something vile sliding off of him in waves. Bile rose in my throat. "Daddy?" I said, using the name I hadn't called him since I was six.

His mouth twisted and his eyes went hollow. "Go! Away!" The voice was loud and booming and definitely not his. His knees began to buckle, but I couldn't move. It was as if someone was holding my arms behind me. Thomas sprinted forward and reached my father before he could hit the ground.

CHAPTER 7

I stood in the back garden watching Sophie's graduate students—the few who agreed to come back—excavate the cistern, staying far enough back so that the whispers of unseen people remained unintelligible. Her graduate assistant, Meghan Black, wore cute bow-shaped earmuffs and what appeared to be a pink tool belt over a quilted Burberry jacket while she bent over a row of muddy bricks with a small brush. I could only wonder what her monthly dry-cleaning bill must be. Maybe her mother paid for that, along with the clothes.

I recalled what Anthony had said about the cistern's bricks having come from the mausoleum at Gallen Hall and knew he was right. Ever since I'd seen the specter of the man holding the piece of jewelry standing by its edge, I'd known something besides buried pottery and silverware was causing the air in the back garden to beat like the wings of a bird. I'd just ignored the truth, something at which I was very proficient. I wasn't sure if the dark shadow in Nola's room was related to the cistern, too, or simply something unpleasant brought forth during an unfortunate (and hopefully isolated) Ouija board game Nola had played with her friends Lindsey and Alston. Or maybe they were connected somehow, the energies of three teenage girls summoning the dark spirits that lurked in all shadows, waiting for an opportunity to invade our lives.

"You sure look sexy when you're thinking."

I didn't startle, having sensed Jack's presence from the moment he entered the garden, my awareness of him like that of the ocean's tides for the moon. Or, as he'd once told me, like the wrong paint color for the Board of Architectural Review. He wasn't wrong.

He kissed the side of my neck, then slid his arm around my shoulders. I hadn't thought to put on a coat, and I was grateful for his warmth. "Aren't you cold?" he asked, pulling me against him.

"I didn't plan to be out here very long. I'm waiting for another designer to interview and thought I'd come check on the progress while I waited. I'd really like this to be done before the progressive dinner. It's such an eyesore."

"Well, even if it's still here, I'm sure your dad can make it look like it was designed to be here by Loutrel Briggs himself. Speaking of which, how is your dad? When I spoke with him last night, he said he was fine by the time he was loaded back into the car and denies any memory of what happened."

"Yep," I said. "Only now he's insisting that he might have blacked out because his blood pressure dipped. And he's still not speaking to me because I insisted that he stay in bed and miss his gardening club meeting yesterday."

"That's pretty serious. Did you have to lock him in his bedroom and bolt the windows? Either that or he really was hurting. That's the only thing that would make him listen."

"Exactly what I thought. You know he loves his gardening club. The only thing that pacified him was Jayne's assurance that she would speak for him at the meeting since she was already familiar with his notes on the subject matter. They apparently spend a lot of time together in the garden."

"Thank goodness for Jayne, then," he said.

"Yeah. Thank goodness." The white-hot seed of *something* that had implanted itself in my stomach yesterday when Jayne had made her offer and my dad had accepted seemed to explode in fireworks of heat as I relived the conversation. I turned my head to look up at Jack. "Aren't you supposed to be writing?"

He averted his gaze, studying the activity inside the cistern with great interest. "I'm just taking a break—I'm allowed breaks, aren't I?" His voice held an unfamiliar edge to it.

"Of course. But I heard you playing with the children in the nursery, so I was just wondering. Everything all right?"

"It's fine," he said quickly. "Just working through a scene with Button Pinckney and her sister-in-law," he said, referring to the former owners of Jayne's house on South Battery. "It's tough creating dialogue for real people, that's all."

"I'm sure it is," I said. "But I have every confidence your book will be the next *Midnight in the Garden of Good and Evil*. Isn't that what your editor said?"

"Former editor," Jack corrected, his expression solemn.

My gaze traveled behind him to Nola's bedroom window, and I wondered if the passing shadow had been my imagination. *It's now or never.* I took a deep breath and did a proverbial girding of my loins. "I need to show you something."

He quirked an eyebrow and gave me a lascivious grin. "Me, too. Do we have time?"

I gave him a playful shove, wondering if he'd ever grow up and hoping that he wouldn't. "That's not what I meant. I have a picture that Meghan took of the back of the house. There's something in it you need to see."

He glanced over at Meghan, happily brushing mud off of what looked like an old stick. "She just came back to work today after having her cast removed. When did she take the picture?" His eyes narrowed as he regarded me.

"Hello?" A tall man wearing an immaculate gray suit stood on the path that led from around the side of the house. "Your nanny was on the front porch with two of the most adorable babies and she told me I could find you two back here." He walked closer with his hand out-stretched. "I'm Greco."

I was too relieved by my temporary reprieve to be startled by the stranger's appearance. He shook both of our hands as we introduced ourselves, then waited for us to speak. When we didn't, he prompted, "The designer. We had an appointment?"

I looked at him with confusion, taking in the yellow silk Hermès tie and the coordinating pocket square in his jacket. He was very tall with intelligent eyes and a warm smile and, even better, came without any spiritual hangers-on. "Yes," I said, "but I was expecting someone named Jimmy—a friend of our handyman, Rich Kobylt. Did I misunderstand?"

He laughed. "My last name is Del Greco, but my first name is James—or Jimmy, according to my friends and family. My sister was the one who said that Greco sounded more like a designer."

Jack grinned, clearly amused. "Can't argue with that. So you and Rich are good friends, huh?"

Greco nodded. "We've been best friends since grade school. We were even roommates at Clemson. Stayed in touch even after I left for nursing school. I'm an RN and MSN, but after all my friends and family started asking for my design help, I realized I was in the wrong profession."

Jack nodded in understanding. "I sometimes wonder the same thing. Mellie has said more than once that I'm always the person to go to when it comes to placing the stray ottoman or accessorizing a bookshelf."

Greco looked at Jack with appreciation. "It's a skill everybody thinks they have, but few actually do."

"Yes, well," I said, leading him toward the kitchen door and wondering if it would be appropriate to ask him what he and Rich Kobylt had in common, since it apparently wasn't fashion.

General Lee, wearing his cone of shame, stood facing the wall when we walked into the kitchen. Even though the cone was clear, he acted as if he couldn't see through it and nobody could see him. Except for eating and drinking and going outside briefly to relieve himself, he'd stayed in that position, stoically accepting his fate. It was sad and sweet at the same time, and I gave him extra treats when no one was looking and gave him a countdown to when he could see Cindy Lou Who. I wasn't sure which perked him up more.

"Good heavens," Greco said, coming to a full stop when he spotted the dog. "Do you do that to everyone who offends you?"

I was a little resentful that he addressed his question to me.

I frowned and Jack came to my rescue. "That's General Lee. He's just had his little procedure."

General Lee moved his head long enough to give us a deep, soulful look before resuming his examination of the wall paint.

"Poor little guy," Greco said. "I'd pet him, but I get the feeling he'd rather be alone right now."

Jack nodded. "He's holding up well, under the circumstances, but he keeps shooting me warning glances not to get in the car with Mellie and allow her in the driver's seat."

Greco raised his eyebrows but, being an apparently intelligent man, kept silent.

After he declined my offer of refreshments, I led the way up the stairs while he took his time eyeing the foyer with obvious appreciation. "So," Greco said as we walked, "have you met with any other designers?"

Jack coughed. "Only about a dozen or two. Mellie is . . ."

"Particular," I offered.

"Picky," Jack said at the same time.

I frowned at Jack. "By 'picky' he means that I like things . . ."

"Her way," Jack offered. "Besides impeccable taste and the ability to work within a budget, any designer we hire will also need to have some knowledge of psychology—especially obsessive-compulsive disorders."

My elbow contacted with Jack's hard stomach, eliciting a satisfying *oomph*.

"And probably self-defense," Jack continued. "It's a good thing you have a nursing degree—that's definitely in your favor. Do you know how to use a labeling gun by any chance?"

Turning my back on Jack, I faced Greco. "Ignore him. He's a writer and lives in a fantasy world most of the time, so you really never know what's going to come out of his mouth next."

"Good to know," the designer said, looking refreshingly unfazed. Several of the other designers I'd interviewed had left before we'd even climbed the stairs, so I took this as a good omen.

The bedroom door was shut, as it had been since we'd moved Nola into the guest room in March, when I'd seen the face in her window and sensed the dark shadow hovering in the upstairs hallway. It was still there, waiting. And watching. I just wasn't sure for what. Or for how long.

When I'd given the excuse of needing to redecorate Nola's room to move her out, I'd had the worry of not having the money to spend on a major redo. But I'd been saved by my mother and Amelia agreeing it was a great idea since Nola was a young woman now and her bedroom should reflect her growing maturity. They'd been so enthusiastic that they'd decided to split the cost as a Christmas gift to Nola.

"So," I said, turning around to face the two men. "This is Nola's room. She just started her junior year at Ashley Hall and we'd like to give her a room that not only reflects her eclectic tastes for her to enjoy now, but will be a warm and comfortable retreat to come home to once she starts college."

We stood smiling at each other in the hallway for a long moment before Jack coughed. "Maybe we should go inside and take a look?"

"Yes," I said. "Of course." I put my hand on the doorknob and turned. Nothing happened.

"Is it locked?" Jack asked, stepping in front of me to try.

"I hope not," I said, "since there's only one key and it's usually kept on the inside of the door." Our eyes met in mutual understanding.

Greco chimed in. "These old houses usually have a skeleton key. Maybe your housekeeper knows where it is?"

"Yes," I agreed, "but I don't think it's locked. It's just . . . stuck."

Jack tried turning the knob again, pushing hard against the door with the side of his body. I could see it give, the outline of light peeking out from around the frame. It definitely wasn't locked, then. But something was holding it closed from the other side.

The front door downstairs opened and closed. "Hello?" Nola called. "Anyone home?" I bit my lip, not wanting her to see the struggle and understand the reason for it. I heard the sound of her book bag being dropped at the bottom of the stairs—I needed to talk to her about that again—and then her feet running up the stairs, and knew I was too late to stop her.

"Need help?" she asked, moving toward her bedroom.

"It's all right . . ." I began, but she'd already squeezed in front of Jack, assessed the situation, and turned the knob. The door swung open. We stood staring into the space, unsure of what to say.

The first thing I noticed was the scent of horse and leather, along with the lingering odor of gunpowder. I wrinkled my nose, wondering why it seemed so familiar when it shouldn't, and recalled that I had smelled it recently. The second thing I noticed was that all the remaining furniture and bedding had been stacked on the rug, a teetering stepladder that reached the top of the posts of the antique bed. What looked like dried mud had been smeared on the walls and at first glance appeared to be random strokes and shapes. But when I looked closer I could see the individual letters formed a single word, splashed on the wall with fury and anger, the mud thick with hate. *Betrayed.*

"Well," Greco said, stepping purposefully into the room, hands on hips, and then turning around to inspect the carnage. "It looks like we have a lot of work to do here."

Jack, Nola, and I shared surprised looks before turning our gazes back to the designer. "You're hired," I said, and then, without thought, I hugged him.

CHAPTER 8

I sat in a plastic folding chair in an empty listing, passing the time with a box of dried oranges, jabbing cloves into them in the pattern Sophie had dictated for the pomander balls she wanted strewn in every wreath and centerpiece in every house for the progressive dinner. It was taking me longer than expected because getting the cloves evenly spaced was more challenging than I'd thought it should be, even using the pocket-sized ruler I thankfully had in my purse. It was also possible that I was dragging out the chore because of the extra pleasure I got in envisioning each orange as a voodoo doll of my former best friend.

I was in no hurry to finish, since Sophie had so kindly stuffed the backseat of my car with boxwood cuttings that needed "conditioning" before we could use them in our Colonial-wreath-making workshop. "Conditioning" meant a lot of cutting, scraping, recutting, and soaking—four steps too many, in my opinion. I was hoping I'd have time to stop by a craft shop and buy plastic ones. A lot less trouble and they'd last forever. Hopefully, Sophie wouldn't be able to tell the difference.

This house was on State Street and belonged to a client whose listing

I'd accepted only because I'd already sold them another home on Gibbes. I usually didn't do open houses because even when I was supposed to be alone in the house, I never really was, and I found it awkward trying to explain my sudden outbursts of singing to unsuspecting home browsers.

But this house was a relatively new (circa 2002) estate home—or, as Sophie referred to it, an aberration of architectural and historic sensibilities—built to loosely resemble the house that had originally been on the lot before being abandoned and then condemned by the city. I remembered how Sophie had dressed in black and wept whenever she passed the empty lot, then became openly hostile when she saw the opulent home being built in its place. It was a Charleston double house on steroids, according to Sophie, whose chief complaint was that the house was new. The owners, my clients, were a nice middle-aged couple from Boston who'd been happy in the house for several years until they heard that the most desirable location to own a home in Charleston was South of Broad. I didn't agree, but a double commission wasn't something I could ignore. Especially not now.

I heard the front gate close and I stood to look through the window, expecting another Realtor and her clients for a second showing. I waited until I heard footsteps on the porch, then opened the door before they had a chance to hear the doorbell chime "Dixie." The owners had thought it cute and that it might make their neighbors warm up to them. It hadn't.

"Anthony!" I said in surprise, taking in the crutches he was using because of a sprained ankle, the bruises on his face, and his arm in a sling—all apparently from the car accident.

"Sorry," he said. "I probably should have let you know I was coming. I called your office, and that nice Miss Jolly told me you were here."

Our receptionist was usually a better gatekeeper, but I was sure Anthony had used his considerable charm. I stood back and held the door open for him, watching as he looked around as if hoping to see someone.

"Is your sister here?"

"No—she's watching my children. She's our nanny."

He looked chagrined. "Of course. I was just . . . Never mind. I came to apologize for the other day, and hopefully make another appointment for us to visit the mausoleum."

I shuddered at the memory of my father and the dark voice that had erupted from his mouth like bile. "I'm not sure. . . ."

"Someone messed with my car, Melanie. I know I won't be able to prove it, but my steering wheel was like something possessed. I couldn't control it—it was like it had its own mind. Like someone was controlling it remotely."

"What has this got to do with me going to the mausoleum?"

"It's Marc—don't you see? He's somehow found out what I'm up to, and he's desperate for us not to find whatever might be hidden there."

I wished I could see, because then I wouldn't have to consider the other very real possibility of what had happened to Anthony's car. "No, I don't. Marc is a jerk, but he's your brother. I doubt very much that he would try to physically harm you."

Despite the chill outside and in the empty house, beads of perspiration dotted his forehead. I led him to the lone chair and he sat down heavily.

"Sorry," he said. "This whole thing has me . . . spooked."

Me, too, I almost said. "Can I get you some water?"

He shook his head. "But thanks. I'll really feel better if you say you'll still help me."

I crossed my arms. "I think you need to tell me more than just 'meet me at the mausoleum.' I need you to tell me the whole story, okay?"

Anthony placed his crutches on the floor, then leaned back in his chair and stretched his legs out in front of him. "When Marc bought the plantation, it was because he thought that's where the Confederate diamonds were hidden."

"I knew that, but not why. What made him think that?" I asked, settling my gaze on one of the oranges and noticing that the spacing on the cloves was off.

"Same reason everyone did at the time, I guess—all those rumors about the Vanderhorst Confederate ancestor who supposedly hid the diamonds. But when Marc was doing research for his book on our ancestor Joseph Longo, he discovered Joseph's business diary at the Charleston Museum in the archives. Since he knew Jack was working on the same subject for a book, he tore out the pages. . . ." He stopped, a look of chagrin settling on his features. "And destroyed them, but there was enough there to make Marc believe the diamonds were somewhere on the plantation—or had been at some point before they were moved to your house."

Unable to stop myself, I picked up the orange with the errant cloves and pulled out my ruler. Anthony stopped speaking, and when I looked at him, I realized he was staring at me. "These are decorations for the progressive dinner. Haven't you ever seen cloves stuck into oranges to make pomander balls?"

He nodded slowly. "Sure. Just never with such . . . precision."

I frowned at him. "You were saying something about why Marc thought the diamonds were hidden at Gallen Hall."

"Right," he said, forcing his gaze away from what I was doing. "Joseph had copied into his diary what looked like some kind of weird drawing, almost like a doodle. Apparently while at a party at the Vanderhorst home on Tradd Street, Joseph did some snooping and found a really old piece of paper with these odd scribblings in Mr. Vanderhorst's desk, and Joseph copied them into his diary. Marc only showed the copy to me once—and I thought it looked like hieroglyphics, but Marc said that was proof the Vanderhorsts had hidden something valuable on one of their properties. I mean, why go through the trouble of using codes if they weren't hiding something valuable, right? Marc assumed it was the diamonds because of the story of Captain John Vanderhorst being entrusted with the diamonds after the war and then turning up in Charleston without them."

"Yes, well, we now know that Marc did, actually, have the diamonds and he hid them in my grandfather clock. So why does he think there's something else that might be hidden in the mausoleum?"

"Because when Marc found out that Jack was working on another book, he thought it could be a sequel, and Marc wanted to make sure that he knew everything and that Jack wouldn't find anything new. So he went back to his notes and saw that on that same page in Joseph's diary, he'd also copied the words 'French treasure.' Not sure what the 'French' part means, but 'treasure' is certainly clear. Marc thought the same thing. The Confederate diamonds weren't from France, which is probably why he dismissed this particular notation when searching for the diamonds."

I bent down to look into the box of oranges, using my ruler to check the placement of the cloves. "And?" I prompted, feeling his eyes on me again.

He cleared his throat. "Marc hasn't figured out what the drawing means—I know that much. He didn't ask for my help, either, because then he'd feel obliged to share any treasure with me. But that didn't keep him from looking. He pretty much tore apart Gallen Hall and used metal detectors over all the floors and walls, looking for whatever might be a 'French treasure.'"

I'd finished with the oranges and begun to pace, picking up stray lint from the bare wood floor as I walked. "I'm afraid you've lost me. All the diamonds are accounted for. There's no more treasure. And you still haven't said what this has to do with the mausoleum."

He sat up and leaned his elbows on his knees. "You're wrong. Maybe not about the diamonds, but definitely about there being another treasure hidden somewhere."

"I don't . . ."

He held up his hand. "Before Marc and I had our falling-out, we were in the library at Gallen Hall, smoking cigars and drinking bourbon. Marc never could hold his liquor, which is the only reason I can think of for him telling me this—and I seriously doubt that he knows he did, or he'd have burned down the house and everything else once it all belonged to me." He stopped, rubbing his sore arm.

"So what did he tell you?"

"He said he had proof that there was more hidden treasure on Vanderhorst property."

I frowned. "So you think he found another diamond?"

"No. He would have gloated about that for weeks. Several months ago when he found out that Jack was already at work on another book, he went to the archives where he'd found Joseph Longo's diary and found personal correspondence belonging to the Vanderhorst family from 1781, which was during the occupation of Charleston, in case you weren't aware."

I just nodded, not wanting to show that I had no idea to what he was referring.

"He stole the letters from the archives, too, just in case they contained something Jack could use for his book. But when Marc read them, he found something else entirely."

I was seething now, on Jack's behalf. We'd always known Marc was a weasel, but we'd thought we'd seen the bottom of his depravity. Apparently, we hadn't. "What?" I prompted.

"It was a mention that a room needed to be prepared for an important visitor from France who wished to lay a wreath on the tomb of the Vanderhorsts' daughter, Marie Claire. Marc pointed out that the Vanderhorsts, like most of the colony of South Carolina at that point, were loyalists. And the French were bitter enemies of the British. So why would a Frenchman be visiting the Vanderhorsts? To lay a wreath on the tomb of a daughter who'd never existed?"

Anthony raised an eyebrow. "Marc showed me the family tree—he was quite obsessed with the idea of more treasure to find and had made his own very complicated drawing—and the Vanderhorsts had six sons, only two of whom lived to adulthood. And let's not forget the words 'French treasure' Marc had seen in Joseph's diary."

I blinked. "So, between the drawing and the letter with incorrect information, he thought a treasure was hidden somewhere on Vanderhorst property? It seems a bit of a stretch."

"Yeah—so did finding the Confederate diamonds in your house." He gave me a sardonic smile. "But there's more. Marc thinks there's a connection to the drawing with some of the bricks inside the mausoleum. Marc's already dug around the floor of the mausoleum and searched and searched but come up empty-handed. He wanted to tear the entire mausoleum down to do a better search, but the preservation people put a stop to it. Apparently, it's protected by the Archaeological Resources Protection Act, which requires federal permits for excavation or removal of material remains of past human life or activities. We can't touch it. Not legally, anyway."

"But you've searched, surely."

Anthony's eyes darkened. "I've tried. But there's someone . . . something . . . keeping me out. That's the weirdest thing—because I'd been inside the mausoleum many times in the past without anything strange happening. But then all of a sudden when I tried to enter to search one more time, things would . . . happen to me. I'd feel punches and scratches. And . . ." He stopped, giving his head a firm shake as if trying to remove a painful memory. "A stone lid on one of the crypts slid partially off and broke, and one of the pieces barely missed landing on my foot. Do you know how heavy those lids are? They don't just slide off. I wanted to believe that I'd imagined it all, but there were purple bruises all over me." He looked away for a moment before forcing his gaze back to me. "And I had bloody scratch marks on my back. Under my clothes. Like someone had raked their fingernails over bare skin."

I didn't even try to pretend I had no idea what might have been responsible. "When was this?" My voice shook.

"It started around the time we had all those heavy rains this past spring, remember?"

Of course I did. That was when my back garden sank, revealing the hidden cistern. Unburying what had been covered for at least a century.

I nodded, my thoughts running a marathon down different paths, trying hard to avoid the most obvious. "And you somehow found out that the nineteenth-century Vanderhorsts used some of the bricks from the mausoleum and old cemetery wall to build the cistern at their Tradd Street house."

"Yeah. By accident. Apparently, Marc hadn't destroyed all the documents and letters he stole from the archives. He left a bunch of them in a shoebox in a garbage can. Luckily, when I discovered I was the hapless owner of a failed winery and took possession of the premises, I found the can in the carriage house. Apparently, whoever was in charge of taking out the garbage had forgotten this one bin."

He shook his head wearily, and I felt sorry for him, for having grown up with a brother like Marc Longo. He continued. "Feeling angry, and wanting some kind of evidence that Marc was doing something illegal, I went through the papers. There was a lot there, all stolen by Marc from the archives—nothing to do with him or any of his business dealings, sadly—and ready to go out in the trash. Which explains why I couldn't find anything about the plantation when I tried to do my own research. That's how I found out about the bricks. I read through everything—but it was just a bunch of ledgers with costs of all the building materials and furniture for both Vanderhorst properties, and a housekeeper's journal about how much tea and sugar she measured out on a daily basis. The only thing interesting I learned was that there'd been an older mausoleum on the same site as the one that's there now, but for some reason it was torn down and then rebuilt within two years of the original. They also replaced the brick wall that surrounded the cemetery with an iron fence at the same time. The Vanderhorsts were building a house on Tradd Street at the time—probably an earlier version of your house now—and the demolished mausoleum and wall would have been a cheap source of bricks."

I raised my eyebrows. "Why would they have done that? Is the new one bigger?"

Anthony shook his head. "No. That's the thing—they used the same blueprint both times. And it was practically brand-new. There were only three bodies interred at the time—all placed there in the same year: 1782."

I stopped pacing. "Please tell me that you still have the shoebox."

He picked up one of the oranges and began to examine it, and it took all my restraint to ask him not to touch any of the cloves. "Of course—I'm not like Marc. I could never destroy a historical document. That's just . . . wrong."

I decided that I liked Anthony Longo a lot. "Can I see the shoebox?"

He began tossing the orange from one hand to the other, and I clenched my teeth. "So this means you're still in?"

I was pretty sure I didn't have a choice. There was no doubt in my mind that what was going on in his mausoleum was somehow connected to my cistern and the specter haunting Nola's bedroom. I unclenched my jaw. "Yes. I suppose I am."

He smiled, then stood. "I'll get out of your way, then. I'll bring the box to your house whenever it's convenient. Or I can drop it by your house now if Jayne's there."

I frowned. "Why don't you just bring it by my office? You can leave it with Jolly. She's completely trustworthy."

He looked disappointed, but I owed it to my friendship with Thomas Riley not to encourage another suitor for Jayne.

"And, Anthony?"

He looked at me expectantly.

"Don't tell anyone I'm helping you with this. It's not something I want people to know."

He gazed at me silently for a moment. "All right," he said with a nod before hoisting himself up with his crutches, then walking toward the front door in the octagonal entranceway. Its scale wasn't of the right period, in contrast with the rest of the house. I almost bit my tongue when I realized I'd started to think like Sophie.

"I wouldn't eat that orange if I were you. It's been dried," I said, eyeing the fruit he still held in his hand.

"Oh, right," he said, tossing it to me.

I somehow managed to catch the orange. "And one last thing."

He looked at me expectantly.

"Be careful. I'd stay away from the mausoleum for now until I can figure out a plan."

We said our good-byes and I watched him exit, closing the door behind him. When I turned around to resume my task, all the oranges from the box were now on the floor, neatly lined up to make a perfect X.

CHAPTER 9

As I locked up my clients' house, juggling the box of oranges and satisfied with the precisely arranged cloves sticking into their skins, I heard my name being called. I turned around and spotted Veronica's daughter and Nola's friend, Lindsey Farrell, and her father, Michael, walking what appeared to be a snowball white husky puppy.

"Need some help?" Michael called as he rushed up the steps to take the box.

"Thanks," I said. "My car's right over here—if you can just stick the box in the back, I'd appreciate it."

I used my remote to pop open the trunk, and while he was fitting the box inside, I turned to greet Lindsey. "It's nice to see you—Nola didn't mention that you got a new puppy."

I bent down to scratch the ball of fluff behind the ears, his gorgeous blue eyes happily staring into mine while his little pink tongue lolled. Ever since getting my own dog, I'd become hyperaware of other dogs. I couldn't walk down the street without smiling at them or asking to pet them, and I would be humiliated if Jack ever found out, because my official line was that I wasn't a dog person. Even though I now owned three and one of them slept on my pillow. I wasn't a person who wanted to advertise that she'd relaxed any of her personal rules.

"He was a birthday surprise from my mom." Lindsey leaned over and whispered conspiratorially, "My dad isn't too happy, but I've always wanted a dog. His name is Ghost."

I looked at her, startled. "Ghost?"

"Yeah. You know. Like from *Game of Thrones*."

I stared at her blankly.

"Like in the HBO series based on the books by George R. R. Martin," she prompted.

I could tell she wanted to roll her eyes when I showed no recognition, but because I was Nola's stepmom and an adult, she resisted. "Yes, well, I don't have a lot of extra time nowadays with the twins and work."

"And the house," she said. "My dad says keeping up with a historic house is like living with a persistent and fat mosquito with a hole in its stomach that keeps sucking you dry."

I pretended to be appalled, trying to forget how I'd once thought much the same thing. And still did on occasion, like when Sophie announced we had wood rot on the front piazza and we needed to restore the wood rather than replace it with something less vulnerable to the elements. Like with anything that wasn't wood.

"You got that right," Michael said as he approached. He jerked his chin in the direction of the car. "Doing more magic tricks with oranges?" His tone was light, but his eyes weren't, and I knew he was remembering the orange thrown at him in my dining room.

I feigned ignorance. "Actually, those are for progressive dinner house decorations. Since your house is one of the dessert course houses, I was about to call Veronica to see if I could get into your house now since it's so close. Sophie wanted me to measure the fireplaces so she would know how much garland we'd need, and also to look around to get an idea of what else we might need for the house. Yours is a Victorian, so it will be a little different than the rest. I'm not really sure how different, but I told her I'd take pictures with my phone and let her figure it out."

"I can do that," Michael said. "Or Veronica. No need for you to take up more of your day."

I was more than eager to agree, knowing I had just enough time to stop by Glazed for a doughnut and latte before an appointment I had at the office. But the sudden scent of Vanilla Musk made me close my mouth. "Actually, Sophie will just make me come back and do it, so I might as well get it taken care of the way she wants it the first time." I forced a big grin, recalling something Jack had once said about me. "You know how some people are—everything has to be just right, and done exactly as they would have done it, or it's just not good enough."

"Mom's not home, but the front door is unlocked if you don't want to wait for us to finish walking Ghost," Lindsey offered.

Michael started to protest, saying something about coming with me, but I spoke over him. I still couldn't put a finger on why I didn't want to be alone with him, and settled on the memory of the orange being thrown across the room at him. "Don't be silly—I don't want to be a bother or interrupt your family time. I promise to be quick, and I probably won't even be there when you get back. Nice to see you both," I said cheerily, trying to ignore the icy touch of the hand on my arm.

I walked the three blocks to the yellow Victorian on Queen Street. I'd passed it many times, even remembered hearing speculation about it going on the market after the former owners, Veronica's parents, had moved to an assisted-living community. Veronica and Michael had moved in instead, making it a home for their only child, Lindsey. I hadn't known any of this at the time, of course, having not yet reconnected with my old college classmate, but I remembered the house.

It was a pretty Queen Anne complete with an asymmetrical façade and a dominant front-facing gable. Until I'd met Sophie, I'd just called this style of house old and would have shown it to every buyer who stopped in my office looking for a piece of Charleston history regardless of which period they specified. Most buyers hadn't known much more about historic architecture than I did, the only impediment to their purchase usually the asking price. Despite many houses requiring extensive renovations, the prices were still higher than that for a four-bedroom new build in Poughkeepsie. But the desire to own a historic house in the Holy City kept me in business, which I was very grateful for even if I did not exactly understand it.

I walked through the front gate and up the steps to the wraparound porch. It didn't matter if the door was unlocked or not because it opened before I reached it, the heavy scent of Vanilla Musk saturating the chilly air. This was the house Veronica and her sister, Adrienne, had grown up in. Although Adrienne had been murdered while living in a dorm at the College of Charleston, it would make sense that this house, where she'd had so many happy memories, would be the place to which she'd return.

Victorian architecture, with its accompanying interiors and emphasis on dark wood, heavy fabrics, and clashing patterns, was my least favorite in my repertoire of old houses. As I stood in an arched doorway leading from the small entry hall into the front parlor, I couldn't tell if the look was intended to appear old or was simply dated. Beneath the lingering scent of Vanilla Musk, the pervading air of the room was of stale emptiness. Any past warmth or hint of comfort and family had long since vacated the premises.

I remembered from one of my earlier conversations with Veronica that Michael wanted to sell the house, saying that the renovations and repairs were too much. But after a box containing the contents of Adrienne's dorm room at the time of her death had been discovered in the attic, along with a new clue in the form of a necklace, Veronica couldn't let it go.

I pulled out my measuring tape—always carried alongside my ruler because one should always be prepared—and iPhone to measure the mantels and take pictures according to Sophie's directions, glad I had Nola as my personal technology manager. I'd never been good with any kind of electronic equipment, mostly because the devices always seemed to die or lose power when I came too close to lonely spirits wanting my attention. But even Nola had faith that I could manage the camera function on my phone and that even if my camera died, the photos would be put on a cloud somewhere so I wouldn't lose them. I figured I didn't need to know how things worked, but should just be happy that they did.

I stepped into the parlor and, after quickly measuring and jotting down the width of the mantel, aimed my camera at the heavily carved fireplace with the wavy mirror above it. A marble urn stood on each end of the mantel, and I hoped they didn't contain ashes, because Sophie would want me to stick greenery in them along with an orange or two for decoration.

A definite presence accompanied me as I walked through the open pocket doors to the dining room and then to the woefully outdated kitchen. Shiny floral wallpaper covered the walls, matching the harvest gold and avocado green appliances and laminate countertops. Although it needed a complete kitchen gut job and some cosmetic fixes, there would still be potential buyers lined up outside the door hoping to be able to call this address home. Invariably, they'd ask if the house was haunted—some enthusiastically and others less so—and I'd give a soft laugh to show them that I was in on the joke, because of course ghosts weren't real.

I sniffed the air, smelling the familiar perfume. I wondered why Adrienne chose not to show herself to me. I speculated whether it had to do with the other presence I sensed, the one that wasn't so friendly. The one whose dark and angry voice had come through my mother's mouth when she'd held the necklace found in the attic. My mother would say Adrienne was saving her energy in case she needed it to protect me.

I continued to measure and snap photos of the downstairs, my Realtor's brain automatically doing the calculations necessary for updating the house, not just for more comfortable modern living, but also for resale. As I passed through the small foyer toward the front door, I found myself hesitating at the bottom of the stairs. The wide steps were covered in dark wood and a somber-hued floral pattern. The heavy wooden balustrade jutted up alongside the steps before turning at the landing under a brilliant stained glass window and then continuing to the upper floors and the attic.

It was neither inviting nor welcoming, yet I felt a firm push on my back, nudging me forward, and when I tried to turn around, I found my way blocked by unseen hands.

"Fine," I muttered. "Go ahead and show me whatever it is you want me to see, but I can't promise anything other than that I will tell my sister and my mother so they can help you if they can. That's it."

Jayne had told me that her argument with Detective Riley had come from her insistence that she advertise her abilities, and he had said it would only bring the crazies out of the woodwork to harass her. I happened to agree with him, which sidelined this investigation and any other cold cases for which he'd hoped to solicit our help. I had enough going on in my life anyway, so I didn't miss being involved. Not that the ghosts were paying any attention to my time-out.

Slowly, I climbed the stairs, holding tightly to the balustrade as I remembered other stairs on other occasions, and a solid push that could send a person hurtling to the bottom. I wasn't eager to repeat the experience. The old wood risers creaked under my feet, lending an uneasy feeling of foreboding and making me long for the creaking floors in my own house, which sounded more welcoming than frightening.

The upstairs hallway with its dark rose runner and mauve walls lent the effect of a funeral home, and, following a cursory glance to show Adrienne I'd done my best, I made to head back down the stairs. But the entity walking with me continued to forcefully guide me toward the stairs leading to the attic door.

I climbed the last flight of steps, then stood staring at the wooden door panels and the ceramic doorknob, hoping the door was locked so that I could turn around and leave. Not that it mattered, as the door swung open in front of me and I was pushed into a musty space. The rainbow of muted colors descending from the dirty stained glass windows on either side of the large room did nothing to dispel the darkness and gloom of the attic.

Hulking shapes of furniture draped with sheets were pushed against the walls, along with a child's miniature kitchen, grocery store, and baby stroller complete with Raggedy Ann doll strapped inside, sightless eyes reflecting the stained glass. The room echoed with what sounded like a sigh, an exhalation of memories and time. It weighted the air, the single sound carrying all the loss and grief of a life cut short. I closed my eyes for a moment, then jerked them open again as I felt a small shove on my shoulder.

I stepped forward, my foot colliding with the side of a cardboard box. Packing tape had been ripped from the top seam and lay curled against the box, the flaps stuck beneath one another to keep it closed. As if knowing what I was supposed to do, I leaned forward and pulled open the flaps, recognizing immediately that this was Adrienne's box. A sorority scrapbook sat pressed against one side, and photographs and invitations to various events were sprinkled like confetti over a small heart-shaped throw pillow and a College of Charleston Cougars baseball hat.

I rifled through the mementos of a college freshman, trying to determine what Adrienne wanted me to see, knowing this was the box Veronica and Detective Riley had already gone through. Frustrated, I straightened. "You've brought me all the way up here, but you've got to be more specific. They found the broken chain and charm already. We're just not sure what it means—if anything."

I felt a small stab of panic. After my mother had touched the necklace and the dark voice had come from her, I'd taken it away. I just had no recollection of what I'd done with it. I remembered putting it somewhere so special that even I couldn't remember exactly where. Or maybe subconsciously I'd known then that I hadn't wanted anything to do with it.

"I have to go, Adrienne. I'll let Jayne know I was here. Maybe she can find out more—"

I was cut off by the sound of the front door slamming shut and a dog barking. "Hello, Mrs. Trenholm." Lindsey's voice traveled up the stairs. "We're back!"

I stood frozen, staring at the door and wondering how I'd explain my presence in the attic. I contemplated hiding there until everyone was asleep and then sneaking out but quickly dismissed the idea. If I was caught, the headlines would be worse than any recounting my ghost-seeing abilities.

I was in the middle of calculating how long it would take me to get down to the second floor when something soft struck me in the back of the head. I looked down to where the object had landed at my feet and picked it up. It was the heart-shaped pillow, covered in red felt with a ruffled edge. The sound of running feet, heavier than Lindsey's, came from the stairway, and before I could think of what I was doing, I shoved the small pillow into my tote bag.

"Melanie? Are you up here?" It was Michael, sounding as if he'd already reached the second floor. I listened as his footsteps, slower now, approached the attic door.

Still immobile, I heard something else, something small and delicate, clatter against the floor at my feet. I looked down at the broken chain and the charm that Veronica had found in the box, the interlocking Greek letters offering a clue we'd yet to understand.

Panicking, I watched as the doorknob turned, then quickly scooped up the necklace and dropped it into my tote before Michael opened the door.

I registered his look of surprise as I walked past him with a smile. "Thank you," I said. "I think I've got all the pictures I need. Tell Veronica I'll give her a call."

I hurried down the stairs as fast as my high heels could take me, gave Lindsey a quick good-bye and the dog a pat on the head, then exited the house as fast as I could, trying to decipher the look on Michael's face. It wasn't until I'd reached my car and met my gaze in the rearview mirror that I realized what it had been. *Grief.*

CHAPTER 10

When I got home, Jack's minivan wasn't in its space in the carriage house. It was dinnertime for the twins, so I doubted that Jayne had taken them out. Usually when Jack was knee-deep in a book, he didn't leave the house in the middle of the day unless there was an emergency. Or he was procrastinating. I frowned as I stepped out of my car, contemplating the possibilities.

The sound of squealing brakes followed by a revving engine brought my attention to the street. I walked to the end of our driveway and peered out to see Jack's minivan hurtling in my direction before coming to an abrupt stop about twenty feet away in the middle of the road.

The driver's-side door flung open and a very annoyed Nola emerged and began stomping toward the house. "I didn't want to know how to drive anyway," she shouted over her shoulder just as Jack exited from the passenger-side door.

"Good," Jack shouted in reply. "I'm sure the entire world will thank you."

Nola burst into tears and ran past me and up the steps to the piazza. I could hear her feet pounding to the front door as her sobs carried back to us on the street.

"Jack?" I'd never heard him raise his voice to his daughter, ever.

There was no remorse on his face as he stared back at me. "She's a menace to society when she's behind the wheel of a motor vehicle."

"Still, that's no reason to yell at her." I pointed to the house. "Go inside and apologize. I'll park the car since I don't think either one of you is capable of doing it right now."

I didn't wait for him to respond as I got behind the wheel and put the car in drive, then parked it in its space next to my car. After waiting long enough for Jack and Nola to have a heart-to-heart, I entered the house through the front door, avoiding the back garden and cistern. It had become such a habit that I'd forgotten what the back door looked like.

I paused in the foyer, listening to Jayne in the kitchen with the twins and trying to hear Jack's or Nola's voice. Instead I heard the distinctive clink of ice in a glass from the direction of the parlor, and I cautiously walked in that direction, my breath held.

Jack stood in front of the bar cart, usually filled with empty decanters. Because Jack and my father both were recovering alcoholics, we kept the decanters empty except when we had company. As I watched, Jack leaned down and, after hesitating for a brief moment, opened the cabinet door. Despite having a brass key in the lock, it had never been locked. Because there'd been no reason to lock it.

Jack reached inside to the back of the cabinet and pulled out what looked like a full bottle of Glenfiddich. Having grown up with an alcoholic father, I recognized the bottle like an old friend. I continued to hold my breath, not daring to move even though I wanted nothing more than to back away and pretend I hadn't seen him.

He held the bottle with both hands, looking at it for a long time, as if it might be the face of an old lover. I guess, in some ways, it was. And then, without a word, he leaned down and put the bottle back where it had been.

"Jack?" I said softly.

He started at the sound of his name but didn't turn around. "I thought you'd go check on Nola."

I moved to stand next to him, staring pointedly at the open door of the cabinet. "And that would give you time for what?" I found myself very close to tears. "What's going on?"

His beautiful eyes bored into mine, but there was none of the humor or love I usually saw in them. They weren't empty, but there was definitely something missing. "What's going on?" he repeated. "What's going on besides my career getting flushed down the toilet?"

I took his hand, and being unaccustomed to having our roles reversed, I led Jack to the sofa, pulling him down next to me. "What's happened?" I asked.

He jumped up and began pacing the room, keeping his distance from the bar cart. "Oh, just the usual in the life of a writer trying to resurrect his career. I write ten pages, then delete nine of them, and after I rewrite them I realize it's all total crap. So I went for a run because fresh air and exercise are supposed to help creativity, but as I'm running down Legare I practically trip over Rebecca and that little dog of hers—with ears dyed pink now, I kid you not—and she asked me how I am in the way somebody asks a person with some life-threatening disease, and then tells me she's sorry, and she seemed surprised that I had no idea what she was talking about or why she should be sorry and then wouldn't meet my eyes. So I rushed back home to check my messages and sure enough, there's one from my agent."

I took a deep breath, preparing myself for what I knew was not going to be good news. I wanted to suggest a time-out so I could find a doughnut or two to bury my worries in and to distract me from the looming problem. But that was what the old, single Mellie would have done. Now I was a married and responsible adult and mother of three. And I loved Jack. I had for even longer than I'd known. I needed to slap down the old Mellie and figure out a way to get us through this. That's what marriage was. We were a team. And if it was my turn to be the strong one, then I'd better figure out how. Even if I had no clue as to how to start.

My voice was a lot stronger than I felt. "And what did he say?"

Jack stopped in front of the grandfather clock, staring at it as if it might still be holding on to secrets. "I didn't get to speak with him—just his assistant. She said my agent's taking early retirement; he's already gone. She said I would be given the option of working with another agent inside the agency or I could find my own."

If Rebecca had known bad news was coming, then there was only one place she could have heard it. I pushed the thought from my head, unwilling to go there, and swallowed, tried to put on a relaxed smile. "Well, that's good news, isn't it?"

He turned around and looked at me with wild eyes. "No—of course it's not. A literary agent is not the same as a real estate agent. They're not interchangeable."

I stood quickly, my temper pushing aside my attempt at being the rational adult. "Excuse me? I'll have you know that not every real estate agent is the same. . . ."

He held up his hand. "I know, I know. I'm sorry. That's not what I meant. I wanted to say that it's a personal connection between a literary agent and an editor and the writer. There has to be a strong belief in the writer's abilities for them to be able to work together. I can't just be handed off to someone who doesn't know anything about me or my books. Like Desmarae, my new editor. Did I tell you that she actually suggested we should aim for a younger audience with this book—the same book that she still hasn't read the first chapters of yet so she has no idea what it's about—and ask Kim Kardashian for a cover blurb?" He slapped his palm against his forehead so hard it left a red mark.

"Oh, Jack." I moved to his side, reaching up to touch his shoulder, hard and tense beneath my hand. "I'm so sorry. I know this is all sudden, and unexpected, and certainly not welcome when you're trying to finish your book. But maybe this will be a positive change. Maybe your new agent will be even more enthusiastic and energetic. And will be happy to tell Desmarae exactly where to put her Kim Kardashian blurb."

Jack frowned. "He or she might have to wait on that—first I need someone to tell Desmarae that we can't wait another year before publication, which is what she's telling me now. Apparently, they're revisiting their publishing schedule and my previous slot has been given to a historical erotica series."

"But—"

"I know. We need the money. I've already spoken with my publisher directly, who was less than receptive to my idea of keeping me where I'm scheduled, so I'm hoping my new agent—whoever that's going to be—will have better luck."

"Do you think . . ." I paused, ready to suggest grabbing the children and taking them for a walk. It was procrastination, sure, but playing with the children was always such a stress reliever, and it was certainly easier than figuring out what we should do.

He quirked an eyebrow. "Were you going to ask me if I think it's a coincidence that Rebecca knew before I did?"

Our eyes met. "Because there's no such thing as coincidence," we said in unison.

"Exactly," Jack said. "And I don't have a doubt in my mind that Marc is behind this somehow."

I didn't want to agree, even though I had a sinking feeling that he was right. It was just too awful to think about right now. I distracted myself by looking at the red mark on Jack's forehead. Touching it gently with my thumb, I said, "Does it hurt?"

His eyes met mine, and a little spark passed between us. He nodded. "A little."

I stood on my tiptoes and kissed it.

"It hurts here, too," he said, pointing to his cheek.

Without question, I placed my hands on his shoulders and reached up to give him another kiss, feeling the bristles of his beard tickle my lips. I stepped back. "Better?"

"A little. It hurts here, too." Jack pointed to his mouth.

Pulling him closer, I happily obliged, ignoring the nagging thought that he was distracting me for a reason. His arms wrapped around me, his hands snaking under my blouse as he pressed me into him. I felt his fingers unfastening the hooks on my bra as he trailed small kisses across my cheek until he reached my ear. His hot breath fanned the bare skin on my neck as he whispered, "I think I need a little stress relief right now."

"Me, too," I whispered back, my hands fiddling with the button on his jeans.

There was a slight clearing of a throat behind us, and we both dropped our hands like teenagers caught in the backseat of the parents' sedan. We turned to see Greco standing in the entranceway, his head nearly touching the top of the molding. I'd forgotten that he was supposed to be at the house, taking inventory of the furniture in Nola's room and the attic to see what he could reuse or salvage for the redo.

"Sorry to interrupt," he said, looking around the room at everything but us. "I can come back at a more convenient time."

"No, no—it's perfectly fine," I said, smoothing my blouse and skirt, hoping that at least one of the hooks in my bra was still intact.

Greco smiled at a spot over our heads. "If you have a moment, I wanted to show you something upstairs."

I groaned inwardly, wondering if he'd found a skull hidden under a floorboard or a human femur behind loose wainscoting. In my world, anything was possible. I feigned a relaxed smile as Jack and I followed the designer up the staircase, going over all responses to whatever it was he wanted to show us that would placate him enough so he wouldn't quit. *Why, yes, I do believe that looks like an ax mark in the back of that skull you found in the air duct. That Nola—such a prankster!*

I realized Greco was speaking and I shut down my inner voice.

"The architectural details in this house, including Nola's room, are really quite spectacular. And the antiques are top-notch. Not that I don't appreciate the business, but except for a few cosmetic changes, I don't think there needs to be the kind of massive redo we originally spoke about."

Jack and I exchanged a glance. Clearing my throat, I said, "Well, when Nola moved in a few years ago, my mother-in-law did a refresh of the room with new fabrics and wall colors. The bed was here—it's too big to be moved unless we cut a hole in the wall and lower it with a crane into the back garden, in which case my house-hugging friend would throw me in the marsh with a cinder block attached to my ankle.

But we added an antique desk Jack's mother found in the attic here, along with a few occasional pieces."

"Like the jewelry chest?" he asked, a small hitch in his voice.

We reached the top step and stopped. "Yes," I said. "I thought it needed to be refinished, but Amelia liked it the way it was—said it added 'character' to the piece."

Greco was frowning, and I didn't want the jewelry chest to be the reason he quit. I was ready to agree to painting everything neon green and adding a Harry Styles mural on the ceiling if that's what it would take to retain him. "But it doesn't have to stay if you don't like it. And I like Harry Styles." I was proud that I knew who that was, if only because Jack had taken Nola and me to see *Dunkirk* and she'd mentioned that the actor sang, too.

Greco smiled, looking a bit confused, but it didn't erase the frown lines over his nose. "No, it really is a beautiful piece and if your daughter likes it, we can certainly incorporate it into the new design. It's just . . ."

Jack walked toward the bedroom and grabbed the doorknob. "It's just such a tangled jumble of chains and baubles that you can't see how she can find anything?" He pushed open the door, then stepped back for us to enter.

We stopped at the threshold. Nola and I had scrubbed the walls clean, leaving only faint traces of the muddy letters that had appeared and had, thankfully, remained gone. But the jewelry cabinet, emptied by Nola when she'd moved to the guest room, stood in the corner now with every drawer open, the lid pulled all the way back like a gaping mouth.

"You want to use it more as a sculpture than a jewelry cabinet?" Jack suggested helpfully.

I smiled pleasantly as if that had been exactly what I'd been thinking, too, instead of what Greco was about to tell us.

"I appreciate your creativity," he said to Jack. "But there seems to be something wrong with it. I'll close all the drawers and the lid and turn my back, and the next thing I know, everything's opened again."

"How strange," Jack and I said in unison.

Greco crossed his arms and regarded us under lowered brows. "Something tells me that it's not."

Jack took a step toward the jewelry chest and pulled a drawer in and out as if testing it. "You know how these old houses are, with uneven floors and varying humidity. . . ."

Greco held out his hand palm up to stop Jack from continuing. "Please. Don't. Ever since my first visit here, I've been getting weird vibes from the whole house—and this room in particular."

I held my breath, preparing myself for his words of resignation.

"I kind of like it," he said. "I find it rather creatively inspiring. I actually grew up in a house on Broad that always had things that went bump in the night. I found it more interesting than frightening, and since I couldn't see whatever it was causing the ruckus, nothing really bothered me."

"Is that so?" I asked noncommittally, feeling a little jealous that the odd sounds never bothered him because he couldn't see anything. Until I'd learned how to block out all the sights and sounds, I'd spent my childhood sleeping with my eyes open. "Well, this is an old house, and Charleston is supposed to be one of the most haunted cities in the world, so I suppose it wouldn't be out of the question that there might be the odd spirit here or there."

"Phew," he said, doing a mock swipe of his forehead. "I was afraid I would scare you. Glad to know you're not easily scared."

Jack put his arm around my shoulder and pulled me close. "Who, us? Never."

"Good. Because I found something else you might find . . . interesting." He walked over to the large four-poster bed, the intricate rice carvings winding their way up to the acorn finials. Lowering his tall frame, he pointed at the ball-and-claw foot, tapping his finger against something near the bottom edge.

As usual, I wasn't wearing my glasses and couldn't see what he was pointing at no matter how much I squinted.

Jack shook his head at me before leaning forward to see. "A carving of a peacock."

"A peacock," I repeated, trying to recall why that seemed significant.

The designer straightened to his full height. "I'm not sure if it's connected, but the peacock was a secret symbol used here in the Carolinas during the Revolutionary War. I do a bit of Revolutionary War reenacting—on the British side—which is how I know this factoid. Of course, it could be something else entirely."

"What do you mean by 'secret symbol'?" Jack asked. He was wearing the expression he used when dissecting reams of information to boil down into something he could write about.

"A spy ring. From what I've read, it was as instrumental in leading us to an American victory as the Culper spy ring, but far less known. Mostly because to this day, historians aren't really sure who the major players were and, of the ones whose identities are known, what side they were on."

"Really?" Jack asked, and I could almost hear the wheels whirring in his brain.

Greco nodded. "I know you said this bed has been here for a long time, but do you know where it originally came from?"

I began shaking my head, then stopped. "The Vanderhorsts were the original owners." I smiled at my own cleverness. "And they also owned Gallen Hall Plantation. My mother-in-law said a lot of the furniture in this house was most likely brought here from the plantation house, since so much of it predates this house. And I bet it was all made on the plantation, too, since it has the peacock mark."

Greco lifted his eyebrows. "Well, then, this would make sense. So it probably doesn't have anything to do with the spy ring at all."

Jack bent down to get a closer look at the carving, touching it with deference. He turned his head to look up at me and smiled, his eyes dark. "Or maybe it does."

Because there's no such thing as coincidence. Neither one of us said it out loud, but we didn't have to.

I had a sudden recollection of the smells that had pervaded the room when we'd discovered the word *Betrayed* smeared on the walls, as well as the scent of horse and leather, along with the lingering odor of gunpowder. Recalled now where I'd smelled it before. It had been at Gallen Hall when Jayne and I had seen the British soldier pointing a musket at us. Right before the cold, dead voice had erupted from my father's mouth.

I leaned against the bed, feeling suddenly weak. "Oh, it definitely does," I said, sinking down into the mattress and wondering if the cold breath across my cheek was only my imagination.

CHAPTER 11

Our mother stood between Jayne and me in the nursery, wearing a red-and-green silk sheath dress instead of the black-and-white referee's shirt she should have donned for a war of wills.

I held a contented Sarah wearing a red velvet dress with a white lace Peter Pan collar and intricate smocking on the chest. White stockings with tiny candy canes covered her chubby legs, and very small black patent leather Mary Janes were neatly buckled on her plump feet. Every so often, she'd stroke the soft velvet of her dress and smile, even twisting around to see the enormous bow I'd spent a good half hour tying to perfection.

A very unhappy JJ was in the midst of a tantrum, complete with head thrown back and all four limbs rigid, as if he couldn't bear the feel of his red velvet pantaloons or matching vest with lace cravat. His beloved whisk was clutched tightly in a small fist like a defective light saber.

Our mother was speaking in a very calm voice, making it hard to hear her over JJ's screaming. "They don't have to match, Mellie. They're twins but very separate individuals. Let him wear what he wants."

"But it's for the Christmas card photo," I protested. "They're supposed to match."

Jayne looked at me with what appeared to be her last thread of patience. "No, not really. And as long as it's not a matter of the child's safety or completely inappropriate—which does *not* include wearing colors besides red and green—he should be allowed to choose what he wants to wear."

I looked in horror at the outfit JJ had chosen and Jayne had placed on the blue glider. "Jeans? And sneakers? For our Christmas photo?" I didn't mention the ridiculous price I'd paid for the pantaloons and vest. If I did, I was afraid we'd all be throwing our heads back and screaming.

Jayne's smile was more like a grimace as she placed JJ on the floor before she might drop him because of his squirming. He immediately lay facedown on the rug and began beating the floor with his hands and feet and whisk. Jayne raised her voice slightly to be heard. "The bulldozer on the sweater is red, all right? So he'll fit right in. And we can borrow Sarah's red shoelaces for his sneakers. That way, we'll all have a cohesive look."

Sarah reached for my mother, no doubt wanting to touch the opera-length pearls that GiGi—what Sarah and JJ called their grandmother—wore around her neck. They had belonged to my grandmother, also named Sarah, and when my daughter played with the necklace, she'd gibber in a language I couldn't understand but definitely had the cadences of conversation. She'd pause at the appropriate times as if another person was speaking to her and would grin and laugh at intervals. I'd accepted this about Sarah, and so had Jack. But that didn't mean I was happy about it.

My mother looked over the large bow barrette on Sarah's head. "It's a Christmas card photo, Mellie. Not an audition for *Southern Charm*—not that I'd allow it, but you know what I mean. This is supposed to be fun, not torture. The twins couldn't look bad if we dressed them in potato sacks. I have to agree with Jayne that we should allow JJ to wear what he wants or we're all going to lose our hearing."

"Fine," I said, looking at my pitiful son thrashing about on the floor like a fish on a hook. "Maybe you can find a hay bale to bring into the foyer in front of the Christmas tree, too, so that blue jeans won't appear out of place."

My disappointment dissipated as I knelt on the floor next to JJ and placed my hand on the back of his head, feeling the heat of his exertion beneath his dark hair. "Sweetheart? Would you like to wear your doh-doh sweater?" He'd been calling bulldozers "doh-dohs" ever since he'd learned to speak, and the word had somehow inundated the vocabulary of the entire family.

He stilled at my touch, his sobs turning to hiccups, before flipping over onto his back, his appendages and whisk spread out so he looked like a beached starfish who liked to bake. His blue eyes—Jack's eyes—stared back at me with hurt and righteous indignation as tears dripped down his round cheeks. "And boo jeans?"

"Absolutely," I said, scooping up my son and feeling his arms wind around my neck, pressing his sodden cheek into my neck and making my heart melt. "I'm sorry you didn't like the outfit I picked out. Maybe next time I'll bring you with me and we can decide together."

"Daddy pick!" JJ said, pulling back with a wide grin, as if five seconds before he hadn't been tearing at his clothes like a penitent in sackcloth. It reminded me a little of Jack's abrupt transformation the day before from crazed writer on the verge of drinking to seductive man with a mission. Maybe there was more to DNA than eye color and face shape. Or maybe the Trenholm men knew how to manipulate women to simply distract or to get what they wanted. I shook my head, trying to erase the thought.

"We can talk about that later." I looked over at where my mother and Jayne were already pulling out the red shoelaces from Sarah's sneakers and replacing the white ones in JJ's. Behind them, I could see into the twins' closet to the shelf where I kept their accessories—hair bows and headbands on the right for Sarah, and bow ties and suspenders on the left for JJ. All neatly labeled by me, for which I'd yet to hear a word of appreciation from anyone. "What about a red bow tie . . . ?" I began.

"No," Jayne and my mother shouted in unison.

"Okay, fine," I said. "At least General Lee and the puppies don't mind dressing up."

As if on cue, the door opened slightly as the three dogs came into the room, walking slowly instead of their usual jackrabbit bounding and general high spirits, followed by Jack.

"Daddy!" both children squealed, reaching out their arms to him.

Jack scooped up both children as I remained on the floor, patting my lap for the dogs to approach. They stared at me with an unfamiliar look in their eyes, their plumed tails, which normally draped proudly over their backs, now touching the ground by their hind legs, their heads held low. They didn't move, no matter how much I slapped at my lap or told them to come.

"I think they're boycotting their outfits," Jayne said.

"What do you mean? They look adorable!"

General Lee wore a knit Santa Claus outfit complete with pom-pom hood and shiny black belt. Porgy and Bess had matching reindeer outfits in green, but their hoods had antlers with Christmas lights draped around them.

"Oh, wait. I know the problem." I reached over to each puppy and found the switch on the battery pack to light up the antlers. "There!" I said. "Isn't that better?"

With a sharp yelp, General Lee bolted out of the door, quickly followed by Porgy and Bess.

"I think you have your answer," Jack said, the hint of a smile in his voice.

"*Et tu, Brute?*" I stood slowly, recognizing defeat. "Fine. I'll go take off their outfits and apologize. Although I think if we all told them how adorable they looked, they might be more excited about wearing their costumes."

I directed this last bit at my mother and Jayne, but they were both shaking their heads sadly, as if *I* were the delusional one. I continued. "We might as well take our Christmas card photo in July or October, because apparently it doesn't matter that we're not all dressed according to a Christmas theme."

"At least the photo can't be used as evidence against you when the animal-cruelty people show up," Jack said with mock seriousness.

I picked up the discarded red velvet pantaloons and threw them at his face, knowing that he couldn't catch them because he was holding a child in each arm.

"I'm going downstairs. Let me know if you all change the theme entirely and I need to put on a bathing suit and flip-flops for the photo."

When I reached the bottom of the staircase, the dogs were nowhere to be found. Either Mrs. Houlihan was giving them a treat in the kitchen or they were avoiding me. I sensed a movement from behind me in the upstairs corridor. I turned to look, but despite the sudden chill, the hallway was empty. At least I knew the dogs weren't hiding from *me*.

Taking a deep breath of what I hoped was courage, I turned and began climbing the steps, taking care not to disturb the draped magnolia-leaf garland Veronica had helped me throw together that morning for the photo. It was filled with plastic pomegranates, lemons, mixed pine-cones, and cinnamon sticks so that the plastic stems of the magnolia leaves weren't noticeable. I'd made Veronica promise not to tell Sophie that the fruit was all fake and we'd used superglue to attach it all. I'd at least stopped at using a hammer and nails on the antique banister, knowing that Sophie would have thrown me into the cistern if I'd put one single tiny hole in the wood. Personally, I didn't care how Colonials had decorated their staircases. I wasn't interested in smelling rotting fruit wafting about the house for a month.

"Hello? Is anybody there?" I waited for a moment, and when I didn't hear anything, I started back down the stairs, relieved that I'd done my duty and could report to Jayne and our mother that whatever was lurking in the upstairs hallways didn't want our help.

A cold breath on the back of my neck made all the hairs on my arms stand at attention. I clutched the banister, getting ready for the inevitable shove from behind. Instead a woman's voice, as piercing and cold as ice, blew into my left ear. *Lies.* The "S" sound reverberated in the air like the hiss of a snake.

I jerked my head around, almost losing my balance. A woman stood on the top step looking at me with angry eyes, the color of them ob-scured by shadow. She wore a low-cut emerald green ball gown with a corseted waist and voluminous skirts indicative of the late eighteenth century. Her rich brown hair was unpowdered, coiled in long curls around her face, and swept high on top of her head with a flourish of entwined ribbons that matched her dress. A large brooch in the shape of a peacock, its eyes and feathers sparkling with colorful jewels, gleamed from the bodice of her dress, and I had the distinct impression that she wanted me to notice it.

As I watched she turned her head until it dipped at an odd angle, allowing me to see her small, perfect ear, the long expanse of her neck. And an angry welt standing out in crimson relief against her pale skin.

"Who are you?" I whispered.

The front door opened behind me, and the vision of the woman wavered, then vanished, but not before I saw the anger in her eyes soften to sadness. And noticed again the raw red welt that encircled her neck like a noose.

"Melanie?"

My father's voice called from behind me. I gripped the banister be-cause I was too shaky to trust myself not to fall as I turned around. "Hi, Dad," I said, walking slowly down the stairs, accidentally dislodging a pomegranate. It fell over the stairs, landing with a hollow thwack as it hit the floor below, then rolled for a few feet before stopping.

He didn't smile back. "What's wrong?" he asked, looking behind me at the stairs.

"Nothing," I said. "Just arguing with JJ over what he should wear for the photo." Ever since the incident at the plantation mausoleum, my father had been staring into dark corners and paying more attention to Sarah's babbling. I just wasn't convinced that he was becoming a true believer; I thought he was either deciding that his family was destined for a freak show or just gathering enough evidence to debunk our psy-chic gifts completely. Despite any sincerity he'd shown Jayne by listen-ing to her explanations, I still couldn't completely exonerate him for my lifelong embarrassment and reluctance to admit my abilities. I still saw them as a flaw, an ugly scar I wasn't eager to show the general public. Or lifelong disbelievers like him.

"Well, you're pale as a ghost." He smiled as if he'd made a joke. "I'm allowed to say that, right?"

"Why wouldn't you be?" Still shaken by my encounter, I wasn't yet ready to let go of my resentment. Eager to change the subject, I asked, "Where's the photographer?"

As if in answer, there was a brief knock on the door. When my father opened it, I was surprised to find our handyman, Rich Kobylt. "Sorry— I rang the doorbell a couple of times, but I don't think it's working again." He looked past my father's shoulder to meet my eyes. "I'd be happy to take a look at it again. . . ."

"No," I said abruptly. He'd already adjusted it several times, at a cost that would have bought me about one hundred new, modern doorbells if Sophie would allow it, but I knew there was something wrong with the doorbell that couldn't be fixed by ordinary means. And I suspected that Rich knew it, too. He'd once admitted to me that he had a little bit of a sixth sense, and I continued to humor him without revealing that he was absolutely right.

I looked at him now with dread. "Why are you here? Did I forget to pay an invoice?" There were so many from Hard Rock Foundations, it wouldn't be impossible that one could have been overlooked, despite my intricate and involved filing system that ensured every bill was logged and slotted for payment on the appropriate date. Jack had once complimented me on my system, saying the planning of the D-Day invasion paled in comparison.

He hitched up his pants. "No, Miz Trenholm. Not tonight. Your daddy was looking for a photographer, so I volunteered my services."

I looked at my dad, not trying to hide the horror on my face. "You said you were hiring a buddy of yours who's a professional photographer!"

"I did—and he called me this morning and told me he's got the flu and didn't want to get anyone sick. I happened to mention it to Rich, and he said he could help."

Rich cleared his throat. "Yes, ma'am. I'm the official photographer at all my family's gatherings—including weddings. I take a pretty good picture, if I do say so myself."

I tried to block out the image of a roomful of Kobylts all with baggy pants and no belts and felt myself involuntarily shudder. I attempted a smile, the last hope for a beautiful Christmas card photo completely obliterated by images of blurred faces and mismatched outfits. "Well, then, I'm glad you could step in. I'm not sure if I could get us all dressed and together in one place again."

"I hear you," Rich said. "It's a real production with a big family, especially if little kids and pets are involved. My sister-in-law even dresses up her dogs in the most ridiculous outfits for their Christmas card photo. They look so depressed I've refused to take their picture anymore. Unhappy dogs don't say a lot about my picture-taking capa-bilities, you know? I told her next time she did that to those dogs, I was calling the ASPCA."

The three dogs chose that moment to emerge from their hiding place in Jack's office, running toward Rich as if he were coming to spring them from prison. Nola, dressed in a red velvet dress that was a grown-up version of Sarah's—I'd known better than to push for a hair bow or Peter Pan collar—followed close behind as Rich gave me an accusing look. "Now, that's just pitiful." Three sets of sad canine eyes looked at me as if the dogs were practicing for those ASPCA TV commercials. I almost expected Rich to burst out singing, "In the arms of the angel . . ."

Nola bent down to remove the dogs' outfits. "I think Mr. Kobylt might have a point, Melanie. How about I ask Dad to put that stuffed round red reindeer nose on your front car bumper and antlers on the side windows and we'll call it a day, all right? I can't imagine your car will complain."

"It probably should," Rich muttered as he lifted a large backpack off of his back and began pulling out camera equipment and setting it on the foyer floor.

Feeling completely defeated and not a little irritated, I crossed my arms. "I thought we'd take the picture by the Christmas tree next to the stairs. It's the tallest and the prettiest, in my opinion. It's also the only one of the six I'm supposed to have that's completely decorated for the progressive dinner. Of course, my opinion doesn't seem to matter around here, so if you'd prefer to take it in the middle of the cistern, have at it."

"No," Rich said a little forcefully. "I mean, I think the Christmas tree next to the banister with all that garland will look perfect. Don't you think, Mr. Trenholm?"

I turned around to see Jack on the landing, a child in each arm as he descended. He stopped next to me and kissed me gently on my temple. "If that's what my lovely wife wants, then that's what we should do."

Feeling slightly mollified, I said, "Just make sure no one leans against the banister. It's a pain to glue that fruit onto the garland."

Nola's eyes widened. "Glue?" She said it with the same inflection some people use to say the word *murder*. "Does Dr. Wallen-Arasi know?"

I was saved from responding by the sound of my phone's "Mamma Mia" ringtone coming from the parlor. "I'll get it," Nola said, racing across the foyer. By the time she returned, it had stopped ringing, but she was looking at it as her fingers tapped wildly on the screen.

Without looking up, she said, "It was Dr. Wallen-Arasi. She sent you a text asking you to look at the photos you sent her from Lindsey's house."

I frowned. "How did you know my password?"

She looked up at me to roll her eyes. "Seriously? You use the same password for everything: 1-2-2-1. Although even if I didn't know that already, I could have guessed it since you're such an ABBA freak." She stopped walking and looked down at my phone, her eyebrows raised. "Wow. That's seriously messed up."

I took the phone from her and looked at the photo on the screen. It was the one I'd taken of the mirror over the fireplace at the Farrells' house on Queen Street. Behind me, in the room where at the time I was completely alone, was a filmy cloud that vaguely resembled a human figure. I squinted, trying to discern any facial features or anything at all that would definitely identify what we were looking at.

"Is that a finger?" Nola asked, pointing to something that appeared to be a human hand floating behind the cloudy form.

I nodded. "I think it is. It's pointing up the stairs." I remembered the attic, and being led to the box against the wall. And the necklace being dropped at my feet.

"Can I tell Lindsey?" she asked quietly.

"No. I mean, not yet. Let me show this to her mother and she can decide."

Nola faced me. "It's her dead aunt, isn't it? Does this mean you're going to help them find out who killed her?"

I looked pointedly at Rich, who was pretending very hard to be focusing on setting up his camera equipment, while listening to every word. "Let's discuss this later," I said, handing her my phone before running after JJ, who now careened toward the banister, his focus on a prominent pomegranate.

"Melanie?"

Distracted from my pursuit, I turned at the odd note in Nola's voice.

"What's this?" She walked toward me with my phone held up to me, the screen filled with tiles of photos I'd taken not only of Veronica's house, but also of Nola's room to document the before and after of the redo.

She made one of the photos bigger and put it closer to my face as Jack came to stand next to me. I'd simply taken the photographs without looking at them, figuring I didn't need to see them until after the project was completed. I squinted, already knowing what she was seeing, and felt my stomach clench.

"Looks like a guy in really old-fashioned clothes standing by the antique jewelry chest," Jack said. "And correct me if I'm wrong, but he doesn't appear to have any eyes in his eye sockets."

I felt Nola, Jack, and Rich staring at me.

"Did you know about this?" Nola asked in a strangled voice.

My answer was drowned out by the sound of JJ squealing as he pulled the pomegranate from the garland, yanking the rope of magnolia leaves off of the banister and sending plastic fruit and greenery cascading to the foyer floor. They rolled in an oddly uniform pattern, all coming to a stop in a perfect circle around me, as the sound of a sibilant "S" curling like a rope around my neck rang in my ears.

CHAPTER 12

I shoved the small shopping bag from the Finicky Filly farther under one of the folding tables set up in the stables of the Aiken-Rhett House museum on Elizabeth Street so Sophie wouldn't see and know why I was late to our scheduled session to organize the wreath workshop supplies before the big event. Sophie wanted to make sure we had enough materials before the actual workshop, and it was my goal to ensure she saw only the boxes of the real stuff and not the faux fruit and garland I'd supplied.

After the previous day's Christmas photo session debacle, I'd been in dire need of retail therapy, and the lovely people at my favorite clothing-and-accessories store had been more than happy to oblige. Despite wanting to buy half the store, I'd had to keep reminding myself that I was on a strict budget and that unlike in my single days, I now had other people to consider before whipping out my credit card. In the end, I'd chosen a skirt on sale as a present for my mother, a cute pair of inexpensive earrings for Jayne, and an incredibly cheap pair of shoes for me that were marked down so far that they were practically free. I felt a lot better when I left the store.

I began sorting through the boxes of Christmas-wreath-making materials, noting with aggravation that many of the oranges donated by other volunteers had randomly spaced cloves and that none of the pomegranates was of uniform size or shape.

"How did the Christmas photo turn out?" Sophie asked as she appeared next to me. I tried not to stare at her ensemble, which looked as if her toddler, Skye, had chosen it. And made it. If she hadn't, then I imagined Sophie must have raided a defunct circus-costume stash to come up with the color-blocked balloon pants with elastic at the ankles (to better display her Birkenstocks) and clashing floral cardigan with oversized buttons of varying colors. Neon green toe socks poked out of her sandals. I'd tried for years to tell her that a pair of Keds or really any other kind of shoe besides sandals would keep her feet warm. I'd finally given up.

"How far did you have to run to get away from the clown once you took his clothes?" I asked, grabbing two more oranges, trying not to shudder at the unevenly spaced cloves.

Sophie picked up some pomegranates and began laying them out on the table to count. "The photo session was that bad, huh? Guess you won't end up on the cover of *Parents* magazine now."

"Better than being on the cover of *Circus Life*," I said under my breath. Louder, I said, "It was awful, if you must know. We ended up taking the photo in Waterfront Park near the Pineapple Fountain so we wouldn't catch any dead people in the pictures, and because it was cold outside, we all wore our coats, which hid our mismatched outfits—JJ and the dogs refused to wear their Christmas clothes, and it was a disaster. Taking the photos outside was a stroke of genius on my part."

"A true disaster," Sophie said. "I don't know how you manage. You're a real survivor, Melanie."

I couldn't tell if she was being serious or not, and I didn't get the chance to ask her before she bent over one of the boxes with the fake boxwood branches I'd found at a wholesale club for ninety-nine cents per branch. She pulled out a bunch and raised it to her face and gave it a big sniff before turning back to me. "Melanie!"

"Don't they look real?" I asked enthusiastically. "By the way, did I tell you that I have an appointment at the historical archives to return old Vanderhorst letters that someone tried to throw away?"

She threw the branches on a table, my transgression temporarily forgotten. "Really? Who tossed them?"

"Marc Longo. He stole them from the archives. And then, instead of returning them, he just tossed them. Luckily, his brother found them and gave them to Jack and me to look through."

Her eyes narrowed. "There's a special corner of hell for monsters like that. Anything important in them?"

"I don't know. Jayne texted me while I was doing a little Christmas shopping just now to let me know Anthony had dropped them off. I asked her to leave them on Jack's desk to go through first as a sort of apology."

"Why were you apologizing?" She held up her hand to stop me from responding. "Let me guess—you labeled all of his drawers again with color-coded labels."

She looked up, waiting for me to respond. When I didn't she said, "Then you organized his desk the way you would organize your own without any thought to how he would want it?"

I kept silent and watched as her eyes widened. "Oh, no, Melanie. Did you try to keep something from him again?"

I turned away from her, finally giving in to the urge to pick up one of the oranges and fix it. "I really screwed up. I feel like a complete failure as a wife."

She was silent for a moment, and I felt her gaze on me. "Melanie." I looked up at the soft tone of her voice.

"You're not a failure, okay? Quirky, sure. Insecure? Yeah, most of the time. But you're a pretty great person all around. You're a great mother and a terrific friend. Remember how you watched Blue Skye when both Chad and I had the flu even though you already had a full plate? You didn't even think twice. And despite what you might think, you're a great wife, too. You and Jack were really made for each other, like Chad and me. Like peas in a pod." She smiled. "Organic, of course."

Even I had to return her smile at that.

She continued. "But you need to remember that marriage isn't something you walk into knowing what to do. It's a learning process. So, yeah, you made a mistake. Just say you're sorry and that you'll try harder, and then move on."

"So you think I need to apologize?"

She gave me a look that didn't need any words.

"Okay. I get it. And thanks." I stared at her for a long moment. "Although I find it hard to listen to you when you're dressed like that."

"Forget what I said about you being a terrific friend. So," she said. "What didn't you tell him?"

I replaced the orange, then blew into my hands to warm them before emptying a box of pomegranates. "Just about the apparition I've seen in Nola's room. And the dark presence I've been sensing in the upstairs hallway that may or not be related to the strange man without eyes that I've seen at the cistern."

Her eyes narrowed. "What strange man?"

"I didn't ask his name, but he's wearing old-fashioned clothing and holding a piece of jewelry. Like a bracelet or something with different-colored stones."

"What kind of old-fashioned clothes?"

I shrugged. "I don't know—old."

She took a deep breath. "Was he wearing pants or knee breeches?"

I thought back, trying to remember an image I'd been desperately trying to forget. "Breeches. Definitely breeches."

"Okay," she said slowly. "What kind of shirt?"

I closed my eyes. "It had a high neck with lots of frills in the front, and a tied bow at his throat."

Sophie nodded. "Was the collar standing straight up or folded over a little?"

"Folded over," I said without having to think about it. There'd been a large dark spot on his shirt, and my gaze had lingered there. But I'd noticed the bow.

"Hmm," she murmured, nodding.

"Hmm, what?" I asked.

"Well, it's just that you told me that the bricks from the cistern came from the old Vanderhorst plantation, right?"

I nodded. "Yes."

"Before the plantation was turned into a winery, the graduate program at the college would use the mausoleum there to train the students on various cemetery preservation techniques—usually involving shoring up crumbling tombs and cleaning headstones. It was hard to get students to go back. A lot of them said they got bad vibes. But a few say they actually saw something." She grimaced. "You know how sometimes people think they see a shadow and then blow it all out of proportion, so others jump on the bandwagon and say they saw something, too? My students and I hang around a lot of old buildings and cemeteries, so I've learned to take it all with a grain of salt."

"And you never mentioned this to me?"

Sophie gave me the same kind of look I imagined she gave Blue Skye when her little girl pushed her plate of organic quinoa onto the floor. "Really, Melanie? Since when do you want to talk about ghost sightings? Like never."

"Whatever," I said, mimicking Nola. "So, what did they see?"

"Apparently it was a full apparition of a man wearing late-eighteenth-century clothing. None of them stuck around long enough to get a lot of details, but they saw it long enough to register that he was missing his eyes. Kind of hard to miss that detail, I'd guess. And there was something odd about his shirt. Like there was a big stain on it."

Small beads of cold sweat formed at the base of my neck. "Was he holding anything?"

Sophie thought for a moment. "I don't remember them saying anything about that—they might have and I just forgot. Or they ran away too fast to notice it. Meghan Black is one of the students who claim to have seen something—since she's working in the cistern, you can ask her. Just don't tell her I told you. I really don't want to give any credence to this kind of thing."

I frowned. "Why? Because you don't believe in ghosts?"

"No. Because I do. I've been your friend for too long to doubt their existence. See, Melanie? Some people actually do learn, change, and grow as they experience new things."

The alarm on my watch beeped. It was one of those new watches that did everything except make dinner and clean the dishes, but the only thing I'd mastered since Jack had given it to me for my birthday was setting the alarm.

"I'm sorry—I've got to go. I have just enough time to get the letters at the house before my appointment at the archives." I glanced around at the Ashley Hall moms hanging evergreen boughs and signs indicating the various wreath-decorating station stops. "Looks like you have plenty of volunteers, so you won't miss me."

"Hang on." Sophie pushed a clump of plastic stems in my direction. "Take these with you. I'll have my grad students condition the real boxwood clippings so we can use them for the workshop." She picked up a plastic stem and held it delicately between two fingers, as if it might be contagious. "Really, Melanie. Even for you, this is pretty pathetic. I should make you work with the students to condition the stems. It would be a good lesson for them to learn what happens when we take shortcuts."

She looked as if she might actually be serious. I spotted Veronica walking across the courtyard toward us and I eagerly waved her over. "Perfect timing—I think Sophie needs you."

I reached under the table and pulled out my shopping bag. "I'll send Jack over with the minivan later to retrieve the faux boxwoods—I saved the receipt just in case."

"Just in case I noticed?"

"I would *never*."

Sophie didn't return my smile. "Remind me sometime why we're still friends."

"Well, it's definitely not because we admire each other's style," I said, indicating her pants before backing away until I was a safe distance from being pelted with a pomegranate, then turned and left.

When I returned home, I stashed my shopping bag in the dining room so it was out of sight until I could safely reclaim it and bury my new shoes in my closet. Not that I expected to fool Jack; he noticed everything about me. I couldn't part my hair a different way or paint my nails a new color without him noticing and saying something nice about it. Several of the women I worked with complained that they could paint their bodies blue and streak naked through their houses and their husbands wouldn't even look up. I supposed I should be grateful, especially when every compliment came with a kiss—or two—but I was always afraid that one day he would stop. Then I'd revert to the old insecure Melanie, who couldn't believe that Jack Trenholm had picked her.

I walked over to Jack's office door and hesitated for a moment before gently rapping on it. "Jack?"

"Come in."

I pushed the door open and was surprised to see him sitting on the floor with papers strewn all around him. He had a stack in his lap and was apparently sorting them. I closed the door and leaned against it. "Are you speaking to me yet?" Since the photo incident, we'd shared a bed but not much else. All our verbal exchanges had been excruciatingly polite, the aura of disappointment surrounding him as thick as the humidity before a hurricane.

He sighed and looked up at me. "I'm sorry, Mellie. I'm not trying to shut you out. I'm just trying to figure out what else I can do to make you trust me. To share everything with me. Even when you don't think it's the best timing."

"It's just that you don't need distractions right now. . . ."

He held his finger to his lips. "Stop. I don't want to rehash the same old thing. It won't get us anywhere."

The sound of screeching brakes outside followed by a quick acceleration brought our attention to the front windows. Jack stood and joined me at the window, both of us wincing as I spotted my dad's old Jeep Cherokee being tortured as it scooted down the street.

Jack turned away from the window. "I can't watch. It might give me nightmares. Your dad must have nerves of steel. Thank goodness Jayne is in the backseat. I think she'll give a calming influence."

A heat wave of some unidentifiable emotion flushed through me. "Jayne's with them?"

Jack nodded. "Your dad asked her, and Nola thought it a good idea. I guess she was looking for backup in case your dad threw himself out of the vehicle."

I watched for another moment before I, too, had to look away, but not for the same reason. "I wonder why Nola didn't ask me." I somehow managed to keep the hurt from my voice.

Jack regarded me, his mouth twitching as if he wanted to smile. "I can't imagine that ending well, can you? It could be very stressful for both of you if she put her seat belt on in the wrong order of things."

I frowned. "Well, there's a right way and a wrong way for everything."

"Exactly," Jack said.

I watched him for a beat, waiting for him to speak first. When he didn't, I asked, "So, are we okay?"

Jack faced me, his eyebrows raised, and didn't say anything.

I pushed myself away from the window and walked slowly until I stood in front of him, then forced myself to meet his eyes. "I'm sor—" I stopped. Swallowed. Remembered what Sophie had said, and that I was trying to be the more mature version of myself. The version of myself who knew how to apologize, regardless of whether she thought she'd done anything wrong. I tried again. "I'm . . . sorry. About not telling you about the apparition in Nola's room. I was just trying to—"

He silenced me with a slow kiss. When he lifted his head, he said, "Saying sorry was enough—I don't need to hear anything else. We're a team, Mellie. Always. I just need you to remember that before you decide again to keep something from me. There's a lot about you that drives me crazy, but that's the one thing that I just can't live with."

I pulled back. "There are other things about me that drive you crazy? Like what?"

"Where would you like me to start?" He kissed me again, his lips lingering on mine. "I didn't mean it in a bad way, since I find most of your craziness endearing. But I suppose we could start with the labeling gun. . . ."

There was a brief tap on the office door before it was opened by my father, looking flushed and rumpled, as if he'd just outrun a pack of wildcats, with wide eyes and hair standing up at attention. He clutched a manila folder stuffed with papers and his hands shook a little.

"Are you okay?" I asked, concerned about his pallor.

"I'll be fine in a moment."

We all turned at the screech of brakes outside. Jack rushed to the window. "You didn't leave her alone, did you?" he asked, his voice full of concern.

My dad shook his dead. "No. Jayne insisted she could handle it. I think she's destined for sainthood." He said it with a note of admiration, making that hot flush consume me again. I wondered if I might be experiencing the change of life already and made a mental note to call my gynecologist the next day.

He looked down at the papers strewn on the floor. "What's all this?"

"From Anthony. He dropped by earlier with a shoebox full of old letters and documents he'd found in the garbage can at Gallen Hall, presumably stolen from the archives by Marc when he found out I was working on another book. Marc apparently tossed them instead of returning them when he discovered there was nothing interesting enough to write about. He and Melanie had hoped there might be some information in there regarding the mausoleum. Sadly, just a lot of receipts and lists—nothing helpful."

My father held out the manila folder. "Well, maybe this will have something for you. When Yvonne was helping me find information about the gardens here and at our house, we found some misfiled paperwork. Yvonne made copies and I stuck them in the back of one of my folders, then forgot all about it until we were on the way to Gallen Hall. Remember, Melanie?"

I nodded, wishing I could forget.

He continued. "They're newspaper clippings and architectural drawings all about the Vanderhorst plantation, but they had been stuck in with the Tradd Street garden papers. Easy to see how that would happen, since they're both Vanderhorst properties. Yvonne said they use a lot of volunteers and interns to do filing and to return papers to the archives after someone has checked them out. So it wouldn't be out of the question that they were simply returned to the wrong folder whenever the last person looked at them—which could have been decades ago."

Jack began thumbing through the papers, a smile growing on his face. "Which means Marc never saw these, or he would have kept them. Or thrown them away." He looked up at me with an excitement I hadn't seen in a long while. He paused, his eyes widening as he gently took a yellowed page from the stack. "Well, well, well," he said. "Looks like we just might have beaten Marc at his own game."

My father and I moved to either side of Jack, looking down at the fragile page in his hand. "Is that . . . ?" I began.

"Two architectural renderings of the mausoleum at Gallen Hall, I think," Jack replied, a wide grin on his face.

My dad started to say something, but his words were lost in the screech of skidding tires and crunching metal from the street outside, followed by the sharp barking of a dog and the incessant scream of a car horn penetrating the house and making my blood run cold.

Jack threw down the folder and grabbed my hand before running from the room, my father close behind. And from somewhere came the heady scent of roses, as sweet and redolent as a summer day, following us outside into the frigid late-November afternoon.

CHAPTER 13

J ack let go of my hand as he raced around the smoking wreck of the two vehicles to the Jeep's driver's-side door, calling Nola's name, while my dad rushed to the passenger side, looking for Jayne. My feet remained where they were, unwilling to listen to my direction, the mixed scent of roses and burnt rubber making me cough.

I watched as both doors opened easily despite the crinkled sides of the Jeep, which more closely resembled an accordion than vehicle panels, then stared as Nola and Jayne stepped out of the car looking stunned but unharmed. I exhaled loudly, my relief loosening my bones. I closed my eyes for a brief moment, only to notice upon opening them the filmy apparition of a woman wearing clothing from the nineteen twenties standing by the tree swing beneath the ancient oak in our front garden. She was gone so quickly that I thought I might have imagined her. Only the lingering scent of roses told me that I hadn't.

I turned toward the other car, recognizing Marc Longo's silver Jaguar, or what was left of it after Nola had apparently T-boned the back half of it in the middle of Tradd Street. Considering the street was one-way, it was difficult to imagine how it had happened, but I had witnessed Nola behind the wheel; anything was possible.

The distant wail of a siren reverberated in the chilly air as I ran toward the Jaguar, steeling myself for what I might see. On the driver's side Marc was hitting the inside of the door in a futile attempt to open it, a deflated airbag hanging limply from the steering wheel. He glared at me through the still-intact window as blood seeped from a deep gash on his forehead. I grabbed hold of the handle and yanked, but nothing happened. I shrugged to show Marc I hadn't had any luck. Panic bloomed in his eyes and he began beating on the window with his palms, yelling something that I was sure I didn't want to hear.

On the other side of the car, Jack had opened the passenger door and he and my father were pulling out a man who had blood dripping from his nose and an ugly scrape across his cheek and was dressed as if he'd been on his way to a pulsing dance club. He had the unwrinkled skin and small build of an adolescent, although when he waved his hands to knock away Jack's hold on him, the corded veins on his hands gave away his age. The shaved sides of his head and floppy wave of bleached-blond hair hanging over his forehead were more suited to a teen or twenty-something than to someone in his mid to late thirties or early forties, as this man probably was. His close-fitting white shirt revealed not only his lack of an undershirt, but also the presence of an impressive six-pack. The shirt was tucked into tight pencil jeans and I couldn't help but notice that he wore cowboy boots. My gaze moved to his face and was met with an ugly scowl that matched Marc's, and for a moment I wanted to ask Jack to put him back in the car and close the door.

He stepped away from Jack and my dad, shouting at whoever would listen. "I guess I shouldn't be surprised that this is how they drive down here in the South." Checking that his shirt was tucked in, he glanced around until he spotted Nola and Jayne huddled together on the sidewalk, Jayne's arm held protectively around Nola's shoulders.

As he moved toward them, I glanced behind him as Jack gave a half-hearted tug on Marc's door, unfazed by Marc's pounding on the window or the muffled shouting. Marc was neatly pinned behind the steering wheel, making it impossible for him to crawl out the other side.

"Sorry, Matt!" Jack shouted with an exaggerated shrug. He cupped his ear to indicate the sound of approaching sirens. "I'm sure the fire department will bring the Jaws of Life to let you out soon." He turned his back, and his smile quickly slipped from his face as he focused on the passenger from the car stalking toward his daughter.

The man stopped in front of the two women, jabbing an index finger in their faces. "Which one of you is the driver?"

Jayne put on her nanny face and spoke firmly and calmly to the man, keeping her arm around Nola. "There is no need to shout, sir. . . ."

"Like hell there isn't! I could have been killed!" He did a figure eight in the air with his pointer finger, moving from Jayne's face to Nola's and then back again. "Which one of you is the idiot who caused this accident?" When no one answered, he leaned closer. "Which one of you?" He was so close, I'm sure spit flew in their faces.

Nola responded by bursting into tears just as Jack reached them and pulled her into his arms, letting her sob against his chest. "You need to calm down, sir. You're all in shock right now. Can we just stop with the shouting until the police and emergency vehicles arrive? Let's just take a moment and be thankful that no one was seriously hurt."

I was standing next to Jayne and moved closer to put my arm around her, but I noticed that my father had reached her first and that she was now safely tucked against his side.

The man let out an expletive. Even though I was sure Nola had heard it before, Jack put his hands over her ears. I could tell that Jack's temper was on the verge of igniting, although he kept it in check as he spoke to the man again. "Really, sir. There is no need to use that kind of language."

Fortunately, the next two words out of the man's mouth, which were probably a suggestion of what Jack could do to himself, were drowned out by the simultaneous arrival of a fire truck, an ambulance, and two police cars.

Everyone began speaking at once as the police officers approached to get statements, and two firemen approached Marc's car, leaving me alone in front of the house, watching everything as if it were unfolding like a movie. I stared at the man as he elbowed his way in front of Jack and Nola to give his statement first, his words carrying back to me.

"I'm going to sue the person responsible for everything they're worth. I'm going to make them pay for this! I could have been killed, or maimed, because of some moron who has no business behind the wheel." He pulled out a cell phone and began stabbing at the screen. "I'm calling my lawyer and he'll be on the first flight out of LA."

"Sir, may I have your name, please?" the officer asked calmly.

He stopped barking into his phone briefly to address the policeman. "It's Harvey Beckner, and I demand to have a complete medical evaluation and I want that driver locked up." He pointed vaguely in Jayne and Nola's direction, not yet having ascertained who the driver had been and not, apparently, overly concerned.

The name sounded vaguely familiar—not in a personal way, but as a name I might have read in a magazine or heard on the news. Jack's gaze caught mine, and I could tell that his thoughts were running along in tandem with mine. I glanced at the cowboy boots, the perfect physique, the Botoxed face and mod hair—the entire package more at home in Los Angeles than in Charleston. I darted my gaze back to Jack as realization dawned on me. Jack's eyes widened and I knew he'd figured it out, too.

A scream of tearing metal brought our attention back to the Jaguar, where a metal arm was prying the door from the side of the car as two firemen freed Marc from his prison. After they pulled him out he brushed them off, ignoring their advice to lie down on the waiting gurney. He staggered toward the cluster of people surrounding the policeman, grasping Harvey Beckner's arm. The man was currently yelling into his phone, presumably to his lawyer, telling him that he was going to sue the person responsible and the whole city of Charleston if he felt like it.

"Harvey," Marc said, attempting a smile. "Glad you're okay."

Harvey pulled the phone from his ear and looked at him as if he'd forgotten Marc even existed. He yanked his arm away, looking with disgust at the blood smear from Marc's hand. "Okay? Are you blind?" He swiped at the blood dripping from his nose, grimacing as dark red drops landed on his sleeve. "I think my nose is broken! And who knows how much therapy I will need? I'll probably have PTSD." He jerked his head in the direction of Nola and Jayne. "What I do know for sure is that I'm suing these yokels. They won't even know what hit them once I'm through with them."

As if suddenly registering our existence, Marc faced us, pausing for a moment before slowly turning his attention to Nola. His face relaxed into a cold smile. It was a ghostly shade of white—a hue I was overly familiar with—making the blood garish in contrast.

An EMT was trying to get his attention. "Sir, you've got a wound on your forehead and you might have internal injuries. You need to lie down. . . ."

He brushed the EMT aside, his grin wider now. "So, Nola, you were driving? You've got your permit, right?"

I wanted to tackle her to the ground, anything to keep her quiet. But she was already nodding, no doubt lulled by the false sense of security of Marc being familiar to her.

"This is perfect," he said, fully smiling now, the sight odd beneath the blood oozing from his forehead.

"You know these people?" Harvey asked, his tone only slightly less belligerent than before.

"Very well, I'd say. Actually, we're related. Aren't we, Cousin Jack?"

Jack smiled, and I wondered if anyone else could see the tension in his jaw or the odd light in his eyes. I assumed they hadn't, or they'd all be moving back to a safe distance.

"No, actually, we're not. *Matt*." He emphasized the name he'd been calling Marc since they'd met.

Marc swayed a bit on his feet, but his grin remained. "No matter." He turned to Harvey. "This is Jack Trenholm. You probably haven't heard of him, so don't worry if the name doesn't sound familiar. But he and his wife own Fifty-five Tradd Street. The house where our movie is set."

Our movie. I knew for sure now. This was the producer of the film based on Marc's book. Or Jack's book, I corrected myself.

Harvey examined us now with interest, and I wanted to grab my entire family, run into the house, and bar the door before he came to the same conclusion that I had already reached, and that I was certain Marc and Jack had, too.

I took a step toward Nola so that Jack and I flanked her as Jayne and my dad looked on, realization dawning in their eyes, too.

Marc continued, his grin never dimming. "And that girl, the one who nearly killed us, is their daughter Nola."

"Is that so?" Harvey said. "So this is the family who've been denying us access to the house for filming?"

"That's right," Nola said, stepping forward, apparently not hearing my silent screams for her not to speak, to admit nothing. "I was driving, but it was an accident. I was just practicing backing out from our driveway and I didn't see you coming." She hiccupped, her voice coming between shallow breaths. "And Marc stole my dad's book idea, and that's why we will *never* allow that movie to be made in our house. *Never.* That's why Melanie said she'd dye her hair purple and restore another house if that ever happened—which means it never will."

She was shouting by the last word and I drew her to me so she could bury her face in my shoulder and catch her breath.

"Is that so?" Harvey said, his grin now matching Marc's. He leaned in close to Nola's ear. "Because I think never is going to be a lot sooner than you imagined." He straightened, focusing his attention on me. "And I sure hope Melanie likes purple."

Jack moved forward, blocking Nola and me. "Are you threatening my wife and daughter?"

Marc threw back his head and made a sound that could have been a chortle, his pallor even worse than before. He ignored the two EMTs on either side of him trying to coerce him into lying on the gurney. "That wasn't a threat, Jack. I think he was just explaining that you lost. Again."

Jack's expression didn't change. "Don't count your chips yet, Marc. Because no matter how many times I might lose, you'll never be a winner."

Harvey was back to shouting to his lawyer on the phone, and the police had begun to take statements from Nola and Jayne. Which was why no one noticed when Jack hooked one of his feet behind one of Marc's. Marc slid to the ground like a kebab without its stick, landing with a small *oomph*.

The EMTs struggled to lift him off the ground and onto the gurney while Jack got the attention of one of the policemen. "Make sure you check him for alcohol. He didn't appear to be too steady on his feet."

Jack didn't wait for a response, instead returning to Nola and me, putting his arms around us both as Nola and Jayne made their statements to the police while I weighed which was worse: being sued for everything we had or learning to like purple hair.

I sat on the floor of the master closet with my labeling gun, organizing the Christmas presents I'd already bought. Before my family had increased exponentially, I'd usually finished with my shopping and wrapping before Thanksgiving. But ever since the twins were born, I no longer seemed in complete control of my life. Not that I ever regretted having children—I couldn't imagine my life without all three of them. It was just that even with a nanny, two sets of grandparents who lived nearby and were involved in our lives, and a supportive husband, there never seemed to be enough hours in the day to do all of the things that had once filled my days.

Like decorating and labeling the new storage bins I'd bought to store gifts in my closet. Part of the problem had been that my labeling gun kept disappearing, but even my gift spreadsheet, where I listed gift recipients along with gift ideas, was still mostly blank, with only the headers along the top. My brain felt pulled in too many directions to settle on any one thing, so nothing seemed to get done, leaving a trail of half-finished projects in my wake.

I sat back and sighed. Despite its already being December, the bins were nearly empty and those gifts that were inside hadn't yet been wrapped. Jayne had bought four tickets for the King Street and Downtown Holiday Shop and Stroll for the following weekend, so I hoped I'd make a dent in my list. Assuming I ever finished making the list.

I rubbed my eyes, exhausted from watching two back-to-back Hallmark Christmas movies with Nola. We'd settled ourselves in front of the TV in the upstairs family room while Jack finished with the police and called the insurance company before driving my dad home. Nola had been resistant at first, but after five minutes she'd been hooked. Four hours and two bowls of extra-buttery popcorn later, she said she felt much better. But that if I ever told her friends what she'd just watched, she would make sure no doughnut would ever cross the threshold of my house again.

I felt Jack's presence before he joined me in the closet and pressed a kiss on the top of my head. He sat down on the floor beside me and smiled, although I could see the tense lines around his eyes and mouth. "You look so cute when you're organizing."

"Thanks. You might try it sometime. It's very relaxing."

His eyebrows rose. "Do you have an extra labeling gun?"

"Is the sky blue?" I leaned forward and flipped off the lid of a shoebox. Like all of my shoeboxes, this one had a photo of the shoes inside taped to the outside to make finding the right pair easier. Except this box had a photo of a pair of shoes I'd given to Nola last year. I reached inside and pulled out my spare labeler and handed it to Jack. "The last time it disappeared, I bought two."

He looked down at it with a frown.

"It's the old-fashioned kind," I explained. "Where you have to dial the disk at the top and click it with the trigger. They're harder to locate than the new digital ones, but I find the clicking very therapeutic." I gently elbowed him in the arm. "Go ahead and try it. Right now I need two sets of numbers one through ten. That's so I can label each of the presents for the twins so they get the same amount."

"Is that really necessary?"

"Yes. You and I were only children growing up so it didn't matter, but I want to make sure I'm always fair."

"But . . ."

I reached for the labeling gun. "And if you argue with me, it's not therapeutic anymore, okay?"

"All right, all right." He began twisting the disk to the number one. "I just got off the phone with Harvey Beckner's lawyer."

My throat tightened. "And?"

"And Beckner is apparently okay with forgiveness and a fat check from our insurance company in exchange for the rights to film in our house. In a surprising move, he also said he would still pay us the going rate for the use of the house. Which is a good thing since I won't see a penny of income for at least a year except for straggling royalties for my older books."

I looked over at Jack, clicking the trigger on the labeling gun with more force than required, lost in his thoughts. "I guess we're supposed to feel grateful, but I can't help but believe there's another shoe somewhere waiting to drop."

Our gazes met before he returned to the labeling gun.

"How's Nola doing?" I asked, eager to change the topic. Jack had knocked on Nola's door as I was leaving after the Christmas movie marathon, just as Rebecca called to let me know that both Marc and Harvey had been released from the hospital with only a few stitches. It was another thing for which I should be grateful, but I just couldn't manage.

Rebecca had started to say that maybe things were going to work out for the best after all, but I'd hung up on her before I could say that things working out for the best would be that the accident had rendered Marc sterile so that he couldn't spawn little Marcs.

"Nola's pretty shaken up," Jack said. "We're really fortunate that no one was killed or seriously hurt. I don't think she will ever voluntarily get behind the wheel of a car for the rest of her life. She told me that all she wants for Christmas is a prepaid Uber account."

I leaned over to my open laptop, where the Christmas spreadsheet was displayed on the screen, before typing "Uber gift card" under Nola's name. "I can't say I blame her. I once rear-ended a CARTA bus on Meeting Street because I'd been distracted by the cutest pair of shoes worn by a woman on the sidewalk—so it technically wasn't my fault, but it took me weeks to be comfortable behind the wheel again."

Jack blinked at me a few times without saying anything before returning to his labeling.

"Louisa was there," I said softly.

"Louisa Vanderhorst? I thought she'd gone to the light, or wherever it is you send restless spirits."

"She did. But she comes back whenever she thinks she needs to protect us. I saw her and smelled the Louisa roses. I've actually been smelling them a lot lately. As if she knows something we don't."

Jack frowned. "It would be helpful if she could be a little more specific. We might have seen this whole fiasco coming." Before I could explain to him that it didn't work that way, he continued. "They've suspended Nola's driving permit, so her not wanting to drive isn't really an issue right now anyway. She was definitely at fault since she was the one apparently speeding backward out of the driveway when Marc drove past, so the fine will be pretty hefty. She and I both agreed that it will come from her royalties from the Apple song commercial," he said, referring to her extracurricular hobby of writing music for other artists and for the occasional jingle. It's what had saved our Tradd Street house once before.

I took a deep breath, forcing myself to confront the elephant in the room. "So, that's it, then? They'll bring their film crews in and we won't lose the house, right?"

Jack put down the labeling gun and turned to me. "Do you remember what I told you outside in the garden on the day we were married?"

I nodded. "About how you wanted to live here for the rest of your life and see your children grow up here?"

"Yes. That's all I've ever wanted. You and me, our family, here. And I cannot—*will* not—allow Marc Longo to take it all away from us. I'd rather die than see that happen."

I grasped his hands. I had a sudden flashback of Rebecca telling me about her dream. Of an unknown man burying Jack alive. "Don't say that, Jack. Don't ever say that."

His lips twitched in a small grimace. "It's not that we couldn't continue our relationship, you know."

"Jack . . ." I said with warning.

"Yes, they're going to film Marc's movie in our house," he said grimly. "We don't have much choice. In the meantime, I've rescheduled our meeting with Yvonne for tomorrow. We're going to dig through every piece of paper and we will find something. I know we will. I've sent a copy of the mausoleum drawings to an architect friend of mine, Steve Dungan, to look at to see if there's something I can't see with my untrained eye. There's a different date at the bottom of each one, so I'm hoping he can compare them and tell us what's different, maybe explain why the first one was built and then rebuilt only two years later." He squeezed my hands. "We're a good team, Mellie. If we work together, we can't lose. In the meantime, we'll pretend our tails are between our legs and we've given up." He reached his hand behind my neck and gently drew me toward him. "Two can play this game, and things are about to get dirty."

I kissed him, but my thoughts remained on Rebecca's dream as an icy chill skittered across my skin like someone walking across my grave.

CHAPTER 14

I loved the way Charleston dressed up for the holidays. From the light-bedecked spans of the Ravenel Bridge and the wrapped trunks and fronds of the palmetto trees in Marion Square to the streetlights on King Street masquerading as gentlemen sporting wreaths with red bows around their necks, nothing put me in the spirit of Christmas more than walking through the streets of my city. I always waited with a child's anticipation for the giant Santa hat to be placed on top of the turret of the house on the corner of Tradd and Meeting Streets. But as Jack and I drove to our appointment with Yvonne downtown, I barely noticed the red bows and greenery sprouting from most doors and iron gates. I was much too preoccupied with spirits other than the Christmas kind.

As usual, Jack had no problem finding parking near the Addlestone Library on the College of Charleston campus, where the South Carolina Historical Society archives were now housed. Yvonne Craig, long past retirement age, had turned down incentives to retire and instead had moved the few miles to the new location along with her precious documents. When she'd announced her decision, Jack had told her that she was one of the most important treasures found in the archives, and followed the compliment with a kiss on her soft pink cheek. I'd thought she might pass out.

Jack carried the shoebox of documents we'd received from Anthony, and I held the folder of misfiled materials Yvonne had given my dad. We'd already combed through all the papers, reading and then reading them again without seeing anything that caught our attention as being something we should investigate further. I supposed the cost of nails and sugar on an eighteenth-century plantation might have historical significance, but did not necessarily contain the seeds to overcome the goiter on the necks of our well-being, Marc Longo.

Neither Jack nor I was willing to believe that there wasn't anything in those files that might lead us to any more hidden treasure. Or at least something that might be valuable enough to protect us against Marc's next assault. We might be in a temporary truce now, but we weren't naïve enough to believe that Marc wasn't out there waiting to pounce like some feral cat outside a mousehole.

Our hopes were pinned on the indomitable Yvonne. She'd gleefully accepted the scanned documents Jack had sent her the previous day to go over before our meeting, just in case we'd missed something; she claimed that at her age she didn't sleep much anyway. Besides, she'd said, she was hoping she could be instrumental in showing karma the way to Marc's front door.

As we walked through the doors of the Addlestone Library, Jack's face was grim, the dark smudges under his eyes making them appear more blue. Along with the dark stubble on his unshaven jaw, those smudges made him look like a marauding pirate on a mission, and I was glad that I was on his side. And in his bed.

I could only wish I looked that good when I hadn't slept. Jack hadn't come to bed last night, wanting to go through the files one more time, and all morning he'd been so preoccupied that he hadn't even noticed the new labeling system I'd given his sock drawer during my labeling frenzy the previous day.

"There's one thing I don't understand," he said, pausing inside the enormous glass rotunda where the previous summer the full skeletal remains of a T. rex had been on display. I'd wanted to bring the children, but Jayne said they were too young, and Nola had added that Sarah would be petrified if it started talking to her.

"Just one?" I asked, not meaning to sound sarcastic.

Not that it mattered. Jack's face remained grim and I wasn't even sure he'd heard me. "We know Marc wants our house. He's admitted as much. So why not just sue us outright so we have to sell the house, and then they could film to their hearts' content? Why make us believe that they'll accept the insurance payout for the accident in return for the rights to film inside, and just let it go?"

We headed toward the third floor, where Yvonne said we'd find her in the historic archives' reading room. We walked slowly as we contemplated the implications. "Good point," I said. We stopped walking and our eyes met. I swallowed. "Unless he needs us."

Jack nodded. "Exactly what I was thinking. He must believe there's something valuable hidden in the house that he has yet to find. And he's hoping we'll lead him to it." His face darkened. "We just can't afford to let him get there first."

I nodded, the unease I'd felt before now blossoming into a full panic. There was no doubt in our minds that Marc had orchestrated Jack's current situation with his publisher, so he was aware how vulnerable we were. Nola's accident must have seemed like an answer to Marc's prayers.

I could almost see the pall of gloomy thoughts surrounding Jack as we entered the reading room, with its dark wood tables clustered in the middle, each one with a reading light. The white walls were crowded with black bookshelves, the tan carpet a sponge absorbing our footsteps.

I spotted Yvonne, wearing her signature rose petal pink and her rope of pearls, emerge from the other side of the room. It was odd seeing her in a place so modern, with lots of glass and concrete, instead of against the backdrop of the centuries-old Fireproof Building, where she used to work. She was frowning as she approached, something else I wasn't accustomed to, her hands outstretched toward me.

"Aren't you both a sight for sore eyes?" she said, accepting cheek kisses from both of us. "I don't think I've seen a person over twenty-five all week. I've actually begun to feel my age—especially against all this . . . newness."

The library was a recent addition to the campus and was a far cry from the elegant balustrades, Ionic columns, and fine architectural details of the Fireproof Building. "It certainly is newer," I agreed, pushing down the Sophie-like thought that the historical archives had no business sleeping beneath concrete and glass.

She sighed. "Yes, that's true." She grinned at Jack over the rims of her bifocals. "But as we all know, youth can be overrated."

Jack grinned back, and I was relieved to see a bit of the light return to his eyes. "And I hope you can prove that, Yvonne, by telling me you found something."

"I do believe I have," she said, leading us toward a table near the back of the room.

Jack let out a breath. "Thank goodness. Because if you didn't have anything new for us, we'd have to resort to our Plan B."

"We have a Plan B?" I asked.

"Not yet," he said, placing a hand on the small of my back as we followed Yvonne through the maze of mostly empty tables.

She indicated that we should sit down at one of them where a thick folder rested, causing my heart and stomach to jump in unison. Jack slid the shoebox toward Yvonne. "Here are the documents that were taken from the archives. We've already talked to our detective friend, who says that even though we're pretty sure Marc Longo took them, it's all circumstantial. But if I were you, I'd put his face with a line going across it on a poster near the entrance to the library."

"And these," I said, placing my own folder in front of me, "are copies of the papers you gave my dad that had been misfiled in the garden papers for the Tradd Street house. They're a jumble of things but include building plans for both mausoleums at Gallen Hall Plantation. The best thing about these documents is that we're fairly certain Marc Longo hasn't seen them because they were filed in error separately from the other documents."

I felt as if we were playing a game of poker, each of us carefully laying out our cards, with Yvonne our clever dealer. Beaming at us from behind her bifocals, she opened her own folder but kept her hand over the paper on top. "In addition to going through the documents you sent, I did a little digging on my own."

She slid the top page toward us like a dealer in a casino, still covering it with her hand. "From what Melanie told me on the phone, Marc has seen, and possibly destroyed, an appointment diary once belonging to his grandfather, Joseph Longo, and in it, a picture of a drawing Joseph copied from a letter he'd found in the Vanderhorst home during a party." She looked at me for corroboration, her eyes bright and shiny like those of a surgeon getting ready to cut.

I nodded.

"Marc's brother also told you that in the archives that Marc stole and then"—she paused, as if in remembrance of a dearly departed loved one—"destroyed, he found a letter dated 1781 stating that a French visitor was coming to lay a wreath on the tomb of the Vanderhorsts' beloved daughter, Marie Claire. I'll keep looking, but sadly, I can't find a copy of it or any other corroborating documentation about any visitors in 1781 to Gallen Hall. Either it doesn't exist or Marc has already found and destroyed it."

"But the Vanderhorsts at that time didn't have a daughter," Jack said.

"Precisely," Yvonne said, finally lifting her hand from the paper. "This next part was easy. Here in the archives we have several tomes dedicated to various Charleston families—the original land-grant Charlestonians, who many still believe are the only true Charlestonians. We're quite proud of our bloodlines, although some aren't as blue as we'd like to think." She winked. "Fortunately, the sheer number of sources makes it rather easy to find family trees and biographical information about them."

We looked down and saw a photocopy of a biography taken from what appeared to be an ancient textbook. "This young woman Elizabeth Grosvenor—known as Eliza to her friends and family—wasn't a daughter but did live with the family at the time as Mrs. Vanderhorst's ward. Her mother and Mrs. Vanderhorst were distant cousins, and when young Eliza was orphaned, she came to live with the Vanderhorsts at their plantation known as Gallen Hall. She was still living there in 1781, the year the letter was written."

Jack reached for the shoebox and began riffling through the contents before he pulled out a thin piece of paper, holding it out triumphantly. "I knew I recognized the name. Eliza was the one who purchased the first peacocks on the plantation. This is a purchase order for three pair, and her name appears at the bottom."

"Well done," Yvonne said, smiling at Jack as if he were her protégé.

I looked down at the paper Yvonne had given us; at the top-left corner there was what appeared to be an image from an oil painting, but the copy had all but blacked out her face.

Yvonne saw what I was looking at and explained, "The original portrait of Eliza is hanging at Gallen Hall. Of course you can't see it here, but she was reputedly a real beauty. She left many broken hearts in her wake, both British and American."

"An equal opportunity heartbreaker," Jack said, examining the smudge of black ink as if to see beneath it.

"Hers was the first body to be interred in the second mausoleum," Yvonne continued. "The first mausoleum remained empty until it was demolished. The first of three bodies interred in the newly built one, all in the same year—1782. To this day, they are the only three bodies in the mausoleum, and there were no further burials in the cemetery after that year, although the house was inhabited for more than two centuries afterward."

"So sad," I said, squinting at the larger print of her birth date on the bio: 1758. I recalled all the ways Sophie had told me a person could reach an early grave back in the days before antibiotics. "She was only twenty-three. Was it illness?"

Yvonne shook her head. "There's nothing in the official record—which made me curious, of course. So I went back through the papers in the shoebox and found a letter from Carrollton Vanderhorst, the owner of Gallen Hall at the time, to the reverend at the local church about a substantial donation in return for a favor."

Jack nodded eagerly. "I remember seeing that—something about requiring a particular area in the cemetery to be set aside for a new mausoleum, and asking the reverend if he could make it happen." He began flipping through the papers again, finally pulling out a yellowed piece of thin paper, delicate ink strokes scratched on one side. "Here it is. 'In such circumstances, whereby church dictates a soul cannot be buried in consecrated ground, my heartbroken wife and I implore you to do whatever is necessary to allow a place where a soul might find peace, despite an unholy demise.'"

"When I read that," Yvonne said, "I could think of only one thing."

"Suicide," Jack said quietly.

Yvonne nodded. "Yes, very tragic. Especially since she was beloved by the Vanderhorsts enough that they would make sure she was interred in the family cemetery. There's nothing mentioning suicide anywhere, of course, because that would have been a terrible scandal. There's simply no reference to what she died from, but back then dying young wasn't as rare as it is now."

"Why should Eliza be important to us?" I asked.

Yvonne said, "I wasn't sure at first, either, so I kept digging. Jack mentioned that there were two mausoleums built in the same place, two years apart, and I saw the plans you sent me. So far, I haven't seen anything that might explain why they tore down the first one, or what that cryptic message about a 'Marie Claire' might have meant. Except . . ." She slid another page in our direction.

Whoever had printed this page from what appeared to be an army supply journal had made sure that the font size had been blown up enough so I could read it. Not that it mattered, because it appeared to be only a list of four items: cognac, feathers of goldfinch, kitchen maid, Burgundy wine. "What is this?" I asked.

"Do you know who the Swamp Fox was?" Yvonne asked.

"Of course," Jack said.

"No clue," I said simultaneously.

We exchanged a quick glance before returning our focus to Yvonne.

"Francis Marion. During the Siege of Charleston he and his men used guerrilla warfare to attack the British. He was never captured and he managed to wreak devastating losses on the British and bolster the morale of the patriots. Many patriot sympathizers hid him in their houses as he moved through the Lowcountry. I'm assuming the Vanderhorsts must have been sympathizers since the name Gallen Hall was mentioned in his personal papers."

"And this list . . ." Jack began.

"Came from Francis Marion's personal documents from the war. I found it when I did an archive computer search using the words 'Gallen Hall.' It's amazing what computers can do these days, isn't it? And to think everything used to be in these little card files. . . ."

"Oh, I still use card files," I began, but Jack cut me off with a throat clearing before turning his attention back to Yvonne. "So, what did this list tell you?"

"Well, nothing at first. These items were apparently a shipment that originated in Virginia and was headed to Gallen Hall, and given to the Swamp Fox for safe transportation." She slid another page in our direction. "Which I might have overlooked, Jack, if you hadn't scanned those papers for me last night. Because this is from the housekeeping journal at Gallen Hall, showing a delivery of the exact same items on March 27, 1781."

Jack's brow furrowed. "And because there's no such thing as coincidence, this must mean something?"

"But of course," Yvonne said. "I haven't had a chance to go through everything you sent yet—I just need a couple more days to do a thorough job—but here's a few more things I think you might find interesting before we get back to our sweet Eliza." She slid three more pages toward us.

She pointed at the first one. "This is a timeline of the American Revolution. I wanted to know what was going on in Virginia in 1781, just in case that might shed some light on all this."

"The Siege of Yorktown," Jack offered.

I looked at him with surprise and admiration, wondering where he'd kept this nerdy side hidden from me and finding it rather sexy.

Yvonne looked at Jack like a teacher encouraging her favorite student. "And who was the commander in charge of the American forces there?"

Jack blinked for a moment, thinking, while Yvonne gave me a courtesy glance to see if I might be able to come up with an answer.

"Look at the list again, Jack. Not the typical list of necessities, is it? But if you had to guess a country of origin for at least two of the items, what would be your best guess?"

We both looked at the list. "France," I ventured.

"The Marquis de Lafayette," Jack said at the same time.

"You both get As." Yvonne beamed.

"Okay," Jack said slowly. "So what does this have to do with Eliza and anything valuable that might still be hidden on the property?"

Yvonne folded her hands primly in front of her. "As you know, the marquis was French and had the full support of the French king, as France had officially recognized American independence in 1778, most likely to thumb their noses at their enemies, the British. It is not documented, but there were rumors that the king of France, in addition to promising troops and ships to support the American cause, had also given the marquis something very valuable to support the Americans financially—namely, to fund spies. It wasn't easy to garner help from well-placed individuals who had so much to lose if caught. Priceless jewels or gold or even art would make a fine incentive.

"There is no official record of this happening, but there are certainly enough rumors and vague letters in various historical archives attesting to the probability that it did happen. However, if the treasure—and we still don't know what it might have been—did make it stateside, there is no record of what happened to it or where it might be today."

Jack slid the list closer. Almost under his breath, he read it out loud twice. "Cognac, feathers of goldfinch, kitchen maid, Burgundy wine. Those four items don't go together. I can almost buy that Lafayette would be delivering cognac and Burgundy wine to supporters in South Carolina, but a bird and a kitchen maid? I don't get it." His eyes widened. "There must be a code in there somewhere."

"Most likely," Yvonne said. "Although I must admit I haven't figured out exactly what yet."

I wanted to say that was exactly where my thoughts had been headed, but that would have been a lie. Instead, I said, "Do you think this is what Marc was looking for?"

Jack slowly shook his head as he regarded me. "It's possible, although there was nothing in the shoebox or the folder that mentioned it. Unless he read something in the papers he already discarded."

"There's more," Yvonne said.

We both looked at her, and it appeared Yvonne was enjoying the suspense just a little too much.

She slid an enlarged copy of a grainy photograph in our direction. I recognized the triangular shape of the mausoleum I'd seen at Gallen Hall Plantation. This was an old photograph of the front of it, showing the names and dates of the mausoleum's residents engraved on the granite.

I recognized Eliza Grosvenor's name, but the other two names, Lawrence Vanderhorst and Alexander Monroe, were unfamiliar, except for the Vanderhorst last name, of course. The only thing that stood out was that all three had died in 1782, Eliza in July and the two men on different dates in October. "Do we know anything about the two men?" I asked.

"We do now," Yvonne said as she slid two more pages toward us, both apparently from the same book as Eliza's biography.

I squinted at the photograph of the mausoleum's plaque while I waited for Jack to read the two biographies. He was silent for a few minutes, then straightened. He took a deep breath. "Well, that's an unexpected turn of events."

"What?" I said without looking up, distracted by something in the photograph.

"Alexander was a British soldier quartered at Gallen Hall during the occupation of Charleston, which began in 1780. And Lawrence"— he paused for effect—"was engaged to marry Eliza."

That made me look up. "So what happened?"

"It's not really clear. It just says that Alexander was found floating facedown in the Ashley River. Cause of death was accidental drowning."

"And Lawrence?"

Jack's eyes narrowed. "He was found four days later, a pistol shot to the middle of his chest. According to the biography, no one was ever charged with his death."

"According to *that* source," Yvonne interrupted. "But in *this* source, an atlas of Revolutionary War spies published in the thirties, their deaths had something to do with a spy ring, and one of the men might have been a double agent, selling secrets."

Jack and I shared a glance, both of us recalling something Greco had told us about a spy ring. He'd been pointing to a peacock carving on the claw-foot of Nola's bed.

"What was the spy ring called?" Jack asked.

"There's not a lot of information on it," Yvonne said. "Some historians even doubt its existence because there aren't any existing rosters of member names. The only way they identified each other was in the use of a symbol shaped like a peacock."

I felt Jack looking at me, but I was focused on the photo in my hand. "I think the rumors were right," I said, not looking up from the photograph of the mausoleum, the graininess of the old photo making details hard to discern.

Jack stood behind me, his warm breath brushing the back of my head as I felt the tension in his body, the pent-up excitement that we might have found something, however obscure, that might help us break free of Marc's hold on us.

"Here," I said. "What does that look like to you?" I pointed to the scrolling design that edged the plaque, so many swirls and curls that it was easy to hide a picture inside the design. Unless you knew what you were looking for.

I heard the grin in his voice. "It looks like the eye at the end of a peacock's tail."

"I agree," I said, smiling back. "Of course, it could just be a nod toward Eliza's passion for the bird, since she's interred there. Or not."

He kissed me briefly on the lips. "I told you we make a great team."

Yvonne gently cleared her throat.

"The three of us make an *extraordinary* team," he corrected himself before turning back to me. "Looks like we need to head back to the mausoleum and see for sure," Jack said with enthusiasm. His smile dimmed a bit. "Although I'm not really sure what any of this means, or even *if* it means anything, but it least it gives me something to focus on other than Marc, and the book, and Desmarae, whose latest idea is for me to get new author photos of me shirtless. To attract that younger demographic."

"But does that demographic even know how to read?" I asked.

"I don't know. All I know is that I just want to be left alone in peace to write, and not have to deal with all of this."

I grabbed his free hand. "I know. Hopefully we'll hear back from your architect friend with something helpful soon. And in the meantime, I'll call Anthony and set up a time for us to visit the mausoleum and hopefully figure this all out," I said with a great deal less enthusiasm as I recalled with a sinking feeling the last time I'd been there, and the lingering stench of rotting flesh that had followed me home.

"Don't forget to let Jayne know, so she can come, too," Jack said, gathering up the photocopies Yvonne had given us before enveloping her in a hug.

"Of course," I said, forcing a smile as I gave Yvonne a kiss on the cheek and a good-bye hug.

Jack actually whistled to himself as we exited the library, despite angry looks from librarians and patrons alike. He took my hand and squeezed, and I willed myself to be just as thrilled as he was at our discovery, reluctant though I was to examine what it was that had dimmed my own excitement like a dark cloud scuttling in front of the sun.

CHAPTER 15

On my way to the kitchen the following morning to grab my coffee before work, I heard the twins' babbling voices coming from Jack's office. I peered around the door and spotted the children, still dressed in their matching Christmas footie pajamas, batting at a crumpled ball of paper while the three dogs looked on, mesmerized. There was a lesson to be learned here, I was sure, as I did a quick tally in my head of the money I'd already spent on presents for Sarah and JJ that would probably never be played with as much as this crumpled ball of paper.

Jack sat on the floor near them, snapping photos with his iPhone. He'd already had to upgrade to a new phone with more memory because of the sheer number of photos he took of his three children. Except for the times when he turned the camera on me, my heart squeezed with every click, making me love my husband even more. Assuming that was possible.

"Good morning," I said, moving forward to kiss Jack. "I was wondering where my babies were and why the clothes I'd laid out for them were still on the bedroom chair." I knelt in front of Sarah and JJ, kissing them on their soft cheeks while they made appropriate smooching sounds. They smiled at me but were quickly distracted by one of the puppies batting at the paper ball.

I frowned as I stood. "And where is Jayne? I would hope that by now she'd know that the children should be dressed before . . ."

"Hi, Melanie."

I swung around behind me, where Jayne stood with a cup of coffee, looking young and rested. Unlike me, who hadn't had my coffee yet and who'd been awakened three times in the middle of the night by Sarah babbling to someone I couldn't see. I'd smelled the roses, so I hadn't been frightened. Just annoyed that as a mother herself, Louisa Vanderhorst didn't recognize that I needed my sleep.

Jayne clutched her mug a little tighter, making me realize I'd been staring at it. "Sorry, Melanie—JJ and Sarah looked so absolutely adorable in their pajamas that I thought we'd have a jammie morning. It's so cold outside that I thought we'd bring pillows and blankets downstairs and piles of books and camp out in front of the fire. When it gets a little warmer this afternoon, I'll dress them and take them to the park."

She took a sip from her coffee, reminding me that I was still staring at it. I forced my gaze to her face. "Um, sure. That's fine." I tucked a strand of hair behind my ear, then quickly replaced it, aware of the sun streaming through the windows and probably highlighting the six layers of concealer I'd smeared under my eyes to hide the dark circles. "I guess I'll, um, go get my coffee and head to work. . . ."

Jack stood. "Wait. I've got some great photos of the kids you'll probably want for the album. Look." He put his arm around my shoulders to draw me nearer, then started swiping his thumb across the screen to show me photos of Sarah and JJ playing with the puppies and wearing their cute pajamas. Jack was right. They were great photos, and ones I'd probably include in their photo albums. Except in every single one, Jayne was there—either with the children in her lap or sitting between them or next to them. I wasn't sure why that bothered me. She was my sister. Their aunt. She belonged in our photo albums because she was part of our family. But the gnatlike whine and itch of an unnamed irritation plucked at my conscience, making it difficult for me to meet Jayne's eyes when Jack lowered the phone.

"You're right—they're all great." I began backing out of the room, hoping that some caffeine was all I needed to slap down that persistent whine in the back of my head.

"And don't forget to call Anthony—I went ahead and told Jayne about what we learned yesterday with Yvonne. She's eager to return to Gallen Hall."

"Actually," I said slowly, looking at Jack, "I already spoke with him. He said later this week would work, and since I knew you didn't have anything on your calendar, I said we'd meet him on Friday at four o'clock."

"But Jayne will be watching the twins then," Jack pointed out.

"Oh, well," I started to say, but Jack spoke first. "I'm sure either your mother or mine will be happy to fill in."

"I'll call Mother and ask," Jayne offered. "Not sure if we should mention this to Dad, though. What do you think?"

Dad? "Um, well, assuming we don't want a repeat of what happened last time, I don't think that would be a good idea."

"Agreed," Jayne said brightly. She drained her mug and put it on Jack's desk before approaching, probably feeling it was safe now that her mug was empty. "While I was at the salon yesterday getting a mani-pedi, I did some thinking about everything that's been going on here at the cistern, and the connection with Gallen Hall and all of that history."

I curled my gnawed fingernails with raw cuticles into my palms so no one would notice how long it had been since I'd seen the inside of a nail salon. "Yes?" I said, forcing myself to listen.

"Remember the soldier we saw pointing the musket at us when we visited the plantation? Well, I find it interesting that one of Eliza's room-mates at the mausoleum was a British soldier. Too much of a coincidence to be a coincidence, right, Jack?"

She looked at my husband for corroboration before continuing. "What's really interesting is that Alexander Monroe was a British officer billeted at the plantation during the occupation. So why would he be interred with a son of the household and his fiancée? They had the entire cemetery at their disposal—why not just bury him in a regular grave?"

"I've been thinking the same thing," Jack said, giving Jayne a look of admiration that made the gnat in my head buzz a little louder.

Jayne continued. "And remember that smell in Nola's room that happened when those letters appeared on her wall? It smelled like gunpowder and horses and leather, didn't it?"

I nodded. I'd thought the same thing but had kept it to myself, hoping to figure out what it meant first. Maybe if I'd had the time to get my nails done, I would have figured it out, too.

"Maybe it's Alexander," Jayne suggested. "Which means there's a definite connection to the cistern and the mausoleum. Although, I don't know." She shook her head. "I didn't get a negative feeling from him, but there's definitely a negative vibe in Nola's bedroom."

"There's a woman, too," I added, avoiding Jack's gaze. "I saw her on the stairs. Just once, and it was very quick. It was the day of the Christmas photo, and I only saw her that once. I didn't connect her to the mausoleum, probably because I saw her here, and . . ."

They were both looking at me with blank expressions, and I knew we were all remembering the argument I'd had with Jack that very afternoon when Nola had found the photos on my phone of the other spirit in her bedroom. The argument that had been about me not telling Jack everything. I swallowed. "It was very quick," I repeated. "But I think she said something—it wasn't very clear. I've been waiting to see her again so I could make sure I heard her right before I told anyone. I wanted to be sure."

Jack's lips pressed together in a tight line. "What did you think she said?"

I could still hear the "S" of the last consonant, slithering like oil inside my head. "Lies."

"Just that one word?" Jack's eyes narrowed.

I went to him and kissed him soundly on the lips, keeping it G-rated on account of Jayne and the children being present. "Just that one word. I promise."

His hands cupped my shoulders. "Is there anything else you think you might want to tell me?"

I shook my head. "I don't tell you about every ghost I see because you might start questioning my sanity. I can't block them all." I looked over at Jayne for corroboration and she nodded. "I didn't think to mention the woman on the stairs because I thought it might be someone who'd followed me from outside and it was a onetime deal. It happens a lot. It might even have been something the girls conjured when they played with the Ouija board—there's really no way of knowing. But now, in context with what Yvonne told us, maybe the ghost is connected to the cistern."

"You look so sexy when you're being earnest," Jack said, his lips twitching into a reluctant smile. He pulled me closer to him and kissed me.

"Not to sound like Nola, but get a room."

We broke apart and looked over at Jayne, whose hands were firmly planted over her eyes, one on top of the other just in case there might be an opening she could peek through.

"Actually, I need to get to work," I said, my words dying as I recognized the Hard Rock Foundations truck pulling up in front of the house. "Did anyone else just hear the sound of a giant cash register sucking in all of our money?"

Jack followed my gaze. "Why is Rich Kobylt here?"

We heard the sound of Nola bounding down the stairs before coming to an abrupt stop outside Jack's office door. "Dad? Can you drive me to school? It's Mrs. Ravenel's turn to drive, but Alston and Lindsey have to be at school early and I don't so I said one of my parents could drive me instead."

Jack looked at his watch. "Don't you have to be at school in twenty minutes?"

She nodded. "Yes. So we have to hurry."

Jack sighed heavily as he reached for his car keys on his desk. "And you didn't think to mention this yesterday?"

"No, sorry. I forgot." She hitched her backpack higher on her back, pulling her long-sleeve purple polo out of the waistband of her gray uniform skirt, then turned to me. "And Dr. Wallen-Arasi stopped by yesterday afternoon to look at the dining room floor again and asked me to tell you that Mr. Kobylt would be here this morning to give you an estimate."

Jack and I exchanged a glance, an unspoken agreement to let it slide. We were still so grateful she'd emerged physically unscathed from the accident that neither of us wanted to call her out about being irresponsible. We'd save it for another time.

"Come on, Nola—let's get in the van." He gave me a brief kiss on the lips, said good-bye to Jayne and the twins, then left with Nola.

"Great," I said, sucking in my breath and mentally girding my loins. "I guess that means I need to go talk to Rich."

Jayne reached down to grab a hand of each toddler. "He went around to the back, so you might want to go through the kitchen. He probably wants to check on the progress of the cistern. Didn't you tell him that you want it filled in by Christmas?"

"Yep. Although I haven't told Sophie because I'm afraid of what she'll tell me." I kissed JJ and Sarah, then headed out through the kitchen, grabbing my coat and a cup of coffee on the way out.

Rich Kobylt wore a thick sweater that was long enough to cover his waistband, something for which I was eternally grateful. I didn't think my stomach could handle the view of his backside without at least a cup of coffee in me.

"Good mornin', Miz Trenholm," he called out in greeting.

I closed the door behind me, my face stinging with the chill. "Hi, Rich." I noticed he wore a large metal cross on a heavy chain around his neck. I was pretty sure I hadn't seen it before. He must have guessed where I was looking, because he put his hand on it.

"My wife gave it to me," he said. "No offense, Miz Trenholm, but this garden gives me the creeps. You'd think finding a skeleton in the fountain and then again in the foundation would have sent me over the edge, but it's this cistern that just makes my skin crawl. I feel like someone's watching me whenever I'm in the backyard. My wife gave me this as a little extra protection." He jiggled the chain.

"That was nice of her," I said, not able to think of anything else to say. Was there a proper response for when someone starts wearing a religious icon to protect them from your backyard?

"Yeah, she's pretty thoughtful." Facing me again, he said, "So, I hear my friend Greco is working for you now. He's got a funny way of dressing, but he's a good guy."

I kept my face neutral. "He's great. Very nice to work with. And definitely not easily spooked."

Rich's eyes narrowed a little at my choice of words, and I bit my lip, wishing I hadn't said that out loud. He faced the cistern, where Meghan Black and two other students were diligently picking at the bricked sides despite the cold. "Between you and me, this is taking a lot longer than I'd thought. If they don't finish this week, there's no way I'm going to be able to fill this in and make it disappear before your big party."

"Could you just get a bulldozer in here and cover it all up and we'll call it an accident?"

He stared at me blankly. "You serious, Miz Trenholm? Because I don't think Dr. Wallen-Arasi would go for that." He emphasized his words by shaking his head. "As a matter of fact, she's nice and all, but I wouldn't want to get on her bad side."

As a frequent victim of her bad side, I had to agree. "No, you certainly wouldn't want to go there. So," I said, eager to get away from the cistern and the pervasive scent of dead, rotting things that lingered despite the cooler air and Sophie's assurances that anything dead would have disintegrated long ago. "You're here to look at the dining room floor?"

"Yes, ma'am. I understand you got some of those nasty wood-boring beetles."

"According to Dr. Wallen-Arasi, we do." I put my hand on his arm and leaned closer. "Could you do me a favor, please? If it's over a thousand dollars to get rid of them and repair the floor, could you get me an estimate on laminate floors? You know—the ones that look like wood but aren't tasty to beetles?"

He pursed his lips. "Dr. Wallen-Arasi won't like that at all. Not one bit."

I stepped back. "True. But she's not the one paying for it, is she?" I narrowed my eyes at him. "And if you breathe one word to her about what I just said, you're going to need a lot more protection than that necklace. Do you understand?"

His eyebrows shot up. "Yes, ma'am. I understand."

"Good. You go on inside. I have a quick question for one of the students first. I'll join you in a minute."

He didn't wait for me to tell him a second time. He'd almost made it to the kitchen door before he bent down to tie his shoe. I almost spit out my coffee and had to avert my eyes.

Turning toward the cistern, I watched as Meghan Black, in the same cute black bow earmuffs and pink tool belt I'd seen her in before, bent forward with a tiny brush to wipe dirt from a protruding brick in the cistern's wall.

"Hello, Meghan?" I called.

She continued with the brush and I noticed the wires from her earbuds snaking beneath the earmuffs. I moved to stand in front of her and waved my hands until she noticed me. She reached up and pulled out the buds and smiled at me. "Good morning, Mrs. Trenholm."

"Good morning." I took a sip of my coffee, the liquid quickly growing cold. "So," I said, indicating the deep hole in my backyard. "Are you all almost done here?"

She looked horrified. "No—far from it. We're finding things every day, but it does take time to make sure nothing is damaged when we excavate." She moved closer to me, and I saw a pink and green Lilly Pulitzer coffee thermos on the ground next to a white blanket, on which what looked like junk lay in careful rows. "Look what we found this morning," she said with excitement as she held up what appeared to be a broken piece of china. "It's a broken piece of china!"

"Fascinating," I said.

"I know, right?" Meghan carefully replaced the shard next to a nearly identical piece. "I think we might have an entire cup and saucer." She moved her hand to something smaller lying on the blanket. "We found this bone, too," she said, holding up something small and white as my throat constricted.

Her smile fell. "Oh, don't worry, Mrs. Trenholm. Actually, we've found a lot of animal bones—mostly chicken bones. Probably from buried garbage. You know what they say—one man's trash is another man's treasure."

She said it with so much enthusiasm that I had to smile. "Do you have a moment? I wanted to ask you about that photo you took. And the man standing near the cistern."

A visible shudder went through her, and I was fairly sure it had nothing to do with the wind. "I deleted it from my phone. Along with the photo of the face in the window upstairs."

This didn't surprise me. I would have done the same thing if I didn't know for sure that the spirits wouldn't stay deleted. "No worries—you e-mailed them to me, so I have them on my phone, and you gave me printed copies, remember?"

She nodded. "Yeah. You should probably delete the photos and tear up the prints, too. It's not like I believe in that kind of thing, but it would seem to me that's not something you should have hanging around your house."

"No doubt," I said. "So, I don't know how much you recall about the photo, but was there anything you noticed that was memorable about the figure?"

"Apart from the fact that he wasn't there in person and only showed up in the photo? That's kind of hard to forget."

"Sure. But what do you remember about his clothing?"

"Oh. It was definitely late eighteenth century."

"Are you sure? Because in the picture, it appeared he wore a cravat with folded collars."

"A lot of people can't tell the difference between seventeenth- and eighteenth-century men's fashions unless they study that kind of thing—unlike women's fashions. You can always tell by the width of their skirts what decade of what century they're from. Cravats were worn for de-

cades overlapping the two centuries. But I know it was eighteenth century because I distinctly remember his hair was pulled back, like in a
ponytail, and not cut short. That's the main difference between the two
centuries."

I'd been harboring a hope that this specter had nothing to do with
the woman on the stairs or the soldier at Gallen Hall. Because then they
would be separate entities, to be dealt with one at a time. But three
eighteenth-century apparitions pointed in another direction entirely.
"Was there anything else?" I asked, forcing myself not to hold my breath
as I waited for her answer.

She began to shake her head, but stopped. "I've tried to forget it, but
there was something about his eyes. At first I thought they were just
hidden by shadows. But then . . ." She stopped, looked at me. "But after
printing the pictures and looking at them closely, it looked as if they
were . . . not there." Her brown eyes opened wide. "I hope I'm not
scaring you, Mrs. Trenholm. It was probably just dirt on my iPhone. My
mom has always said I have an active imagination, so I naturally made
a smudge into a person. Because ghosts aren't real."

"So they say," I said. As if in afterthought, I said, "Did you ever do
any work at the cemetery at Gallen Hall?"

"Oh, yeah. When I was an undergrad, we went out there a few times
with the FARO laser scanner in our digital documentation class to document the headstones. It was really fun."

"Sounds like it," I said. "So, did you or any of your classmates
ever . . . see anything there? Any dirt smudges on camera lenses that
looked like a ghost?"

She went very still. "Maybe."

"Maybe, yes?" I prodded.

"Yeah. A bunch of us saw something once and everyone ran, including me. But I tripped—I'm a little clumsy—so I got a better look. He
was standing by the mausoleum."

"Did it look like the same person that you saw here?"

She took a moment, then nodded. "Yeah—it was definitely the
same . . . thing. I know because there was a . . . stain or something on

his shirt, where you could see beneath his jacket. It must have been unbuttoned or something, because I could see the white shirt underneath." She rolled her shoulders as if to shake off the awareness of someone staring at her. "I don't talk about it because I'd rather just forget it."

I forced a bright smile. "Totally makes sense. If I'd seen something like that, I'd want to forget all about it, too." I finished my ice-cold coffee. "Well, thanks for speaking with me. I don't want to hold you up, so I'll let you get back to work. Have fun."

She nodded enthusiastically. "Don't worry—I will!" She replaced her earbuds as I stepped away from the yellow tape and made my way back to the house, the awareness of someone watching me making my skin crawl. I entered the kitchen without looking back, content with telling myself it had been Meghan.

CHAPTER 16

I held the step stool for Veronica so she could place the angel at the top of the dining room Christmas tree. I hoped no one would notice that half of the angel's yellow yarn hair and one of the felt wings were missing thanks to Sarah, who'd mistaken the angel-doll tree topper for a chew toy. I had no idea how she'd reached it since I'd had to put it in a closed box after she'd spotted it in the dining room, but it had managed to find its way into her crib. I wondered if Louisa might be exercising her indulgent-grandmother instinct postmortem.

"Perfect," Veronica said, stepping down from the stool. "I think all of the trees look lovely, but this is the prettiest in my opinion."

I stood back, admiring the effect of handmade dolls hanging from pine boughs, and strings of popcorn and pinecones wrapping around the tree. "My arms are so short. I'm glad you were here to hang the ornaments on the upper branches."

She smiled, but her eyes were sad. "Adrienne was five feet eleven inches by the time she was seventeen. She was always the go-to person for tree decorating or getting something off a high shelf. Everybody thought she played basketball or volleyball, but she wasn't athletic at all.

She preferred to read and play the piano. It was really unfair—all that height wasted."

"I bet," I said, aware suddenly of her sister's perfume settling in the air around us. I pretended to continue studying the tree while I tried to decide if I should say something. "I, uh . . . When I was in your house taking photos for Sophie, I ended up in the attic."

She looked at me without surprise. It was almost as if we were challenging each other to see who could pretend the longest that they didn't see the elephant standing in the middle of the room.

"I know. Michael told me. He said he thought you were only planning on taking pictures of the first floor."

"I thought so, too. But your house is so beautiful, I couldn't stop. I hope you don't mind me being so nosy."

Veronica shook her head. "Not at all. I hope you got what you needed."

She kept her eyes leveled on me, and I knew she wasn't talking about the pictures. "I think so." I stopped, then found myself feeling the need to say more. "I found the box full of Adrienne's things."

"I know. I saw that her little heart pillow was missing."

My cheeks reddened. "I don't know why I took it. I just sort of . . . panicked when I heard Michael and Lindsey come in the front door, and it seemed the logical thing to do at the time. If you'll hang on a second, I'll go get it. . . ."

"No, please don't. I think Adrienne must have wanted you to have it. Unless you have a habit of taking things from people's houses." She smiled so I wouldn't take offense.

"No, not usually. I just felt . . . compelled to put it in my purse." I chewed on my lip for a moment, straightening a string of popcorn and pinecones. I wanted to get a ruler to make sure each strand was evenly spaced, but I was fighting the impulse. Jack said it was the only way I could get better, to fight that impulse for precision—unless I decided to become a Formula One mechanic or a brain surgeon.

"Was the pillow important to Adrienne?"

Veronica smiled. "Yes. Our mother made it for her before Adrienne went to college. Even though she was nearby, Mom said she wanted Adrienne to remember that she was loved."

The surge of perfume stung my eyes and I had to blink back tears. "Your poor mother," I said, thinking of Nola and how it would feel if something happened to her. I couldn't go beyond that thought.

"We were all devastated, of course, but especially our mother. I don't think she really ever recovered." Veronica brightened. "There was another box that we retrieved from her dorm room, full of clothes she'd made. She wanted to be a fashion designer—ever since she was a little girl. She was always making clothes for Mom and for me, and most of her friends. She was incredibly talented with a needle. I donated the clothes to a women's shelter, knowing Adrienne would approve. It's funny. . . ."

When she didn't continue, I prompted, "What?"

Veronica shrugged. "You know how you said you felt compelled to take the heart pillow? I felt the same thing when I saw that box of clothes. It was like Adrienne was speaking in my ear."

She probably was, I wanted to say.

"You still have the necklace, right?" she asked.

I couldn't tell her how I'd rediscovered it, so I just nodded.

Still looking at the tree, she said, "I've been meaning to ask you for it, but I thought . . ." She stopped for a moment, lifted her hand to touch a small wooden nutcracker ornament wearing British regimental red. "But I thought that as long as you held on to it there was a chance you would agree to help us."

"Us?"

Veronica met my gaze. "Adrienne and me. Michael just wants to put it behind us. But I can't move on." She lowered her voice to a near whisper. "I sense her near me all the time. I don't think she'll rest until we find out what happened to her. To punish the person responsible. Which means I can't give up. It's just that Detective Riley hasn't been able to turn up anything new despite the necklace and what it might mean. We're back to where we started before I found that box." She shrugged but I heard the hitch in her voice. "You were my last resort. I don't know where else to turn."

I turned back to the tree, focusing on a small robin's nest ornament, the single egg made from a wooden button. My cheeks heated as if she'd just scolded me, which, I suppose, she had. "So," I said. "Hypothetically speaking, if I were psychic, what would you ask me to do?"

"Hypothetically, if you were psychic, I'd want you to ask Adrienne who killed her."

I thought for a moment, remembering the apparition I'd captured on my phone while taking pictures in her house. But I didn't want to scare her. I paused, trying to find the right words. I cleared my throat and said, "From what I've been told, it never works that way. It's like the living and the dead still speak the same language but just use a completely different dialect. And there's, like, a . . . time delay. Remember what it used to be like speaking long-distance on a landline before fiber optics? Where one person asks a question, and by the time the other person hears it, they've already started asking their own question? So, no. It's never as easy as just asking."

I almost mentioned the Hessian soldier who'd once haunted my mother's house on Legare Street. I'd had complete conversations with him, and I hadn't understood why I'd been able to until my mother explained that he must have also been able to communicate with spirits when he was here on earth. But I couldn't tell Veronica that. Because I wasn't supposed to know what it's like to speak to the dead.

I realized Veronica was staring at me.

"So I've heard," I quickly added. "And a lot of times, the spirits aren't strong enough to convey an entire message. It takes a lot of energy just to make themselves seen." *Or smelled,* I almost added. "Then they have to find a way to deliver the message as quickly as they can, which usually lasts for a brief second. It's why so many messages from the other side seem coded. It's just quicker for them to say what they have to say."

"So you've heard."

I nodded. "Right."

"In that case, I'd ask you to keep the lines open, then pay close attention when she gives you a message. Like compelling you to walk upstairs to an attic where you hadn't planned on going."

"And if I did, and I somehow managed to figure out who did this to Adrienne, what would you do?"

"I'd tell Detective Riley and leave out any mention of your name in any publicity that might surround the story of solving a twenty-year cold case. I'd never find the words to adequately express my thanks, but I'd promise to never stop trying."

My eyes stung and I quickly blinked them. "That's good to know."

"So you'll help me?"

Our eyes met and I swallowed. "If I were a psychic, I'd find it very hard to say no."

Any response she had was lost as repeated loud knocks sounded on the front door. I rushed to open it, then wished I hadn't. Rebecca stood on the front porch looking flustered and a little disheveled, which, for her, consisted of a hair out of place and her pink hair bow slightly askew. She carried a silver flocked tabletop Christmas tree, complete with a bedazzled star tree topper and a pink feather garland.

I moved back to allow her and the tree inside the vestibule. "I don't know why you can't get that doorbell fixed, Melanie. I've been ringing and ringing and freezing to death outside. Did you forget I was coming?"

"Funny—it worked for Veronica. And, yes, I did forget. Veronica and I have been busy all morning finishing up all the fireplace mantels and we just completed decorating the last tree in the dining room."

Her pink-lipsticked mouth formed a pout. "But Sophie said I could put my tree in the dining room."

I shook my head, pretending to think. "No, I'm pretty sure she said laundry room. Since it's tabletop size, we all thought it would look best sitting on top of the washing machine."

Her lips pinched together. "Marc and I are donating a *lot* of money for this event. I would like to think that gives me *some* kind of bonus."

"Of course it does," Veronica said gently as she took the hideous tree from Rebecca so my cousin could take off her pink faux fur coat. "That's why we're putting your tree in the laundry room. It will be the center-piece since no other decorations will be in there to compete with the beauty of your creation."

I wanted to high-five Veronica for not mentioning that the reason it would be the only Christmas-themed item in the laundry room was because the laundry room wasn't likely to be seen by any of the guests.

"Thank you," Rebecca said, sounding slightly mollified. Addressing Veronica, she said, "I've got a whole bag of ornaments in the shape of little dogs that I bedazzled in my car. If you'd like to go ahead and bring the tree to the laundry room, I'll go get them. You can help me put them on the tree."

"Will do," Veronica said, as I admired her ability to keep her eyes from rolling. "Oh, and please thank your husband again for that generous donation to Ashley Hall. I've already spoken with the school, and since I know Melanie is crazy busy this time of year with work and her family obligations, I told them I will be happy to host the film crew at my house for my portion of the progressive dinner so they won't have to bother Melanie. Can you please let him know?" She smiled brightly, then left, leaving Rebecca to just mutter, "Sure," as Veronica disappeared into the back of the house.

When Veronica was out of earshot, Rebecca put her hand on my arm. "How's Nola doing?"

I stiffened. "Physically, she's fine. Mentally, well, she says she's never going to drive a car again. Especially not after what that horrible Harvey Beckner said to her."

"I know." She leaned closer to me in a conspiratorial way. "He's not my favorite person, either. Marc's writing the screenplay, you know, because nobody else is really qualified to tell the story—"

"Except for Jack," I interrupted.

"Yes, well, be that as it may, Marc's working on the script and Harvey keeps on asking for more sex and violence and all sorts of things that weren't a part of the original book. He wants to show a love scene between Joseph Longo and Louisa Vanderhorst."

"What?" I said, horrified. "But she loved her husband. That never happened—never. That's just a horrible fabrication—and skews the whole story!"

"I know, I know. Poor Marc. He's really stuck between a rock and a hard place, isn't he?"

"Excuse me?" I asked, sure I'd misunderstood. "Are you saying Marc is the victim here?"

Rebecca's round blue eyes blinked slowly. "All I'm saying is that Harvey is being really unreasonable. Marc's book is perfection as it is—otherwise it wouldn't have hit so many bestseller lists, right? I don't know why Harvey is requesting so many changes. But, anyway, I've been worried about Nola and I'm glad to hear she's doing better."

"At least until the film crews arrive in January to start filming the movie. I think she's more upset about this deal than Jack and I are. She thinks it's all her fault."

"That's silly. Just tell her it would have happened sooner or later. Marc always gets his way."

"Really?" I said, crossing my arms. "Because he told me that he was going to own this house."

"I don't know why he wants this old, creaky house, but if he said he wants it, sooner or later he'll get it."

I waited a moment so she could let her own words sink in. "You do understand you're talking about my family home, right?"

"Sure—but you never really wanted it, remember? Didn't you use to refer to it as a goiter on your neck?"

"Yes, but that was before I married Jack, and before Nola came to live with us and the twins were born."

Rebecca looked skeptical. "All I know is that you never wanted this house. That you've always hated old houses. That's the only reason why I'm not fighting Marc on this. Because I know that it's really what you both want."

I was so angry that I couldn't find any words to argue. She must have taken my silence for agreement, because she put her hand on my arm again, and said, "I had another dream."

"About something bad happening to Jack? I'm starting to think you're making this all up just so we won't fight Marc anymore."

"No. This one wasn't about Jack."

She was scrutinizing me so closely that I had to step back. "Was it about me?"

Rebecca gave a quick shake of her head. "No. It was about Nola."

My stomach and heart squeezed. "Nola?"

"Yes. At least I'm pretty sure it was her. It was a young woman about her age, and she's the only person I know who fits that description, so I assumed it was her. There was . . ." She reached her hand up to her neck in a defensive gesture. "There was . . . there was a rope around her neck."

My breath came in shallow gasps as my hand slowly drifted up to my own neck, as if to make sure there was nothing there.

Rebecca patted me on my arm. "I know—it's hard to hear. But I also know you'll figure it out in time to protect her. I'll let you know if I have any more dreams." She flashed me a bright smile. "Right now, I'm going to get those gorgeous ornaments from my car and help Veronica set up my tree. It's going to be the most beautiful tree in the house, if not all the houses!"

I watched her leave, then stood where I was in the vestibule for a long moment, staring at the closed door. I'd heard Nola come in from school about an hour before and had the sudden need to see her, to make sure she was all right.

I took the stairs two at a time, surprised to find her door open and voices coming from inside. I peered into the room to find Nola on the bed with a large and very thick book on her lap and her laptop in front of her, the three dogs perched at the foot watching her. Greco stood by the wall between the windows, impeccably dressed as usual in suit pants, shirt, and tie, his jacket draped neatly over a chair. His shirtsleeves were rolled up, and he appeared to be examining ten paint swatches on the wall.

He looked at me and smiled, then went back to frowning at the wall. "Who knew there were so many shades of gray?"

"I thought there were only supposed to be fifty," Nola said with a smirk.

"You're not supposed to know about that book," I said.

"There was a book? I only know about the movie."

"Actually there were several—of both. Maybe we should look at the convent school in Ireland your dad keeps talking about."

"But then you'd miss me too much." She gave me a grin, then returned to her laptop.

I stood next to Greco, trying to ignore the jewelry cabinet with its open lid and all the doors and drawers wide open. "I thought gray was just black and white mixed together."

"Sometimes," he said, tilting his head. "But in different light, some can appear to be more blue, or green, or beige. Miss Nola would prefer a strict black-and-white gray. And it is my job to make sure that's what gets put on her wall."

I looked over at Nola, who was reading something on her laptop. "Why are you in here, Nola? Don't you have a nice ergonomic desk and chair set up for you in the guest room?"

Without glancing up, she said, "Yes, but Greco is in here, and he's the expert on the American Revolution, which is what we're studying now. He's a Revolutionary War reenactor. Did he tell you that?"

"He did," I said. "But he's not here to help with your homework."

"I'm rather enjoying it," Greco said. "I like talking about my favorite subject with such an interested and intelligent student."

I grinned with pride, as if he were complimenting me. But I couldn't take any of the credit where Nola was concerned. "Well, she does love history—which is a good thing since her father pretty much lives and breathes it."

"He should try reenacting."

Just the thought of Jack wearing a uniform did funny things to my stomach. "I'll mention it to him."

Greco picked up a sample quart of paint and screwed on the lid. "This one is definitely out. It's much too beige—and Miss Nola is just not a beige person."

As he spoke, Nola shifted her legs on the bed, making the three dogs adjust their reclining positions, resulting in the thick textbook beginning a nosedive off the side. I caught it midslide, slapping it against the bed on the page where Nola had it opened.

Nola pressed her hands against her heart. "Good save, Melanie. I hope it's not damaged. It belongs to Greco and it's really old."

"No worries," the designer said. "I've practically memorized it. It actually belongs to my great-uncle, a professor of history at Carolina back in the day. Quite well respected in his field. His expertise was focused on spies throughout American history, particularly during the Revolution."

I looked down at the splayed page and stopped, noticing the large picture at the top of the page. "That's Gallen Hall. Nola, did you know that it was owned by the same Vanderhorsts that owned this house?"

"Yes, Captain Obvious. You and Dad have only been talking about that nonstop for days."

Greco was saying something about blending two of the paint samples to make the perfect true gray, but I was listening with only half an ear as I read from the textbook. "This is interesting," I said, my heart beating a little faster as I saw the small picture beneath the one of the mansion. "Another reference book I saw also mentions that Lawrence Vanderhorst might have been a spy and was discovered shot in the chest, and that his killer was never found. But this is new." I stopped for a moment to find the part in the text again, and squinting so I could see it, I read out loud.

"'When Lawrence Vanderhorst's body was discovered on the morning of October twenty-eighth, the only thing clear about his death was that it had been caused by a single bullet to the chest. Several people from the house rushed outside at the noise but could only find footprints in the dew leading to and from the house, one set apparently being the victim's. All servants and family members were interviewed, but no clear evidence suggested that any of them were involved. His murder has never been solved.'"

I read it again to myself, thinking how strange it sounded that no one was arrested despite the evidence pointing to someone who'd been in the house at the time of the murder. I looked up to where Greco was painting another swatch of color on the wall, and then over at Nola, who was looking down at her laptop and absently rubbing her neck. I became aware of a scratching sound in the room, like a small animal trapped inside the walls, trying to get out.

"Do you hear that?" I asked.

"Hear what?" Nola looked up at me.

"That sound. That scratching sound."

Greco shook his head, but it was too late to pinpoint where it had come from, as it had already stopped. I placed the book back on the bed in front of Nola. "Could you please bookmark that page? I want to make a copy of it when you're done so I can show your dad. I have no idea if it means anything, but it couldn't . . ."

I forgot what I was saying. On the wall behind Nola, above the headboard, the word *Lies* had been scratched into the paint.

Nola looked at the word, then back at me, her eyes wide. Slowly we both turned to Greco.

"Well," he said, smiling, "it's a good thing we're planning on painting the entire room."

CHAPTER 17

I stood at the threshold of Jack's office, listening as Nola plucked out a desultory tune on the piano. It wasn't the ideal spot for the instrument, but both Jack and Nola insisted being together in a shared space was good for their shared artistic vibe. It made my heart happy to watch them work in the same environment, knowing it was one of the reasons for their close father-daughter bond. Considering they'd been separated for most of Nola's life, their bond was no small feat. Nola and I were close, too, and I tried not to take offense that she never dared roll her eyes at her father, saving all that for me. Nor did she deprive him of his favorite foods. Nola insisted this was her way of showing me affection, but I wasn't convinced.

Jack huddled over his desk, poring over documents related to Gallen Hall and the three people buried in the mausoleum. He still hadn't heard back from his architect friend, Steve, and we were holding out hope that the architectural renderings would contain the one thing we needed.

As I entered the room Jack and Nola sighed in unison, pushing up the hair off their foreheads with the heels of their left hands as they stared down at their individual work spaces.

"You about ready to go?" I asked Jack.

It took him a moment to answer, as if he were unwilling to pull himself away. He moved his chair back before looking up at me. "Sure. Let me grab my jacket." He looked back at the papers on his desk, then slid his gaze over to Nola. She'd had a doctor's appointment at noon and then managed to convince me afterward that she could just go home instead of back to school because all she had left were PE and music.

"Need to take a creative break?" he asked.

"Even if it's not creative, I need a break. I keep coming up with absolutely nothing new here. I've been adulting all day, and I'm done."

"Adulting?" I asked, pretty sure that if I looked that one up in *Webster's*, I wouldn't find it.

Both Jack and Nola looked at me with matching frowns.

"You know—being an adult," Nola said, speaking slowly as if explaining something to the twins.

"I don't think that's a real word," I said.

"It is." Jack stood and took his jacket off the antique coat rack behind the door. "If you watched any reality TV or subscribed to certain channels on YouTube, you'd know that."

"YouTube?" I asked, thinking I'd heard of it before—probably during carpool with Nola and her friends, which was generally a huge font of knowledge.

"I'll tell her in the car on our way to Gallen Hall," Jack reassured Nola. "If only so she won't embarrass you in front of your friends."

"Whatever." Nola dropped her hands from the keyboard and let her shoulders fall. "I need some creative inspiration. Are you sure I can't go with you?"

"Absolutely not," Jack said. "I'm sure you've got homework."

"It's Friday."

"Right," Jack said distractedly, as he patted his jacket and jeans pockets. "Has anyone seen my . . ." He stopped, then reached forward to grab his phone from his desk, pausing just a moment before picking up a piece of paper and walking over to Nola.

"Here," he said, holding it out to her. "You were so good figuring out Hasell Pinckney's snow globe puzzle, maybe you'll have better luck with this than I have. Feel free to search the Internet or any other source you can think of, although I'm pretty sure I've seen them all." He pointed to the books on the floor by his desk. "And there's a whole pile of books about ciphers going back to the Egyptians. Have at it."

Nola took the paper and stared at it, then read aloud, "'Cognac, feathers of goldfinch, kitchen maid, Burgundy wine.'" She looked up, her brow furrowed. "What's this supposed to mean?"

Jack gave her a grim smile. "We're hoping you can tell us. You said you needed a creative break, so you're welcome."

"Great," she said with a heavy sigh. "Can I invite Alston and Lindsey over to help?"

I nodded. "Sure. And you can order pizza. Just make sure it's not vegetarian and you save some for me. Jayne's coming with us, and the twins are with my parents, so your friends will be good company. They can spend the night if they want."

"I'm sure they'll come over, but they won't spend the night. They say our house after dark is creepy."

"Only after dark?" Jack asked.

I elbowed him. "That's fine. We'll be happy to drive them home when we get back—shouldn't be too late, if that makes you feel better."

"Finding out who that was in my bedroom window would make me feel better, but no pressure."

"We're working on it, Nola," Jack said as he bent to kiss the top of her head. He indicated the paper with his chin. "Maybe that will help. All we know so far is that it might connect a treasure from the king of France to the Americans during the Revolution."

"All right," she said, her fingers already flying on her phone as she texted her friends. "Have fun at the cemetery."

I grinned, finding it somewhat amusing that a comment like that in our house sounded perfectly normal.

We took my car, since Jack's minivan was full of baby toys, cracker crumbs, and spare diapers. He'd come a long way since his Porsche days, and he never seemed to have any nostalgia regarding the lost days of his bachelorhood. For his Christmas stocking, I'd purchased a bumper sticker that read REAL DADS DRIVE MINIVANS. Nola had been with me and had wanted to get one that read CONDOMS PREVENT MINIVANS, but I wouldn't let her.

Jayne was waiting outside her house on South Battery as we drove up, and she slid into the backseat.

"You ready?" Jack asked, looking at her in the rearview mirror.

"As ready as I'll ever be." She buckled her seat belt as Jack pulled out onto the street. "Mother gave me the rundown of what to do, so I feel confident that Melanie and I can handle whatever's waiting for us. And don't forget I have a little experience from that incident in my attic."

I felt Jack waiting for me to say something. "Yes. Absolutely. And Mother and I have faced enough evil spirits on our own that it's practically second nature now."

"I'll follow your lead," Jayne said with conviction.

Feeling a little embarrassed, I said, "As Mother says, we're stronger together. We just need to remember that."

"Good plan," Jayne said. "Speaking of Mother, have you thought yet about what to get her for Christmas?"

I turned slightly in my seat to get a better look at my sister. "Yes, actually. I already got her a skirt at Finicky Filly that I know she'll love. And she adores the Woodhouse Spa, so I decided to give her a spa-day gift certificate. The owner, Kim, is amazing and said she'd wrap it up in a gorgeous gift basket with candles and skin products."

"That's a great idea. How about I contribute and add stuff to the basket—maybe a whole weekend of pampering? Mother would love it."

My throat felt as if it had been coated in sawdust, and I couldn't speak for a moment, even though I could feel the weight of the silence in the car.

"That's a terrific idea, isn't it, Mellie?" Jack prompted. "Your mother has been so great with the twins and Nola—I think double the pampering from her daughters would be the perfect gift."

I nodded, trying to swallow the sawdust so I could speak.

"Great," said Jayne. "And for Dad, I thought we could arrange for a master gardener to give him personalized instruction in his own garden. Sophie said she knows someone from the college who would be perfect and she gave me his number—I just wanted to check with you first."

I finally managed to open my airway so I could speak. "Sounds wonderful. For both of them. I'll call Kim at Woodhouse if you want to take care of setting up the master gardener."

"Actually, I already did. And I have this great design software, so I made this really cool laminated poster that explains it all so we'd have something to wrap."

Jack poked me on the side of my leg. "Thanks," I managed. "That will save me a lot of time, and I'm sure he'll love it."

Thankfully, I was saved from coming up with anything else to say when Jack's phone rang. Jack looked at the dashboard screen. "It's Yvonne. I'll put her on speaker." He clicked a button on the steering wheel. "Hello, gorgeous. I'm in the car with my wife and sister-in-law, so don't say anything compromising."

Yvonne laughed, and I pictured her soft hands patting her white coiffure. "Oh, Jack Trenholm. You're incorrigible."

"Thank you. I try. We're on the way to Gallen Hall now. I hope you have good news for us."

"I'm not sure if it's good news, but it is interesting. I was out power walking this morning with my posse. . . ."

"Your posse?" Jack asked with a grin.

"Yes, Jack. I've had to learn a whole new vocabulary since working here at the College of Charleston. They do say that studying a foreign language is the best way to keep your brain young."

"That they do. Please continue."

"Yes, well, remember when we were speaking I told you how I couldn't find anything regarding how Eliza died?"

"Yes," Jack said slowly.

"Well, the Charleston Museum has a huge collection of personal correspondence and photographs that they use interns to sort and file, so it's usually hit or miss. Plus, they get more and more documents each month as people empty attics and the like. So when I passed the museum this morning, I just had a feeling that I should go see if there was anything about the Vanderhorsts from Gallen Hall in there. I was pretty sure I'd found all there was, but it couldn't hurt to look again."

When she didn't continue, Jack gave me a sidelong glance, then said, "And?"

I could almost see Yvonne's pink cheeks and sparkling blue eyes. "I found something—it was filed with other documents from the Grosvenor family, which is probably why it was overlooked when Marc Longo was busy stealing the Vanderhorst letters."

She didn't say anything more, so Jack prompted, "And what did you find?"

"Well, I found a letter from the doctor who was called to the scene of Eliza's passing. It was addressed to his wife, which most likely explains his candor. In it he expresses his sadness at the loss of such a vibrant young woman, 'cut down in the bloom of her youth.' Those were his exact words. I wonder if the pun was intended, seeing as how she literally had to be cut down."

I leaned closer to the speaker, wanting to make sure I'd heard correctly.

"She hanged herself?" Jack said.

"Yes, sadly. According to the good doctor, Eliza hanged herself from an oak tree in the cemetery on the plantation grounds."

He rubbed his jaw, his face dark in thought. "It's very unusual today for females to commit suicide by hanging, or shooting or anything that violent. I wonder if it was different then."

"I would think it would have been less so," Yvonne offered. "Women were considered more delicate back then. Not that I've done the full research, but from what I recall from all my reading, of all the suicides and murders involving women in the last two centuries, women tended to favor poisons." Yvonne's voice brightened. "I read of an interesting case recently from the early eighteen hundreds where a nanny killed her mistress using oleander leaves—"

"Thanks, Yvonne," Jack said, cutting her short. "What are you thinking this might mean?"

"Isn't that your job?" she asked with a chuckle.

"Yes, but I always feel that I have a better chance of being right if you agree with me."

"Smart man. I knew there was a reason I liked you. And one thing that you've taught me is to go with my gut feeling. And when I read that letter about Eliza killing herself, and knowing that hanging is rare for female suicides, guess what I thought."

"That she hadn't killed herself at all," Jack said.

"Exactly."

Despite the seriousness of the subject, Jack smiled. "I sometimes wonder if we might have been separated at birth, Yvonne."

Yvonne clucked her tongue. "Now, Jack, don't be silly. Because then it would be wrong for you to have this tremendous crush on me."

Jack laughed out loud at that one. "So true. Thanks, Yvonne—this is definitely something to think about. We're headed to Gallen Hall now to see her tomb, so maybe we'll discover something new that will make sense."

"Keep me posted. Good-bye, everybody."

Jack clicked the button on the steering wheel to hang up. He reached for my hands, which I'd placed around my neck without being aware of it. "You okay?"

I nodded. "Yes. I'm fine. It's just . . ."

Jayne cleared her throat, as if to remind me of my promise to Jack to tell him everything.

"It's just that Rebecca told me about another dream."

Jack frowned. "What now? Were you being strung from a rope? Because I wouldn't trust anything Rebecca says. I'd bet that Marc is feeding her things to tell us."

"I know. I've thought that myself. But whatever Rebecca is, she's still family, and despite everything, she puts family first. Remember that she's the one who told us what Marc was planning after that horrible book-launch party. She's just kind of stuck in the middle because she's married to him. It's not in her makeup to harm us intentionally. But, no. It wasn't about me."

He gave me a sidelong glance, and I caught a glimpse of worry.

"It was Nola. At least she thinks it was—Rebecca said it was unclear, but it was a young woman around Nola's age." I recalled Nola sitting on her bed, doing homework, her fingers absently rubbing her neck. "Rebecca dreamed that . . . that Nola had a rope around her neck."

His jaw began to throb. Jayne reached from the backseat and put her hand on his shoulder. "We got this, Jack. Melanie and I are here. You figure out all the clues, and we'll talk to the dead people. We'll get to the bottom of this and won't let anything happen to Nola. All right?"

For the first time, I felt reassured by Jayne's presence, glad that Jack and I weren't tumbling into the abyss alone. I reached over and put my hand on top of Jayne's. "Stronger together, right?"

She nodded, then sat back in her seat. I did the same, watching the scenery go by as we crossed the Ashley River, resisting the impulse to touch my neck.

As we bumped over the road leading to the house, I was relieved that no specter of a soldier pointing a musket at us blocked our way, although an unsettled feeling, not unlike the one I'd felt the first time I'd been here, coated my skin like acid. I looked back at Jayne and knew she was feeling the same thing.

Jack parked the car in front of the steps, and we all exited. The first thing I noticed was the scent of gunpowder. The second thing I noticed was the underlying earthy odor of freshly turned dirt. I watched as Jayne held her hand over her nose, and once again I felt the nudge of reassurance that I wasn't doing this alone. Having Jack and his strength and brains with me was always helpful, but it wasn't the same as having a psychic sister. Although I wasn't sure I was ready to admit that out loud.

The front door opened, and Anthony stepped out onto the porch. He still wore a sling on his arm from the car accident and still needed crutches because of his sprained ankle, but he now sported a bandage across his nose and had two black eyes. "Thank you all for coming," he said, his eyes lingering on Jayne for a long moment before turning to me.

Jack reached out his hand to shake. "I hope the other guy looks worse than you."

Anthony reached for his nose as if he'd forgotten it was there. "Oh, right. Yes. Sadly, I wish I could say it was a valiant attempt to defend myself, but it was . . ." He stopped. "Actually, it was the oddest thing. I was standing on the steps leading to the wine cellar when I found myself tumbling forward. I was alone at the time, so I have no idea how that happened. I suppose I'm lucky I didn't break my neck." He held out a crutch. "This saved my life. It got stuck in the hand railing, preventing me from plummeting to the bottom."

Jayne and I exchanged a glance.

"We'll head to the cemetery in just a minute. I had no idea it was so chilly. Come on inside where it's warm while I go find my jacket."

He began leading us inside, but Jayne rushed to his side. "Can I get it for you? If it's not in your bedroom, I mean. Because that would be where you're not wearing clothes." She pressed her eyelids shut.

"I think she means to ask if she can get your jacket for you to save you from hobbling on your crutches."

Jayne's face had turned crimson, but she managed a nod.

A clearly amused Anthony nodded. "That would be nice. I do get tired hobbling around. There's a small coat closet under the stairs. Just pull on the knob—it gets stuck easily."

Eager to escape, Jayne walked away while Jack and I looked around us. Despite the Italianate exterior, the departure from architectural norms of the day hadn't influenced the interior. It was designed as a center-hall Colonial, with formal rooms on either side of the foyer, each separated from the one behind it with pocket doors. From what I could see of the parlor and drawing rooms, the furniture reclined within spectral sheets, ghostly inhabitants of an all-but-abandoned house. It reminded me of my house on Tradd Street the first time I'd seen it, complete with cobwebs and mold stains. *It's like a piece of history you can hold in your hands.* Mr. Vanderhorst's words always came back to haunt me just as my inner voice started tallying up all the repair costs when I entered an old building.

I was about to ask Anthony about his plans for the house and land when my gaze traveled up the wall along the circular staircase, where uncovered oil portraits of unknown people stared down at us from crumbling plaster. "Am I the only one who thinks by their expressions that we're not . . ." I stopped, my gaze having settled on the largest portrait, separated slightly from the others as it hung on the roundest section of the wall.

It was a portrait of a dark-haired woman wearing a green silk dress, her hair piled high on her head. She was young, late teens or early twenties. Her dark eyes seemed to gleam from the portrait, the kind of eyes that appeared to follow the viewer. But it wasn't her beauty or the skill of the painter that caught my eye. That made me stare. It was the jeweled peacock on her bodice that made it impossible to look away.

"Who is that?" I asked, although I was pretty sure I already knew.

Anthony shook his head. "I don't know—there's nothing on the frame or behind the portrait that indicates the subject of the painting. Although . . ."

Jack quirked an eyebrow. "Although?"

"Although I feel as if we know each other . . . intimately. She has those eyes that follow me wherever I go. I find myself hurrying up the stairs at night just to get away from her."

I continued to stare at the portrait, recalling the woman I'd seen on the stairs at my house, the dark-haired woman in green with the peacock brooch. I remembered, too, the odd way she'd held her head, and the red welt that encircled her neck. When a person is hanged, Jack had once told me, most don't suffocate, as a lot of people think. If they're lucky, they die when their neck is broken by the fall, their bodies left dangling.

I turned to Jack. "I think that's Eliza. Eliza Grosvenor." And before I could stop myself, I raised both hands to my neck, just as Jayne walked up to me and whispered the word *lies*.

CHAPTER 18

I gaped at my sister, wondering if I'd imagined she'd just spoken that word out loud. "What did you say?" I asked Jayne.

Her eyes were dazed, like those of someone who'd just woken from a long sleep. "I said something?"

I nodded. "It sounded like you said 'lies.'" I looked back to where Anthony stood next to Jack. If he wanted our help, there was no point in sheltering him from any of the sinister aspects of what it meant to see dead people. "Which is what the woman said to me on my stairs at home before she disappeared."

I looked down at Anthony, surprised to find his demeanor more of anticipation than of apprehension. "Did you try to touch her?"

"Amateurs," I said under my breath. Jayne elbowed me, giving me a look of reproach.

Louder, so Anthony could hear, Jayne explained, "Usually, any sort of physical interaction will make them go away. Eventually, so will ignoring them—which is what Melanie likes to do—but that takes longer."

Dark brown eyes stared at me from the portrait as I crossed the foyer, and I tried to convince myself that it was the artist's talent that caused the effect. I climbed the stairs, stopping in front of the painting. I let my hands fall to my sides as I examined the woman in the green dress, her creamy skin contrasting sharply with her dark hair, the delicate nose set in a slim face defined by high cheekbones and sharp angles.

But her mouth couldn't be described adequately. Rosy pink lips were half-open, as if she'd just finished speaking, the corners of her mouth turned up in a *Mona Lisa* smile. With those lips, coupled with her mesmerizing eyes, she wouldn't have surprised me if she had stepped down from the frame and continued down the stairs. I probably would have been less surprised than the average person, but still.

"It's the woman in Yvonne's book," Jack said. "It was a black-and-white copy, but it's definitely the same portrait. And am I the only one who sees the resemblance to Mellie?"

"Not at all," I said, flattered but not convinced. Even from the confines of a portrait, it was clear that the beauty, elegance, and poise this woman possessed were inborn. If I had any of those qualities, it could only have been accidental and only on my best days.

"No, he's right," Jayne said as she moved to the bottom of the stairs. "It's not so much a physical resemblance per se—although you both have those awesome cheekbones, and there's something to the shape of the eyes. It's more your expression. I see it on your face a lot—that look that says you don't have a clue as to what you're supposed to do next, but you're going to pretend that you do."

I frowned down at my sister, wanting to ask her when she'd become such an expert on human behavior, but stopped when I realized that she might not be too far from the truth.

"You might be right, Jayne," Jack said, looking past me at the portrait so he didn't see my annoyance. "And Yvonne was right, too. Eliza was pretty hot."

I gave him the look I gave to other Realtors who insisted their poaching of a client was accidental. "Really, Jack? Is that how you'd want men to refer to your daughters?"

He cleared his throat. "I meant to say Eliza was a remarkably beautiful woman. Just like you. Probably intelligent, too."

We all turned to look at the portrait together, my eyes drawn to her neck and its lack of jewelry. And the absence of a red welt marring the perfect skin.

"That's definitely her?" Jayne asked, coming up the stairs to stand behind me. "The woman you saw on the stairs at home?"

The sound of Anthony's crutches crossing the marble floor echoed in the large space. "It was her ghost you saw?"

I met Jayne's eyes briefly before turning to look at Anthony. "Yes. I'm pretty sure it was her. She looked just like she does in this portrait. Except . . ." I paused, wondering what was different besides the missing ligature marks. My gaze traveled to the peacock brooch, the four multihued gems catching the light from an unseen source.

"Except?" Anthony prompted.

I frowned at the portrait. "I'm not sure. I saw her for such a brief moment that it's hard to recall. But I do remember her eyes. At first they were angry. And then, right before she disappeared, they seemed so . . . sad."

My eyes dropped to the brooch, and I had a sudden recollection of how I'd felt that she'd wanted me to notice it. To pay attention to it. "There's something about the brooch, I think. Something she wants us to notice."

Jack leaned closer, his eyes narrowing as he studied a thin gold chain that was wrapped around the ribbon and her dark curls, then turned his gaze to the brooch. "Maybe it's the light the artist wanted to paint in, but it doesn't look like the metal in the brooch is gold, does it? The color is off—and definitely different than the gold chain in her hair."

"It looks almost orange," I agreed. "Not gold at all. And it's uniform throughout, with the same orangey color, so it doesn't appear to have been altered by whatever reflected light the artist might have seen and wanted to replicate."

"It looks like copper," Jayne and Anthony said together.

They looked at each other and Jayne smiled. "Jinx."

Anthony grinned back and I resisted the urge to roll my eyes at the cuteness of it. But my loyalty to Detective Riley held me back.

"Assuming those are real stones," Jack said, "I can't imagine why they'd use a less expensive metal than gold. Copper is a base metal, not a precious metal. It could be pinchbeck."

"Pinchbeck?" I asked, hoping I wasn't the only uninformed person in the room.

"It means a cheap imitation," Jack explained. "It's a mixture of copper and zinc and was originally used in costume jewelry and watchmaking. It's supposed to look like gold, but when you hold them up together, you can usually tell which is the real McCoy."

"Eliza wasn't a daughter of the family," Jayne said. "She was Mrs. Vanderhorst's ward. So maybe those are semiprecious stones set in pinchbeck."

"Then why is her portrait in such a prominent location?" Anthony asked. "If she wasn't considered a member of the family, I mean. From what I understand, nothing's been moved or changed since the Vanderhorsts owned the house, so these portraits have been here for a couple of centuries."

"Well, she was engaged to be married to Lawrence Vanderhorst, so she was soon to be a member of the family." Jack's gaze spanned the staircase wall. "It doesn't look like his portrait is here. The rest of the male portraits are from different eras." He climbed a few steps higher, stopping in front of two smaller oval portraits in gold frames. "Look at this. There's a whole story here—two men about the same age wearing Civil War uniforms. One is navy blue and the other gray—probably brother against brother. It's like the Vanderhorsts exist to give me book plots."

"True," I agreed. "And our house."

"For now," Jack said under his breath as he began to walk back down the stairs.

Before following him I paused for a moment, looking back at Eliza's portrait. Her gaze seemed to meet mine, and I had the sense that she was somehow disappointed in me. As if she were speaking loud and clear in a language I should understand, and I was still missing the point.

Quietly, I asked, "What lies, Eliza?"

I startled at Jack's hand on my arm. "We'll find out. Hopefully, it will lead us to whatever hidden treasure Marc Longo is after. And if not, to a bestselling book that gets made into a movie. I hear that happens sometimes."

"Yeah. I've heard that, too," I said, allowing him to lead me down the steps, feeling Eliza's eyes following us down the stairs.

As we headed out the door, Jack and I filled Anthony in on the details of what we'd learned so far from Yvonne, and then Jayne told him about my encounter with Eliza. She spoke calmly and concisely, which was why I allowed her to tell him about it, and because I wanted to make sure that Anthony knew Jayne had all her faculties. Not because I thought they should be dating, but because Rebecca was his sister-in-law, and I wanted to be sure he knew we weren't all crazy.

The late-afternoon sun slanted shadows across the drive, warping the shape of the house's shadow on the shell-and-dirt drive. What little warmth the sun offered disappeared as we walked toward the cemetery gates, the temperature dropping by degrees as we got closer.

The gates were closed but unlocked, and we stopped in front of them by unspoken agreement. Jayne and I shared a glance with each other, my concern mirrored in her eyes. I didn't smell anything or see anything unusual. But the chill in the air had nothing to do with the season. It worried me. Someone—something—was here, waiting and watching. And the absence of everything but the chill meant the unknown entity was storing its energy.

Jayne turned toward Anthony. "When do you normally sense you shouldn't go any farther?"

"Right here. As soon as I reach out to open the gate, I feel pressure on my chest. Like someone has a hand on me, holding me back."

"Is it just pressure, or a punch?" Jack asked.

"Just pressure—at first. But if I keep going farther, the force of what-ever's holding me back becomes stronger, almost like someone's trying to protect me. But if I keep pressing forward, the pressure on my chest . . ." He stopped, taking a deep breath. "It becomes almost suffocating. Like I'm being squeezed between rocks. And the few times I was able to make it inside the mausoleum, it became full-blown punches and scratches."

We all looked toward the mausoleum as if expecting someone to step outside and challenge us.

"And Marc was able to go inside without a problem and dig around?" Jack asked.

Anthony nodded. "I was, too—up until recently."

"Around the time of the heavy rains," I said. "When the cistern collapsed in our backyard."

Jack looked at me. "I'm sure that's not a coincidence."

"Probably not," Jayne said. "Since the cistern's bricks came from here."

"And because there's no such thing as coincidence," I said sharply. I wasn't sure if it was the growing unease that made me snap at her or just her general air of confidence in almost every area of her life. I hadn't been that way when I was her age. I had doubts that I was that way now.

Her eyes met mine with understanding, which was even more irritating. I loved my sister; I did. I remembered being a little girl and telling whoever asked that what I wanted for all birthdays and Christmases was a sister. I was thrilled she was in my life. I just wasn't as thrilled to find her moving into it like Goldilocks into Baby Bear's bed.

Feeling ashamed at my own thoughts, I gave her a big smile. "According to Jack, I mean."

She smiled back, making me feel even worse. "And you're both right. Thanks for reminding me."

I caught Jack watching me with a questioning look and quickly turned toward Anthony. "I'm going to suggest that you wait here with Jack while Jayne and I try to get inside the mausoleum. Do you have the key?"

He shook his head. "I haven't been able to get close enough to relock it since the last time I was there. The gate is shut, but it shouldn't be locked."

I noticed for the first time the oak tree looming over the fence on the opposite side of the cemetery. Its ropelike roots pushed up the iron spindles of the fencing, slithering under the ground like invisible snakes, forcing headstones to lean haphazardly and give the impression of crooked teeth.

"That's probably the tree," Jack said quietly.

I nodded, liking the way our thoughts often worked in tandem. I examined the circumference of the tree, the heavy elbows of the branches bent to hold drapes of Spanish moss, and I estimated the tree's age to be close to three hundred years old. "It's definitely old enough," I agreed.

"Old enough for what?" Anthony asked, his voice too loud.

"To be the tree from which Eliza hanged herself," Jayne said. Her voice was quiet, but it carried through the empty cemetery like a last breath.

Lies. I wasn't sure if I'd imagined the word whispered again in my ear. I looked at Jayne and she was staring back at me with wide eyes, and I knew she'd heard it, too. She reached for my hand and I took hers. "Stronger together, right?"

I nodded and we took a step toward the mausoleum. A breeze that scattered only the leaves on the ground but didn't stir the Spanish moss on the trees swirled around our legs, pushing at our backs and propelling us forward.

We took another step.

"Stop." We turned at the sound of Jack's voice.

"I don't feel right about sending you in alone. I'm coming with you." He took a step toward us, but I held up my hand.

"It's all right, Jack," I said. "We know what we're doing."

"We do?" Jayne spoke under her breath so Jack couldn't hear.

"Why don't you and Anthony examine the rest of the cemetery, look for anything unusual on any of the headstones?" I suggested.

"Some of Eliza's favorite peacocks are buried here," Anthony said. "But we'll stay close to the mausoleum so we can keep an eye out."

Jack frowned, torn between studying headstones—one of his favorite pastimes—and staying close to me, one of my favorite pastimes.

"I'll be fine," I said, sounding more assured than I felt. "You're close enough that if we need anything, you can be with us in seconds."

Wanting to get it over with before nightfall, I tugged on Jayne's hand, leading her toward the entrance to the mausoleum. As Anthony had said, the doorway gate, with a square wrought-iron design at the top, stood slightly ajar. We peered into the dark interior through the slats of the rusting bars, seeing nothing but the dim outline of a single crypt opposite the opening.

"The other two crypts must be on the sides," I said, noting the plaque on the front of the triangular structure listing Eliza's name along with the two men's. I held up my phone and snapped pictures of the plaque and the gate to study later. I wasn't interested in hanging out in this cemetery any longer than I needed to.

"Let's go," I said as we flipped on the flashlights on our phones. I shone my light inside the space, stopping short at a rustling noise like that of a mouse or a bird. Or a long dress sweeping across a stone floor.

"Did you hear that?" Jayne asked.

I nodded, peering inside and hoping I wouldn't see anything. The circular spots from our lights illuminated dusty bricks and thick mortar on the walls, then square stone tiles on the floor. In three alcoves stone crypts nestled in the brick walls, lying in supposedly quiet repose. The light from my phone allowed us to see a broken corner of one of the lids, then trailed down to the bricks beneath each crypt.

"Looks like hieroglyphics," Jayne said.

"Yeah, that's what Anthony said. And Marc thinks it's some kind of a code. Or it could just be fancy brick details because the bricklayer was feeling artistic."

"Do you really think so?" Jayne asked.

"Not really. I'm just wishing this were all a lot easier so we could make it go away faster. We'll take pictures to show Jack." I reached up to push the gate open, just as it slammed shut in front of my fingers, the sound as final as that of a crypt lid being slid into place.

I knew better than to blame Jayne for closing it and began to tug on the bars, hoping that common sense would prevail and the unlocked gate that had been ajar seconds ago would actually cooperate and open. It wouldn't. I began shaking it until Jayne placed her hand on my arm.

"Maybe what we need to see isn't inside." Jayne pointed at the complex design on the top half of the mausoleum gate, the swirls and lines as intricate and deliberate as those of a spiderweb. I lifted my phone and began snapping more photos.

The breeze had picked up, dead twigs and leaves now hurling themselves at us. I looked up at what had been a brilliant blue winter sky and saw instead an ominous black shelf cloud hovering over us like a grim smile.

Not completely convinced that we couldn't gain access to the mausoleum, I stuck my hand through the bars, hoping to find some kind of latch I could release from the inside.

I heard the crunch of running footsteps coming toward us, then Jack's voice behind me. "It's about to storm—we should get inside. . . ."

I didn't hear what else he said. Something yanked on my hand from inside the mausoleum, pulling so hard that my head banged against the iron gate. As spots gyrated in front of my eyes and my ears rang with a metallic echo, I heard a man's voice, deep and gravelly, shouting loudly inside my head. *Traitors deserve to die and rot in hell.*

"Mellie? Mellie!" Jack's voice was frantic, his hand grappling with the gate, trying to force it open. "Jayne—help me!"

Jayne's hand squeezed mine as my knees hit the concrete step in front of the gate, my arm now numb, my head bruised. The stench of rot filled my nostrils as the heavy stomp of boots thudded across the mausoleum toward me. I closed my eyes in terror, prepared for the worst. And then whatever had been pulling on my arm suddenly let go, sending me backward into Jack's arms. I looked up upon hearing the unsettling sound of squealing hinges as the gate of the mausoleum opened slowly. The specter of a British soldier in a bright red coat slowly faded into the dark abyss, leaving behind the scent of gunpowder and the unmistakable feeling of despair.

I sniffed as I turned back to stare at the bricks. "There's probably a lot you still don't know about me."

"Then I can't wait to find out."

Anthony cleared his throat. "I'd suggest you two get a room, but the bedrooms in the house are pretty dusty."

I slanted a look at Jack, then aimed my flashlight at the bricks in front of me.

"Where did Marc do his digging?" Jayne asked Anthony.

Anthony moved the beam of his light toward the crypt on the center wall with the broken corner on its lid. "According to the plaque, this is Eliza. For whatever reason, probably just a guess since she's in the middle, Marc began digging here after his scanning with a metal detector turned up nothing."

"Why did he stop?" I asked, shivering as I read ELIZABETH GROSVENOR on the plaque, her short life memorialized by the dates beneath her name.

"The same crypt cover that had slid off and almost landed on my foot before did the same thing to Marc—it barely missed him. That's why he tried later to have it demolished, but the preservation people stopped him." Anthony frowned. "The last time I was here, it was because Marc wanted help in opening the coffin. He figured once the lid was replaced, he'd never have a chance."

"Did you find anything?"

He gave me an odd look. "Not what we expected. When we returned, the lid was back on the crypt. The only thing that made me believe what Marc told me about it falling again was that the corner had been broken off and the broken piece was still on the ground." He pointed at a tile in the narrow border around the dirt floor in front of the crypt. "You can see where it hit—this tile is pretty much pulverized." An strange smile crept across his face. "You have no idea how refreshing it is not to have to try to explain the unexplainable."

We were all silent as we examined the odd markings, the sound of our fingers brushing brick melding with the splat of rain on the ground outside and the occasional sound of phone cameras clicking. I sat back on my heels for a moment, trying to pinpoint a stray thought. I tilted my head one way and then the next, and then again.

"If you want, I can hold you by your feet so you can see them upside down," Jack said.

I frowned at him, then looked back at the stripe of bricks. "It looks like one of those slide puzzles, doesn't it? You know—those square puzzles with the plastic squares inside with one missing space where you slide them around to make a picture?"

Jack nodded, a slow smile beginning to form. "Yeah—I used to get them in birthday party gift bags when I was a kid."

"I remember those," Anthony said. "And you're right. It's like every brick is in the wrong place, judging by how all of the lines on the edges don't match up with any of the adjacent bricks." He scratched his head. "I wonder if these were left over from something else, so it didn't matter what order they were placed in."

"Or they were put like that on purpose." Jack leaned closer, rubbing his fingers on the rough line of mortar between two bricks. "Considering this was built way before cameras, the only way to figure out the pattern—assuming it's intentional—would be to take out all the bricks and put them together."

"Have you heard back from Steve Dungan—your architect friend? Maybe he can shed some light on this," I asked.

"I'll call him as soon as we get home." He pulled out his phone. "In the meantime, let's each take a section of the wall and snap photos of the individual bricks. I figure we can enlarge them and print them out so we can lay them all out like puzzle pieces and see if they fit together."

I could hear the excitement in his voice, something that had become a rare thing in recent months. Even the trauma of being yanked through a mausoleum gate by an unknown entity made it worth it.

"Good idea," Jayne said. "I'll take this wall." She pointed to the wall on the left. "Jack, why don't you take the one in the center, and Anthony, you take the one opposite mine?"

"What about me?" I bristled, feeling left out and being reminded yet again of the trauma of PE class when it was time to choose teammates for volleyball.

"You need to be on the lookout for any drop in temperature or weird breezes that might signal that our visitor is back. Your abilities are a lot stronger than mine."

Feeling mollified, yet guilty for being too quick to judge, I sent her a smile. "Good plan. And since it's stopped raining, I'll stand right outside the doorway. Just in case it locks again. I'd hate for all four of us to be trapped inside."

They all regarded me with wide eyes. "Smart," Jack said, his gaze not leaving the gate until I was safely on the other side.

I crossed my arms over my chest to hold in as much warmth as I could. The chill of the mausoleum seemed to have crept into my bones, unwilling to release me. I was glad, as it kept me alert, since I was unable to shake the feeling that someone—or something—was watching me.

"I'm freezing," I called inside the mausoleum. "I need to keep moving—I promise I won't go far."

I didn't wait to hear Jack telling me to be careful, and I took off in a sprint around the perimeter of the cemetery. I hoped my new smart watch was keeping track of my steps so they wouldn't be wasted effort. I slowed as I reached the oak tree, its sad limbs now dripping raindrop tears, and I felt a downward drift in the temperature. I wasn't afraid, though. The air had a softness to it, a sense of suspension, as if I were diving into the sea but my body was caught in midair. The smell of death and rot was gone, replaced with the scent of rain and wet grass. But I wasn't alone. Of that I was sure.

A movement caught my attention, nothing more than a shift of shadow, except no sun shone overhead. I didn't see her at first, her green gown blending into the overgrowth on the other side of the cemetery fence. As I continued to look, her form became less transparent, her face and clothing easily discernible. I felt my attention drawn again to the brooch worn on her bodice, the jewels in the peacock's tail and eyes sparkling despite the lack of sunlight. I wanted to step closer to see it better, but I was afraid of making her disappear. I wasn't wearing my glasses, so I couldn't see her in crisp detail, and for about the hundredth time I cursed my own vanity.

I recalled the first time I'd seen her, on the stairs at my house on Tradd Street, how I'd felt as if she'd wanted me to notice the brooch, and I remembered there was something about it that didn't look right. Maybe it had been the metal, which didn't look quite gold. I squinted to see better, then took a step backward as I realized her feet weren't touching the ground but were suspended at the level of the top of the fence. And when my eyes traveled upward, I saw the rope around her neck, the other end of the rope tied around a thick tree limb.

Her eyes never left my face, and her lips didn't move, but the word *lies* threw itself at me as if it had been shouted, startling two black crows from a tall patch of grass where they'd been hunting drowned worms. They flew away in a sharp flutter of wings just as I heard Jack, Anthony, and Jayne emerge from the mausoleum.

"Did you hear that?" I asked, staring at the empty tree.

Only Jayne nodded, reassuring me that I hadn't imagined it.

"Hear what?" Jack asked as he approached. He pulled me close and kissed the side of my head.

"Eliza was here. And I think . . ." I screwed up my eyes, trying to recall exactly what I'd seen.

"What?" Jack prompted.

"She definitely wanted me to notice her peacock brooch. I'm not exactly positive, but I'm pretty sure it's the same brooch in the portrait, with four jewels in the eyes and feathers."

"Let me guess. You weren't wearing your glasses so you can't say for sure. You know, Mellie, they have these things called contacts nowadays. . . ."

"I know, I know. It's just that my eyes get so dry and I find them uncomfortable. I've been meaning to make an appointment with my eye doctor, but haven't found the time. I will, though. Soon."

"Well, hopefully you'll run into her again when you're wearing glasses and can get a better look." Jack glanced up at the darkening sky. "We should get home. Nola's friends don't like hanging around after dark."

"Why's that?" Anthony asked. We all looked at him to make sure he wasn't joking.

"Same reason you run past Eliza's portrait," Jayne suggested. "This would all be so much easier if Marc was afraid of things that go bump in the night."

"Oh, he's afraid," Anthony said. "He just thinks that Rebecca has some kind of power over ghosts and can control them. Rebecca's happy to go along with it, too. But she only has premonitions, right? It's not like you and Melanie, where you can see and talk to them."

Jack was staring at him, but his thoughts seemed to be miles away. "No kidding," he said, turning to me. "I think we might have found Marc's Achilles' heel."

"What do you mean?"

"You once told me that bringing in a film crew might agitate some of the resident spirits. This might be a very good thing."

I frowned. "Since we've maybe found a way to make Marc less interested in stealing our house, are we giving up trying to figure out this puzzle?"

Jack shook his head. "Heck no. We will use every brain cell to figure this out and to make sure Marc never gets his hands on our house or any hidden treasure. Aggravating him while scaring his pants off will just be the icing on the cupcake."

We dropped Jayne off at her house, then drove the short distance home, fighting over the radio station, more out of habit than out of any desire to listen to music. I didn't recognize the car parked at the curb in front of our house as Jack pulled into our driveway. "Is Lindsey or Alston driving already?" I asked as we walked around the house to the piazza.

"Not that I know of. They all just have their permits." Jack walked toward the unassuming sedan, stopping behind it to read the bumper sticker. His lips pressed together in a firm line. "Citadel," he said curtly.

I knew to tread lightly. Alston's older brother, Cooper, now a senior at the Citadel, was a frequent visitor to our house, but always with his sister or a group of friends. His visits had been less frequent over the last year due in part, I was sure, to Jack's frostiness. I actually liked Cooper. He was tall and good-looking, and he was also polite, smart, and nice to his sister and his mother. I'd always thought the latter was an indicator of good-husband material, my opinion solidified by watching Jack with his mother. Not that Nola was looking for a husband, or that Jack would allow her to date before she was thirty, but I was fairly confident that Nola was safe with Cooper. The craziest thing they'd ever done together was binge-watch all eight episodes of the *Star Wars* franchise over a weekend in our upstairs TV room. Jack had insisted on leaving the door open and then brought up fresh popcorn and drinks at regular intervals to make sure they weren't sitting too close.

"Cooper probably drove Alston and Lindsey—he's a good brother, you know."

"Humph." Jack stomped up the piazza steps. "He's a guy. That's all I need to know."

I rolled my eyes, waiting until he unlocked the front door and held it open for me. As we stood in the foyer, taking off our coats, we heard Nola's laughter from upstairs, followed by a male voice. We waited for another moment, anticipating hearing the sound of other female voices. When we didn't, Jack took the stairs two at a time while I followed at a more sedate pace.

I passed the three dogs at the top of the stairs, staring at a corner of the hallway. Stopping short, I followed their gaze, hoping I wouldn't see anything, and then worrying because I didn't. General Lee let out a low growl to let the unseen intruder know who was boss, then immediately ran behind me, quickly followed by Porgy and Bess. It was a good thing they were cute, because they were complete failures as protectors.

I continued to stare at the corner, willing myself to see whatever it was, aware suddenly of the scent of roses. I relaxed slightly, knowing that whatever was there, Louisa was there, too, protecting us. "Thank you," I whispered, backing away slowly toward Nola's room and Jack's raised voice.

"You know the rules about closed doors, Nola."

I stood behind Jack in the doorway, his hands on his hips just like Mrs. Houlihan's when she'd find me in her kitchen stealing cookies. Nola sat on her bed with her laptop and scattered books, and Cooper stood in front of the armchair he'd apparently been sitting in before Jack threw open the door without knocking.

"The dogs were acting weird, but they didn't want to go out and weren't interested in any treats, but they kept distracting us, so I just shut the door."

"Distracting you from what?" Jack asked. I couldn't see his face, but I imagined his eyes were narrowed in a perfect interpretation of the avenging father.

Cooper offered his hand to Jack. "Good to see you, sir. We were brainstorming about those words you gave Nola earlier, trying to see if we could interpret them."

After a brief hesitation, Jack shook the young man's hand. "Um-hm," he said. "I told her she could invite a few friends over for pizza."

"Yes, sir. But my sister wasn't feeling well, and Lindsey is in Pawleys Island this weekend with her parents. So I volunteered to come help and keep Nola company."

"Well, isn't that convenient . . ." Jack began.

I elbowed my way past Jack to greet Cooper. "That's wonderful. Thanks so much. And were you two able to figure anything out?"

Nola gave me a relieved look. "Nothing yet. We can't find anything that connects these things, so Cooper thought that we should make identifying lists of each object, starting with color, since three of them—just not *kitchen maid*—can be identified with specific colors."

Jack looked at Cooper with grudging admiration. "I hadn't thought of that. You might be onto something—although I have no idea where *kitchen maid* would fit into that equation."

"That's the same conclusion we reached, sir. But until we think of something else, we're creating four lists—since we're working with four items—of descriptive words, beginning with colors, to see if we can come up with anything. It's a process. Like writing a book, I would assume."

Jack actually smiled at Cooper. "Yes, you could certainly say that."

"Did you find anything at the cemetery?" Nola asked, looking a lot more relaxed now that Cooper and Jack had shared a cordial exchange of words.

"We're not sure," I said, pulling out my phone. "Jayne and Anthony will be sending me theirs, but basically we took lots of photos, including pictures of two rows of bricks with odd markings on them. If we print them individually, we should be able to put them together like a puzzle. It's going to take forever since I'll have to find a way to print every brick exactly proportionally and then find a surface large enough to put the puzzle together."

Cooper cleared his throat. "I might not be able to find the floor space for the actual puzzle, but I have access to some pretty cool software that should make the sizing-and-printing part a little easier. I'd be happy to take a look if you want to send the pictures to me."

Nola and I both beamed at Cooper, but Jack narrowed his eyes. "And what would you expect in return?"

"Dad!" Nola cried out as I punched Jack in the shoulder.

"Nothing, sir," Cooper said, his cheeks blazing red. "I'm just wanting to help. I think this whole puzzle thing is really cool—especially when I think it might end up in one of your books. I've read them all, by the way. I'm a huge fan."

"Hmm," Jack muttered.

I grabbed hold of his elbow and began pulling him out of the room before he could say anything else. "Thanks, Cooper," I called from the hallway. "I'll have Nola forward all of the photos to you to see if you can come up with anything. And we really can't thank you enough, can we, Jack?"

I yanked on his arm and dragged him down the hallway toward the stairs, aware now of pounding on the front door. We looked at each other before continuing down to the foyer, the dogs at our heels and General Lee growling. Jack stepped in front of me as if to shield me, then peered through the sidelights by the door. "Just when I think my day can't get any worse."

Before I could question him, he yanked open the door, revealing the smooth face and plucked eyebrows of Harvey Beckner. "It's about time someone came to the door! I've been ringing the doorbell for twenty minutes."

He made to step forward, but Jack blocked him. "The doorbell only rings when someone the house wants inside is ringing it."

Harvey sneered. "Right. Because houses have souls." He turned around to shout to a group of men unloading equipment from two vans illegally parked at the curb. It was street-sweeping day on Tradd Street the following morning, which meant a guaranteed tow, but I wasn't going to mention it.

Jack continued to block access to the house. "It's getting late, and we're about to have supper—"

"Perfect," said a voice from the door at the end of the piazza. "I'm starving."

Jack tensed. "Matt," he said, his jovial tone at odds with the set of his jaw. "Why are you darkening my doorstep?"

Marc moved to stand next to Harvey. "We need to get a few still shots of the interiors at night and test for lighting before it's time to begin filming. And Harvey hasn't seen the inside yet, so he's brought his lighting people and location scouts to get their opinions."

"I don't know about this." Jack looked back at me. "Mellie, was this on your calendar?"

"No . . ." I began, feeling like a two-foot dam in the path of a tsunami.

"I don't think you're in a position to argue, Jack," Marc said. "It will go easier for all of us if you'll just let us get to work."

"But I'm hosting a progressive dinner here in less than two weeks," I protested. "Rebecca told me she'd worked it out with you so that there wouldn't be any cameras and equipment in the house until after Christmas."

Marc pushed on the door, but Jack was unyielding. "We'll be out by Sunday. Until we're ready to begin filming sometime around the first week of January. You'll need to take down all this Christmas stuff by then." He frowned at the magnolia garland that Veronica and I had spent hours making. My blood began to heat at the affront.

"That's really not convenient . . ." Jack began, but he stopped when I tugged on his arm.

I whispered in his ear, "Let it go, Jack. They've won this battle. But not the war."

After a pause, Jack stepped back. "Then welcome to our house," he said, graciously opening the front door as wide as it would go. "So good of you to come."

Both Marc and Harvey eyed Jack suspiciously, and I wondered if it had anything to do with the sudden chill in the air that had nothing to do with the temperature outside, or the sound of running footsteps across the empty foyer behind us. I also wondered if either one of them was remembering what Harvey had said about houses having no souls. And if they were about to find out how wrong he was.

"Please," Jack said, beckoning the men to enter. "Make yourselves uncomfortable. My family and I will be sitting down for a delicious meal in the kitchen and you are not invited to join us. And just so you know, it's lights-out at ten, sometimes earlier if our twins are here. Trust me, you don't want to be here after dark."

He said this just as the crew from the vans began to fill the vestibule. Jack put his hand on the small of my back and began guiding me toward the kitchen, where Mrs. Houlihan had left our dinner warming in the oven. He pushed open the door to the kitchen and allowed me to pass in front of him, giving a good impression of an evil Vincent Price laugh as the door swung closed behind us.

CHAPTER 20

I blew warm air into my gloved hands as I walked with Jack the short distance to Jayne's house on South Battery.

"Cold?" Jack asked, drawing me close to his side.

I turned my face toward his, sure he could see the trembling of my lips. "I'm at the point of turning numb, so I don't have to worry about feeling the cold anymore." I tried to smile, but the cold pierced my teeth. "I don't know why we couldn't take the car."

"Because there's only satellite parking for the Shop and Stroll, and we'd probably be walking just as far. I'm sure Jayne has hot chocolate to warm us, and there will definitely be plenty to eat and drink along the route once we pick up our tickets at the Francis Marion Hotel."

"If I don't die of hypothermia first," I muttered, attempting to wriggle my toes inside my shoes. I aligned my stride to his, pressing closer to him. "You're the best heated blanket a girl could ever ask for."

I could hear the smile in his voice. "Is that the reason why you married me?"

"One of them. I wouldn't say it's the number one reason, but it's pretty close to the top."

He kissed the crown of my head. "Mercenary."

"A girl's got to do what a girl's got to do." We'd reached Jayne's house, stopping at the bottom of the driveway. I stared at the wreath on the front door and the garland wrapped around the banisters that led up to the front portico. I squinted. "Are those . . . ?"

"Pink." Jack finished for me. "They're definitely a frosted pink. I'm guessing Rebecca's been here."

"Ugh. Just because she donated a lot of money to the Ashley Hall fund-raiser, she thinks she can do whatever she wants. At least she was able to talk Marc into filming the progressive dinner at Veronica's instead of at our house, so I guess I owe her one. But I certainly don't want to be here when Sophie sees this. I tremble to think what she'll do to retaliate."

"Take off Pucci's pink nail polish and sweater and make her look like a real dog, maybe?"

I glared up at him. "Okay, I agree that the polish is too much, but there's nothing wrong with dog sweaters."

"Let's just agree to disagree, shall we?" Jack asked as he led me down the front drive.

Speaking through chattering teeth, I said, "What on earth do you think Jayne's surprise is? She knew we had tickets for the Shop and Stroll tonight, so I hope it's something spectacular to justify our being thrown out in this weather longer than we needed to be."

"You know it's only about fifty degrees, right?"

I plastered an indignant look on my face. "To some of us, that's the same as freezing." I began climbing the steps. "Come on before I turn blue."

The door opened before I had a chance to ring the bell, my mother appearing in the opening. "What are you doing here?" I asked as we hugged. "Are you the surprise?"

"I've been here all afternoon with Jayne and your father preparing the surprise." She glanced behind me to where Jack stood. "Good job, Jack. I know how persistent Mellie can be when she suspects something's up."

I whirled to face my husband. "You know what it is?" I stepped forward into the foyer, barely recognizing the brightly lit space from when I'd first seen it right after Jayne had inherited the old house, every inch of it filled with cobwebs and peeling plaster. I knew Jayne had been working with Sophie to restore the house to its former grandeur, and after looking at the gleaming banister—peeking out from beneath a frosted pink garland—and mold-free walls, I had to grudgingly admit that Sophie knew what she was doing.

I spotted Jayne by the dining room door. "Please don't tell me you have a pink Christmas tree hidden somewhere," I said. "I just can't believe you let Rebecca do this to your house."

"I know, I know. But she was so upset when she came here. She knows that the laundry room at your house that you allowed her to decorate won't be seen, but she hid her disappointment from you because she knows you're dealing with 'issues' right now—her word, not mine. She said she had a lot of decorations left over and asked if I would allow her to decorate my house. Since it's still under renovation and I'm not hosting one of the courses for the progressive dinner, I agreed. She seemed really sincere."

I wasn't sure if I'd ever heard Rebecca's name and the word *sincere* uttered in the same sentence before. But the fact that she'd hidden her disappointment from me did loosen some of my resentment toward her. Just a little bit.

"Hello, Peanut," my father said, emerging from the dining room. I peered past him, almost expecting to see swaths of moisture-speckled wallpaper drooping from the cracked cornices. Instead, the walls were scraped clean, waiting for either paint or reproduction wallpaper. Knowing Sophie, I figured she'd probably brought artists from Italy to hand-paint the original wallpaper design, and Jayne had willingly allowed it.

"So, what's going on?" I asked while my father hugged me. I kept my gaze focused on the dining room, where I could see Jayne and the foot of another person standing at the dining table.

I stepped into the dining room and was met with a loud "Surprise!" from Jayne. I turned my head and was speechless for a moment as someone held up an iPhone to take my picture. "Cooper?"

"Yes, ma'am. Nola's babysitting, so she asked me to take a picture of you being surprised."

Before I could ask a question, my gaze was drawn to the surface of the enormous table and the neat rows of five-by-seven photographs.

"Are these . . . ?" I began, looking around at the faces now clustered around the table.

Cooper cleared his throat. "I pulled an all-nighter to get them all downloaded, then sized so they're all the same, and then printed them. Nola brought me breakfast, though, so it was worth it."

I could feel Jack glowering at Cooper, so I said, "I'm sure it was all vegan and gluten-free, so no chance she was out to impress anyone."

Cooper shook his head. "Actually, it was a cinnamon bun with a side of hash browns Mrs. Houlihan made. She even drove Nola over to deliver it. Best hash browns I've ever tasted . . ."

As if sensing the tension, Jayne moved to stand next to me, straightening one of the photos. "Mother told me about Marc and that horrible Harvey guy invading your house, so when Nola told me that Cooper had printed out all of the photographs, I thought bringing them to my house would be safest. That way, Marc can't snoop."

"Brilliant idea," I said, meaning it, although a tone I hadn't expected emerged.

Jack nodded. "Jayne also suggested that I clear out my office for the same reason. She offered her house to store everything for the time being."

"Jayne certainly thinks of everything," I said, tapping lightly on one of the photographs. "Can't imagine how we survived before she came to Charleston." I looked at the single photograph, then picked it up, studying it closely. "I think this goes in one of the corners—you can tell from the design because only two sides have finished patterns, and the other two have truncated lines that must continue onto other bricks."

I looked up to find all sets of eyes focused on me. Except for one—Jayne's. Her eyes were blinking rapidly, her bottom lip clenched between her teeth. She jerked her gaze up to the table and to the photograph I held pinched between my fingers. She swallowed. "I think you're right, Melanie. Good job—now we have a place to start." She began clearing one corner of the table, then pointed to the empty spot. "I think you should have the honor of putting the first piece here." She smiled at me and I felt as if I'd been kicked in the stomach.

"Actually," I said, feeling the looks of censure from around the table, "you should do the honors. You're the one who had the foresight to set up the puzzle in your dining room." I handed her the photograph. "Here."

She hesitated just for a moment before taking the picture. "Thanks," she said, putting it in its place of honor in the corner of the table. "I want you all to feel free to come here at any time and work on this puzzle. When I'm at Melanie's looking after the twins, just stop by and get my key. The more, the merrier, I say."

An antique carriage clock chimed from the fireplace mantel, making me glance at my watch. "I don't want to be late picking up our tickets at the Francis Marion. It will cut into our shopping time."

Jack was eyeing the table, and I knew he was thinking his time would be better spent playing with the puzzle than Christmas shopping on King Street. "Jack," I said with a warning in my voice, "you know they have a special service tonight to help men take care of their shopping. I'd hate for you to miss that."

He looked up, surprised at being caught. "I just thought . . ."

"Come on," I said. "Let's call an Uber or something. It is way too cold to walk all the way to Calhoun." I glanced around the room, aware of someone missing. "Where's Anthony? Isn't he supposed to be coming tonight?"

Jayne shook her head. "He's sick. He said he hasn't been feeling well since he left the cemetery. I told him he should come to his house in town just in case it's something at Gallen Hall, but he said he was too sick to move. I asked if I could call his doctor, but he said he'd be fine by morning. I'll check in then."

I exchanged a glance with my mother but didn't want to say anything in front of Cooper about how Anthony should stay away from stairs and open windows while alone at the plantation house.

"And if it's all right with you, Miss Smith, I'd love to stay here for a bit and work on the puzzle. Just for an hour or two." Cooper looked at Jack. "I mean, if that's all right with you, sir."

"As long as you're here, and Nola's not, I'm fine with that arrangement."

"Jack . . ." I started to say, but I was interrupted by the ring of the doorbell.

We watched as Jayne walked across the foyer to open the door. There was a slight pause and then: "Thomas," she said, her voice an octave higher than it had been five seconds ago. "What are you doing here?"

Detective Riley stood in the doorway, his tall figure filling the space. He looked behind Jayne and met my gaze. "Sorry. I didn't know you'd have company. I just wanted to stop by and see how you were doing." He grinned. "And if your house is behaving."

Cooper and my dad looked confused, but the rest of us, who'd witnessed the spirit cleansing in Jayne's attic, understood.

"It's doing fine," Jayne said, pulling the door open wider. "And you have shoes; please walk them inside."

Feeling the need to rescue my sister, I placed my hand on her shoulder and squeezed, a reminder to take a deep breath before trying again. "So great to see you, Thomas. We're getting ready to leave for the Shop and Stroll, but come in for a minute to warm up. If that's all right with Jayne?"

I glanced at my sister and she gave one decisive nod.

"I really don't want to intrude. I can come back later . . ." Thomas began.

"Don't be silly. We're all old friends here." I pulled him inside and closed the door behind him. There was an awkward silence, filled with Jayne's deep breathing, as we all looked at one another.

My dad clasped his hands together. "What are we thinking? We have a trained detective in our midst and a whole mystery spread out on the dining room table." He indicated the dining room. "Would you like to take a gander, Detective?"

I thought I saw a bright gleam in Thomas's eye. "I'd love to," he said, following my dad and stopping in front of the table. "Wow. It's like a giant jigsaw puzzle. Are these bricks?"

"From the inside of the mausoleum at Gallen Hall," Jayne said slowly, considering each word. "There was a horizontal design two bricks wide encircling the interior, but none of them matched."

"And you figured out that the lines on the bricks might match up if you could separate them into individual puzzle pieces." Thomas looked at Jayne as if she were Einstein himself standing in the dining room.

"Actually, it was my other daughter," my dad said, beaming. "I sure hit the lottery with three brilliant women in my family."

Other daughter? I smiled and nodded appreciation, unable to feel truly grateful at his compliment. I didn't scrutinize my feelings, fairly confident that I was certain I knew the exact reason.

Thomas began unbuttoning his coat. "This actually looks like fun. Although it could be that these were just leftover bricks and don't have any connection to each other at all."

"Oh, we've definitely considered that possibility," Jack said. "But we're determined to remain hopeful."

Thomas leaned over the table to get a better look. "I see someone's found a corner piece already. Nice going."

"That was me," I said, a little too eagerly, because apparently I thought I was still in kindergarten and required approval and reassurance for every small task.

"Yes, it was," Jack said, rubbing my back and making me feel even more like a child. I turned to express my annoyance and was immediately met with a gentle kiss on my lips.

"Has anyone considered staying in tonight and working on the puzzle?" Thomas looked around for collaborators, his eyes hopeful.

"Yes," Jack said at the same time I said, "No."

My mother stepped forward to intervene. "We have an extra ticket for the Shop and Stroll, Thomas. Why don't you join us?"

Both Jack and Thomas looked longingly at the photographs. Turning his head back to address my mother, Thomas said, "That sounds like fun. I've got all those nieces and nephews I have to buy gifts for, so the Shop and Stroll could be just what I need."

"And they have a service just for men, to help them select gifts," my mother said as she sidled up to my dad. "Although I must say that some men don't need any help at all."

I started to roll my eyes but stopped when I saw Jayne looking at them with adoration. I was thrilled my parents had found each other again and were so much in love. And, yes, our relationship with each other had a difficult past, but we'd moved so far beyond those old resentments and hurts. Or we should have. Even I recognized this. Maybe negative emotions were like bad habits, and I needed a twelve-step program to cure myself so I could move forward without all that baggage tethered to my ankles that kept me firmly planted in the past. I made a mental note to add that to the top of my New Year's resolutions spreadsheet.

"Great," I said. "Everyone get bundled up. I'd rather take an Uber, but I don't feel like arguing with Jack, who apparently enjoys the cold. We've got a long walk in the frozen tundra, but I understand there are warm drinks waiting."

"It's not that cold," everyone said at once as I wrapped my scarf around my neck twice and tucked my hair and ears under my knit cap.

"Humph," I said, shoving my gloved hands into the pockets of my coat and leading everyone out the front door.

We'd made it only to the end of the drive before Jack's phone rang. He looked at the screen and groaned. "It's Harvey. I'm going to let him leave a message."

We'd left him and his crew at the house for the second night in a row, the previous night being a complete wash because none of their equipment would work for some reason. Nola and the twins had been forced to camp out at my parents'—a small price to pay, according to Nola.

I frowned. "I think you should answer it. Maybe he's just telling you he's leaving forever and wants to know how to set the alarm."

Jack frowned back at me but hit ANSWER on his phone. I couldn't hear what was being said, but the growing smile on Jack's face told me it was good news. When he'd hung up, he put the phone back into his jacket pocket.

"Are they done?" I asked.

"Nope. First of all, he needed to complain about the man with his crack showing above his pants who was working in the dining room and wouldn't leave."

"That's Rich Kobylt," I said. "He wanted to finish the dining room floor before Christmas so he could spend time with his kids, who will be home from college, and I told him he could take as long as he needed." I grinned at the success of my plan.

"And then he said the power kept going off but that the breakers were still in the on position and none of the other houses on the street were without their lights." He sounded practically jovial now. "Then he said most of his crew ran out of the house after the lighting guy said he saw a woman standing behind him in the mirror in the front parlor, but when he turned around no one was there."

"Go figure," I said, my smile matching his.

He looked up into the clear night sky and put his arm around me, pulling me close. "Have I ever mentioned what a brilliant team we make?"

"I think so. But I don't think I'd ever get tired of you saying it."

We stopped on the sidewalk, allowing the others to walk around us as Jack bent his head to kiss me. "I think we're on the home stretch now, Mellie. I think we're right on the cusp of getting Marc Longo out of our lives forever." He kissed me again. "We're going to bury him alive."

He pulled me close to his side, walking fast to catch up to the rest of our group. "Still cold?" he asked.

I nodded, unable to tell him that the trembling of my lips had nothing to do with the air temperature, and more to do with remembering Rebecca's dream and how it hadn't been Marc being buried alive.

CHAPTER 21

We stood in the elegant lobby of the Francis Marion Hotel beneath antique crystal chandeliers, soaring ceilings, and tall columns with gilt acanthus leaves on their capitals. The hotel had undergone a face-lift in the late nineties, winning a twelve-million-dollar restoration award from the National Trust for Historic Preservation and, more important, the approval of my friend (and sometime nemesis) Dr. Sophie Wallen-Arasi. The restoration team had brought the hotel back to its nineteen-twenties elegance, which, although beautiful, was one of the reasons I usually avoided this particular hotel.

"Do you hear that?" I asked Jayne.

"The twenties music?" She nodded. "Have you spotted the girl dancing the Charleston in midair where a table must have once been?"

I almost didn't turn, not wanting to attract the spirit's unwelcome attention, but couldn't stop myself. There was something about seeing unadulterated history as it had been lived, even in brief snippets, that was the one and only part of my sixth sense that I didn't hate.

The girl, not much older than Nola, had blond, bobbed hair peeking out of a net cap with dangling pearls over her ears. Her drop-waist dress and long ropes of pearls swung in sync with her kicking legs as she danced the Charleston, the low heels on her ankle-strapped shoes making soft thudding noises each time they landed on the invisible table.

I wanted to turn away, but I couldn't, because now her dance movements had slowed as she became aware that someone was watching her. That someone could see her. She stopped completely and slowly turned toward us so that we could see her entire face, including the dark bruise that covered one cheek and the red blood dripping from her nose and lips.

We watched each other for a long moment, as if each was expecting the other to make the first move. "We should go," I said softly to Jayne, who was also unable to turn away from the sad eyes of the flapper.

"We could help her, you know," Jayne whispered back. "Not right now, but later. We could ask the hotel to allow us access so we can find out what's keeping her here and send her on her way."

"Send who on her way?" Thomas appeared at our sides with a glass of wine from the lobby's corner bar in each hand.

"No one," I said, accepting a glass and taking a gulp. I felt Jayne's gaze and recalled that her breakup with Thomas had been due, in part, to his insistence that she shouldn't go public with her abilities. Doing a ghost cleansing in a public hotel lobby wasn't a good way to keep our light under a bushel, I was fairly certain. I glanced back to where the flapper had been and saw only the beautiful lobby, filled with warmly bundled holiday shoppers eager for a fun evening in Charleston.

"Rebecca," Jayne said in answer to Thomas's question, raising her own glass to her lips.

"If she were here, I would definitely want to send her on her way," I said, taking another sip, which I almost spit back into my glass when our cousin appeared as if conjured, looming behind Jayne in a pink fur coat and matching pink Uggs.

"I didn't expect to see you here," I managed to say after I choked down my wine. "Seeing as how you need to get up so early tomorrow for the wreath-making workshop. I know how you like your ten hours of beauty sleep."

"True," she said. "I like it but don't need it, thankfully. No worries—I'll be bright-eyed and bushy-tailed tomorrow morning at eight sharp." She gave a little salute while I furtively glanced around for any sign of Marc.

"Hello again," Thomas said to Rebecca. "I don't think I've had the pleasure of seeing you since we met at Cannon Green, at your husband's book-launch party." He gave a show of scanning the crowd. "Speaking of which, is Marc here?"

I wondered if he was trying to give us a head start to find Jack, my parents, and our tickets before making a beeline out the back door.

"Sadly, no. He was supposed to be, but he's at Melanie's house trying to calm down Harvey Beckner. Seems they're experiencing a lot of equipment failure and they can't get anything done. Harvey thinks it has something to do with inferior Southern infrastructure."

"I hope he said that out loud so anyone listening could hear," I said.

"Interesting." Jayne's face was expressionless. "What did Marc tell him?"

Rebecca shrugged. "I'm not sure. He's been having issues with the battery on his phone—it keeps dying right after it's charged. I could hear that Rich person in the background shouting at Harvey to keep his equipment off the newly repaired dining room floors, and then it cut out."

Jayne and I shared a glance. "So, Rebecca," I said. "Don't you think this is a sign that Marc's not meant to be filming in my house?"

"Oh, I don't think he really cares about filming. . . ." She stopped talking, her eyes widening as she realized whom she was speaking to and what she'd just said.

"So what does he care about?" I asked, stepping closer to her so that I could almost feel the pink fur tickle my nose.

"It's nothing—I didn't mean to say that. Of course he wants to—"

"Rebecca." I cut her off. "If all the stuff you say about family being the most important thing to you is true, then you need to tell us what Marc is up to."

Her bright blue eyes filled with moisture. "But Marc is my family, too. And I love him. He's kind and gentle, and not anything like the monster you think he is. He's my husband."

Bile rose in my throat but I swallowed it down. "Well, the fact that you actually married him is your fault. And now his actions are partly your responsibility. Marc is trying to ruin my life—destroy my husband's career and steal my house. I think it's clear where your loyalty needs to lie."

She began tugging on the fingers of her pink knit gloves in a nervous gesture.

"If he's doing anything illegal," Thomas said gently, "then you could be an accessory to a crime and punished accordingly. I don't know if you watch television, but *Orange Is the New Black* is something you should be watching to prepare yourself for women's prison. Where wearing pink isn't an option. And I don't think orange is your color."

Her eyes widened as her skin blanched. "You don't need to threaten me."

"I'm not threatening you. I'm just giving you a heads-up." Thomas crossed his arms as the three of us stared at Rebecca, waiting for her to break.

She tucked her chin like a turtle taking a defensive stance. "It's not illegal to take something that once belonged to you, is it?"

"Like what?" I narrowed my eyes at her.

She looked around discreetly before leaning closer and whispering, "A piece of paper."

"What kind of paper?" I asked, growing impatient. Behind her shoulder I spotted my parents and Jack crossing the lobby, and I was fairly sure Rebecca wouldn't be as forthcoming in Jack's presence.

"Something he'd thrown in the trash at the plantation. But when he went to get it, everything was gone."

"You mean the papers from the historical archives that he stole and then threw away?"

She drew her shoulders back defensively. "I don't know anything about that, but I'm sure Marc wouldn't have stolen anything from the archives. Maybe it was an accident and when he went to return them he saw that they were gone."

We all stared her down with the same dubious expression. "They were found in a garbage can, Rebecca." I glanced behind my cousin to see that Jack and my parents had been stopped by a middle-aged couple and were chatting. I looked back at Rebecca. "Can you be more specific about the paper he's looking for? Maybe I know where he can find it."

Rebecca pressed her lips together, contemplating, her eyes moving from me to Jayne to Thomas, then back to me. "It's a drawing. The design matches what he thought was some kind of drawing in Joseph Longo's diary. It was one of a bunch of papers in a folder he'd *borrowed* from the archives. He didn't realize it the first time he saw it, but when he saw the copy of the diary drawing again recently, he was pretty sure it was a match."

"Where did he see it again?" Jayne asked.

Rebecca sucked in a deep breath. "Marc thought he'd accidentally thrown out a bunch of the notes he'd gathered at the archives to research his next book." She looked at us to see if we knew that he'd gone to the archives only because he'd learned Jack was working on a new book.

We remained expressionless as she continued. "Anyway, the drawing and several other papers must have fallen behind his desk, because there they were when we had to move it when I decided he needed shiplap in his office. It's all the rage now on that HGTV show—"

"Rebecca . . ." Jayne interrupted, and I saw her watching my parents and Jack resume their approach behind us.

"Anyway, he didn't find anything he thought was important in those papers he'd borrowed from the archives, which is why he'd *misplaced* them, meaning to return them to the archives later, but when we found his own research papers behind his desk and he saw the diary drawing again, he had second thoughts. So he went back to the plantation to retrieve the box of papers from the archives and found it was missing."

"What kind of drawing?" I asked.

Rebecca shrugged again. "It was weird—lots of scrolls and lines."

"Can you show it to me?" I asked quickly, but Rebecca had already stepped back and was smiling and greeting my mother while keeping a wary eye on Jack.

"Rebecca," Jack said. "Where's your dog?"

"It's so cold out that I felt Pucci would be more comfortable at home. It was so sweet of you to ask."

"I wasn't referring to Pucci," Jack said with a smile that could rival glaciers.

Rebecca frowned. "I just don't understand how the two men I've had the most meaningful relationships with don't like each other. I'm convinced that if we spent more time together—the four of us—we'd be the best of friends."

If her reminder that she and Jack had once dated hadn't brought up my lunch, this last comment certainly would have. I was suddenly very glad that I hadn't eaten anything yet, but the wine sloshed unhappily in my stomach.

Jack continued with his glacial smile, his eyes focused on the ceiling as if he were actually considering her suggestion. Finally, he said, "Or I could dip myself in oil and light myself on fire. I imagine the outcome would be the same in either case."

Rebecca's large eyes blinked slowly. Twice. "And what would that be?"

It was Jack's turn to blink. "Reaching the same level of fun."

Before she could think of anything else to say, Jack made a show of waving to someone across the room. "If you could excuse us, please? There's someone I'd like Melanie and me to say hello to." He smiled at the rest of the group. "We'll be right back. And I'm sure Rebecca has a Christmas list of new sweaters and accessories for Pucci she needs to go buy, and we don't want to keep her."

Without waiting for a response, Jack took my hand and began leading me across the room, while I attempted to make eye contact with Rebecca to let her know that we weren't done talking. I had the distinct impression that she was avoiding my gaze, focusing her attention on rebuttoning her coat.

I ran into Jack's back when he stopped suddenly in front of an elegant older couple. The gentleman, wearing a proper felt hat like men had worn in the fifties, was helping a platinum-haired woman with her coat. After gently settling it on her shoulders, he handed her a soft-hued silk scarf from his own coat pocket and she smiled up at him as she placed it over her head.

"Yvonne," Jack said, and I did a double take, believing that Jack had been lying about seeing someone he knew so that he could get away from Rebecca.

"Yvonne?" I repeated, almost not recognizing her out of context. It was as if I expected her to be surrounded by thick and dusty reference volumes wherever she went.

"What a lovely surprise," she said, accepting a kiss on her cheek from Jack and then me. Facing the man standing next to her, she said, "Allow me to introduce my beau, Harold Chalmers." She glanced up at her date with sparkling eyes. "Harold, I'd like you to meet some of my dearest friends, Jack and Melanie Trenholm."

I was too surprised to speak for a moment as I realized that I knew very little about Yvonne's personal life. I looked up at the tall, elegant man, scrutinizing him more closely than was warranted, my curiosity winning out over my good manners. Harold Chalmers's eyes were a warm brown, the hair beneath his hat a George Clooney salt-and-pepper. There were lines in the corners of his eyes indicating that he probably laughed a lot and spent a good deal of time in the sun.

I gave him my hand and he took it in a warm and firm clasp. "It's a pleasure to meet you, Mr. Chalmers."

He chuckled, a low, deep rumble in this throat. "Please don't make me feel older than I am. It's Harold," he said, squeezing my hand. "And may I call you Melanie? I feel as if I already know you after everything Yvonne's told me about you. All good, I can assure you."

Jack pressed the heel of his hand against his heart. "But what about us, Yvonne? I thought we had something special."

Yvonne's cheeks pinkened, making her eyes sparkle even more. She slapped at Jack's arm with her gloves. "We do, Jack. But I think it's best if we just admire each other from afar, don't you?"

"That's probably best," Harold agreed. "I wouldn't want to challenge you to a duel for the lady's favor. They once did that a lot in Charleston. In lots of places, I imagine, but quite a lot nearby in Philadelphia Alley."

I smiled and nodded, familiar with the thoroughfare. I'd made the mistake of going down the narrow bricked walkway only once and found myself watching in horror as two men dressed in eighteenth-century clothing stood back-to-back before pacing away from each other, pistols drawn.

"No, sir," Jack said, extending his hand to shake. He was smiling, but I saw him shooting furtive glances at the crowd around us.

"Don't worry," I said. "Marc's not here. Rebecca said he was still at the house, taking the brunt of Harvey's anger over the sporadic power and equipment failures."

Jack gave me a slow, warm grin. "What a shame."

"That's exactly what I thought." I grinned back, sliding my hand into the crook of his elbow.

"Oh, speaking of Marc Longo," Yvonne said, her tone bitter enough that if she'd been anyone else I'd have expected her to spit on the ground at the mention of his name, "I've been doing more research about the Vanderhorsts and Gallen Hall in particular, trying to see if there was anything else that might help you find what you're looking for. I haven't had time to photocopy and e-mail you this yet because I had my appointment at the beauty parlor today and time got away from me." She patted her shining helmet of hair.

"Anyway," she continued, "I couldn't stop thinking about that note from the marquis to the Swamp Fox, and the rumors of a treasure from the French king to the Americans that was never found. I haven't even been able to find anything definitive that would clarify what the treasure actually was. However . . ." She closed her mouth, and her cheeks puffed out slightly as if they were finding it hard to contain the secret.

"Yes?" I prompted, afraid Jack might lose his mind if he had to drag out every word.

"So I decided to focus my search on specific treasurelike words, like jewels, gold, and metal."

Once again, her cheeks filled with anticipation, and even I had a hard time restraining myself from shaking her a little to get the words to pop out of her mouth. "And?" I prompted.

"And," she said, drawing out the word in a way that would make any Charlestonian proud, "I happened to get a hit on something very unexpected. It might not mean anything, but then again, since there's no such thing as coincidence, it might." She winked at Jack. "I found an article in an ancient Charleston architecture text that focused on the various craftsmen and metalworks in and around the city. We do have the most beautiful iron gates and fences, don't we?"

We all nodded, but I could see the tic starting in Jack's jaw. "Anyway, I saw mention of a Samuel Vanderhorst, a respected metalworker in the city around the end of the eighteenth century. The name popped out at me, of course, so I did a little digging and found a small biography of him in the antiquated volume that also mentioned Elizabeth Grosvenor." She shook her head. "I shouldn't have missed it the first time I went through the book, except he didn't have his own listing, because . . ." She paused but quickly continued when she spotted the manic look in Jack's eyes. "Because Samuel was a freedman and former slave on the plantation and therefore was mentioned only briefly, his name tucked in amongst about twenty other craftsmen on the plantation. His owners freed him when they discovered what a gift he had for metalworking. All the gates and fences at the plantation, including the cemetery, were designed and made by him. I might not have taken note of his name and occupation, except that the listing mentioned that he also made jewelry." She raised her eyebrows and I fully expected her to waggle them for effect, but she didn't. "Aren't you going to ask me what keyword I used in my search that ended up on the listing?"

With a tight smile, Jack said, "Yes, please. I don't think I can take any more suspense."

"Pinchbeck! After the Revolution, Samuel left the plantation and set up shop in Charleston, where most of his work involved forging gates and fences in and around the city. But in his spare time, he also made costume jewelry for less affluent clients, most of it with pinchbeck."

Jack and I stared at each other. "The brooch," we said simultaneously.

"It wouldn't be out of the realm of possibility that he made the peacock brooch Eliza Grosvenor is wearing in her portrait at Gallen Hall," Jack finished.

"Does that help?" Yvonne asked.

"I hope so," Jack said. "I don't know, but I'm sure it's a piece of the puzzle. I'm just not sure yet where it fits." He looked up at Harold. "Is it all right if I hug Yvonne?"

"Go right ahead. I think she'd be disappointed if you didn't."

Jack hugged the older woman and kissed her on the cheek. "Have I told you lately how wonderful you are?"

"Now, hush, Jack. Harold can hear you," Yvonne said, giggling.

We all laughed, then said our good-byes, with Yvonne promising that she'd e-mail the photocopies of what she'd discovered.

As Jack and I walked across the lobby to join our group, I looked around to make sure no could hear, then said, "Rebecca just told me that Marc is looking for one of the papers we found in the box Anthony gave us. It's a drawing, and apparently Marc has one that matches it—it's the one copied by Joseph Longo at the Vanderhorst house. All Rebecca knows is that Marc believes they're connected. Do you think he has any idea what he's looking for?"

Jack stopped walking and met my gaze. "I doubt it. The only thing I *do* know is that Marc doesn't know anything more than we do—yet. Meaning we're probably still a few steps ahead of him. I think the brooch is important—you said that Eliza wanted you to notice it. Regardless, we need to find it before Marc does. Remember how Anthony said that Marc had used a metal detector on the floor of the mausoleum? A metal detector can't detect pinchbeck—it's made of copper and zinc, which are both nonferrous metals."

"Meaning?"

"Meaning that there'd have to be a heck of a lot of it to be detected with a metal detector. And the amount of pinchbeck used in a brooch wouldn't be enough. It also means that Marc doesn't know what he's looking for." He was thoughtful for a moment. "Do you think you could ask Eliza about her brooch?"

"You know it doesn't work that way . . ." I began.

"I know. But I thought you could maybe try, see where it goes. I'm sure Jayne would love to help, too."

I swallowed. "Sure," I said. "Because Jayne's always happy to help."

Jack gave me an odd look.

"She is," I said, squirming under his gaze. "That's a good thing, right? And don't say what you're thinking."

Jack held up his hands in surrender. "I didn't say anything."

"You didn't have to." I began walking toward the group, my pace quickening as I spotted the young Charleston dancer moving toward me from the other side of the room, her bruised and bloody mouth open as if she were trying to speak.

"Come on," I said, sliding my arm into Jayne's. "Let's go—we're missing out on some Christmas shopping." I hurried toward the exit without turning back, feeling the disappointed gaze of the dead woman following me out the door.

CHAPTER 22

The high heel of my shoe got stuck for the third time in the dirt courtyard of the Aiken-Rhett House museum as I moved among the various wreath-decorating stations set up inside the carriage house and around the courtyard. As I twisted my foot back and forth to remove it from the rocky soil, I looked up to see Sophie standing by the coffee and doughnut table watching me before dipping her head and staring pointedly at her own Birkenstock-clad feet.

I hobbled toward her, intent on diving into the box of doughnuts on the table in front of her; I had ordered them from Glazed, making sure there were plenty of my favorite flavors, the Purple Goat and tiramisu. I'd already placed two in a napkin and hidden them inside my purse beneath the table.

"Sure," I said, "you might be more comfortable, but at least I don't have to worry about being mistaken for someone needing a handout. You should probably put a glass jar in front of you—you can always give the proceeds to Ashley Hall." I eyed her mom jeans with the tapered ankles and high waist circa 1990, the turtleneck with tiny whales all over it that was definitely a nineteen eighties holdover but had been subjected to Sophie's tie-dyeing obsession, and the leather-fringed vest that was more circa eighteen eighty.

When Sophie had told me her parents were downsizing and her mother was sending her a bunch of clothes from her closet, I'd tried to prepare myself. But the sheer scope of Sophie's windfall had been worse than I'd thought. I'd tried to tell my friend that just because her mother had given her all those clothes didn't mean she actually had to wear them, but Sophie was as dedicated to reusing and repurposing everything as she was to restoring old homes. Unfortunately.

"It's a nice turnout," I said, looking around at the groups of people standing at each wreath-making station. I leaned down and reached beneath the red-draped table. "Thank goodness for the good weather—maybe we'll raise enough money today that we can skip the progressive dinner."

Sophie blew out of her face a strand of green-streaked hair that had slipped from its braid. "Right. And that would happen just after they canceled Christmas."

I pulled out a small shopping bag from Sugar Snap Pea and handed it to Sophie. "Against my better judgment, I bought this for Skye. I was in the store looking for yet another replacement for Sarah's favorite book, *If I Were a Lamb*—JJ keeps tearing off the covers—and I saw these and had to get them."

Sophie opened the bag and peered inside. With a happy exclamation, she pulled out a small yellow knit cap with peace signs stamped all over it in neon colors. "I have one just like this!" she said.

"I know. But I thought it would look cute on Skye anyway."

"Thank you!" she said, taking me by surprise and hugging me. "I've always known you're not the curmudgeon you pretend to be."

"Humph." I looked across the courtyard to where Veronica was at the orange-and-clove station, helping customers attach the fruit to their boxwood wreath frames before they moved on to the holly-berry station.

"Aren't you supposed to be helping Veronica?" Sophie asked, pouring coffee from an industrial percolator into a recyclable paper cup for a customer.

"I was, but then she said she could handle it by herself, so she sent me to Jayne, who's at the ribbon station, and she said the same thing. So I came over here to see if you needed any help."

We looked over at the growing lines in front of Veronica's and Jayne's stations, where it was obvious they needed another pair of hands. Sophie faced me. "You were reorganizing all their supplies, weren't you?" She looked pointedly at the stack of cups I'd picked up and was placing on the opposite side of the table.

"Maybe," I said slowly. "Is there something here I can help you with?"

"Sure. Why don't you organize the sugar packets in the little basket by expiration dates printed in tiny writing on the back of each pouch, oldest in front?"

I would be lying if I said the thought didn't excite me. I replaced the cups and reached for the sugar. "All right," I said. "Although it looks like my talents could be used elsewhere." I indicated the growing lines now spilling out into the courtyard.

I looked at the milling crowd, wishing Rebecca would hurry up and get here so I could ask her more about the drawing Marc had. I'd told Jack what Rebecca had told me the previous evening, and we'd gone through the papers from the archives after we'd returned from the Shop and Stroll, eventually finding the photocopied page of what Rebecca had described as lines and scrolls. It meant nothing to us, and I'm sure Marc had reached the same conclusion about his drawing. But we needed to see it, just in case it did mean something. All I needed to do was to make Rebecca show it to me.

"Dr. Wallen-Arasi?"

Sophie and I looked up to see Meghan Black standing in front of us. I might not have recognized her out of context, except she wore her usual pearls and Burberry quilted jacket, her hair in a high ponytail. She didn't have on the cute earmuffs, but I recognized the J.Crew pants and flats from a recent shopping expedition with Nola.

"Meghan!" I said. "Good to see you out of the cistern. I was starting to think you were only three feet tall. Here to make a wreath or two?"

"I might—I live in a carriage house on Rutledge and the door isn't visible from the street, but I bet my mom in Atlanta would like one. I'm actually here because Nola mentioned this is where I could find both of you this morning." She looked around for a moment, then stepped a little closer. "Is Mrs. Longo here?"

I shook my head. "My cousin won't be here for at least another hour. She said her husband came home late last night and woke her up, and it took her a while to get back to sleep. She's exhausted." I forced my expression to remain neutral as I recalled the two trips to the nursery I'd made the previous night, one because JJ's whisk had fallen through the slats of his crib, and the second one because Sarah was babbling so loudly I thought someone was in her room. She'd settled down by the time I'd reached her, the sweet smell of roses telling me it had been Louisa. The third time, Jack had gone and I'd fallen back asleep immediately so I had no idea who or what had caused the interruption to my sleep, and at that point I'd ceased to care.

Meghan nodded, her brown eyes wide. "Don't take this the wrong way, but I'm not sure she should hear this." She leaned in a little closer. "I found something in the cistern yesterday that I thought you both might want to see. That film guy and Mr. Longo were hanging around a lot, asking questions and requesting that if we find anything we show it to them first. Please don't take offense, but I'm not sure I'd want them around anything fragile or historically important. I don't think they appreciate the importance of old things, you know?"

Sophie and I nodded emphatically. I'd liked Meghan from the moment I'd first met her, and now I understood why. "We couldn't agree more," I said, peering at the Anthropologie shopping bag she held in her hand, balls of newspaper shoved inside and around a newspaper-wrapped object. "What did you find?"

Glancing around one more time, she placed the bag on the ground next to her, then took out the newspaper-wrapped package before placing it on an empty corner of the refreshment table. It was rectangular, but thinner than a brick, and seemed lightweight. "It's not super fragile, but it's old, so be careful when you open it." She slid it toward Sophie.

"I don't have gloves."

Meghan smiled. "I always carry extras." She reached into her coat pocket and pulled out a clear surgical pair.

Sophie snapped them on her hands, then began to unfurl the newspaper while Meghan and I played lookout. Two older women approached and I poured coffee for them without charging them just to make them leave faster.

"Oh." Sophie's head was bent over the paper and I joined her to peer into the opening.

"I know, right?" Meghan said. "It's amazing that it's so well preserved. Probably because it's made of mahogany, which is naturally bug and moisture resistant, but also because it found its way inside a leather traveling bag with a wad of what we think might have been a fabric coated with linseed oil that made it partially waterproof. It's what floor mats were originally made of, and it's just our luck that one may have been discarded around the same time this ended up in the cistern. It's amazing what really old garbage we can salvage because it was accidentally thrown away with something that worked to preserve it." She sounded as excited as I imagined a bride would when discovering the perfect wedding dress.

A small slab of wood, about the size of my car's rearview mirror, lay in the middle of the newspaper. One side was finished in the remains of a dark stain, the wood dull and split from years of being buried. Sophie flipped it over, the wood lighter and unstained on this side, and in worse condition without the protection of the stain and varnish of the front. On one of the short sides, a mottled brass square that might have been a hinge hung precariously to its spot near the top, two small nail holes near the bottom showing where a second hinge might have been. "It looks like a tiny door," I said.

Meghan nodded. "That's what I thought, too. I brushed it clean before wrapping it so Dr. Wallen-Arasi could have a better look. It's so different from all the pottery fragments and animal bones that I thought it was unusual enough to make sure I brought it to your attention."

"Nice work, Meghan," Sophie said, making the young woman's cheeks pinken. Sophie leaned a little closer. "What's this?"

I wasn't wearing my glasses—no surprise there—and when I squinted it appeared that there was just a dark smudge of dirt in the corner.

"I saw that, too," Meghan said. "So after I got it cleaned up, I got out my magnifying glass and took a look. It's a carving of a peacock. With its tail feathers opened. I have no idea what it might mean."

Sophie and I met each other's gaze. "It probably means that whatever piece of furniture this came from—and I'm assuming it's part of a piece of furniture because of the fine wood—was made at Gallen Hall Plantation." Sophie ran her finger over a small indentation at the top corner, her finger fitting neatly into the space. "I'm thinking this might have been one of those hidden doors we find all the time inside old desks and dressers. This door would have been flush against the back or side of a drawer opening and could be opened with a single finger." She flipped it over in her hands again. "This would have been a fairly small place to hide things. Most likely letters or documents." She glanced briefly at me. "Definitely something small."

"So not gold bricks?" Meghan asked.

"Definitely not." Sophie shook her head. "What makes you ask that?"

"Several times Marc Longo has come out to the cistern to check our progress, asking us whether or not we've used metal detectors to find anything metal." Meghan rolled her eyes. "Like we don't have better equipment than that." She held up a foot, now without a cast, to remind us of the XRF machine that had fallen on it earlier in the year. "The thing is, I overheard him saying something to that producer guy. I didn't mean to eavesdrop, but you know how loudly he talks."

I nodded, encouraging her to continue.

"Anyway, I was in the dining room and Mr. Kobylt was showing me the repairs he was doing to the floor in there, and Mr. Longo was telling the producer guy something about how he was sure the Confederate gold was on Vanderhorst property." Meghan rolled her eyes again. "Which is kind of ridiculous, really. There has been so much research on the subject and the conclusion is that the bulk of it was stolen from federal troops in 1865 by unknown persons and disbursed." With an insider grin, she said, "And we've all read about the Confederate diamonds found in your grandfather clock, Mrs. Trenholm. They're all accounted for, so I guess Mr. Longo just wants to believe that the gold must be there, too." She tilted her head in question. "They are all accounted for, right?"

I nodded. "Yes. We know what happened to all of the diamonds, and found the remaining ones that hadn't been given away or sold. I wish there were more." I hadn't meant to say that, at least not out loud to an almost stranger. There was just something about Meghan's open and eager face that encouraged confidences.

"Are you sure?" she asked.

"Very," I said slowly. "Why do you ask?"

She continued to look speculative. "Well, there was a reporter from the *Post and Courier*—Suzy something—who came by yesterday. She's writing a story on hidden historical treasures that might be found in the Lowcountry. She mentioned the pirate treasure supposedly buried on Sullivan's Island, the Confederate gold and diamonds, and the connection of the last two to your house. I told her you would be the best person to ask about that because all I knew was that I was supposed to be excavating the cistern and so far had only discovered broken bits of pottery and bones."

"That's all, then? She didn't say anything else?"

"Actually, she did. Something about another treasure—from the American Revolution. Something given to the Americans by the king of France maybe? She said there are plenty of rumors about what the treasure might be, but nobody knows for sure. She wanted to know if I'd heard anything about that, or if you'd mentioned it to me."

My mouth went completely dry. I had had a dozen or so phone calls and texts from Suzy Dorf, which, as usual, I'd ignored. She'd been nothing but a thorn in my side since I'd inherited the house on Tradd Street. Besides being nosy and too inquisitive about the rumored possibility that I could speak to the dead, her worst fault was being friends with Rebecca. Now I wondered if I should have been so hasty with the DECLINE button on my phone.

"I see. And was Mr. Longo there when she stopped by?"

Meghan shook her head. "No. He'd been sent out to get more batteries and lightbulbs since everything was losing power and every time they flipped on a light, the bulb would explode." She raised her eyebrows, as if she expected us to reassure her that this was perfectly normal. Which it was, of course. For us.

"Interesting," Sophie said, her tone indicating that the subject was anything but. "Did she happen to mention why she thought Mrs. Trenholm would have any knowledge about the French treasure?"

Meghan shook her head again. "She didn't, and I didn't ask. It was getting dark and I still had a lot more work to do in the cistern while there was still daylight. None of us like to be there after the sun goes down." She didn't need to explain that the reason was only partially because it was hard to excavate without full light.

"That's fine," Sophie said reassuringly. "You're doing a great job, by the way." She indicated the wooden door resting on the newspaper. "And thanks for bringing this to me—I'm sure it's important; I just can't figure out why yet."

"Yay," Meghan said, giving a little clap with her hands. "You'll let me know when you figure it out, all right?"

"Absolutely," Sophie said. "Now, go make a wreath for your mom and have fun. Nola and her friends are here to help get you started. . . ." Her words trailed off as we followed her gaze to the first table in the opened carriage house, where Nola, Alston, and Lindsey were supposed to be welcoming the participants, taking tickets, and explaining how the whole process worked. Instead, the three girls were sitting at the table with their heads bowed over a thick textbook that was opened between the three of them while people milled about in front of them trying to figure out where they should start.

I exhaled a deep breath. "Hang on—let me go find out what's going on with those three Gen Zers."

"Hey, don't knock millennials—we're not all bad!" Meghan looked genuinely upset.

"Sorry," I called as I walked across the courtyard to where the girls sat at a long table under one of the arched openings, my heels slowing me down as I tiptoed over the dirt in an attempt to save my shoes. I stopped in front of the table, waiting for one of the girls to look up. When no one did, I cleared my throat.

"Oh, hi, Mrs. Trenholm," Lindsey said sweetly. "We didn't see you standing there."

"Or the other twenty or so people who are looking for a little guidance here." I frowned at the three of them, wearing matching black Ashley Hall cardigan sweaters with long-sleeved purple polo shirts, plaid skirts, and black tights. They never intentionally coordinated what color polo or tights they were going to wear, as allowed by the school, but somehow they always ended up looking like fraternal triplets. Personally, I liked that they always matched. Maybe because I was the thwarted mother of twins who preferred things to match but whose efforts were never appreciated.

Nola sat back heavily in her chair. "Sorry. It's just that Lindsey reminded me this morning that our art history teacher told the class on Thursday that we were having a quiz on Dutch painters on Monday and I forgot to bring my art history book home. It's going to be a big part of our final exam, too, so we have to know it."

"I forgot my book, too," Alton said. "And it's like ten percent of our grade, so we need all the time we can get to study."

I glanced down at the thick book with shiny pages and a photograph of a painting of a woman wearing a Dutch cap and a bright blue apron, pouring what looked like milk from a pitcher. I frowned, remembering how obsessive I'd been about grades at that age, and even felt a small tug of panic in the pit of my stomach. I glanced at my watch. "You're supposed to be here for two more hours. How about I relieve you for an hour so you can go study? But only an hour. I've got work to do today, too." I didn't mention that part of that work would involve solving the photo puzzle on Jayne's dining room table.

The girls shot up from their seats at once. "Thanks, Melanie," Nola said, giving me a quick hug. "I'll dedicate my A in the class to you."

Nola scooped up the heavy book with both hands, and the three of them took off toward the house. I hoped they were aware that the Aiken-Rhett House was preserved and not restored—a distinction drilled into my head by Sophie—and that there was no furniture they'd be allowed to sit on. I turned away, intent on allowing them to figure it out.

I smelled coffee and turned to find a recyclable cup held in front of me. I smiled up at Veronica and accepted the cup. "Thank you. You must be a mind reader," I said.

"I needed a coffee break and figured you probably did, too." She took a sip from her cup. "I wish you'd been here earlier when we had a customer demanding plastic greens for her wreath so that she could keep it up as long as she wanted to without it turning brown. I thought Sophie might have a heart attack."

I laughed out loud. "I can't believe I missed that. I didn't get a lot of sleep last night, so I'm moving slowly this morning."

Veronica nodded. She didn't say anything, although I could tell by her air of anticipation that she wanted to. I remained silent, sipping my coffee, and waited.

Eventually, she said, "Should I be concerned if the attic door opens on its own all the time now?"

"Are you asking if you think there's something structurally wrong with your house? I'd say probably not. Although I'm not an expert on that sort of thing."

"Adrienne's trying to tell me something, isn't she?"

I closed my eyes for a moment, smelling the dark coffee and enjoying the warmth on my bare hands. "Probably. Especially if this is something new."

"It is, and I don't think it's a coincidence. It started the night Michael said he wanted to put the house on the market."

I looked at her. "When does he want to do that?"

"After the first of the year." She met my gaze. "He gave me an ultimatum. Either him or the house. He said if I valued our marriage, I'd sell and allow us to start over." She took a sip of her coffee. "I'm afraid that if we move out, we'll lose Adrienne forever. And I'll never know what really happened to her."

I stared into my cup, tilting it in my hand and making my reflection swirl on the dark liquid. "I'm crazy right now with all this Christmas stuff and the filming going on at my house—not to mention the excavation in my backyard."

Veronica's face fell, and I briefly thought she might cry. "I don't know what to do."

I thought for a long moment of the young dancer in the hotel the night before. Of all the times I'd been forced to sing ABBA songs to block out cries for help. I took a deep breath. "I might be able to help you—or at least buy you some time. Why don't you call my office and set up an appointment with me? I can certainly list your house, just as I can certainly make it go as slowly as possible." My boss, Dave Henderson, would kill me for hanging on to an unproductive listing, but I couldn't tell Veronica that I couldn't help her. Besides, I wasn't promising that I could find out what Adrienne was trying to tell her. All I was saying was that I could buy her some time.

Veronica grabbed my free hand and squeezed, her eyes moist. "Thank you, Melanie. Thank you so much. I don't care what Rebecca says about you—I think you're wonderful."

I opened my mouth to ask her what she meant, but a group of mothers from the school whom I recognized had approached the table and were already busy chatting to me and asking questions. I drained my coffee and turned my attention to them, all the while aware of the faint scent of Vanilla Musk perfume and the ribbon of icy air that caressed my cheek, leaving no doubt that the new activity in Veronica's attic had nothing to do with coincidence.

CHAPTER 23

I woke up to a single ring of the landline telephone that was no longer plugged in but remained on my bedside table for occasions like this. I sat up quickly, not wanting to disturb General Lee or Jack, and held the receiver to my ear. "Hello?"

The snap and crackle of empty space filled my ear. I pressed the phone closer, hoping to hear my grandmother's voice. She'd been dead for years, but she still preferred the phone to communicate with me. And only when she thought I might be in trouble. "Grandmother?" I whispered into the receiver, my stomach feeling as if multiple rubber bands were wrapped tightly around it. My greeting was met only with the electric sizzle of an ancient telephone line that shouldn't be making any noise at all.

"Grandmother?" I said again, still straining to hear. I waited for another moment, then slowly pulled the receiver away from my ear but stopped; the sound was as strident as a baby bird's cry, beaming its way to me as if from another galaxy.

Jack.

"What?" I pressed the phone against my ear again. "Did you say 'Jack'?"

Another moment passed, and then I heard it again. *Jack.*

"What about Jack?" My question was met by silence, even the crackling sound fading. "What about Jack?" I repeated. But the phone had gone completely dead; there were only the sounds of the old house and General Lee's snoring for company.

I hung up the phone and turned around to see if Jack was awake. A sliver of moonlight cut across his pillow, accentuating the white of his empty pillowcase. "Jack?" I said out loud, looking at the bathroom door for any light from beneath it. But the door yawned wide, an empty black shadow indicating no lights were on inside.

I slid out of bed, making General Lee snuffle and adjust himself on my pillow, then go back to sleep. I glanced at the video monitor, but the nursery was empty except for the two sleeping babies in their cribs. Sliding on my slippers, I grabbed my robe and thrust my arms into it before hurrying out the door, the rubber bands around my stomach squeezing tighter. My grandmother never called just to chat.

I hurried down the corridor and paused at the top of the stairs. A light was on downstairs, and a few of the rubber bands slid off my insides. When Jack was writing, he often woke up in the middle of the night with a story idea that couldn't wait until morning. I placed my foot on the top step, then stopped, aware of an odd sound coming from Nola's bedroom behind the closed door. She was still sleeping in the guest room as Greco continued with his redo of her room, the paint and sawdust from the new built-in bookshelves and window cornices making it nearly unlivable. The restless spirits, too, if one wanted to count them as disrupters of sleep.

After a quick glance toward the light downstairs, I moved slowly down the hall to Nola's bedroom, brushing past the two miniature Christmas trees filled with tiny children's-toy ornaments—one for a girl and one for a boy—that Sophie had insisted we needed. One shook and nearly toppled when my robe snagged on it, and I had to grab it by the stuffed teddy bear tree topper to keep it upright. I promised myself for the millionth time that next year we were going on a cruise and skipping the holidays completely.

I paused a moment to flip on the upstairs hallway lights, and was not completely surprised when nothing happened. One of the screaming phone calls Jack had received from Harvey that past evening had been about these exact same lights. Apparently, there was something wrong with the Southern wiring (his words, not mine, and he used a few more descriptive adjectives before the word *Southern*) that was causing the lightbulbs to blow out as soon as the switches were flipped.

I thought for a moment about getting Jack but stopped myself. If he was writing, that would be a good thing, and nothing I wanted to interfere with. I was an adult. And a mother of toddler twins and a teenage girl. There shouldn't be anything left that could scare me. Surely I could handle whatever was behind that door. And if not, I could close it and then go get Jack.

I gingerly touched the door handle, for some reason thinking it would be hot. The brass felt cool to the touch, so I wrapped my fingers around it, then pressed my ear to the door. I couldn't identify the sound at first, probably because it seemed so out of context in my house in the dead of winter. A buzzing, like a man's electric razor several decibels louder than it should have been, vibrated through the door, traveling from my head to my fingers and making them tingle.

With a deep breath, I turned the handle, then pushed the door open enough for me to peer inside. Moonlight filled the unadorned windows, lighting the room with a blue-white glow. I reached around the doorframe for the light switch and flicked it on. Nothing happened.

The buzzing was louder now, unbalanced, the source concentrated on one side of the room. The dusty scent of gunpowder drifted toward me and I glanced furtively into the dark corners for the musket-carrying British soldier I'd seen twice before. Except for the moonlight, the corners were empty, the room bare.

Pushing the door as far as it would open, I stepped a little farther into the room, listening as the buzzing took on a new rhythm, a *thud-thump, thud-thump*. Like a beating heart. I swallowed, unwilling to let go of the doorknob just in case I needed to make a hasty retreat and needed to find the door. My eyes gradually adjusted to the moonlight, my gaze moving from one side of the room to the other, stopping when it reached the bed.

Greco had stripped it of all its bedding and had been draping fabric samples over it for Nola and her grandmothers to pick and choose from. But the noise wasn't coming from the mattress. It was coming from higher up. I looked at the foot of the bed, where the two carved bedposts jutted toward the ceiling like fat fingers. I blinked, my eyesight even worse in the dark, but good enough to tell that one of the posts was different from the other. It was thicker at the top, it seemed. Rounder. I blinked again. *Moving.*

I stepped back quickly, my heels bumping into the edge of the open door. Taking a deep breath, I looked at the top of the bedpost again, trying to decipher what I was seeing, hoping against all hope that it wasn't those flying palmetto bugs that were terrifying when they were solo. I had no word to use for when they traveled in packs.

But they were buzzing. Like bees. Forcing myself to let go of the doorknob, I stepped closer to the bed to get a better look. One flew in front of my face as if on reconnaissance, and to my relief it was much smaller than a palmetto bug and most likely a bee. It buzzed and jerked, then flew back to join the cluster of buzzing insects swarming along the entire length of the bedpost.

I walked across the room to examine the windows, wondering if one had been left open. Then I remembered. It was December. From what my father had explained to me about bee behavior, during the winter months bees stayed in their hives, keeping the queen warm until spring. There was another reason there would be a swarm of bees inside my house in December. An unnatural reason. My grandmother had once told me that bees were messengers from the spirit world. How appropriate, then, that I would have just received a phone call from her. As I stared through the hazy darkness at the buzzing, swarming mass on Nola's bedpost, I wished she'd simply told me on the phone what she wanted me to know instead of sending bees. Apparently, *simple* wasn't a word anyone in my family was familiar with.

A shape drifted across the cistern below, a fall of light followed quickly by darkness. I stepped back, not wanting to be seen, and waited for whoever it was to show up on the other side. I squinted, wondering if it was an intruder of the flesh-and-blood type or of a ghostlier sort, unsure which one I'd prefer. I waited for whatever it was to emerge, but the night remained still and dark. But I knew there was someone—some*thing*—out there. I felt malevolent eyes on me, like sticky tar that clung to my skin.

I backed away quickly, unwilling to wait for whatever it was to show itself. I continued to walk in reverse until I reached the doorway, not brave enough to turn my back on the window. I saw her then. Eliza. She stood by the bedpost, staring at it as if she were as surprised by the bees as I was.

I remembered Jack telling me to ask Eliza about her brooch. I knew it didn't usually work that way, but I was tired of waiting for the message to come to me. I wanted to be left alone, to focus on Jack and our family and my career again. To resume normal lives that didn't involve swarming bees, specters haunting the backyard, and reporters asking questions I didn't want to answer.

Eliza was more shadow than light, but the green of her dress gleamed like an emerald in the moonlight, the sparkle of the jeweled brooch on her bodice winking at me. "Eliza." I kept my voice light, mingling it with the buzzing of the bees, not wanting to scare her into vanishing.

She looked directly at me. At least I sensed that she was looking at me. I wasn't sure—her face and body were swathed in shadow—but I felt her gaze on me. Despite the darkness that enshrouded her, the jewels on her brooch seemed lit from within, small beacons of light. I felt compelled to look at it, to notice something. I squinted out of habit but was close enough to see the shape of the bird, the fanned tail. The four stones seemed to mock me as I struggled to understand what Eliza was trying to tell me.

"What is it?" I whispered. "What do you want me to see?"

Lies. For a moment it was if the buzzing of the bees had mimicked the sound, the cold breath of a corpse washing over me as the word swirled around the room telling me that it hadn't been.

"Eliza?" I whispered, but she was gone, along with the bees and the buzzing and the smell of gunpowder. I waited for a moment, attempting to catch my breath, and then, with trembling hands, I reached for the door and left the room, gently latching the door closed behind me. I spotted the light in the foyer and ran down the stairs, knowing Jack was on the other side of that light and could make it all better.

Jack's study door was open, the green-shaded banker's lamp on his desk giving pale light to the room. I stopped on the threshold, breathing heavily, not seeing Jack at first. Yet I definitely smelled . . . pipe smoke? "Jack?" I called, hoping another ghost wasn't waiting for me. One per night was more than enough.

"Over here."

My gaze followed the voice, stopping at the corner behind the piano where Amelia had placed a lovely leather Chesterfield chair and otto-man, for times when he wanted to read quietly or just think in his office. I rarely saw him use them, as he did most of his thinking either walking around the room or sitting at his desk. But he was sitting in the chair now, in the near dark, his feet on the ottoman. And smoking a pipe.

I had so many questions that it was hard to pick one to start with. "Why are you smoking a pipe?" I managed.

He took it from his mouth and looked at it as if surprised to see it. "I know you disapprove of cigarettes, and cigars stink, but I thought you'd be okay with a pipe. My grandfather left me his collection when he died, and Mr. Vanderhorst was kind enough to leave several tins of tobacco in the freezer."

"But you don't smoke."

He shrugged. "No, I really don't. But I didn't want to start drinking again, and smoking was the next best thing. And it worked for Sherlock Holmes—he always smoked a pipe when solving complex puzzles. Besides, after I'm gone, the pipe smoke will let you know that I'm hanging around." He offered a half smile.

"Don't say that, Jack." I wasn't sure if my concern was more over him mentioning his death or over his need for a drink. I walked across the room and stopped near his chair. "What's happened?"

A crease formed above his nose as if he was trying to remember. "Well, for starters, when I woke up at three in the morning, the first thought in my head was that I needed a drink." He took a long puff from his pipe, then coughed a little. "It's been years since I had that thought first thing." His eyes met mine, and I felt the heat of his gaze. "I usually have better things to think about when I wake up."

A flash of heat spiraled up from my core, nearly making me dizzy as it reached my head. He'd had that effect on me since we'd first met. I took a deep breath. "Has something happened?"

"Do you want the good news or the bad news first?"

"Let's start with the good news," I suggested, thinking in the back of my head that maybe I could distract him from telling me the bad news.

"I heard from Steve Dungan, my architect friend. He finally looked at the building plans for both mausoleums, examining all the measurements, comparing the width and length of all the walls, the angles of the triangle that forms the structure, looking for any differences." He sucked on the pipe, his eyes closed briefly. When he blew out the smoke, I smelled a not-unpleasing mixture of sweetness and spice.

"And?" I prompted.

"He found only two changes from the original. The first is that the original mausoleum had spaces for ten crypts, not just the three that are there now. The other thing he noticed is that the second mausoleum is exactly two brick widths taller than the first."

I thought for a moment. "The row of bricks with the strange markings is two bricks wide. Which tells me that the whole purpose of rebuilding the mausoleum was to add that double row."

"Yeah, so that might be the reason why the first mausoleum was demolished and replaced with a nearly identical one two years later. Hopefully we'll figure out what the reason was when we finish the puzzle on Jayne's dining room table." He raised his eyebrows. "Maybe you can ask the ghost of Sherlock Holmes for help on that one for me?"

I frowned. "You do know he's a fictional character, right?"

Jack leaned his head against the back of his chair and looked at me through half-closed eyes. "Sure. Just trying to keep my fantasy world intact so I can still write books." He tilted his head slightly. "You look real sexy with your hair like that—all rumpled from sleep."

I smiled, glad not only that distracting Jack was going to be easier than I'd thought, but also that I didn't have to listen to the bad news. I took a step closer, his eyes following me.

"And then there's the bad news," he said, and I stopped.

He lifted his head. "I made the mistake of checking my e-mail instead of trying to go back to sleep. My brilliant editor, whom I'm beginning to believe really must be a twelve-year-old boy in disguise, told me that in a marketing meeting where all the powers that be discuss what to do with problem children—books they don't know how to market, that is—the brilliant suggestion had been made to convert my next book into a graphic novel."

"A graphic novel? What's that?"

"Basically? A cartoon. They're going for that younger market."

"But your book is about a mentally ill mother with Munchausen syndrome by proxy who kills her daughter. Not sure how that would translate into a cartoon."

"Bingo. You don't know how refreshing it is to hear the voice of reason. It's rare in the publishing business, apparently."

"But they can't do that if you don't agree to it, right? And if you don't, you'll just find another publisher."

He barked out a laugh, a dark, ugly sound. "If it were only that easy. If there's such a thing as being blackballed, that's what would happen to me. Nobody is taking my phone calls or returning my e-mails. I couldn't find a new agent right now unless I could prove I was the reincarnation of Margaret Mitchell. It's like I'm the plague and nobody wants to be infected."

I sat on the edge of the ottoman, unsure of my role. He was always the one with the answers. The first person I ran to. It was hard to reconcile the accomplished man with the chiseled face and piercing eyes with this man referring to himself as an infectious disease. For an instant I considered looking past this moment to the next, of closing my eyes to a problem I had no idea how to solve and telling him what I'd just seen upstairs, hoping that answering the question of Eliza would make him forget about his own.

But I couldn't do any of those things. Because Jack needed me. Needed me to be strong and to shoulder some of the problem solving on my own. I had a small fantasy where I figured out what Eliza was trying to tell me tonight and it was the key to everything. I imagined solving it all and handing it to Jack and him immediately turning it all into a bestselling novel. Maybe that's why my grandmother had called. To tell me I needed to take care of things, to protect Jack while he dealt with his personal demons.

Placing my hands on his leg, I leaned forward and said, "This is all temporary, Jack. You've got a great book already written, and the idea for another one—you're not out of the game. Not by a long shot. You've got a respected body of work and that alone speaks volumes."

He blew out a puff of smoke, temporarily obscuring his face. "I want to believe that. You have no idea how much. But, Mellie, my career is my identity. I'm a writer. A bestselling author. Without that, who am I?"

I leaned closer. "You're a father, a son, and a husband. And you're damned good at all three of those roles, and those are a heck of a lot more important than anything else." I tried to think of what else might jolt him from his despondency, but I was woefully lacking in the ability to give a pep talk. As an only child and a single woman for most of my adult life, I hadn't learned that skill. Maybe, just this once, I'd revert to the old Mellie and pretend that Jack's despondency didn't exist. It was simple, really. I just wouldn't allow it.

"Do you mean that?" he said, his voice smoky.

I stood, took the pipe from his hand, and placed it in a crystal ashtray on the table next to him. Then I straddled his lap, his hands moving under my robe and resting on my waist. "I do. I couldn't pick a better father for my children. I am also hopelessly and ceaselessly in love with you, Jack Trenholm. Whatever profession you choose."

His hands caressed my sides through the thin fabric of my nightgown, doing wild things to my nerve endings. "Show me," he whispered in my ear.

So I did.

CHAPTER 24

When I got home after work the next day, I threw open the door to the piazza, intent on rushing upstairs to Nola's room to see any lingering evidence that Eliza or the bees had been there the previous night. I'd been running late for work that morning and both Sarah and JJ had been out of sorts, begging to be held, and I hadn't had the time to investigate. I stopped short at the sight of Greco hanging a Christmas wreath on the front door. I walked more sedately toward him, then stood back so we could both admire it.

"What happened to the wreath that was there? I made it, you know. At the workshop I ran benefiting Ashley Hall."

Greco stepped forward to rearrange a strand of holly berries and adjust the enormous, intricately knotted red velvet bow. "Oh, it's in there. I loved your color scheme—you did a nice job of that. It just needed a bit of . . . zhushing."

"Zhushing?"

He nodded. "It's a technical term designers use that means 'adding to' or 'expanding.' In layman's terms, it's taking something skimpy and inelegant and re-creating it as something a client might actually be proud to have in her home. Or to hang on her front door."

I probably should have been offended, but he was annoyingly right. Compared to this elegant and gorgeous confection, mine had been a puny impostor. Even Jack had had a difficult time coming up with a convincing compliment. Nola had just called it sad.

I peered closely at it. "So my wreath is somewhere underneath all this . . . zhushing?"

He nodded. "Yes. Somewhere very deep." He turned around to indicate the glass hurricane lamps that lined the perimeter of the piazza. "And I switched out your luminaries. I didn't think paper bags were the best look, and the fake candles inside looked, well, fake. I found these electric candles that not only appear real but aren't nearly as tacky as some of those less expensive ones."

I started to protest, but he held out his hands. "My treat. Your mother and mother-in-law are being so generous with the redo of Nola's room that I felt I needed to up my game a bit. I hope you don't mind."

I looked at the hurricane lamps, each one spotless and sporting an ivory candle in a brass candlestick. It was impossible to tell the candles weren't real. "Do the flames flicker like actual candles?"

Greco looked offended. "Of course. They're also on timers so that they turn on at dusk and turn off at sunrise. The best part is that Dr. Wallen-Arasi approves. She says they look like the sort of lighting they had during Colonial times, so they will be appropriate for the progressive dinner—and safer than real flames. She actually likes them so much that she wants more to be placed throughout the entire house so there won't be a need for more obviously electric lights the night of the dinner."

"Great," I said, picturing diners stumbling around my house in the near dark, the spirits rousing due to the lack of bright lights to deter them. I looked up at him. "Did you say Dr. Wallen-Arasi? Did you see her?"

"She's inside. She arrived about twenty minutes ago and I let her in. I hope you don't mind. She didn't see the replacement window brochures on the hall table, if that's what you're worried about. Although I'm not sure I shouldn't have mentioned them to her, since everyone knows repairing your historic windows is much more economical in the long run."

"Thanks, Greco. And if you'd like to pay for the repairs, I'll ask Nola to start one of those GoFundMe accounts and let you know."

He picked up two shopping bags from Hyams Garden and Accent Store, several boughs of fresh pine poking out of the tops. "I'm going home to make potpourri with these, and I'll bring it tomorrow inside some of my vintage silver pomander balls—all very kosher, as I explained to Dr. Wallen-Arasi. Nothing on the inside or outside of my potpourri isn't authentic to the Colonial period."

"That's a relief." I pretended to wipe sweat off my brow. I was fairly certain that Greco knew about my lukewarm feelings toward authenticity when it came to the bottom line. I was all about the bottom line and convenience. I think he appreciated this and might even have been enjoying his role as referee between Sophie and me. "Did they even have potpourri back in the day? I thought that was more of a modern invention by stores like Abercrombie & Fitch to get people to come inside."

He stared at me for a long moment, and I wondered if his eyes looked funny because he was trying very hard not to roll them. "No, actually. Potpourri has been around since early civilizations. I think its usage correlates to the level of hygiene practiced by humans of the time period. In Colonial days, with no running water and certainly very rarely heated, people didn't bathe much, especially in the winter. Try to imagine body odor on top of that of wet wool, and you can perhaps come close to what it must have smelled like in the average home. Hence potpourri."

It was my turn to stare at him. "I didn't know that, and I might even have been happy continuing in my ignorance, but thank you."

"You're welcome." He twisted a blue cashmere scarf around his neck. "By the way, that word that was scratched into the wall that I sanded out is back again. I wanted to let you know that I'm aware of it, and I'm on it." He smiled, touched his forehead in a mock salute, then walked toward the piazza door.

"Thank you," I said to his retreating back, amazed that he was more concerned about concealing the word than why it was there or what it might mean.

I glanced at my watch, then hurried through the front door, letting it slam behind me. I had quickly taken off my coat and hung it up, buttoning every single button because that's the way it should be done, when I turned around and nearly ran into Jayne.

"Sorry!" I said. "I was running a bit late and then stopped to chat with Greco outside. But I'm here, so you can leave now. Twins good today?" I thrust my hand into the closet and grabbed her coat, having to unbutton only the top button.

"Little angels, as usual. That Sarah is running all over the place and babbling up a storm. JJ prefers to be carried everywhere and to build stuff with whatever he can find. Hard to believe they're related, except they both look like Jack."

"Hard to believe," I repeated, placing my hand on her shoulder and gently propelling her to the door.

"They're catnapping in their cribs, so they should be good for another thirty minutes or so." She looked at my hand on her shoulder, then into my eyes. "Why are you so eager to get rid of me?"

I looked past her toward the small carriage clock on the table in the foyer and walked a little faster. "I'm not trying to get rid of you, but didn't you say you had to leave a little earlier today? That's why I rushed back."

She stopped. "It's not an emergency or anything, Melanie. I'm just going to see Anthony in the hospital."

I paused with my hand on the doorknob. "He's in the hospital?"

"Yeah—they're not sure what's wrong with him. It's some kind of virus, they think, but they can't figure it out. He can't keep down any food or liquid, so he's hooked up to an IV."

I met her concerned gaze. "And he's been that way since we were all in the cemetery?"

She nodded. "I think he's . . . susceptible to evil spirits. Remember his car accident?"

"But I thought Marc had done something to his car."

"Could be, but he did tell Thomas he saw someone or something in his backseat right before the accident, and then he was pushed down the stairs when he was alone in the house, and now this. I can't imagine how Marc could cause Anthony to be this sick. I'm thinking the negative presence we keep sensing is having an effect on Anthony because he's trying to dig for answers that whatever it is doesn't want him to find." She took a deep breath. "I'm going to tell Anthony he should move into my house when they stabilize him enough to release him from the hospital. It's a big house, and I'll be there to make sure nothing happens to him. And he'll be away from the cemetery."

"You want him to move in with you?"

"No, not like that. It's to protect him, and only until he's one hundred percent better."

I peered closely at her. "Was this your idea or his?"

Her gaze slid to the space behind me. "It was sort of both of ours." She paused. "Although he may have mentioned it first. I think he's scared. And this way, someone will be home to work on the puzzle all day long. We've only got about one-quarter of it done. There are way too many bricks with nearly identical patterns, with only tiny swirls or lines to make them unique. I'm beginning to wonder if there's an intentional design at all."

I'd had the same doubt but had been keeping my thoughts to myself. It was as if I really believed that if I didn't say anything out loud, it couldn't be true. Instead, I said, "I don't think Thomas is going to like this very much."

Jayne pressed her lips together. "I don't think he has any say in the matter."

The carriage clock chimed, and I yanked open the front door. "I don't want to keep you—tell Anthony I said hello and call me later and let me know how he's doing." I closed the door, then waited until I could hear her retreating footsteps.

I raced to the dining room window and peered out, looking for my mother on the sidewalk. When I didn't spot her, I ran up the stairs, taking them two at a time, and hurried into Nola's room.

Sophie looked up from where she knelt in front of the jewelry cabinet. "Is there a fire I should know about?"

"No, sorry. Jayne just left and my mother's not here yet, so I only have a few minutes to come see Nola's room."

She looked confused. "I have no idea how those three things are supposed to be related to each other."

I sighed. "My mother and I are supposed to take JJ and Sarah to Hampton Park this afternoon. The weather's so nice. . . ." I paused, wondering at the expression on her face.

"And you didn't want Jayne to go with you?"

I closed my mouth, realizing that, yes, not wanting Jayne to accompany us had been the reason I'd been rushing around, making sure she was out of the house before our mother arrived. I swallowed. "Maybe."

"Don't be ashamed to admit it, Melanie. It's understandable. You've only recently rediscovered your mother and built a strong relationship. You never thought you'd have to share her, and now you do. And nobody asked you first."

It felt as if a bowling ball had been lifted from my chest. I took two deep breaths, enjoying the new sensation of lightness. "I hadn't really put it into words, but, yes. You're right. And this afternoon I just wanted it to be my mother and me. Not because I don't like Jayne or don't want us all to have a good relationship; it's just that I wanted some alone time with my mother and the twins. Is that so wrong?"

Sophie shook her head. "Of course not. And admitting to yourself what you need is the first step toward building stronger relationships with others."

"Thanks," I said. "I appreciate you telling me things I need to hear. Most people don't have the nerve." My gaze took in her crazy green-streaked hair, her 1980s Benetton sweater with enormous shoulder pads, the same mom jeans she'd worn to the wreath-making workshop, and her Birkenstocks. "So, despite your questionable style sense, you still qualify as my best friend."

"Ditto," she said, using the bedpost to help her stand. "And remind me to pick up some chakra stones for you. You seem stressed."

"Gee, really? I can't imagine why." I walked toward the bed, recognizing the rectangular piece of wood Meghan Black had found in the cistern; it was still resting in a nest of newspaper. "I guess this has something to do with why you're here? Besides dispensing advice, that is."

She grimaced. "And deflecting nosy reporters, too, apparently. That Suzy Dorf was here looking for you. Seems she went to your office but was told you weren't there, either."

"Good to know that Jolly at the front desk is doing her job. What did you tell her?"

"That you weren't here and I had no idea when you'd be back. She did have one question for me, though."

I raised my eyebrows.

"She wanted to know why we're friends. I told her I have no idea."

I gave her a half grin. "Me, neither."

"You know, Melanie, you should probably speak with her. Find out what she knows about the French king's gift. Because it's only a matter of time before she finds out everything we've discovered so far and tells Rebecca. Then Marc will swoop in for the kill like a palmetto bug on a bread crumb."

I sighed. The last thing I wanted to do was speak with the inquisitive and diminutive Suzy Dorf. But Sophie was right. As usual. "Fine. I'll reach out to her tomorrow." I indicated the piece of wood. "So, did you find out anything?"

"Yes and no." She walked over to the jewelry chest, the drawers and lid all open. "I'm pretty sure I know where that small secret door is from." Putting down the newspaper, she removed the top drawer of the chest and placed it on the floor before flipping on her iPhone flashlight and beaming it inside. "Look on the right-hand side here—there's still a broken hinge clinging to the wood of a small cavity, and the size of it matches the holes in the piece Meghan found. When I held up the piece of wood, it was an exact fit." She looked at me, and our gazes locked. "It appears it was ripped off its hinges. It's not lockable, so there'd be no reason to rip it off to get to the contents of the narrow cavity."

"Unless someone was in a big hurry."

Sophie nodded.

"But the cavity is empty?"

"Yep." She picked up the drawer and placed it back inside the jewelry chest. Facing me again, she said, "Do you remember where the chest came from? Is it possible it came from the Vanderhorst plantation?"

"It came from the attic—it's full of Vanderhorst furniture. It's like a time machine up there. I don't think the family ever threw away anything." I remembered the peacock Greco had shown me on the bed, and the story of how everything made on the plantation had been marked with the peacock icon. I indicated the claw-foot at the bottom of the bedpost. "Does the peacock carving match the one on the little door?"

"Yep. But that only means that they were both made at Gallen Hall, and most likely used as furnishings there before being moved here. This house isn't as old as Gallen Hall, and the carpenters and craftsmen would have been making the furniture for that house first." She gently kicked at something on the floor. "Any idea why there are so many dead bees in here?"

I stepped closer to get a better look, the sole of my shoe crunching something beneath it. I looked down and saw a cluster of dead bees, their wings and legs frozen in eternal flight. "They were here last night. Swarming around this bedpost but nowhere else. The windows were closed, and it's been too cool for the bees to be out of their hives anyway."

She tapped her chin. "I'm sure there was something hidden in that jewelry chest. I'm not certain how that little door ended up in the cistern, but it was probably considered garbage after it was broken off and discarded. That's how most things end up in a cistern. Now, it's anybody's guess as to where whatever that chest was hiding might be now, but if this bedpost has the same carving, and they're both made in the same period style and wood, meaning it's *possible* they were created to be in the same room, and there were bees buzzing around this post last night, inside, in the dead of winter, I'd bet here would be a good place to start."

Being careful not to step on any of the bees, she leaned over and knocked on the post in several places, her expression not changing. "Pretty solid." Without a word, she slid out of her Birkenstocks and climbed on top of the bed, moving aside a lilac drapery panel with her foot. Standing on her tiptoes, she reached toward the pineapple finial at the top of the post and lifted it off. "These finials are removable on all antique four-poster beds so the canopy can be attached in the winter for warmer bed hangings." Smiling down at me, she stuck her fingers into the opening and swished them around. "Nothing," she said, frowning. "I'd be lying if I said I wasn't disappointed. Were the bees only around this post?"

"Yes—definitely. The finial was as big as a basketball, there were so many bees."

"Hmm." She stuck her fingers inside the bedpost one more time before replacing the finial, then gingerly stepped around the mattress to check the other three. With a grunt of defeat, she lowered herself to the floor. "Sorry, Melanie. I don't know what to tell you. I could have sworn that small door cover would lead us somewhere."

"Me, too. Thanks, anyway, for trying."

She began wrapping the piece of wood in the newspaper. "Let me know what the reporter says, okay? Or if you would like help replacing all the plastic fruit on the stairway garland."

I was saved from responding by the appearance of my mother, looking beautiful and elegant and not nearly old enough to be my mother. "Sorry to barge in, but the door was open, so I just walked right in. You know, Mellie, it's not a good idea to leave the door open."

"I didn't." I met her gaze, then waited for her and Sophie to greet each other. "Are you ready to go? I just need to get the children up from their naps and put their sweaters on."

She wasn't listening, her eyes focused on the bed behind me. "There's something . . ." She stopped, shook her head. "There's something here we can't see. I'm being drawn to this bedpost for some reason." Looking down on the floor, she spotted the pile of bee carcasses. "Oh."

"Exactly," I said.

"They were swarming around the bedpost last night," Sophie explained. "I've already looked inside the top of each post and knocked on the rest to see how solid they are, and found nothing."

"And," I added, "Eliza was here last night. Briefly."

Our eyes met. "Did she say anything?"

I hesitated a moment. "'Lies.' She's said that before."

My mother stepped closer to the bed, then held her gloved finger to her lips before pressing her ear up against the wood of the bedpost. "I hear something. Someone. A woman." She pressed her ear against the bedpost again and closed her eyes. "It's too garbled. I can't hear her clearly." She began to peel off her gloves, finger by finger.

I moved forward to grab her arm, to stop her, but she'd already wrapped her hand around the post. Her body went rigid and her face contorted as if in pain, before her chin dipped to her chest and I couldn't see her face anymore.

"Mother . . ."

Her head jerked back and for a moment I didn't recognize the mottled face that glared at me now, with bulging eyes and bloody skin. The voice that erupted from my mother's small body made Sophie and me step back as if we'd been struck, but neither of us could look away.

Traitors deserve to die and rot in hell!

The putrid stench of rotting flesh leached in through the floor and plaster walls, and my stomach roiled, but I couldn't leave, no matter how much I wanted to. "Mother!" I screamed, reaching for her hand and peeling her bare fingers off the bedpost, feeling what seemed like an electric current pulse against her skin.

Her eyes widened as she looked into my face, her expression of confusion softening slightly as she seemed to recognize me. "It's me, Mother. It's Mellie."

She nodded, letting me know she heard me. I held on tightly to her arms as her body relaxed and I led her to the bed. Just before we reached the edge, her eyes jerked wide, and, as clear as air, my grandmother's voice shouted from my mother's mouth. *Jack.*

CHAPTER 25

The following morning, I stepped around the small frosted Christmas tree in the middle of the lobby at Henderson House Realty and stopped at the tinsel-bedecked receptionist's desk, surprised to find it empty. "Jolly? Jolly Thompson? Are you here?"

"Right here," called a voice from beneath the desk. "I'll be right with you."

I moved around to the back of the desk and spotted our receptionist wearing yoga pants and a bright blue tunic, sitting cross-legged in the knee well. Her eyes were closed, allowing me to admire her turquoise eye shadow and sparkly mascara. "What are you doing?"

Her eyes snapped open. "Hang on." She rolled over onto her hands and knees and crawled out from under her desk. She reached out her hands and I helped her to stand. She shook her head as if to clear it. "Sorry—just trying to do more homework for my online psychic class. It's about channeling, so I was giving it a try."

"Any luck?" I asked.

"Not yet. I'm not really surprised, though. I think my strength is intuition. And touch." She rubbed her hands together. "Like right now, I felt nothing when you pulled me up. There was no tingle or anything, which just confirms my suspicions that you have no psychic powers whatsoever."

"Really?" I said. "How interesting." Her psychic statements were more miss than hit, so I tried not to encourage her, despite the fact that a few times she'd come eerily close to hitting the nail on the proverbial head. I peered at the top of her desk. "Any messages? Cancellations?"

I was hoping that Veronica would call and cancel our morning appointment. I'd told her I would help her buy time, but I knew that sooner or later I'd need to confront the ghost of her sister and find out what was keeping her here. I just couldn't manage adding one more thing to my overflowing plate without my head exploding.

Jolly leaned over her desk, her dragonfly earrings temporarily replaced for the season with light-up Christmas bulbs. "You have two new appointments for showings—both with out-of-towners—and Veronica Farrell called to confirm an appointment at nine o'clock regarding a new listing. And . . ." She drew out the word slowly for dramatic effect. "That Suzy Dorf stopped by yesterday while you were at a house showing and then called twice after you left for the day. I don't know how much longer I can hold her off. She has a hard time taking no for an answer."

I recalled what Sophie had said, how I needed to speak to Suzy and find out exactly what she knew. I blew out a heavy sigh. "Fine. Send me the call next time. Maybe that will make her stop pestering us."

"Only if you're sure," Jolly said, her disappointment at my apparent caving showing on her face. She was enjoying being my gatekeeper maybe just a little too much.

"I'm sure."

She picked up one of her never-ending lists—she made lists for everything, which was one of the reasons we got along so well—and crossed something off. "Well, then, here you go." She handed me the messages. "Oh, and one more." She reached for a pink memo pad and tore off the top note. "Your mother called. She said instead of the park at noon, to meet her and the children at Belmond Place to see the Christmas tree and the toy train in the lobby. The weather has turned a bit nasty for a walk in the park."

I nodded, recalling my mother's collapse the previous afternoon and the aborted trip to the park. "Did she mention if Jayne would be joining us?"

"No, she didn't." Jolly lowered her chin, looking at me over the top of her glasses. "Does that make a difference?"

I waved a hand in dismissal. "Of course not. She's my sister."

"Um-hm," Jolly said, looking like someone who knew way more than she should and probably attributed it to her "psychic powers." I wondered for a moment if I might be mentally broadcasting my mixed feelings about Jayne, and made a note to think only about babies and puppies while in Jolly's presence.

I forced a smile, eyeing the coffee and doughnut on the credenza behind her; they were almost hidden behind a giant Santa Claus that would say, *Ho, ho, ho* and ring his bell if a person clapped. She saw where I was looking and blocked my view of the doughnut. "I'll be in my office," I said. "Let me know when the Farrells get here."

"Will do."

I began to walk toward my office but stopped when Jolly called me back. I turned around. "Yes?"

"When that adorable husband of yours stopped by yesterday to drop off your glasses, I saw that man again standing behind him."

"That man?"

"Yes, remember? A while back, I told you both I'd seen a dark-haired man holding a piece of jewelry standing behind Jack. But then I said he had a mustache, and now I'm not so sure. I think he just has a dark shadow like he hasn't shaved in a few days."

"Yes, of course." I did remember, mostly because Meghan Black had managed to capture a photo on her phone of a man standing by the cistern and matching the same description. "Tell me again what he looked like?" I asked, hoping she'd say something completely different this time.

She closed her eyes. "Well, like I said, he had dark hair, which I could see because he wasn't wearing a hat. And his clothes were old-fashioned, with those short pants men used to wear that ended at the knees." Her eyes popped open. "He was holding something, too. I think the first time I saw him, I thought it was a bracelet, but this time I saw it wasn't a bracelet at all."

"So what was it?" I pressed.

"Some kind of a bird, I think. With four really big jewels, which was why I thought it was a bracelet at first. But this time I could tell it wasn't. Maybe a pendant?"

"Or a brooch?" My voice cracked.

"Yes! I think that's it." She nodded to emphasize her realization. "And whoever it was must have come from wherever Jack had just been, because he followed Jack out when he left."

I didn't mention that Jack had been at home working, or that I knew where the spirit had come from. Nor did I mention that I had no idea why.

"Did you tell Jack about the apparition?"

"Of course." Jolly chewed on her bottom lip. "Especially because there were some definite unfriendly vibes coming from the man. And when I looked at his face, his eyes were just dark, hollow circles. So I thought Jack should know." Her expression was sympathetic. "I will admit that Jack seemed a little startled—not everyone expects to hear that they're being shadowed by an evil spirit."

I realized my jaw was nearly numb from clenching my teeth. I almost didn't recognize the sound of my own voice when the words finally tumbled out. "Did the spirit . . . say anything?"

Jolly's bright green eyes stared straight into mine. "Ghosts don't talk, dear. You've been watching too many reruns of *Ghost Whisperer*." She leaned forward, Christmas bulb earrings swinging. "It's more of a . . . mental connection with the spirit. And let me tell you, this was an angry spirit and I was pretty sure I didn't want to hear what he was saying. Except . . ."

"Except?" I prompted.

"Except I felt something beneath his anger. Something that felt a lot like . . . heartbreak. Not just a broken heart, but a *seared* heart. Like he was a man who'd been horribly betrayed by someone he'd deeply loved. So I decided to listen to what he was trying to communicate to me."

The phone rang, startling us both. "One moment," she said as she answered the phone, then placed the call on hold.

"And?" I asked impatiently.

She pressed her lips together. "I don't usually use this kind of language. . . ."

"Just tell me, please."

"I was pretty sure he was trying to say, 'Traitors deserve to die and rot in hell.'"

Icy fear dripped down my spine as I recalled the same words in my own head at the mausoleum, and then coming from my mother's mouth in Nola's bedroom. I swallowed. "Was that all?"

She paused, then shook her head. "No. There was a name, too. But I got the impression that he was thinking it was Jack's name, except it wasn't."

"What was the name?"

Jolly's green eyes widened. "I'm pretty sure it was Alexander."

There was only one Alexander I knew. Alexander Monroe. The name on one of the crypts in the mausoleum. The British soldier billeted at Gallen Hall during the occupation of Charleston.

"Hmm," I said, pretending that the name didn't mean anything. "Very interesting. And you told all this to Jack?"

"Yes, of course. I assumed he would mention it to you, although he did say you were under a lot of stress right now with the holidays and the film crew in your house and getting ready for the progressive dinner. Jack said you're hosting twenty-four couples for the main course? And all on top of you having two little ones and a teenager and a full-time job. I'm exhausted just thinking about it." She gave me a sympathetic smile. "That Jack is such a wonderful husband—so compassionate and caring. That's probably why he didn't bring it up. It's not an emergency or anything. I mean, it's not like ghosts can hurt you, right?"

I stared at her for a moment without comment. "Right," I said noncommittally. "Well, thanks for letting me know. And for these." I held up the pink message slips. Walking back to my office, I was left to wonder why Jack hadn't mentioned any of it to me. As I closed my office door, I felt a small surge of anger. It might be petty, but feeling left out was the one thing I couldn't live with and that always made me revert to the old Mellie. Even with that knowledge, the hurt didn't dissipate, making me decide that when Jack was ready to share what Jolly had just told me, I'd tell him about the bees in Nola's bedroom and what had happened when my mother touched the bedpost.

I hung up my coat on the coatrack, buttoning it up to the collar and checking the pockets even though I'd just checked them before I'd left the house. It was an old habit, started when I was a young girl taking care of my alcoholic father, checking his pockets for flasks or small bottles so I could destroy them before he remembered where they were. It was the kind of old habit that was difficult to break. Along with drawer labeling so my father didn't have to struggle in the morning picking between black and navy socks.

When Jack laughed at some of my quirks, I sometimes had the urge to explain why I did these things. But then I'd have to explain to him why I still did, even after all these years of my father being sober. If only I knew the answer, then maybe I could stop.

I moved to the Keurig machine—a birthday gift from Jack—on my credenza and was selecting which flavored coffee I wanted from the rack of alphabetized K-Cups when a flash of red caught my attention. Keeping my body still, I shifted my gaze toward my desk and froze. The heart-shaped red pillow that I'd taken from Veronica's attic sat on my chair, propped up so I couldn't help but notice it.

Putting down my coffee mug, I walked over and picked up the pillow, thinking—hoping—it was a different one. But because of how things worked in my neck of the woods, I knew hoping was a lot like planning on putting out a forest fire with a single puff of breath. I studied the pillow, noticing the neat hand-stitched seams along the ruffled edge, the nubby red material that appeared as new and vibrant as it probably had thirty years before. I brought it to my face and sniffed, recognizing the faint scent of Vanilla Musk perfume.

I pressed the intercom button on my desk phone and waited for Jolly to pick up. "Jolly, has anyone been in my office since I left it yesterday?"

"No, Melanie. Just the cleaning people. Why? Is something missing?" I stared at the small pillow still clutched in my hand. "No, actually. It's—"

"The Farrells are here. I'm sending them back now."

"Thanks—" I started, but she'd already hung up, the sound of dead space quickly replaced with that of tapping on my office door. "Come in."

Michael opened the door and stepped back to allow Veronica to enter first, his hand solicitous on the small of her back. Veronica startled when she saw what I held in my hands, her eyes questioning. When Michael noticed it, too, I saw him do a double take, but otherwise he gave no sign that he recognized it.

I indicated the chairs in front of my desk. "Please, have a seat." Not knowing where else I could put the pillow, I tossed it on the seat of my chair, then sat on it, hoping I wasn't offending anyone. "Sorry," I said in explanation. "Bad back."

They both stared at me, expressionless. To break the awkward silence, I offered them both coffee, and when they declined I pulled out a brand-new yellow lined notepad from my top desk drawer. I had a laptop, a desktop, and an iPad, but nothing could beat plain paper and pencil. And whatever I wrote never disappeared into a cloud, or whatever that thing was where Nola continued to tell me I should be storing documents.

"So," I said, getting ready for my sales pitch. "I'm glad that my friendship with Veronica has brought you in today, but I also hope that you've done some research into my sales record to know that I'm the best agent to list your historic home."

"Of course," Michael said, uncrossing his legs and leaning forward with his arms on his thighs—what my boss, Dave Henderson, called the "power stance," meaning a client was ready to sign on the dotted line. Except I hadn't gotten that far yet. "So can we dispense with the chitchat and get the house on the market today?"

I placed my perfectly sharpened number two pencil on the pad and looked up at Veronica, who was staring at her lap. "Today?"

"Yes," Michael said. "I see no reason for delay. We think it will move fast, so we'd also like to look at options for a good family home to move into. We'll include Lindsey in the decision, of course, but it will be mostly Veronica's choice."

He put his hand on her arm, but she was now looking directly at me.

"I see." I picked up my pencil again. "So, let's start with that so I can begin thinking about available houses. Veronica, what would you like to see in a new house?"

Michael spoke before Veronica could open her mouth. "We're flexible on location—Mt. Pleasant and James Island are possibilities. Probably not downtown or South of Broad because we definitely want something more modern than what we have now." He smiled at his wife, oblivious to the fact that she was neither smiling nor nodding but sitting stoically and staring into space.

He continued. "We're both tired of the maintenance and upkeep on an older home. And with Lindsey going to college soon, we'd like to spend our downtime traveling and doing things together instead of spending all that time and money repairing things on the house." He pointed at the pad of paper. "Aren't you going to write that down?"

I looked up at Veronica to gauge her reaction, but she'd returned her gaze to her lap. I replaced the pencil on the pad with a decisive snap. "Look, why don't we work on this part later? I've already got about a dozen homes in mind—we'll narrow it down by location later. Right now, I think we should visit your house on Queen Street and make a list of things that might need to be changed or updated before putting it on the market, so you can get top dollar."

"Oh, please," Michael said. "There could be a gaping hole in the roof with rain pouring in and someone would still want to buy it because it's historic and in Charleston."

"Well, while there is some truth in that, if the house needs expensive repairs or major updates, it will be reflected in the sale price. And if you're wanting to replace it with another house in Charleston, you'll want as much money from the sale as you can get."

Veronica finally spoke. "She's right, Michael. I don't want to skimp on the new house, since we'll be there for a very long time. We have to think of the future, of possibly having grandchildren and making sure there's room for them and yard space. It won't be cheap."

His face softened, as if the mention of the word *grandchildren* had given him a new perspective. Or maybe it had been the words "it won't be cheap." "I see what you're saying. But that doesn't mean we should be dragging our heels."

"Of course not," I said. "But we need to make sure that we take enough time to do it right, however long that takes. Try to think of it in terms of money—the more move-in ready your house, the higher the asking price."

When Michael smiled, I realized we were finally speaking the same language. "Fine," he said as he stood. "Then bring your pencil and paper and let's head home so we can get started. Hopefully, it won't take too long."

Michael was already walking toward the door and didn't notice Veronica's thumbs-up, which she gave me behind his back.

"Hopefully," I said, shoving the pad and pencil into my briefcase and retrieving my coat. "Just for good luck, let's all cross our fingers that there's nothing major that needs to be done on the house before we put it on the market."

Michael opened the door and held it for us, dramatically displaying his other hand to show his crossed fingers. "I got us covered."

Veronica exited in front of me, delivering a brief kiss to Michael's cheek and distracting him just long enough that he didn't notice the red pillow fly across the room and hit me in the back before falling to the floor.

Michael glanced behind me briefly as if the flash of color had caught his eye. Then he followed me out the door, pulling it shut with a soft snap.

CHAPTER 26

I took a pedicab from the Farrells' house on Queen Street to Charleston Place to meet my mother and the children because if I'd had to walk in my heels after exploring all three floors of the Farrells' Victorian, I would have had to self-amputate at the ankles.

I also had bruises on my rib cage and back from Veronica prodding me every time I said something was fine, and she'd continued poking me until I had ratcheted up the needed upgrade or repair to her satisfaction. By the time I left, my list was ten pages long, enough to keep the house off the market for at least a year unless Michael had his say. He certainly hadn't looked happy as he'd closed the front door, and I doubted he would go along with even half of the suggestions I'd made.

As I sat in the pedicab, I had the brilliant thought of calling Sophie and sending her over to Veronica's to make a few structural suggestions, along with dire warnings. She was a college professor and quite good at intimidation and wearing down those who disagreed with her regarding old-house restorations. Which was why I'd spent more money than I had ever thought possible on a new roof and foundation, along with hand-painted wallpaper and hand-sanded floors. All because I couldn't say no to Sophie, even though she dressed like a toddler who'd chosen her own clothes.

I plucked my phone from my purse just when it started to ring. There was no name next to the familiar telephone number because I was too optimistic in believing that I'd never have a need to add her name to my contact list. I slid my thumb across the screen, then held the phone to my ear. "Hello, Suzy. This is Melanie."

"I can't believe I'm actually speaking with you! You're a hard person to pin down."

"So sorry," I said, mimicking the bored tones I'd heard my coworker Wendy Wax using with one of her ex-husbands. "'Tis the season to lose one's mind, and all that."

"That's for sure." Suzy giggled, sounding like the twelve-year-old girl she resembled. "I understand you have a full house right now with a film crew, a decorator, and a classroom full of preservation students in your backyard. How *do* you do it all?"

"Is this an interview about my life? Because if it is, I can save us a lot of time up front and tell you now that I'm not interested."

She giggled again, setting my teeth on edge. "Oh, I'm sure your day-to-day life is fascinating, Melanie, but I'm calling about something else. Are you familiar with the series I'm writing in the *Post and Courier* about lost treasures in the Lowcountry? It's a weekly serial in the Sunday edition."

I was too embarrassed to admit that I only had time to pull the real estate section from the paper and that, despite promises to myself that I would read the rest and become a better-informed member of society, the rest of the paper would usually end up in the recycling bin unread. Jack usually read the whole thing cover to cover, but I'd noticed recently he'd been too immersed in puzzle solving and going over the research materials that Yvonne would send over on an almost daily schedule to find the time to read the paper.

"I think our neighbor's dog has been taking our Sunday paper, because we haven't received it for several weeks now. Her name is Cindy Lou Who, and she's just the sweetest dog, but she does love a juicy newspaper."

I prepared myself for another giggle, and when I didn't hear one, I pulled my phone from my ear to make sure the call hadn't been dropped.

"You know, Melanie, journalists and editors work very hard on the newspaper. We would all appreciate a little respect."

"Sorry. I didn't mean that Cindy Lou Who was chewing on it, Suzy. I was thinking she was probably taking it to read. She's a very smart dog." I wasn't sure why I said that, only that my feet were hurting and the woman annoyed me.

"Glad to know you have a sense of humor, Melanie. Rebecca says you're probably going to need it."

I sat up. "What do you mean?"

I could imagine the reporter shrugging her narrow shoulders. "You'll have to ask your cousin. Now, do you have a few moments to answer some questions?"

We were creeping down King Street, the traffic slower due to the heavy volume and the number of pedestrians doing their holiday shopping. "That would depend. About what?"

"Lost treasures. For my series."

"Right. I'm not sure if I have anything to add, unless you're referring to the cistern in the backyard. They've found lots of broken pottery, if that's what you're looking for. I'd suggest asking one of the grad students working on the excavation, named Meghan Black. . . ."

"I'm looking for something lost since the Revolution, something valuable given by the French king to the patriots, presumably to pay American spies."

I kept my voice even. "Well, we certainly haven't found anything valuable—"

"Yet," she broke in. "While doing research on buried pirate treasure along the coast, I came upon the story in the national archives of Barbados, if you can imagine, of a treasure given to the Marquis de Lafayette in 1781 by the king of France. You're probably wondering why Barbados—"

"No, actually, I'm not. Look, Suzy, I don't have any idea—"

She continued as if I hadn't spoken. "I was researching 'the Gentleman

Pirate,' Stede Bonnet, who was born in Barbados and hanged in Charleston—or Charles Towne, as it was known prior to the Revolution. That's why I was looking in the national archives of Barbados, and there it was—an obscure article about missing treasures that included Blackbeard, Bonnet, and"—she gave a dramatic pause—"the Marquis de Lafayette!"

She paused again, apparently waiting for applause. When I didn't respond, she continued. "Anyway, the article claimed that the marquis had been entrusted with delivering the French king's gift to an unnamed American who'd been charged with the task of enlisting influential citizens in Charleston as spies for the patriot cause. Whatever it was must have been easy to transport and quite valuable, as most of the influential citizens in South Carolina at the time were wealthy landowners, and to be caught planning against the Crown would mean certain death in addition to the confiscation of all your property and leaving your family destitute."

We passed a storefront window, a cute dress catching my attention, so I missed the first part of Suzy's next sentence, my focus snapping back when I recognized the name Vanderhorst. "I'm sorry—what did you say? About a Vanderhorst?"

A heavy sigh reverberated in my ear. "I said that I also went through and read old records regarding the detainees at the Provost Dungeon during the British occupation in the early seventeen eighties. The records included depositions of accused American spies prior to their executions. One of the men who was about to be hanged thought to save himself by naming names and mentioned Lawrence Vanderhorst of Gallen Hall Plantation. You can only imagine how excited I was to hear that and to know that I had an in with the owner of a Vanderhorst property."

I wanted to tell her she was delusional if she considered me an in but kept my thoughts to myself. They were too busy running back and forth over Lawrence's name, the name of the third occupant of the mausoleum at Gallen Hall. Not that I had any intention of mentioning that to Suzy Dorf.

"For the record," she said, "Lawrence was known as a staunch loyalist and had turned in American spies, so his reputation was pretty clean. He was never arrested, so the prisoner was either making something up to get a lighter sentence or he got the name wrong."

"Okay," I said slowly. "I'm not really sure why you're calling me about this. I'm not really into history." We were approaching the intersection of Market and King, where I'd be getting out of the pedicab. I hoisted my purse strap onto my shoulder in preparation, eager to end the call.

"That's not what Rebecca Longo told me."

I stilled. "What do you mean?"

I imagined I could see her satisfied smile at getting my attention. "She said that you and your sister and husband were working with her brother-in-law, Anthony Longo, on something involving Gallen Hall Plantation. You can probably guess how thrilled I was when I read that deposition that mentioned Lawrence Vanderhorst. The accuser claimed Lawrence was a member of an American spy ring. Which was quite a blow, I'm sure, since the Vanderhorsts were supposedly such staunch loyalists. They even quartered British officers in their home."

She paused, as if waiting for me to agree or claim knowledge or even surprise. But I remained silent. I wasn't sure whose side she was on, and I wasn't about to give anything away that might filter back to Marc through Rebecca.

"Anyway," Suzy continued, "the name of the spy ring has been lost to history, but one thing I was able to clarify was that members used the peacock as their symbol when communicating with one another. There are a few wax envelope seals embossed with a peacock still in existence in the Charleston Museum, but nothing to show who sent them, so members of the spy ring cannot be confirmed. But Lawrence's family owned the only plantation on the Ashley River with a large population of *peacocks*"—she emphasized the word—"and my journalist's brain would not let me think that's a coincidence."

"Of course it is," I said brightly. "The world is full of coincidences."

"Funny you should say that, Melanie. Because Rebecca told me that your husband's favorite thing to say is that there's no such thing."

I swallowed, hoping she couldn't hear it over the phone. "He may say something like that from time to time. Regardless, we haven't found anything valuable in our cistern, and I know next to nothing about the American Revolution, the marquis, or the king of France, so I think you should find someone else to interview if you want something juicy to print."

"But you know about Eliza Grosvenor."

I paused, considering my next words, knowing that pretending to be completely ignorant would confirm that I was evading the whole truth. "I know she was engaged to Lawrence Vanderhorst. But why would you think I should know more?"

She giggled, and my teeth ground together. "When I came to your office a couple of weeks ago to see if you were available, that handsome husband of yours was there with the children and had placed a stack of photocopied documents on the receptionist's desk while he prevented World War III from erupting in the double stroller. I couldn't help but notice the biography of Eliza Grosvenor, where someone had helpfully highlighted both Lawrence's name and the words *spy ring*. If that's the story your husband is working on now, I can't wait to read it."

Despite all the evil spirits and vengeful ghosts I'd faced in my life, nothing put more fear in my heart than hearing those words come from Suzy's mouth. As casually as I could, I asked, "Did you mention that to Rebecca?"

"No. Not yet, anyway. Would you not want me to?"

The pedicab took a right on Market Street and stopped in front of Charleston Place. I held up my finger to indicate I needed a minute. I closed my eyes, remembering Jack's face when he'd learned about Marc's subterfuge, and when Jack's book had been canceled and Marc's book on the same subject had been published to so much acclaim. I wasn't sure if either one of us could bear it for a second time. "No, Suzy. To be honest, I wouldn't want you to mention it to anyone, but especially not someone with the last name of Longo."

"I don't know, Melanie. That's a lot to ask a journalist who's trying to get answers."

"Hold on," I said, digging in my purse for money to pay the pedicab, thankful for the few moments it gave me to think. I was silent as I watched the pedicab leave, the phone pressed to my ear.

"Melanie? Are you there?"

"Yes. I'm here. What kind of answers are you looking for?"

"Oh, I don't know. Maybe exclusive access to whatever is going on in your backyard and how it connects to Gallen Hall. I know that the legendary treasure entrusted to Lafayette has some connection to the Vanderhorsts, and I want to be the first to know about it."

"But if there's no connection, and nothing to be found in the cistern or anywhere else?"

"Then I want to interview you. I want to witness you talking to the dead and I want to tell my readers. Or put it in a book. I've been working on one for a while, about interesting Charleston residents of the past and present, and I think you'd be a perfect fit. Anyway, I'd say access to you would be a fair trade for my not sharing any of this with Rebecca, don't you think?"

"Mama!"

I turned at the sound of the little voice, my heart softening when I spotted JJ and Sarah in their double stroller as my mother pushed them toward me on the sidewalk, two sets of chubby little hands reaching for me. "Look, I've got to go. Can we talk later?"

"Sure. Just don't wait too long. I've got deadlines, and I'll need to print something to keep my readers wanting the next installment."

I began walking toward my mother and the stroller, feeling a flash of anger at Suzy Dorf, this virtual stranger who could destroy everything I loved. "You're all heart, Suzy."

After a short pause, she said, "I'm just trying to do my job. For the record, I'm not a fan of Marc Longo, either. He ruined my brother, bankrupted him in a sour business deal. I know how he operates and I'd rather see you and your husband end up on top of this. But I've got newspapers to sell."

"I just need to think about it," I said as I reached the stroller, then bent down to look at my beautiful babies.

"You do that. And, Melanie?"

"Yes?"

"I wanted you to know that I saw Jack a couple of nights ago at the Gin Joint. He was by himself, and he only ordered ginger ale. But he kept looking at the menu again and again, asking the bartender lots of questions. And I don't think it was for book research. Just thought you should know."

Something that felt like a block of ice gripped my heart. "But he left without ordering anything, right?"

"Yeah. He did."

"Thanks, Suzy."

"You're welcome. Talk to you soon."

The call ended, and I immediately pressed my face against the soft cheeks of my children, smelling them and feeling their soft breath on my face. The overwhelming need to save Jack, to save our family, suddenly consumed me. I had to find the answers, even if I had to do it by myself.

"Are you all right, Mellie?" My mother's solicitous tone nearly brought tears to my eyes.

I straightened. "Let's go sit down in the lobby so we can chat and JJ and Sarah can see the train."

"Choo-choo," JJ screeched, waving his whisk in the air and making a young couple chuckle as they passed by us.

We headed into the beautiful lobby with the double staircase festooned with lush garlands, bows, and clusters of glass ornaments. Both children bounced up and down in their stroller as we neared the enormous display beneath the stairway, the fabricated snow-topped mountains surrounding an alpine village, the toy train chugging its way down the tracks and through a mountain tunnel. A row of poinsettias stood sentry before the magical scene and I could almost feel my blood pressure drop.

Even before I'd had children, I'd always thought the Christmas display at Charleston Place was magical, easily imagining that this miniature world of houses with actual lights, tiny people waving, and vehicles with open doors was real. Both JJ and Sarah were watching with wide eyes and open mouths, and I felt a little bit of the fear that had gripped me since my conversation with Suzy dissipate.

"Has something happened?" my mother asked.

I shrugged. "Yes and no. We're not getting anywhere with any of the information we've discovered—not with the mausoleum puzzle or the four words that Nola and Cooper have been working on every spare moment. Even the little drawer cover that Meghan found in the cistern turned up nothing. And Jack, well, he's understandably upset about what's going on with his publisher's plans for his book and very frustrated that he can't sink his teeth into this next book without a single clue to go on."

"Amelia mentioned something to that effect yesterday. Jack stopped by Trenholm Antiques to help his parents place all the new items from their recent European buying trip in the best spots in the store, and he said he had no opinion one way or another."

I raised my eyebrows. "This could be more serious than I thought." I'd meant it as a lighthearted comment but realized too late that it wasn't. The way Jack relaxed and de-stressed was to rearrange furniture and accessories. He had an excellent eye and always knew where the overlooked étagères belonged, or where to place the spare chinoiserie biscuit jar. He hadn't so much as dragged an ottoman across a room for weeks.

"There's more," I said. "Grandmother called me."

"Oh."

"Exactly. She only calls when there's trouble."

"I know. Did she say anything?"

I met her eyes and felt a sinking feeling when I recognized the fear and worry in them. I nodded. "She said Jack's name. Just like you did when you touched the bedpost in Nola's room. Right after you said, 'Traitors deserve to die and rot in hell.'"

She frowned. "I wish I could tell you why I said either thing, but I don't remember any of it." Softening her voice, she asked, "Is Jack drinking again?"

I leaned over the stroller handle to straighten the large red bow in Sarah's hair. "No. Not that I've seen, anyway. But Suzy Dorf said she saw him at the Gin Joint. He wasn't drinking, but I think it was pretty clear that he wanted to."

My mother straightened her shoulders, making her seem larger than her petite frame. "We need to tell your father. Jack is his sponsor, so it would make sense that he should be the one to confront him."

I shook my head. "No. Confrontation never works with Jack. We can definitely tell Dad; maybe he can just have conversations with him. But don't confront him. In the meantime, I'm trying to find some answers to this whole peacock–spy-ring thing. If I could just gift Jack with something concrete for this new story idea, he should be able to find a new publisher who will publish him the way he deserves."

"I'm not sure that will help, Mellie. Jack prides himself on being the smartest person in the room. His whole career has been built on digging up and figuring out buried mysteries of the past. Being that man feeds his confidence and his ego. I'm not sure if handing him answers on a platter will help."

I bristled. I'd always hated being told what to do, or that my thought processes might be wrong. Sophie said that was proof I was stubborn and too independent, a product of how I was raised. She also insisted they were bad characteristics I needed to shed. I wasn't completely sure I agreed with her, and being married had certainly taught me compromise. On some things. But not this. We were talking about Jack here, the man I loved almost to distraction. The man who, according to Rebecca, might be in serious danger. I had to do what I thought best.

"I can take care of this, Mother."

"Of course you can. But you shouldn't do it on your own. Your father, Jayne, and I are all here to help. You just need to ask."

I bristled again at the mention of Jayne's name. My mother must have noticed, because she placed her gloved hand on my sleeve. "Mellie, you do know that your sister is on your side, right? And that your father and I love you both equally. I realize her sudden appearance in our lives must have been a bit of a shock to you, but I think having a sister should be a good thing. I disliked the loneliness of being an only child. And Jayne is such a friendly and loving person. . . ."

I sent her a stony look and she stopped waxing poetic about my half sister.

She continued. "What I mean to say is that a little jealousy on your part is understandable. But you have so much in common and such potential to be close. I hope you recognize that and move forward accordingly. Remember, Mellie. We're stronger together."

Everything she said after the word *jealousy* evaporated quickly. "Me? Jealous?" The forced laugh sounded so odd that both children turned to look at me with apprehension on their little faces.

My mother regarded me with solemn eyes but didn't say anything.

I grabbed the stroller handle. "Let's go look at the Christmas tree. Maybe it will give me a few ideas on how to 'zhush' the trees in my house for the progressive dinner. They're looking kind of skimpy."

We walked in silence around the display toward the enormous tree, JJ fretting because we were leaving the choo-choo train behind, his frustration matching my own as the ability to identify and grasp the one thing I wanted evaded me.

"Mellie?" my mother said quietly.

I faced her. "Yes?"

"I know we didn't find anything in the bedpost. But there's something there. I felt it too strongly. Have you told Jack?"

I shook my head. "I didn't see a need since there was nothing there."

"I think you need to tell him. Maybe he can figure it out. Because there is definitely something there."

I nodded noncommittally, returning my focus to the Christmas tree and all the sparkling ornaments, pretending I couldn't sense my mother's stare of disapproval burrowing within me, where my conscience lay sleeping.

CHAPTER 27

I lay back on my pillow panting as Jack's bare arm pulled me against his similarly clad body. General Lee was burrowing somewhere in the room, having sought a quieter place to sleep earlier in the night. I'd forgotten the one form of relaxation and de-stressing that Jack enjoyed besides furniture arranging, and I was grateful that he'd remembered.

"Wow," he said, kissing my neck.

"I was about to say the same thing. I'm guessing that was enough aerobic exercise that I can skip my jog this morning, right?"

"Nice try." He gave my earlobe a nibble, sending shivers down my back. "It's almost six o'clock and time for my run. You could join me."

I turned my head and opened up one eye. "Are you trying to kill me?"

"Jayne said your stamina has really improved and you've increased your pace. You should be very proud of yourself. She says you're on track for the Bridge Run in April."

I turned away at the mention of Jayne's name, recalling my conversation with my mother. And Sophie. I wasn't saying that they were wrong, but I certainly wasn't agreeing that they were right. My feelings about Jayne were far more complicated than what they were implying, and something I needed to figure out on my own without everyone offering advice. "I'm thinking about taking up yoga instead."

Jack's chest rumbled against my back as he chuckled. "You tried that with Sophie, remember? Before the twins were born. You said every time you closed your eyes and tried to open your mind, some lost spirit would wander in."

"Yeah, well, at least it doesn't hurt my knees. I think I'm too old to run. Yoga's more my speed. Or maybe I'll try Pilates. I don't think that involves any meditation."

He was kissing my neck again, and I felt my brain slowly melting. "Pilates sounds good. It could make you even more flexible." The way he said the word *flexible* made it sound dirty.

I rolled in his arms to face him, placing my palms against his cheeks and enjoying the warm scratchiness of his beard. "I'm so glad you're feeling better."

He pulled away slightly, his eyes darkening. "Better? I wasn't aware that I was feeling poorly."

Too late, I realized my mistake. "I meant, I know how upset you've been with the whole publishing nightmare and Marc Longo bribing us to agree to film in our house, and the rest of it. You've been really down lately, but you don't seem to be in such a dark place this morning."

He let go of me and lay on his back, his arms folded beneath his head. "Dark place? Have you been watching *Star Wars* with Nola and Cooper?"

I could tell he was trying to dismiss my worry, but I was a mother now, my worry not easily waved away. "You've just been a bit down, that's all. And with your history . . ."

"As a drunk?"

I leaned up on my elbow so I could look him in the face. "That's not what I was going to say. You're a recovering alcoholic, and I know from my dad that it will be something you will need to confront every day for the rest of your life. But I'm here, Jack. If you feel the need to talk with someone . . ."

Before I was even aware of him moving, he'd flipped me over on my back, his frame pressing me into the mattress, his blue eyes staring into mine, and I was reminded again of his powers of persuasion and how he knew just what it took to distract me.

"I find you irresistible when you're trying to be serious."

"But I am serious," I said, trying not to focus on the heat of his bare skin against mine, or how I knew it was all intentional. "I'm worried that all this pressure is affecting you. . . ."

He nibbled on my neck, moving up to my earlobe with small kisses. "There's only one thing affecting me right now, Mellie, and that's you, naked, in my bed. I don't think I'll ever get tired of this."

I struggled to remain coherent. "Jack, please. Listen to me. Maybe you and I should go away for a long weekend—to Palmetto Bluff, maybe. To get away from everything."

He didn't lift his head as he continued his attention on every nerve ending in my neck. "We can't afford to get away, remember?"

I focused on my breathing, wondering if I should try to use the Lamaze techniques I hadn't had a chance to put into practice when the twins were almost born in the backseat of a minivan.

"Just promise me one thing, Mellie."

"Mmm?" I mumbled, unable to articulate a coherent word.

"Please don't think you need to solve all of our problems, all right? When you get it into your head that you and you alone can fix everything, your tendency is to react rashly and independently, and that never turns out well."

"But . . ." My words of protest were quickly forgotten as he moved his lips against mine, neatly erasing all thought and worry.

My blissful and oblivious satiation lasted until an hour later, when I was awakened from a deep sleep by the sound of Jack sitting down on the edge of the bed and lacing up his running shoes before closing the door gently behind him. The last thought I had before I fell back asleep was that he hadn't kissed me good-bye.

"You might find this easier with your glasses on," Anthony suggested.

I glanced up at him over the top of Jayne's dining room table. Despite having been in the hospital for almost a week and not being able to eat any solid food, he looked surprisingly robust. His coloring seemed healthy and his hair was thick and shiny, the crutches and arm sling gone. Maybe it was a male thing. I remembered what I'd looked like following my hospital stay after giving birth, when I resembled an extra from *The Walking Dead* instead of a youngish new mother. I would have hated him if he hadn't been so affable.

I sighed, then reached inside my purse under my chair for my glasses. "I'm just not in the habit of wearing them."

Anthony nodded sympathetically. "So they're new?"

I considered lying, then changed my mind. It was stupid, really. "No. I've had them for a couple of years. I just haven't gotten in the habit of wearing them."

He smiled. "Well, for the record, I think you look just as beautiful with them on as you do without them. Just in case you were wondering. And you don't look like Jayne's older sister at all—more like her twin. But I suppose with a mother like Ginette Prioleau, it's in the genes."

There it was again, that little pang in my gut at the mention of Jayne. We'd just had a lovely tea party with the twins in the garden, taking turns pushing JJ and Sarah in the new double swing. I'd enjoyed being with her and loved the relationship my sister had with my children. It was clear she loved them, and the sentiment was returned twofold. But the ball of resentment lodged in my stomach wouldn't budge. Obviously, I was the worst person in the world.

I forced myself to smile. "If I didn't know any better, Anthony, I could swear you were buttering me up for something."

"Ha—got me," he said, standing up with one of the brick pictures and bringing it to my side of the table. "I want you to say nice things about me to your sister."

"I do that anyway."

He met my eyes for a moment. "Yeah, well, Jayne and I are just friends. I'm hoping we can move beyond the friend zone."

"Ah. Have you mentioned this to her?" I picked up a photograph and leaned over the table, holding it next to other photos to see if it matched.

"No. I can be pretty shy around women." A slight blush tinged his cheeks. "Marc was always the one who got the girls when we were growing up. Or maybe he just bullied me enough that I wouldn't go after the girls he wanted. And if I had a girlfriend he found interesting, he usually ended up dating her."

"Sounds like a wonderful big brother."

"You think? He certainly had the potential. He's always had the kind of personality that makes people do what he tells them to."

There was an odd note in his voice, one that I was beginning to recognize in my own when I talked about Jayne. Something that could be either love or hate. Something unexplainable. "Even now?"

He was silent for a moment, his eyes unable to meet mine. "Well, we don't speak anymore, remember? It's easier without him in my life."

"I'm sorry," I said, meaning it. Despite all my weirdness where Jayne was concerned, I couldn't imagine my life without her now.

He waved his hand dismissively. "Nah—don't be. Maybe when we're old men we'll reconcile enough to be chess partners in the same nursing home. Who knows?"

Before I could say anything else, he yelled, "Bingo! Got one." He slid one of the photos up next to another three, making it a perfect match on the top, bottom, and one side.

"Thank goodness. At this rate we'll be lucky to be done by the time we're all ready for the nursing home."

"So it's a good thing I'm living here for a bit while I recuperate. I intend to spend every spare minute working on it until we've found where all the pieces fit." Anthony's voice had a hard edge to it, and I wondered if it had to do with Jayne keeping him at arm's length.

"Yeah," I said. "It's a good thing. Because everything else we've discovered has led us nowhere in a hurry."

"Seems like it," he said. "Jayne's caught me up to speed on every-thing—thought that maybe I could help. Sadly, I can't offer anything new. Except . . . Well, did Jack find the drawing in the box of papers I gave him?"

"Yes, he did. But it means nothing to us. We need to see the one Marc copied from your grandfather's diary, put them together, maybe, to see if they form a picture or code or something that might make sense."

"Remember I told you that Marc showed it to me? I might remember it if I could see the other picture. It's a long shot, but worth a try, right?"

For the first time in a long while, I felt a glimmer of hope. "Yes," I said brightly. "It's definitely worth a try. I know Jack hid it, but I'm not sure where. I'd call him and ask, but I know he's working and I hate to disturb him, but I promise to ask him tonight. Not to worry—it's out of sight, so Marc can't find it. And if you can't offer any hints after you've seen it, I'll try to get Rebecca to help."

"Rebecca? Good luck with that. She's definitely drunk the Kool-Aid where Marc's concerned."

"Yeah, well, she's still my cousin. And they say that blood's thicker than water."

"So they say," Anthony said, already back to studying the photo in his hand, searching for where it might belong.

The doorbell rang, startling us both. "Maybe it's the UPS man," I said. "Jayne does a lot of online shopping." That was only half the truth. I actually did a lot of online shopping—or had before our financial situation had deteriorated—and had most of it delivered to Jayne's house so Jack wouldn't realize exactly how much.

I peered through the sidelights, surprised to see Meghan Black, holding her Kate Spade purse against her chest with both arms wrapped around it, the shoulder strap around the back of her neck. I pulled open the door and ushered her inside.

"Meghan! It's good to see you. But what are you doing here?"

"Your sister, Miss Smith, said I could find you here. I hope you don't mind, but I needed to see you right away."

Fear tiptoed its way down my spine. "Has something happened?"

She looked past me to the dining room, where she could see Anthony sitting at the table. He glanced up and waved. Her large brown eyes widened with concern. "Can we speak privately?"

"It's okay," I assured her. "He's on our side."

She nodded, but the look of concern didn't leave her face. Lifting the strap off her neck, she said, "We found something."

The scrape of the chair in the dining room announced Anthony's approach. "In the cistern?" he asked.

Meghan nodded. "It was actually my friend Rachel Flooring who discovered it. She wasn't sure what it was, so she showed it to me. I probably wouldn't have had any idea, either, except that I've seen that portrait of Eliza Grosvenor at Gallen Hall—back when we were doing work in the cemetery there, we were given a tour of the house. I remember how creepy the painting was, how the eyes kind of followed me around, you know?"

Anthony nodded emphatically. "I know exactly what you mean. I will admit to hurrying past it as fast as I can every time I need to use the stairs." Anthony reached out his hand. "Anthony Longo. Pleased to meet you."

Meghan's eyebrows shot up as she jerked her head toward me.

"He's Marc Longo's brother—but it's okay. Anthony doesn't see eye to eye with Marc on what he has planned for our house on Tradd Street and is trying to help us."

Meghan relaxed a little and shook his hand. "Good to know. But, yeah, that portrait with the scary eyes . . . Well, it's not something a person forgets. Especially that peacock brooch she's wearing. Something about it draws the eye. Like she's asking you to look at it." She began fumbling with the latch on her purse. "Speaking of which." After pulling a small bundle wrapped in cloth from her purse, she looked toward the dining room. "Can I put this on the table? You should probably see it under better light."

I led her into the dining room, Anthony following close behind.

Meghan's eyes widened when she spotted the rows and columns of photographs. "Wow—what's going on here?"

"These are bricks from the mausoleum at Gallen Hall," Anthony said. "We think they're all supposed to fit together like some kind of a puzzle. It's a total guess, but as you can see we've already matched up quite a few, so it's possible we're not completely out of the park."

Meghan smiled. "It reminds me of a Nancy Drew book. I was obsessed with them when I was younger—I've read them all about a dozen times."

"Me, too," I said, liking Meghan more and more.

"So," Anthony said, reminding us of why we were there, "what did you find? The Confederate gold or another diamond?" His laugh sounded forced, and both Meghan and I looked at him.

With a serious face, Meghan said, "You know, Mr. Longo, all the diamonds were located and the story of how the gold is buried somewhere waiting to be discovered by some lucky person is a complete fabrication."

Anthony chuckled. "Yes, of course. Just making sure you'd done your homework."

I wasn't sure, but I thought Meghan might have rolled her eyes as she placed the wrapped item on an empty corner of the table, then carefully peeled back the layers. She stood back so we could see it under the light of the chandelier.

"Wow," Anthony and I said in union, our hands stretched at the same time.

"Please put these on before you handle it," Meghan said, pulling out a pair of gloves and handing it to me. "Sorry, Mr. Longo. I only have one pair, so you'll have to wait your turn."

I quickly slid on the gloves, then hesitated a moment. "It's the brooch, isn't it? Eliza's brooch from the portrait." I carefully lifted it in one hand, fitting it inside my palm while I traced the outline of the peacock's head and body and the splayed tail feathers, as if to reassure myself that it wasn't my imagination.

Meghan nodded. "I pulled up a photo of the painting I took on my phone and compared it. It's definitely the same. Well, either an exact replica or the same one."

"But all four stones are missing," Anthony said, as if he couldn't quite believe it.

Meghan glanced up at him before redirecting her attention toward me. "We're pretty sure it's pinchbeck—that's why it didn't show up on any of our scans. And because pinchbeck was almost exclusively used for costume jewelry, we're assuming that the stones were glass or paste."

"Have you found any of the stones?" Anthony asked. "I mean, even if they're not valuable, it would be nice to put them back in the brooch. For posterity."

Meghan shook her head. "Not yet. But if they're in there, we'll find them. We're literally sifting through every ounce of dirt. We'll be lucky to be done by next Christmas." She laughed but stopped when she realized no one else was laughing with her. She cleared her throat. "Flip it over and look closely at the back of the bird's head."

I squinted and saw only blurry gold before holding it up for Anthony to see, and he did the same. Even with my glasses it was too small for me to read. This time I was sure Meghan rolled her eyes. Pointing toward a spot on the back of the brooch, she said, "The initials S.V. are engraved on the neck of the bird. So, even if it's pinchbeck and it's missing its stones, it could have some value just because of who the jewelry maker was."

"Samuel Vanderhorst!" I shouted, as if I were a contestant on *Wheel of Fortune*. "He was the metalworker who did all the gates in the cemetery at Gallen Hall, right? And later became famous as a freedman after the Revolution when he set up shop in downtown Charleston."

"Exactly," Meghan said. "It's further evidence that this might be Eliza's brooch, since both she and Samuel lived at Gallen Hall around the same time. It's possible she commissioned it, or someone else did for her. Maybe he did it as a favor in return for his freedom."

"Why do you say that?" Anthony asked.

Meghan shrugged. "Well, it was unusual for a slave to be freed because he was good at something. His owner could make a profit from the slave's skills. Samuel Vanderhorst was incredibly skilled—and Carrollton Vanderhorst definitely knew it. It's curious, that's all. Something lost to history, I suppose. Or buried in a cistern."

"True," I said, gently placing the brooch on top of the cloth. "Have you shown this to Dr. Wallen-Arasi yet?"

"No. I wanted to get it to you as soon as possible, and I figured I'd let you show it to her." She glanced at Anthony again. "Marc Longo and that Harvey person were hanging around the dig again this morning, making sure we knew to tell them if we found anything interesting."

"Did they see this?" I asked in alarm.

"Nope. My Burberry jacket has these great, deep pockets so I stuck it in there as soon as Rachel showed it to me."

"Good job, Meghan," Anthony said.

"I agree. Thanks, Meghan. You've been a big help."

She beamed at us. "Anytime—happy to help." She glanced over at the dining room. "And if you think you need more help with that puzzle, please let me know. I'd love to work on it, and I bet my friend Rachel would, too."

I walked her to the door and opened it for her. "Thanks. I'll keep that in mind next time I've spent three hours at the table without finding a single piece."

We said good-bye and I closed the door behind her. Rubbing my hands over my arms, I walked back to the dining room, where Anthony stood looking down at the brooch. "A cold front's coming in. The weatherman said this morning there was a chance of snow by this weekend. I sure hope not. It's a rare occurrence, thankfully, but Charleston is worse than Atlanta when it comes to snow."

"Hmm," he said, making me wonder if he'd heard anything I'd said. "You should probably keep this here, just to make sure Marc doesn't see it."

"I thought about that, but I really need to show it to Sophie, get her expert opinion. Not to worry—I have a good hiding spot in mind. He'll never find it."

"Oh, sounds fascinating. Where?"

I carefully rewrapped the brooch in the soft cloth it had arrived in. "If I told you, it wouldn't be a good hiding spot, would it?"

He laughed. "No, I suppose not. Just hide it well. At least until Marc and Harvey are done."

"If they'll ever be done. They're having so many technical problems I've suggested they find a soundstage somewhere and make it look like my house. Because then they'd be out of my hair."

"Good plan," Anthony said, settling himself into a chair and picking up another photograph. "In the meantime, let's get this puzzle solved so we can all move on."

I regarded Anthony for a moment, his mention of moving on striking a chord with me. "Can I ask you a personal question?"

He peered up at me without moving his head. "I suppose. As long as it's not too personal."

"Well, maybe it's because this whole sibling thing is new to me, but have you ever considered what sort of permanent damage it might cause to your relationship with Marc when he finds out that you've been helping us?"

He looked down at the table, immersed in his study of the lines and circles on the photograph in his hand. "No," he said. Looking up to meet my eyes, he repeated, "No. If there's anything Marc has taught me, it's that to be successful, you need to be prepared to make enemies. Even if they're your friends. Or your brother."

I wasn't sure what I'd been expecting him to say, but I was pretty sure that wasn't it. I thought of Jayne, and despite any of the weird feelings I'd been experiencing where she was concerned, at least I knew I could never deliberately do her harm. Maybe that meant I wasn't the worst person in the world after all.

"Well," I said, "I've got to run by the office and pick up a set of keys for a showing tomorrow, so I'll leave you to it. Good luck."

He lifted his hand in a wave without looking up at me, and I backed out of the room, not wanting to interrupt his concentration. I pulled on my coat, scarf, gloves, and hat before stepping outside. I paused and looked up, the gray clouds seeming to shutter the bright blue sky of early afternoon, closing out the sun. A wind burst blew at me, making me shiver as I contemplated the difficult relationship between siblings and how I was grateful, for a moment, to have something to worry about besides Jack.

CHAPTER 28

Mrs. Houlihan peered out the window of the kitchen at the back garden, where my father and his friends from the gardening society were doing their best to decorate the black hole to make it look more festive for the progressive dinner. I'd hoped the gaping presence would have qualified my house for an exemption from the event, but Sophie had merely asked my father to do something with the cistern that would make it look in keeping with the holiday while not impeding the progress of the excavation.

Not that much was happening in that regard right now, anyway. The semester had ended and the students had returned to their respective homes for the holidays. Meghan had sent us a Christmas card with a photo of her and her dog, which was a doppelganger of General Lee. That's when I knew the excavation had lasted way too long. As had all the renovations in the house, since Rich Kobylt's Christmas card had arrived the same day and it hadn't taken me long to realize that the background behind his smiling family was my front garden.

I took advantage of Mrs. Houlihan's being distracted to pinch one of her famous ginger cookies cooling on a rack.

"I saw that." She hadn't turned her head, confirming the fact that the woman did, indeed, have eyes in the back of her head. "And if you take another, I'll tell you how many calories are in each one."

I finished chewing and wiped the crumbs from my mouth. "I don't know why you're insisting on doing all this baking. You do know the dinner is being catered, don't you?"

She shook her head in disgust, her jowls quivering with disdain. "In all the years I've worked for Mr. Vanderhorst and for your family, I have *never* seen the need to hire *outsiders* to bring food into my kitchen. I'm afraid I'm taking it personally."

"I'm sorry—I really am. Sadly, I don't seem to have any control as to what's going on in my house these days." I thought of the excessive number of Christmas trees and the over-the-top decorations, of the progressive dinner and of Harvey Beckner and his people, who continued to invade my home and refused to give up in their attempts to do the prefilming work that should have been accomplished in a single day. I wondered if they'd be here on Christmas morning and if I should get them gifts so they'd have something to open under the tree. I stared longingly at the cookies. "I can only hope we'll have our house back soon."

"Are they still planning on filming here starting in January?" Mrs. Houlihan asked.

"Not if I can help it."

She looked almost disappointed. "That's a shame. I heard George Clooney was signed up to play Nevin Vanderhorst's father, Robert, and Reese Witherspoon was to play his mother, Louisa. I'd already started planning my menus in my head."

The timer on the oven beeped and she slid on her oven mitts before sliding out what looked like her chocolate-and-mint holiday brownies. My mouth watered as I followed the movement of the pan, watching the housekeeper place it on a cooling rack. Mrs. Houlihan moved to the kitchen sink and began filling it with hot water and suds. With her back to me, she said, "Keep your fingers off of those brownies. Those are for Mr. Kobylt and his family."

I dropped my hand, sufficiently chastened.

There was a brief knock on the kitchen door before it opened, and I was glad I didn't have food in my mouth, because I probably would have choked. Standing in the doorway was a very tall man wearing a scarlet red British regimental uniform complete with shiny brass buttons, white breeches, and shiny black knee-high boots. I blinked a few times to see if he would disappear, eventually registering the iPhone he held in his hand.

"You better not be scuffing up my floors with those boots, Mr. Greco." A warm smile across Mrs. Houlihan's pudgy face eradicated her stern tone. "And if you just give me a sec, I'll have your favorite ginger cookies all wrapped up for you to take home."

"That's very kind of you, Mrs. Houlihan. Thank you."

"Greco," I said, my voice full of relief.

He must have seen the panic on my face, or maybe it was my hand pressed against my heart. "Melanie—I'm so sorry. I almost forgot I was wearing this." He patted the white crisscrossed straps across his jacket and chuckled. "Several of my reenactor friends and I have been hired for an event at the Old Exchange building tonight, but I needed a fabric swatch I'd left upstairs, so I figured I'd stop by on the way."

"No worries. I can't say I haven't seen stranger things in this house."

He raised his eyebrows but didn't say anything. He accepted a brown paper bag from Mrs. Houlihan—complete with a red satin ribbon she'd tied in a bow. "I promise to save these until after dinner, and only eat one at a time so I can savor it and appreciate your culinary talents as they should be appreciated."

She waved her hand at him. "Oh, don't be silly. I'll just make more for you. Eat as many as you like." Her smile was big enough to show the deep dimples on her cheeks.

I frowned at her, but she'd already turned back to the sink to wash dishes.

Greco cleared his throat. "Uh, Melanie. I was actually looking for you. Can you come upstairs to Nola's room for a moment?"

As I followed him upstairs, I kept picturing more words carved into the plaster walls, or a human skull protruding from a cornice. And wondering how much Greco would be okay with before he gave up and quit.

He held the door open for me and waited for me to enter before following me inside. He cleared his throat again. "So," he said. "When I came upstairs a short while ago, I could have sworn I heard, well, the sound long skirts make when a woman is walking across the floor. I knocked on the door twice, and when I didn't hear anything, I walked in and found the room empty."

I kept my expression neutral, not sure if I should mention that odd noises in empty rooms were part of my daily life. I spun around to verify that, yes, the room was actually devoid of people, especially women in long skirts. I followed his gaze to a new pile of bee carcasses clustered around the leg of the bed, the claw-foot nearly covered with them.

I made a show of checking the windows to ensure they were closed, flicking the locks to verify that the windows were, indeed, locked and couldn't accidentally slide open. "I guess we have a hive in the wall somewhere, so I'll have to call a bee removal specialist. You don't want to kill bees, you know—it's bad for the environment."

"It's also bad luck," Greco said, walking toward the bed. "But bees are dormant in the winter, which makes their presence in the room that much stranger." He knelt by the foot of the bed and began running his fingers around the back of the claw-foot, gently flicking the bees out of the way.

"My grandfather was a beekeeper," he explained. "That's how I know a little bit about bees and bee behavior. He always told me that a smart person listened to the bees because they always had something important to say. And this"—he indicated the pile of carcasses—"was telling me something. A pile of dead bees in the middle of winter clustered around one single area spoke to me. So I figured I should investigate."

He continued to move his fingers around the back of the claw-foot leg until I heard a small click. His eyes widened and I knew that he'd found what he'd been looking for. "I was just running my hands up and down over the wood until I felt something—and when I pushed it, a small door popped open right at the spot where the leg is attached to the footboard, to protect it from being seen when the bedclothes are removed, and this fell out."

He stood and carried something to me in his closed fist. When he reached me, he slowly unfurled his fingers and revealed a gold ring with a flat top, with something engraved on it. Without a word, Greco reached inside his waistcoat and pulled out a pair of reading glasses. I slid them on, then picked up the ring to see it better.

I ran a finger over the flat top. "It's a peacock," I said, and I could hear the excitement in my voice.

"Indeed it is. And I do believe it was used as a wax sealer—I've seen them before. That's why it's flat on top. You don't have to take it off to dip in the wax."

"It's a peacock," I said again, not sure how else I could articulate how much I thought this was a Good Thing. I had no idea why, but I was pretty sure Jack would.

"I know," Greco said, his tone matching mine. "Remember how I mentioned the spy ring that had a peacock as its symbol? I think this ring must have belonged to a member, which is why it was hidden, to keep the owner's identity a secret." He reached over and gently flipped the ring over in my palm. "Look on the inside of the ring—there are two initials. I'm wondering if they're the owner's."

Leaning closer and squinting even with the reading glasses, I was able to make out the initials S.V. I met Greco's eyes. "I don't think these are the owner's initials—I think they're the initials of the man who made it, Samuel Vanderhorst."

Greco nodded excitedly. "I've heard of him! He's quite famous for his metalworking and jewelry designs, isn't he?"

"Yes. And he was a former slave at Gallen Hall Plantation, too, which is where this bed was mostly likely made." I looked at Greco's red coat as if noticing it for the first time. "Is your great-uncle—the one who was the American history professor at Carolina—is he still alive?"

"Absolutely. My mother says he'll outlive us all. My father suspects his longevity is due to the fact that he spends so much time studying dead people that it's convinced him that he's better off in the land of the living." He tilted his head. "Why? Is there anything you'd like me to ask him? I'm going to see him tomorrow at a living history encampment at the Camden battlefield. He interprets Major General Horatio Gates."

"Another redcoat?"

He looked offended. "Certainly not. Major General Gates led the American forces at the battle and was responsible for their resounding defeat. Ruined his military career, actually."

"Oh, of course," I said, although I'd never heard the name before. "If you're willing, that would be wonderful. When Nola was using the textbook she'd borrowed, there was a mention that Lawrence Vanderhorst had been shot. Was that because he was a spy? But if the Vanderhorsts were known loyalists, would that make him a spy for the Crown or for the Americans?"

"That's a very good question, and one I'm sure my great-uncle should be able to shed some light on. You might remember that was his expertise—spies during the American Revolution. Actually, if you're all right with me taking a few photos of the ring on my phone, I'd love to send them to Uncle Oliver."

"Absolutely." I held up my palm, showing the front, side, and back of the ring so Greco could photograph it.

"One other thing," I said as I slid the ring on my largest finger, where it was still loose, then folded my fingers over it so it wouldn't slide off. "There was a British soldier quartered at Gallen Hall Plantation, an Alexander Monroe. He was found drowned in the Ashley River four days before Lawrence was shot." I could almost hear Jack's voice in my head. *There is no such thing as coincidence.* "I have no reason to suspect they might be connected, but could you ask your great-uncle, just in case, if he knows anything about either death?"

"No problem—I'm sure Uncle Oliver will be thrilled to help. He lives for that stuff." He glanced back at the claw-foot and the bees; he was silent for a moment, as if contemplating his next words. "There's something else I should probably mention."

I waited in silence, just in case he was looking for a reason to change his mind.

Greco continued. "The weirdest thing about it all is . . . Well, I'm not sure how to explain this." He stopped and a small flush crossed his handsome face. "Although for some reason, I think you could take this better than most."

"What do you mean?" I asked, although I was pretty sure I knew.

He gave me a knowing glance before continuing. "When I found the ring I did what most people would do, I suppose, and I slid it on my pinkie finger. I figured that's where signet rings go, right? Anyway, it fit me perfectly, and just as I was thinking that exact thought, I felt someone—I'm pretty sure it was a woman. . . ." He paused, rubbed his hand across the back of his neck. "I felt someone kiss my cheek. It was definitely a kiss; I could feel it and hear it, you know? Except, instead of being warm, like from someone's lips, it was icy cold."

"And there was no one else in the room?" I was imagining Mrs. Houlihan trying to hide behind the door, since she had been the only other person in the house at the time.

"No. At least no one I could see." His gaze settled on me, and I was surprised it wasn't one of expectation. Like he didn't need any explanations from me, and I was fine with that.

"Hmm," I said noncommittally, eagerly filing away the information to use later.

He glanced at the screen of his phone. "Sorry—I've got to run. Let me go grab the fabric swatch and my cookies from the kitchen and I'll see myself out. I'll be in touch after I speak with Uncle Oliver."

"Thanks so much, Greco."

I listened to the sound of his boots heading down the stairs as I began to scoop up the dead bees onto a paint-swatch board, disappointed that Greco had remembered he'd left his little bag of cookies in the kitchen. When I was done, I dumped the dead bees into an empty paint can being used as a trash receptacle and headed down the stairs, eager to share with Jack the signet ring and the brooch Meghan had found in the cistern.

A loud, hacking cough came from the direction of my bedroom. I ran back up the stairs and pushed on the partially open door. Jack lay huddled under the covers, his teeth chattering. I moved quickly to the bed and placed the back of my hand on his forehead.

"Jack—you're burning up!" I looked at the digital thermometer on the bedside table. "Did you already take your temperature?"

He nodded, his teeth continuing their chatter. "It's one hund-d-d-dred and f-f-four." He attempted a smile, but it looked more like a grimace. "I h-h-have a f-f-fever because you're st-st-standing so n-near."

Despite how horrible he looked, I smiled. "Right." I leaned forward and kissed him on the forehead, my lips burning where they contacted his skin. "I'm going to get something to give you to bring down the fever, then call your doctor. This could be the flu that's been going around, and I don't want to take any chances."

I took a wool throw from the back of one of the two armchairs and placed it on top of him, tucking it around him before sitting down on the mattress. "Is there anything else I can get for you? I could read to you. Or sing."

His eyes widened in alarm. "N-n-n-no. P-p-please." He widened his eyes hopefully. "Ch-ch-chicken s-s-soup?"

"Sure. I'll ask Mrs. Houlihan. If she can't make you some, I'll open a can for you."

He smiled, then closed his eyes. I kissed him again, then stood, absently wondering if I could stick a Santa hat on his head and leave him in the bed just in case he wasn't better in time for the progressive dinner. "I'll be right back. I'll leave the door open in case you need something, and you can shout. The bell I used when I was on bed rest with the twins somehow disappeared before they were born."

Jack began coughing again and I hurried from the room toward the stairs, my steps slowing as I reached the hallway outside Nola's bedroom. The door was open, although I was positive I'd closed it to keep the dogs out. I took a step forward to close it but stopped as my stockinged foot landed in a puddle of liquid.

I immediately thought of Bess, who still occasionally had accidents in the house when the weather conditions and temperature weren't to her liking and therefore not conducive to her using the outdoor facilities.

My gaze traveled past the threshold and into the room, where the puddles continued in a pattern. The kind of pattern wet feet would make. I looked down at where I'd stepped into one of the footprints, noticing how big and solid it was. Definitely not a bare foot, then. Most likely a booted foot, the narrower heel of each footprint making it clear that the wearer had been headed from the room toward the stairs. I thought for a moment I should call Greco and ask him if he'd stepped in anything, but I stopped when the unmistakable scent of gunpowder and leather saturated the air in the room.

"Alexander?" I whispered.

The only response was the buzz of a lone bee as it flew around my head before colliding with the window, its body plummeting to the windowsill, where it lay still and quiet.

CHAPTER 29

I searched behind all of the greenery draped around the front door of my parents' house on Legare Street for the doorbell. I knew it was there, just well hidden beneath the fruits of the zealous administrations of the decorating committee. I recognized the enormous and stunning wreath as the one my mother had made at the workshop, and I tried not to compare it to my own pathetic attempt. Of all the gifts I'd inherited from my mother, apparently talents for singing and wreath making hadn't been included. Not for the first time, I wished I'd been given a choice as to which genes I wanted. And which ones I didn't.

The sky sat leaden and ominous above us, the scent in the air unfamiliar to us Charleston natives. The meteorologists on every channel kept predicting snow, but the models weren't exactly clear as to when or how much. One even said it would miss us entirely and head straight to North Carolina. I just kept hoping the storm would hit hard Saturday so that the progressive dinner would be canceled and I could get back to work on figuring out what was hidden in the mausoleum.

When my finger finally found the doorbell button, I pressed it, then waited for the dulcet tones of the chime. After trying two more times and not hearing anything—typical in the damp and salty climate of the

Lowcountry—I knocked. Then knocked again. Finally, I resorted to pulling out the key that my mother insisted I have and let myself in.

"Mother," I shouted from the foyer. Despite her constant reminders that this was my house, too, and I didn't need to make an appointment to see her, I'd sent her a quick text to let her know I was coming. Just in case she and my father were busy. Doing exactly what, I didn't want to know, but I did want to give them fair warning.

I walked through the foyer, which was bedecked, similarly to mine, in garland and fruit, my grandmother's furniture a warm and familiar backdrop to the decorations. She'd loved Christmas and had always made it a special time for me despite the tension between my parents. Her antique miniature English village had been set out on the center-hall table, the small figures of a caroling choir dressed in distinctive Victorian garb. I wondered if Sophie knew about this and had given her blessing. Not that it mattered. My mother had a way of doing what she wanted while making others think it was their idea. And Sophie, a huge opera fan, was always a little starstruck where my mother was concerned.

"Mother!" I called again, peeking into the front parlor with the stained glass window, then back through the foyer toward the dining room. "Mother!" I shouted, more loudly this time.

"Back here," called a small voice toward the back of the house.

I made my way through the kitchen and a narrow hallway into a glass-walled sunroom that my father had transformed into a greenhouse. My mother used it as a morning room to drink her tea and listen to her music, piped through brand-new speakers hidden within the walls according to Sophie's advice. The room had been a later addition to the house, but that was no reason to desecrate (Sophie's word) the integrity of a historic house with unsightly modern conveniences.

My mother, wearing a thick red velvet lounging robe and matching slippers, reclined on a chaise, delicately sipping from a teacup. "Hello, Mellie. I'm sorry—I didn't hear the doorbell."

"It didn't . . ." I began, then stopped when I realized she wasn't alone.

"Hi, Melanie." Rebecca sat opposite my mother in an upholstered armchair that had been my grandmother's but was recently re-covered in a gorgeous Liberty of London floral print. Rebecca looked small and wan within its brightly patterned cushions, and I wondered if she might be sick. Or if something had happened to Pucci, since her ubiquitous four-legged companion wasn't with her. Her eyes looked puffy and red rimmed and I wondered if she might have lost her favorite pair of pink gloves.

"Oh, hello, Rebecca. I didn't expect to see you here."

She gave my mother a quick glance. "It was sort of last-minute."

"Have some tea," my mother offered.

I removed my coat, then poured myself tea from my grandmother's antique Limoges pot into a matching teacup. Sitting on the edge of the armchair next to Rebecca, I allowed my gaze to move from one woman to the next, finally settling on Rebecca, noticing again how pale she was. "I've been trying to reach you ever since I saw you at the Francis Marion on the night of the Shop and Stroll. I didn't think we'd finished our conversation."

"Yes, well, I've been busy." She took a long sip from her tea, avoiding my gaze.

"I'm sure. A part-time job at the paper and no children must leave you exhausted by the end of the day."

My mother sent me a warning glance and I immediately felt ashamed. It made me wonder how old I'd have to be before that look no longer affected me. Or how long it would take before I'd no longer need it.

She cleared her throat and asked, "How is Jack, Mellie?"

"Still very sick. The doctor suspects it's the flu, so he's being quarantined in our room. I'm sleeping in the second guest room, which hasn't been updated or changed since Mr. Vanderhorst lived in the house. I'm giving Jack flu medication prescribed by his doctor and taking his temp at regular intervals. Mrs. Houlihan keeps him fed with her homemade chicken soup, and Cooper's been keeping him well stocked on all the spy-thriller movies that have been released in the last ten years so that at least he's entertained." I looked accusingly at Rebecca. "Not that he can stay awake very long to watch an entire movie. I think the stresses of the last year have really taken their toll on him and this is his body's way of telling him to slow down and recharge."

I didn't mention how Cooper was also bringing Jack every book he could find that Jack didn't own or hadn't already read on code breaking through the centuries. Jack was desperate to keep working on figuring out what Gallen Hall was hiding, but he barely had the strength to hold one of the books up for longer than it took him to fall asleep.

"I hope you're not using Jack's illness as an excuse not to fill him in on any developments," Mother said softly. "I know he needs his rest, but I'm sure he'd appreciate you keeping him in the loop."

"Of course," I said, making sure my indignant tone was loud and clear. I hadn't exactly shared everything with Jack, because he really was too sick. And the medication made him groggy, so that he was barely coherent anyway. As soon as he was better, I'd tell him everything. I would. "And I don't think this is the appropriate time to bring this up," I said, my eyes darting over to where Rebecca sat.

"Rebecca understands the importance of family, Mellie. Despite what you might think. We've just been talking about that very thing."

"Really?" I asked, turning my attention to my cousin. "So, about our unfinished conversation . . ." I began, then stopped when I noticed fat tears rolling down her pale cheeks. She grabbed a small tea napkin from her lap and dabbed at her eyes.

"I'm sorry," she said. "I came here to get some advice from your mother—she's much more worldly than my own mother, which is why I came to her first."

My mother *had* been a world-famous opera singer, but I couldn't imagine any of Rebecca's troubles needing any kind of worldly advice. I made a point not to roll my eyes, my gaze drifting instead to the antique Dresden desk clock on the side table by the chaise. I had a house showing in an hour and I still needed to speak with my mother.

"Maybe I can help," I suggested, trying to move the proceedings further along.

"Why don't you tell Mellie what you just told me?" Mother suggested gently.

I sat up in alarm. "Have you been having more dreams about Jack or Nola?"

Rebecca shook her head. "No. I can't. I'm . . . blocked, it seems."

I sat up straighter, remembering how that had felt when it had happened to me twice before. And the reasons why.

"Go on," Mother prompted.

"Are you sure? It's not like she's a fan of Marc's to begin with."

"That's true. But is anyone, really?" Mother smiled benignly, taking the sting out of her words. "Besides, Mellie understands discretion. Don't you, dear?"

"Of course."

"And we're all family here," my mother continued. "I'm sure we're all in agreement that blood trumps everything, correct?"

I waited until I saw Rebecca nod before I did the same.

With a small voice that I needed to strain to hear, Rebecca said, "Marc's cheating on me."

I couldn't even feign surprise at this revelation. He was such a cheat and a liar in all of his dealings, it would follow reason that he couldn't remain faithful in his marriage. Still, I felt a glimmer of compassion for her, recalling how tied up in knots I'd been the year before when I thought that Jack and Jayne were having an affair.

"Are you sure?" I asked.

She nodded. "He's been acting . . . weird lately. Not himself. I know this whole filming thing has been a huge distraction, and Harvey Beckner is good at making everyone around him miserable. But still . . ." She dabbed at her eyes again. "Last week, Marc fell asleep on the couch, and his phone fell to the floor. It dinged when I walked in the room, and I went to pick it up to see if it was important and if I needed to wake him. It was . . ." She shuddered. "It was a photo of a woman. A *brunette*," she said with distaste, apparently forgetting that she was in a room with two brunettes. "She barely had on a blouse—and definitely not a bra—and she was saying she couldn't wait to see Marc again, since the last time was so amazing." She stifled a sob with her balled-up napkin. "I felt so . . . defiled."

"You poor thing," my mother said, getting up to refill Rebecca's teacup.

"I didn't say anything, wanting to be sure first. So I did a little digging and found out she's a grad student at the college—in psychology or something. And they've been seeing each other for months. For *months*."

"Are you going to leave him?" I asked.

Her shoulders hunched forward as she began to sob and shake her head. "I . . . can't."

"But why n—" I stopped. Recalled what she'd said about how her dreams were blocked, and I remembered when that had happened to me. "You're . . . pregnant?"

Rebecca glared at me with reddened eyes. "You don't have to sound so surprised, you know. Marc is a very virile man."

I swallowed down the bile that rose in my throat. "I'm sure he is. But that doesn't mean you have to stay married to him, you know. If you have the right support system in place, it's possible to raise the baby on your own."

A fresh torrent of tears streamed down her face. "But I love him. I will never love another man as much as I love him." She slumped down so completely she was almost folded in half, looking as pathetic as a kitten in the rain.

I sat back in my chair, completely defeated. I would be lying if I said I wasn't thinking of using the situation to convince her to share with me the piece of paper Jack and I so desperately wanted to get a look at. But seeing Rebecca's desperation made me quash that idea. The mere thought of trying to make a life without Jack made me sick and crazy at the same time. It was inconceivable, really. I understood her pain, and I couldn't take advantage of it, no matter how much I wanted to. Or how much Marc deserved it.

"I'm so sorry, Rebecca. But like Mother said, we're family. We're your support system. We will help you get through this whether you decide to stay with Marc or not."

My mother moved to sit down on the arm of Rebecca's chair, pulling her close. "Mellie's right. We're here for you."

Rebecca's phone in her purse announced a text. Slowly, she pulled away from my mother and reached for it. She stared at the screen for a long moment, blinking only once and very, very slowly. I thought she might start to cry again, but then I saw her expression change to disbelief, then anger, and finally fury. Without responding, she threw her phone into her purse. "That was Marc. He said he won't be home tonight for dinner again. He's got a *business* meeting and said not to wait up."

She sat still, breathing deeply, her expression slowly returning to neutral while my mother and I watched, unsure what we should do. "Are you all right?" my mother asked.

Rebecca shook her head, a new, determined glint lighting her reddened eyes. "Not really. But I will be." She reached into her purse again, pulled out a piece of paper folded into a square, and held it close to her chest. "I put this in my purse right after I saw you at the Francis Marion, not really thinking I could go through with this. But Marc has left me no choice." After an exaggerated pause, she stood and handed me the paper. "Just in case you weren't aware that Marc has already ransacked your house looking for your drawing while he's supposedly helping Harvey. And don't worry—this is a copy. I could see you already worrying about how to tell Sophie about the creases."

I wished I could tell her she was wrong. Instead, I quickly opened it up and saw what looked like a page identical to what Jack and I had found in the papers from the shoebox. "Thank you," I said. "Won't Marc be angry?"

She slid her purse strap over her shoulder. "He won't find out, will he? I might still love him more than he deserves, and I will do what I can to fight to get him back, but that doesn't mean that I can't enjoy a little revenge for what he's done to me. And our baby." She rested her hand on her still-flat abdomen.

Rebecca embraced my mother. "Thank you both. Right now, I'm in dire need of a spa day and I'm headed to Woodhouse Spa. I'm charging it all on Marc's credit card. And then I'm going to figure out how to win him back—right after I find a way to punish him."

We said our good-byes and she left, saying she'd see herself out, and for once I didn't roll my eyes behind her back, regardless of how much she'd just reminded me of Scarlett O'Hara after Rhett Butler's departure. This was the first time since I'd known Rebecca that she'd demonstrated that she had more brains and gumption than the Barbie doll she closely resembled.

"Well," my mother said, "that was illuminating." She indicated the piece of paper in my hand. "Do you think that will help?"

I shrugged. "I have no idea. I'll compare it to the matching piece of paper that we have and see if it means anything." I looked down at the page, at the weird lines and swirls that resembled the bricks of the mausoleum but were somehow different. I'd have to put them side by side to know for sure.

I carefully refolded the paper and placed it in my purse. "I came over to discuss the schedule for Saturday night. I'll have Nola bring the twins and dogs over to Amelia's house—and remind her to make sure JJ has his kitchen whisk. She forgot it last time and Amelia gave him one from her kitchen, but he apparently can tell the difference. Anyway, I know you'll be busy doing one of the appetizer sessions here, but I was hoping you could hurry to my house before the dinner to help me with last-minute preparations since I won't have Jack."

My mother sat up and pulled her notepad from the side table before adjusting her reading glasses on her nose. "Of course, dear. I'm sure your father can handle any stragglers so I can leave. And I'll make sure Mrs. Houlihan makes more of her gingerbread cookies just for Jack—they might cheer him up, and the ginger can't hurt. Did you know that she sent over a little gift bag of cookies for us? She's just the sweetest."

I looked at my mother to see if she might be deliberately tormenting me, but she was busy writing on her notepad.

My phone buzzed, alerting me that I had a text. I glanced at it to see who it was. "It's just Nola," I offered. "She's not supposed to be using her phone at school, but occasionally she'll text me about things she needs at the store or for a homework project. She likes to be prepared."

"Sounds familiar," Mother said as she bent over her notepad. "So, since yours is one of the dinner houses, you'll need to lay out the appropriate serving pieces for oyster stew and bone-in ham. I'll stop by your house later to get a count of dinner plates, but I'd suggest using the Vanderhorsts' beautiful antique Imari china. All of that gold will look beautiful with the decorations, plus I know there are a ton of serving pieces."

The phone buzzed again, and I pulled it out to make sure the message was from Nola. As I yanked it out, it caught a purse strap, which caused the purse to tip over, spilling the contents.

My mother stood to help, but I held up my hand to stop her. "You don't want to touch something you might react to," I warned.

"What's that?" She pointed near the skirt of the chair Rebecca had just vacated.

I recognized the signet ring that Greco had found. I'd brought it to show Sophie when I met her for lunch and had thought it was secure in the pocket of my purse. I had planned to tell my mother that we'd found it and where but had no intention of actually showing it to her. "Don't touch it," I said. "It was in the bedpost, just like you suspected. Greco found it."

Ignoring my warning, she moved toward it, reaching it before I could get up off of my hands and knees. "Mother . . ."

"I didn't get bad vibes from it, Mellie. It was practically begging me to find it. I think it's okay for me to touch it." She bent down and picked it up, holding it tightly in her palm. I waited for her to scream or for some otherworldly voice to come from her mouth or for her face to become unrecognizable. Instead she closed her eyes serenely, her face softening as she tilted her head to the side as if she were listening to a voice that only she could hear. And then her other hand flew to her neck, pulling at something I couldn't see, and she began to cough.

"Mother!" I grabbed her hand, pulling at her fingers to get her to release the ring, but they were like steel straps, unwilling to let go of their prize.

I was wondering if I should call Jayne for help, when my mother stopped coughing and her breathing returned to normal. Her eyes moved under her eyelids like those of a person having a vivid dream, but she was no longer agitated.

She stayed that way for a full minute, until her hand relaxed and the ring fell onto the rug with a small thud. She opened her eyes as if to reorient herself, then sat back in the chaise. I went to her quickly, taking her hand and finding it surprisingly warm.

"Mother? Are you all right?"

"I'm fine—I promise. The whole process is just exhausting—and gets even more so the older I become." She gave me a reassuring smile. "But I'm fine. Really."

I bent down to pick up the ring from the floor, then slid it onto my finger so I couldn't lose it. "Did you see anything? Did you see the man it belonged to?"

She tucked her chin as if confused by my question. "The man?" She shook her head. "No, Mellie, it didn't belong to a man. It was a woman. Definitely a woman."

"A woman?" I said slowly, recalling what Greco had said. How when he'd slipped the ring on his finger, someone had kissed him on his cheek.

"Yes." She reached up and brushed her neck with her fingers. "She . . . couldn't breathe. She was choking. But she was hurting elsewhere, too." Her palm pressed against her chest where her heart was. "Not like the pain from a heart attack. More like . . . a broken heart."

We stared at each other while I tried to find room for this particular puzzle piece. "Is that all?"

Mother shook her head. "No. She kept repeating the same word, over and over. I believe she's said it before."

"What?" I asked, although I knew exactly what she was going to say before the word passed her lips.

"Lies."

CHAPTER 30

I hesitated on my mother's porch, the chilly wind buffeting me, the scent in the air definitely something odd. Something that smelled a lot like a word I dared not say out loud. Down south, where snow was treated with the seriousness of an erupting volcano and its subsequent lava flow, it was often referred to as a four-letter word.

I looked at my watch again. I'd already called Jolly and had her cancel lunch with Sophie and change my appointment, so I wasn't worried about being late. But I was torn between heading over to Jayne's house—where Jack had told me he'd moved the box of documents—to compare the drawing Rebecca had given me with the one from the archives, and going home to see how Jack was and to go over the most recent developments with him.

The wind hit me full on, so cold that my cheeks burned and I could no longer feel my nose. There was definitely going to be something freezing and cold dripping from the sky, so it simply made more sense for me to head to Jayne's first, so that if it did begin to snow, I could head home to hunker down and talk with Jack then. Assuming he was even up to any kind of discussion.

Telling myself I was doing this in Jack's best interest, I slid behind the steering wheel of my Volvo, glad I'd driven the short distance instead of walking. I'd learned my lesson that morning when I'd walked the dogs—Jack's usual duty—and I'd felt an odd sort of solidarity with the mushers racing the Alaskan Iditarod as the wind pierced my coat and three sweaters and froze my mascara.

I rang the doorbell of Jayne's house, even though I had her key, too. But with Anthony temporarily living there, it felt like an invasion of privacy to just walk in. He opened the door and smiled widely, in contrast with his bedraggled appearance and bleary eyes.

"You look like you've just pulled an all-nighter," I said as I stepped inside.

"That's because I have," he said, shutting the door behind me.

"Working on the puzzle?"

He nodded. "Yeah. It's a little obsessive, I know. But when I do find a brick that fits, I can't help but think the next one will be easier, and then off I go again."

"Well, it looks like you're doing much better—despite the exhaustion you look perfectly fine."

"You're right. Recuperating here at Jayne's was a very good idea. Nobody pushing me down stairs, at least."

"That's a good thing," I said as I took a step toward the dining room.

"Jayne's not here," he said quickly.

I stopped. "Of course not. She's at my house with JJ and Sarah. She's the nanny, remember?"

He gave a little chuckle. "Sorry, of course. I'm just exhausted, so I suppose my brain's not functioning completely."

"No worries—I go a little crazy after just ten minutes staring at the bricks. Did you get very far?"

"Not really. I think it's going to take another week."

I made a move toward the dining room and he stepped in front of me, so that for a moment I thought he was trying to block me. Realizing his mistake, he stepped aside, then followed me into the dining room. I stopped in front of the table, surprised at what I saw. "You've got more than seventy-five percent of it done. Surely it won't take that long to finish—especially since there are fewer pieces now."

Anthony scratched the back of his head. "Yeah, I guess you're right. Cooper was here for a bit early this morning before class—I guess he did more than I thought."

"Why don't you go take a nap?" I suggested. "You'll be able to think more clearly once you give your brain a rest. And you'll want to be rested for the progressive dinner tomorrow."

"Is that tomorrow?"

"Yes, sadly. Unless it snows," I said hopefully. "Although knowing the organizers, they'll make it happen no matter what gets dumped on us from the sky."

He looked longingly toward the stairs, as if already envisioning his bed and crawling into it. "Are you here to work on the puzzle?"

"No, actually." I reached into my purse and pulled out the piece of paper. "Rebecca just gave this to me. This is the drawing Joseph Longo copied from Robert Vanderhorst's desk. I just need to compare it to the one you found with the other papers in the garbage."

Anthony followed me as I moved toward the front window with the large curved window seat. "Pretty clever hiding place, right? Even though it's not even locked. Jack figured that besides Jayne having an alarm system, Marc wouldn't have thought to look here." I slid off the seat cushion, then pulled open the lid. "And apparently he didn't figure it out."

I reached inside and pulled out the box.

"Wow. So it's been here the whole time? Very clever."

"Pretty much the only thing that hasn't been hidden is this." I held out my hand, where the signet ring sat on my finger. "I think this belonged to a spy in the peacock spy ring—but I'm not sure. Still so much we need to figure out."

Anthony was shaking his head. "So none of the pieces are coming together for you yet?"

"Not yet. As soon as Jack gets over this flu bug, I'm confident that he'll see the connection. It's how his mind works."

"But you both think it'll lead you to Lafayette's treasure."

"We certainly hope so. That would really be the answer to everything for us. It would solve our financial issues, give Jack a brand-new book idea to start fresh with a new publisher and contract, and get Marc off our backs for good." I looked at him closely. "What about you, Anthony? What do you hope to gain?"

He looked uncomfortable. "I just want to see him not get what he wants for the first time in his life." He looked away, staring at the photographs on the table. "He's always gotten what he wanted, regardless of who he might hurt in the process." He indicated the box I was holding. "Let's see if this tells us anything."

I placed the box on the table and sat down. It took me only a few minutes to thumb through the documents until I found the drawing I was looking for. I pulled it out, then placed it on the table next to the one from Rebecca.

"They look the same until you see them together, don't they?" Anthony said.

I nodded, then moved them around, perpendicular and then parallel, to see if that changed the perspective. It didn't. I stared at them, knowing I'd seen something similar. Recently, even. Similar, but not the same. I was silent for a moment, trying to think of where I'd seen it, the memory dangling in front of me like a carrot.

I squinted, getting closer to the page from the archives, and saw something I hadn't seen before. I tapped on the spot with my fingernail. "Anthony—can you see this? Does this look like anything?"

He leaned over the drawing, then looked at me with a grin. "It's initials. S.V. Like on the brooch."

I nodded excitedly. "Exactly. Samuel Vanderhorst, the metalsmith at Gallen Hall. Maybe this was the pattern for something he was working on." I sobered a bit. "Which means it's probably not going to help us. He made all the wrought-iron gates and fences at the plantation, so it would make sense that his sketches would remain either in the archives or in a Vanderhorst desk. Which makes me wonder why Marc was so eager to find our drawing."

"Probably because he knew that our grandfather had made a copy of something he saw in Robert Vanderhorst's desk, so it must mean something, right?" Anthony picked up the pages, moving them around like he'd done with the photographs in the brick puzzle. When none of the sides matched up, he placed one drawing on top of the other, then held them up to the chandelier, turning the one on top several times before stopping. "It appears to be something like a primitive map—just lines and angles," he said. "But they need to be converted to the same size so that they match up better. Maybe then we can figure out what it's a map of."

"It's just . . ." I closed my eyes, desperate to remember.

"What?" Anthony prodded.

"I know I've seen this pattern before—or one very similar. And recently."

"Where?"

I glanced up at the sharpness in his voice. "It'll come to me. I just need to stop thinking about it. My subconscious does a lot of my thinking for me."

"Right. Sorry—I really am so tired. Forgive me."

"I understand. I'm the mother of twins under the age of two, remember? I know what mental exhaustion is like."

Anthony nodded, his gaze moving past me to the stairwell behind me. "I think I'm getting delirious in my fatigue. I keep imagining I see Elizabeth, even though I'm not at home with her portrait. And I have the distinct impression she doesn't like me. I'm pretty sure she's the one who pushed me down the stairs."

"Really? And you're sure you didn't trip?"

"Positive. I had the bruises on my back to prove it—in the shape of a small woman's hands."

"Did Marc have any experiences while he was living there?"

"Nope. I seem to be the lucky one."

"Right. The lucky one. It's just odd that she's picking on you and no one else. She seems to be more of an insistent spirit than a malevolent one, from my experiences with her."

"Maybe I just remind her of someone she didn't like when she was alive."

"Maybe. It's been known to happen." My phone rang. I plucked it from my purse and looked at the screen, surprised to see it was Nola calling. She never called. I didn't think her generation knew their smartphones could actually be used to make phone calls. "Hang on," I said to Anthony. "It's Nola—it might be important."

I slid my thumb across the screen to answer, but before I could offer a greeting, she demanded, "Where are you? Didn't you read my texts?"

"I'm at Jayne's house, and no, I haven't read your texts yet. Is everything all right?"

"I'm at home. I figured something out, so I left school so I could get home to show you. But you're not here."

"You left school?"

"Melanie!" Her tone was part frustration and part exasperation. "So sue me—but trust me, this is important. Can you come home right now? I've already texted Cooper and he's on his way, too."

"I can be there in about five minutes. But can you first tell me what this is about?"

"The code!" She nearly screamed the word, and I had to hold my phone away from my ear. "Those four words, remember? In the letter from Lafayette that Dad gave me to work on? Cognac, feathers of goldfinch, kitchen maid, Burgundy wine? We were going over our Dutch painters quiz in my art history class—I got an A, by the way—and it hit me. I know what the words mean. And it's definitely a code."

My fingers were so cold from my race down Jayne's driveway that I could barely fumble in my purse for my keys or pry the car door handle open. I'd almost managed to close the door when it was wrenched from my grasp. Anthony stuck his head inside the door opening. "Let me come with you. I can help."

"Thanks, Anthony, but we'll have Nola and Cooper and Jayne, and even Jack if he's up to it. Right now, I think you'd be most helpful finishing up the brick puzzle. You're really close."

He looked so disappointed that I almost changed my mind and sent him back into the house for his coat and shoes. But then my phone dinged again and I glanced at it on the seat next to me. The message was from Nola. PLS HURRY!

I shook my head. "Thanks—but we've got this covered. I'll check back with you later. Go inside now and take a nap."

"Fine, you're right. But keep me posted." He closed my door and shoved his hands into his jeans pockets, then stood watching me as I backed out of the driveway and onto South Battery.

I'd barely made it a block when I was met by flashing lights and a policeman rerouting traffic toward Water Street. It was apparently just a fender bender involving two cars, but it was enough to block traffic going in both directions. Biting back an expletive, I waited behind five cars to take the directed U-turn, drumming my hands impatiently on my steering wheel.

My phone beeped again. I glanced over at the seat again, expecting to see another text from Nola, but that wasn't what it was. Instead, my screen was rapidly scrolling through all of my stored photos, mostly of JJ, Sarah, and Nola, slowing down when it got to the photos I'd taken at the Gallen Hall cemetery. I started to get annoyed—now was not the time for my phone to go on the fritz. But then I noticed the photo it had stopped on and understood that my phone wasn't malfunctioning at all.

A car honked behind me, and I jerked my head to face forward, noticing the policeman waiting for me to make my U-turn. I smiled and waved, hoping he wouldn't stop me for texting and driving—not that that's what I was doing, but it might have looked that way. Beyond it being dangerous and stupid to text while driving, texting was a skill I could barely perform sitting at a desk and using two hands, much less using one hand while trying to control a car.

I smiled as I passed the officer, then hit the dial button on my steering wheel and called Anthony's cell. I skipped all formalities as I blurted, "It's on my phone—where I saw that pattern before!" I took a deep breath to slow down my words. "It's on the small square inside the larger wrought-iron gate in the mausoleum. I took a picture of it, and I've still got it on my phone."

"Can you send it to me right away?"

"I'll text the picture in just a minute—I'm not home yet."

Another text came from Nola. HURRY!!!!!

I found myself clenching my jaw and forced myself to relax. Ignoring the text, I said, "I was thinking that maybe you could convert the three patterns to the same dimensions and see if putting them together means something."

"Great idea, Melanie. And I'll absolutely do that. I'll keep you posted—and do the same with whatever Nola's discovered, too, all right?"

"Deal." I hit the disconnect button, then found myself detouring my way back to Tradd Street, the short distance taking forever because of all the one-way streets not going the one way I needed to.

When I pulled into the driveway, I immediately texted the photo to Anthony, then raced inside the house. Nola met me in the foyer and began pulling me back toward the kitchen. "I thought we'd work on the dining room table, but Mrs. Houlihan said you'd probably blow a gasket if we messed up any of your table settings for the party."

She dragged me through the kitchen door before I could defend myself, which was a good thing, since Mrs. Houlihan was probably right.

"Jack!" I said in surprise. He sat at the head of the table wearing his pajamas, robe, and slippers, with a thick blanket wrapped around him. A box of tissues sat near his right hand, a wadded tissue shoved in the collar of his pajamas. His hair looked like he'd been stuck in a wind tunnel, and he had three days of stubble on his chin, yet when he grinned at me, my heart beat a little faster and he was still the most devastatingly handsome man I had ever seen.

I raced over to his side of the table, but he held a hand up to block me. "Not too close, Mellie. You can't get sick, too."

I looked around the table and noticed how all the chairs were clustered at the other end. I greeted Cooper, then glanced around for Jayne and the children. I was a little addicted to two sets of pudgy arms around my neck and sloppy kisses on my cheeks when I came home each day. Even with the three dogs scurrying around my feet in greeting, it just wasn't the same. Still, I bent down to scratch behind each set of ears, spending longer on General Lee because he was the eldest.

"Jayne's upstairs with the twins, but when they go down for their nap she'll join us," Jack said. Despite wanting to see JJ and Sarah, I felt a tiny twist of relief that Jayne wouldn't be a part of this. I told myself that I would dissect my feelings later. When I had time.

Jack continued. "We were going to have the twins in the kitchen with us on their blanket with their toys and the dogs, but they kept wanting me to hold them. I don't know who this quarantine is harder on—them or me."

"It's pretty hard for me, too," I said, giving him a meaningful glance.

Nola sighed heavily. "Okay, you two. Can we focus, please?"

I moved to stand behind her while she opened the same art history textbook I recalled seeing her and her two friends with at the wreath workshop. Cooper pulled out a notebook and opened it to a blank page.

Nola began. "So, if you'll recall, when Dad first gave me those four words to make some sense out of, Cooper and I sat down to try to categorize them, see what they had in common." She looked around the table, meeting everyone's gaze, the blue intensity in hers just like her father's when figuring out a tangled mystery with obscure clues. It's what he did best, and apparently, he'd passed it on to his older daughter. Maybe his younger daughter, and son, too, but it was too early to tell.

"Melanie?"

I realized Nola had turned around to look at me, while I'd been staring at Jack and thinking about our children. "Yes?"

"Are you with us?"

I nodded. "Of course. Go on."

"So, Cooper and I made these columns and wrote down adjectives to describe each word and see if we could find any similarities. We did that for days, going over and over the columns, coming up with new words that I wouldn't even know existed if I hadn't used Google. Or had been working with someone besides Cooper."

They shared a glance and Jack frowned. Either he was getting better or his radar where Nola was concerned wasn't affected by the flu.

Nola continued. "The only thing we noticed was that three of them could be identified with a color—cognac is brown, goldfinch feathers are yellow, and Burgundy wine is often red. But that left us with the kitchen maid. Even back in the seventeen hundreds, they probably came in different colors. It made no sense, so Cooper and I just figured that we were pointed in the wrong direction."

Dramatically, she picked up the book and held it open for everyone to see, splay backed like a book an elementary school teacher was reading to her students. I recognized the painting showing a woman with a white cloth hat and what appeared to be a clay pitcher pouring milk into a bowl. "This is a famous painting by the Dutch artist Johannes Vermeer. Its official name is *The Milkmaid*. But"—she paused for dramatic effect—"perhaps because of what most people think a milkmaid should look like—a young woman out with the cows gathering milk, maybe—the painting is more commonly known as . . ."

She paused again, but instead of gritting his teeth, Jack smiled. "*The Kitchen Maid*."

"Bingo!" Nola's smile matched her father's. "I felt really dumb because we've been studying Vermeer all semester, so I knew a lot about him, so this should have clicked a long time ago. What was *really* interesting and caught my attention finally was his color palette."

Nola's arms were drooping from the weight of the book, so Cooper stood and took it from her while I took his vacated seat at the table. "Thank you," she said, and I hoped Jack couldn't see the look on her face when she smiled at the young man.

Nola's brows knitted. "Where was I?"

"Vermeer's color palette," Cooper said gently.

"Right. So each painter pretty much had their signature palette. During the seventeenth century, when Vermeer was painting, there were only about twenty pigments available to him, and he chose to work mostly with just seven." Her smile broadened as she used her index finger to indicate the background in *The Milkmaid*. "His palette was unusual because of the pigment he used to create shadows on white-washed walls that were warmer than those created with black pigment used by other artists."

"And that pigment was . . ." Cooper announced like a master of ceremonies, and I wondered if I should do a drumroll on the table.

Jack and I stared blankly at Nola and then Cooper, as if waiting for them to turn the page and reveal the answer, because apparently we had no idea.

"Umber!" Nola shouted.

Cooper placed the book on the table. "So, basically, we now have four objects with identifiable colors: brown, yellow, umber, and red."

I sat up. "And that means . . . ?"

Cooper and Nola shared a glance before looking back at me. "We're not sure. That's why we were hoping we could brainstorm a little bit now."

Jack reached for the notebook and pen and Cooper slid them down the table. Across the top of a blank page, Jack jotted down the four words and their four corresponding colors. "What we need to do now is put this all in the context of the Vanderhorsts at that time. What they would have been familiar with and what connection to those four words and/or colors they might have had. A familiarity known by Lafayette so that his letter would be understood by them and hopefully not by any others."

"Our thoughts exactly, sir," Cooper said. "And since we're working on the premise that this might be connected to the French king's treasure, we've been looking at those four colors in that context."

Jack was still scribbling but looked up at Cooper. "And what have you found so far?"

"Nothing yet, sir. But I'm prepared to stay here all night with Nola and help figure it out."

Jack's eyes narrowed. "I'm sure that won't be necessary."

"Dad!" Nola shouted, her face a mask of mortification.

"No, sir," Cooper said, a pink stain on his cheeks. He cleared his throat. "We did figure out one thing, sir, in regards to the umber. Mrs. Vanderhorst was an avid art collector. There are actually quite a few paintings she acquired while living at Gallen Hall that were later donated by the family to the Gibbes Museum. It was well-known that her favorite artists were Rembrandt and Vermeer. So it would make sense that she'd know about Vermeer's preferred palette."

"And the marquis would have made it his business to know this," Jack said, thumping the end of his pen against the notebook before dropping it, then slumping back in his chair, his face taking on a waxy sheen.

"Jack—you need to rest." I stood and went to him. Cooper and Nola moved toward him, too, but I waved them back. "No sense in three of us getting exposed—I promise to be careful." I helped Jack stand, and I could hear his teeth chattering again. "Come on, let's get you into bed."

"I love it when you say that," he croaked.

"Dad!" Nola shouted. "We're still here, you know."

Jack grinned through his chattering, then reached back toward the table. "I need my notebook. For later," he said after he saw my alarm.

Nola grabbed it and handed it to me, and I carried it upstairs while my other arm was wrapped around Jack's shoulders. I gave him an Advil, then tucked him into bed, adding another blanket at his request.

"Put the notebook and pen here," he said, indicating the space where I usually slept in the bed. "For when I wake up and feel better."

"Sure," I said, "but don't work too hard. You really need to rest so you can get better." I sat down on the edge of the bed, smoothing the hair from his forehead. "Is there anything else you need?"

He raised his eyebrows in a familiar gesture.

"Jack—you're sick, remember?"

"Doesn't mean I'm dead," he muttered. "Anything else I can be mulling over while I'm stuck here?"

The word *dead* reminded me of something Anthony had said. "Maybe. Anthony and I were talking earlier, and he mentioned how he's pretty sure it's Eliza Grosvenor who pushed him down the stairs at Gallen Hall. He gets really bad vibes when he passes her portrait, so he thinks she hates him. He suggested that maybe he resembles somebody from her life that she didn't like."

"Or maybe she just hates men."

I shook my head. "No, I don't think that's it. It's only Anthony she seems to pick on. And she definitely doesn't hate men. I think she kissed Greco."

Jack lifted his head from the pillow, then immediately laid it back down. "When did this happen?"

I couldn't remember what I'd told him and what I hadn't. He still hadn't told me what Jolly had mentioned—the evil presence from the cistern that had followed Jack into my office. In a fit of pique I'd decided to keep the bee incidents and my mother's outbursts from Jack until he shared with me what he'd learned. It was childish and stupid, and I'd already decided that I was going to tell him everything. As soon as he was better, when he could process it all. That's what I kept telling myself, anyway. I looked down at my hand where I wore the signet ring and placed my other hand over it.

"He had to stop by to pick something up before heading out to a living history event and was dressed in his complete British regimental uniform. He was standing in Nola's room when he said he felt a woman kiss his cheek. I'm pretty sure it was Eliza—I sense her a lot in there."

Jack was thoughtful for a moment. "So, Alexander was the British soldier quartered at Gallen Hall, but Eliza was engaged to Lawrence, the son of the family." His eyelids were beginning to droop. "It's interesting that she'd kiss a British soldier, don't you think?"

I looked down at the signet ring again, remembering how Greco had told me he'd felt the kiss after he'd slipped it on his finger. And how my mother was certain the owner of the ring was a woman. I lifted my hand to show him. "Greco found this in the bedpost. . . ."

I stopped. Jack's eyes were closed, the muscles in his face relaxed, his breathing even. "Never mind," I said. "I'll tell you later." I stood, then leaned over the bed to kiss his forehead. "I love you," I whispered, watching him sleeping for a moment before quietly letting myself out of the room.

CHAPTER 31

On Saturday morning, the day of the progressive dinner, I was up early so I could steer the final preparations. The night before, Nola had helped me pack up the twins and move them and all their equipment to Jack's parents'. I'd argued at first that they wouldn't be in the way, until Nola reminded me of how much JJ loved to throw all round objects he could get his little hands on as if they were baseballs, and how Sarah had taken to climbing into the Christmas trees in search of the shiniest ornament. I'd quickly acquiesced.

Mrs. Houlihan, Nola, and Jayne would be on hand to help. Jack was still too sick to be out of bed, but Cooper said he'd be available if we needed extra help setting up the rented tables to accommodate the twelve couples who couldn't fit around the table in the dining room.

I'd printed out spreadsheets with a time schedule and tasks to be accomplished and by whom in the appropriate rows and columns. I labeled each one with the person's name and then printed extra copies just in case anyone lost theirs, which seemed to happen a lot. The main dining room table was already set with my grandmother's antique Belgian lace tablecloth and matching napkins and the Vanderhorsts' stunning Imari place settings, the brilliant gold, red, and dark blue standing out like jewels against the white tablecloth.

I hated to admit it, but the homemade centerpieces of oranges, pineapples, and pinecones that Sophie had forced me to make were a festive and gorgeous touch. As were Greco's hurricane lanterns on the piazza, which he had returned to festoon with evergreen sprigs of pine, sapphire cedar, and boxwood. He'd even prepared enough to include in the centerpieces of the smaller tables, so they were as elegant as the main table.

My phone beeped and I saw a text from Greco, and I was relieved that he texted like a real person and used full sentences and punctuation.

I heard back from Uncle Oliver with a bit of information for you. Lawrence V. and his father were basically estranged although living under the same roof. It was rumored in some circles that one of them supported the patriot cause while the other remained loyalist. Not clear which one was which as historical information is conflicting. Whatever the truth, he believes it's the reason Lawrence was killed.

While I was still attempting to text the word *thanks*, another text popped up on my screen.

You might also be interested to know that St. Gallen was the patron saint of birds. Uncle O. finds it interesting that the name change happened around the time of the Revolution and Eliza's purchase of the first peacocks.

He added a smile emoji to the end of that sentence and then a fist-bump GIF.

Jayne was emerging from the dining room when I came down the stairs. I showed her the text from Greco. Her eyes widened. "The plot thickens," she said. "And the whole Gallen thing—right under our noses."

"Apparently we weren't the only ones, since nobody seems to have made the connection between Gallen Hall and peacocks."

I read the text again, remembering what I'd read in Nola's borrowed textbook, about the only footprints leading to Lawrence's body coming from the house.

"So who killed Lawrence?" Jayne asked, giving voice to my own thoughts.

"Someone close to him. Someone in the house. The only thing we know for sure is that it wasn't Eliza or Alexander, because they were already dead." I frowned. "But I know Eliza is connected somehow. She brought the peacocks to Gallen Hall, and then the name of the plantation was changed."

"Definitely not a coincidence," Jayne said.

I nodded. "All we know for sure is that she was engaged to Lawrence. But when Mother held the signet ring, she said the owner had been female."

"Then . . ." Jayne began but stopped as Mrs. Houlihan bustled past us clutching a feather duster on her way to the front parlor.

"Let's talk about this later—we've got a lot of work to do."

Jayne nodded, then held up what looked like an orange in her hand. "I found a bunch of these under the table and behind the draperies in the dining room. Are they part of the decoration?"

I remembered a few of them flying around the table when I'd been in there with Michael, but I thought I'd removed them all. "No, not exactly. I think Veronica's sister sent them to remind me that she's still here and waiting to move on. Or JJ was let loose with a bowl of oranges." I marched into the dining room and began to pick up the errant oranges.

"And?"

"And, what?" I lifted the long silk drapes and rescued two more oranges.

"And are you going to help her?"

I moved to the other window and checked under the drapes, finding one more piece of fruit. "I guess I'm going to have to. I told Veronica I would but that I couldn't it do it right now. Michael wants to put their house on the market now so they can move, but Veronica feels that if they move out of the house, they'll lose some vital clue to Adrienne's disappearance."

"So you agreed to help her?"

"Against my better judgment, I did—but not until after Christmas. I'm so insanely busy right now I just couldn't add one more restless spirit to my plate. I think I've thrown in enough brakes on the house sale so that we have until after the first of the year before I have to actually do anything."

"Maybe I can help you."

I didn't meet her gaze. "Maybe. Let's cross that bridge when we come to it."

I began walking around the perimeter of the room, searching for any missed fruit.

"She's right, you know," Jayne said. "About losing some vital clue. I see Adrienne, too, sometimes, and I feel that time is of the essence. I've seen her a few times when I've been working with Veronica. They must have been very close."

I stood and faced my sister. "I guess so. Veronica still misses her and it's been more than twenty years."

Jayne's face looked wistful. "It must have been nice to grow up with a sister, don't you think? Sharing confidences. And makeup. Clothes."

"And fights," I added. "Most sisters I know have always done a lot of fighting." I immediately regretted my words. For a brief moment I pictured Jayne and me with matching black patent Mary Janes having ice cream sundaes at the curved booth in the front of Carolina's with our grandmother. Grandmother would have known that we'd each want our own since even now as adults neither Jayne nor I ever shared a dessert with anyone. And we would have been aware of the silent spirits around us at the other tables and standing nearby, but we wouldn't have been afraid because we would have had each other.

I softened my tone when I saw her wounded look. "Yeah, it would have been nice not to grow up alone. And I'd rather have a sister than a brother. Especially for the sharing of clothes."

As if she'd heard only the first part, Jayne said, "I don't think we would have fought." She peered behind the dining room door and plucked out an orange I'd missed. "Because you and I have this thing we share—this gift or whatever you want to call it. It would have bonded us together. Kind of like how it's bonding us now."

"True," I said, wishing I felt as reassured as I sounded.

She smiled and I smiled back, feeling only a little tinge of remorse that I couldn't completely agree with her.

I indicated the oranges we both held. "Why don't we put these in the kitchen for Mrs. Houlihan? She'll probably use them to whip up another batch of wonderful cookies that she won't let me have." I walked toward the kitchen to deposit the oranges in the bowl in the middle of the center island, Jayne right behind me.

Jayne grimaced. "Probably. I find it's easiest to resist sweets when they're not in the house."

The look I gave her made her quickly switch the subject. "I missed you on our run this morning. You're doing so well, and I feel it's my duty as a coach to keep you motivated."

We returned to the dining room, where I glanced out the window. "Yeah, well, I was more motivated to get this day over with than to get frostbite. It's really getting ugly out there."

"Oh, it was a little cold. But it's all about the proper gear. I was well insulated and I brought my little hand warmers to stick inside my running gloves." She considered me for a moment. "I think I know what I need to put in your Christmas stocking."

I forced a smile. "I like chocolate Santas, if anyone's asking. Dark chocolate and solid—none of that milk chocolate hollow stuff. I might as well eat tofu."

The doorbell rang, announcing the arrival of the party-rental people, and Jayne, Mrs. Houlihan, and I got busy directing the placement of the six extra tables in the front parlor, placing a white tablecloth on each. I began putting the centerpieces on the tables and attempting to zhush them as Greco had taught me, but I stopped when I realized Mrs. Houlihan was going right behind me and redoing them. And making them look much better.

Wonderful baking smells wafted from the kitchen while we worked, making it hard to concentrate. Mrs. Houlihan had insisted on adding to the caterer's menu with her famed tomato bisque, topped with chilled shrimp that her husband had caught off of Edisto the past summer and she'd set aside and frozen "just in case."

She'd also persuaded me to allow her to gift our dinner guests with small bags of goodies, including her praline pecans, homemade truffles, lemon cranberry tarts, and spicy iced peppermint shortbread cookies. I'd yet to taste a single bite of any of it, as Mrs. Houlihan seemed to have a sixth sense where I was concerned, always facing the kitchen door as if expecting me each time I tried to sneak in for a sample. She claimed that I didn't know what a sample was and every time she'd allowed it in the past, she'd had to make another batch of whatever it was I'd sampled. I denied it, of course, blaming it on whoever else happened to be in the house, but she never believed me.

My mother arrived around ten, after going with my father to the gardening store for tarps for his beloved Daphne evergreen shrubs and camellias to protect them from snow. They were hardy, winter-sustainable plants, but Dad wasn't convinced that his Southern beauties would know how to handle icy rain or a thick coat of snow. I'd called him on his cell, asking him to get more tarps than he needed because Sophie was concerned about the cistern and exposing anything old to the frigid cold. I'd bit my tongue before I could make a comment about how it wasn't possible to make a piece of garbage less valuable, refraining from speaking when I reminded myself that we were friends.

Nola came downstairs around the same time my mother arrived. Nola wasn't an early riser, so I was impressed she made it downstairs before noon on a Saturday. Mrs. Houlihan placed a cup of tea in one hand and I put a spreadsheet in the other, and then waited another fifteen minutes for her to completely wake up and get to work.

She began with helping Mrs. Houlihan and me set the small tables with a mix of the Vanderhorst Imari and my mother's borrowed Cartier wedding china with the narrow gold edges, which blended beautifully with the other pattern. The mix and match had been suggested by Greco, and I shook my head in wonder at how I'd found him on a recommendation from his good friend Rich Kobylt of the low-slung pants and pickup truck.

I continued to keep an eye out the window as we worked, constantly checking the weather outside and on my phone and occasionally turning on the Weather Channel for corroboration that it wasn't going to snow before Sunday morning. My life's mantra was that if it was worth doing, it was worth doing three times.

Nola and I were folding napkins in elegant tepee shapes following Jayne's directions—she'd apparently learned how to fold any material into any shape in nanny school—when Jack appeared at the top of the stairs. "Mellie?"

I quickly dropped the linen square and took the stairs two at a time. He still looked pale and not at all well, but there was a little flush of color to his cheeks. "You shouldn't be out of bed."

"Probably not," he agreed, "but I think I just figured out what those colors mean." He leaned into me and I put my arms around his shoulders. His knees seemed to bend a bit and I struggled to keep him upright. Jayne ran up the stairs and stood on his other side, slipping her arm around his waist.

"Should I come up, too?" Nola called.

"No, your aunt Jayne and I can handle this."

"But I was the one—"

"Yes, you helped us figure out about the umber." It was hard to forget since she'd been bringing it into every conversation since the previous evening. "And we're grateful—but those napkins won't fold themselves. You can borrow my ruler to make sure the sides are all equal—I left it on the table next to you."

Jayne and I carefully led Jack back to bed, although I had to move the notebook and about ten crumpled balls of paper off first. I frowned down at him as I adjusted the pillow beneath his head. "Did you work on this instead of sleeping?"

The half grin he gave me was so devastatingly familiar that my anger quickly evaporated, as I'm sure had been his intention. "Maybe."

"Jack! How are you going to get better if you don't take care of yourself?"

"All I need to do is look at your beautiful face, and I immediately feel better." He looked behind me to where Jayne stood, her arms folded. "How was that?"

Jayne attempted to hide a smile beneath her frown. "Terrible. And Melanie's right, Jack. You need your sleep."

I gave her a quick nod of gratitude. "Now go to sleep and we'll talk later. We've got to get ready for the party." I reached for the lamp, but Jack put a hand on my arm. "Let me show you first—and then I'll go to sleep. Promise."

I slid the notebook out from under the pile of rumpled paper and handed it to him.

"See," he said, jabbing his finger at what appeared to be a lot of gibberish. "My mistake is that I thought this should be more complicated than it is."

"Like looking for zebras instead of horses," Jayne said.

"Exactly." Jack sent Jayne an appreciative glance.

As if guessing I had no clue what she was talking about, Jayne explained, "I used to work for a doctor and her family, and she told me that new doctors are always looking for the bizarre diseases when examining symptoms rather than considering the everyday, common-cold-type thing."

"Ah," I said, looking at the jumbled words on the notebook.

Jack coughed and I handed him a glass of water I kept filled on his nightstand. "So," he said, "I spent a couple of hours going over all the code books I have to see if I could break this out. It's only four words, and Nola had already done the hardest part, figuring out the color connection, so I figured I should be able to figure out the rest." Jack paused a moment to lay his head back against the pillow and catch his breath.

"Anyway," he continued, "after a lot of wasted time, I just went back to the most basic of all codes—letter substitution and first letters. Looking for horses instead of zebras, so to speak. It's pretty elementary, but I suspect that whoever came up with the original list of supplies thought it was a good enough coded hint that any additional cipher was just a precaution and didn't need to be as involved."

I followed his finger down the page, where I saw his attempts at making words using various letter orders, then watched as he turned the page, where a single word was written in shaky block print. R-U-B-Y. "Red, umber, brown, and yellow," I said out loud. "So simple, yet so diabolical when you're looking for something so much harder."

Jayne rubbed her forehead. "So the French king gave the Marquis de Lafayette a valuable ruby to secretly give to someone—possibly a spy—at Gallen Hall to support the American cause. And I'm only saying 'spy' since the Vanderhorsts were loyalists, correct?"

Jack nodded, as if the effort it took to speak was wearing on him. But I knew I couldn't stop him at this point. Being tenacious and smart was one of the things I loved the most about him, and I knew it would be pointless to make him stop talking now and relax.

The deep V above his nose suddenly cleared as his eyes widened with realization. "But not just one ruby," he said excitedly. "Four. And what place better to hide valuable jewels than in a piece of costume jewelry? Remember the brooch Eliza is wearing in her portrait—the peacock. I'm sure it's the same brooch I told you about from the vision Jolly had. It had four jewels in it."

Jayne nodded while I tried to keep relaxed. Jolly had told me about her vision of the man with the brooch following Jack, but Jack hadn't. Up until that moment, I'd still been waiting. But apparently he'd told Jayne. Part of me wanted to believe it was an oversight—he'd been sick and everything was so crazed right now—but part of me felt the old sense of being left out.

"The jewels weren't all red, though," I said, remembering the portrait and the times I'd seen Eliza. I sounded bossy and realized this might be my attempt to feel relevant.

"True," Jayne said. She looked at Jack. "They could have been disguised, right? Maybe some kind of stain or watercolor paint?"

Jack smiled with approval. "That's what I was thinking. Stick multicolored jewels into a pinchbeck brooch, and nobody would know what they were hiding."

"Then where are the four rubies?" I asked.

Jack shook his head slowly. "I know it has something to do with the mausoleum—the way it was destroyed and rebuilt two brick rows higher. It has to mean something. It can't be a coincidence that it was rebuilt the year after Lafayette supposedly brought the treasure into the country."

"And the three people interred there have to be connected, too," Jayne added. "Since they all died the same year that the treasure was supposedly delivered to Gallen Hall."

I sat down on the edge of the bed, suddenly aware of the signet ring I still had on my finger. It felt very warm, almost burning my skin with its heat. I remembered what my mother had said when she'd held it, the feeling of heartbreak, and the kiss Greco had received while wearing the ring. The wet boot prints after Greco had left. And I recalled, too, what Jolly had told me about the man following Jack, and the specter's own broken heart.

I looked up with a small gasp, knowing with certainty who the spy was. And the meaning of the word *lies*. More important, if I didn't know exactly where the rubies were hidden, I knew where to look to find them.

"What?" Jack asked, his eyes barely slits as he fought his exhaustion.

"It can wait. We have a party to get ready for." I stood and tucked the covers around him. "You get some sleep. We'll talk more tomorrow."

"Mellie . . ." My name was a word of warning, but I pretended I didn't hear it as I bent down to kiss his forehead, then ushered Jayne out of the room.

"What was that all about?" Jayne asked as I led her to the stairs.

"What do you mean?"

"You gasped, and I don't know if it's because I'm psychic or because we're sisters, but whatever it is you're thinking, I don't have a good feeling about it."

"The only thing I'm thinking about right now is this party and getting everything ready before the first guest arrives. And then we can figure out where the rubies are."

Jayne right behind me, I continued my hurried pace down the stairs, aware of her worried gaze following my every step.

CHAPTER 32

I clasped my grandmother's pearls behind my neck, feeling odd to be doing it alone. Jack and my usual going-out ritual involved me lifting my hair and Jack lingering on the fastenings of my necklace, then finishing with a soft kiss beneath my ear. He was only in the adjacent bedroom, but I missed him as if he were in another country on an extended trip. I'd never seen him have so much as a cold, so to have him confined to bed for nearly a week was unsettling. It was as if the carousel we'd been riding had suddenly switched directions, and I couldn't quite get my bearings.

I stopped by the bedroom to see if Jack needed anything before I went downstairs. He was propped up on pillows so he could breathe better; pill bottles and a filled water jug sat next to him on the bedside table. He had a large textbook open on his lap, and I recognized it as Greco's great-uncle's book about spies.

He watched me approach, that gleam in his eye only partially clouded with medicine. "You look beautiful," he said.

I sat down on the edge of the bed, making sure I avoided the trash can that was halfway filled with used tissues even though I'd emptied it only a couple of hours before. "Feeling a little better?"

He nodded. "Mrs. Houlihan brought me up some of her tomato bisque and a plate of her cookies. I actually had enough of an appetite to enjoy them."

I looked around for the plate. "Did you eat them all? Or at least save me a crumb?"

"Sorry—I ate every last bite. I'm sure there are more downstairs."

"Oh, yes. Tons. I'm just not allowed to have any." I folded my arms. "You do realize Mrs. Houlihan works for you, right?"

"Yes, but . . ." He was right, of course. Having been raised by a military father, I had an almost unnatural respect for authority, and going against her wishes always seemed a bit like insubordination. "It's complicated," I said. Changing the subject, I tapped the book in front of him. "Find anything interesting?"

"Not sure. I'm trying to determine who the major players were in the peacock spy ring. Carrollton Vanderhorst, Lawrence's father, was a known loyalist, but after the Revolution, he retained all of his lands on the Ashley River. Nothing was confiscated as punishment for supporting the wrong side."

"Interesting," I said. "What about Lawrence?"

"Defender of the Crown, through and through. A little fanatical about it—which could be why Carrollton kept his true beliefs secret from his son."

"Speaking of Carrollton, Greco's uncle, the historian, says that father and son were estranged. And apparently Lawrence's murderer came from Gallen Hall—two sets of footprints leading from the house, and only one returning. But no one was ever arrested."

Jack raised his eyebrows. "That certainly fuels the fire of the stories of how they were rooting for opposite sides."

I nodded. "And one more thing. St. Gallen was the patron saint of birds. I don't think that's a coincidence."

"Definitely not." He leaned across the bed and picked up a photo-copied page. "Yvonne faxed this to me this morning—Nola brought it up for me so I didn't have to bother you. It's from an architectural design book she found in the archives about Charleston's cemeteries. There's quite a large section regarding the mausoleum at Gallen Hall."

He handed it to me, but when he saw me squinting, he took it back. "Should I just paraphrase?"

"My glasses are downstairs, just so you know. I was using them this morning to measure napkin folds."

He was silent for a moment before he continued. "Carrollton Vanderhorst was the one who had the original mausoleum built in 1780, as a family crypt, which is why there were ten niches in the original plan. But he's also the one who ordered it destroyed two years later and had his son, his son's fiancée, and the British soldier interred there. Carrollton planned the addition of the two rows as well as commissioned all of the wrought iron for the fence around the periphery, the front gate, and the mausoleum door gate. There were two more gates designed for the cemetery, but they disappeared after Hurricane Hugo in 'eighty-nine. The remaining iron fencing miraculously survived."

I squinted at the page, wishing I could see. "So there were three gates designed for the redo, but only the front gate along with the mausoleum door survived?"

Jack nodded. "Apparently. Samuel Vanderhorst designed and made all of them. But there's one last bit of info that I find the most promising."

He plucked his reading glasses off the collar of his pajamas and then reached under the heavy textbook to pull out a small leather-bound volume. "This rare gem was actually discovered by Cooper at the Citadel library. They have an impressive collection of books about South Carolinians with military backgrounds—of which Carrollton Vanderhorst was one. Apparently, he led several militias up in Virginia during the early years of the French and Indian War. George Washington himself referred to Vanderhorst as his 'great strategist.' When I read that, the next part started to make sense to me."

He flipped the book open to where a clean tissue was being used as a bookmark. "Carrollton died in January 1783 of a"—he paused for a moment to find the correct wording—"'bilious liver.' Apparently he'd been ill for several years, so his death wasn't unexpected. That's why he'd had the original mausoleum built to begin with, along with a brick wall to surround the cemetery." Jack's gaze met mine. "So, let's assume that Carrollton finds himself in possession of four valuable jewels for the patriot cause. But he's dying, and whoever the spy was isn't there to help him, and maybe he doesn't know who to trust with the jewels. After all, Alexander and Lawrence have been murdered by a person or persons unknown, so there's real danger if he's found with the rubies. Remember, the genius military commander Washington referred to Carrollton as a 'great strategist,' so I'm thinking he's pretty clever. So he figures a cunning way to hide the jewels and uses clues to lead the way just in case he dies before he can find out what to do with the rubies."

"Except maybe he was too clever, and no one did." I thought of the drawings I'd given to Anthony, along with the photo of the gate insert and how now would be the time to share what I knew. "I . . ."

Jack spoke at the same time, and I allowed him to continue. "Why would the ghost of a man holding the brooch—and I'm assuming it's Lawrence since of the three buried in the mausoleum, he's the only male who wasn't a soldier—be at the cistern? It's nowhere near Gallen Hall. Maybe he's there protecting the jewels."

"It's possible, I suppose. Even though this house wasn't built until the earlier part of the nineteenth century, there was another house here before it, owned by the Vanderhorsts. When they tore down the first mausoleum and brick wall at the Gallen Hall cemetery, Sophie believes they probably used some of the bricks to build this cistern. People reused bricks all the time back then simply because it was more economical. So, a spirit connected to the old cemetery could possibly feel a connection to the cistern because of that." I gave him a crooked smile. "Just because I see them doesn't mean I understand them."

Jack threw his glasses onto the bed beside him. "Marc's looked everywhere at the plantation for those jewels. I'm beginning to think they're in the cistern. Maybe hidden inside one of the bricks. I'm so tired of being sick, I've half a mind to get out of bed tonight and start digging myself."

I placed a restraining hand on his shoulder, sensing his renewed desperation and frustration. The New York publishing world virtually shut down in the month of December, so Jack was back in limbo land, stuck with stewing and mulling over the fate of his career. "Don't be silly, Jack. It's freezing outside and you're sick. And don't worry—I'm working on things while you're down for the count. I might be able to give you a nice Christmas surprise."

He narrowed his eyes at me. "Remember what I said, Mellie. Don't do anything rash."

"How can I?" I said flippantly. "I've got twenty-four couples coming to our house for dinner tonight. The only thing rash I can picture is me raiding Mrs. Houlihan's party bags so I can finally get a cookie."

Jack smiled, but he didn't look completely convinced. I wondered if he'd always been able to see through me, or if this was what marriage did to couples.

"Lawrence followed me one day, according to Jolly," Jack said. "Did I mention that to you? I might not have. That was around the time I was starting to feel sick, and I don't think I was thinking straight. And she's not the most reliable of psychics, you know? I might not have wanted to scare you. You've had a tough month."

"We both have," I said, taking his hand. "I think I'm getting really close to solving this, Jack."

"'I'm'?"

"We are," I corrected.

The doorbell rang downstairs. I glanced at my watch and stood. "It's the caterers. I've got to go and let them know where everything goes. Mother and Jayne left to get dressed, and Nola went to your mother's to help with bath time for the twins, and then she'll get changed and come here to help. I let Mrs. Houlihan go home an hour ago since the caterers can take over now, but someone still needs to be in charge."

"And you're so good at being in charge," Jack said, almost looking like his old self. "But what were you about to say? Earlier, before I interrupted."

The doorbell rang again. I leaned down and kissed him on his forehead. "I've got to get that. We'll talk later."

I put the TV remote in his hand and ran out of the room, pausing at the top of the stairs to text Anthony, asking him if he'd had any luck with the drawings and the photo of the gate panel. I had to do it twice because autocorrect kept translating it into something that looked like Swahili.

When I opened the door to let in the caterers, Jayne came in behind them. Her coat was open and we both stopped in the foyer to stare at each other. Finally, Jayne laughed out loud. "People are going to think we called each other to coordinate our outfits."

We both wore dark green velvet dresses with low V-necks and slightly flared skirts. "I saw this one in the window at the Finicky Filly and had to have it," I explained.

"Me, too," Jayne said, holding in a giggle. "It's my favorite store."

I didn't bother telling her that it was my favorite store, too. "I guess I'll go change," I said, heading for the stairs. "Tell the caterers not to do anything until I get back."

"Don't be silly," Jayne said. "I always wanted a sister so we could wear matching outfits."

I almost admitted out loud that I had, too, but stopped just in time. I looked behind her. "Where's Anthony?"

"I'm assuming he's on his way, because I've been trying to reach him, but I haven't heard back. Last time I spoke with him, he said to come on over without him because he was running late and had gone home to get dressed. He knows you've assigned him to hang up coats instead of going to the first house for appetizers, and he seemed okay with that."

I frowned. "I could have assigned him to toilet-paper-refill duty, but I didn't. I can still change the spreadsheet—I've got it open on my computer screen."

She grabbed my hands. "Did he call you? He said he would."

I looked down at my phone. No recent texts or phone calls from Anthony. "Nothing from him at all. What is it?"

"He finished the puzzle. Sometime last night. His bedroom door was closed when I got up, so I have no idea when. Let's go tell Jack—this will make him feel better."

"No. I mean, wait," I said, holding her back. "He's probably sleeping. But tell me—what does it look like? Does it tell us anything?"

She shook her head. "No. Not yet, anyway. But it must mean something, right?"

"Hopefully. Let's wait until we talk to Anthony—maybe he'll have more to tell Jack."

She looked at me dubiously, then down at her dress. "I have time to run home and change. Will you be okay without me for a little bit? I promise I'll hurry."

I looked at my watch, then back at Jayne. "I'm coming with you. Let me get the caterers situated, then text Mother and ask her to get here a little earlier than planned. I have to see the puzzle and I don't really think I can wait."

"Really, Melanie, I think it can—"

"I've got an hour and a half before the first guests arrive, and I'm dressed, and the house is ready, and Mother will be here. It will be fine."

Without waiting for her to respond, I ran to the kitchen to talk with the caterers, then texted both Nola and my mother to let them know where Jayne and I were and that we would be back in half an hour at the most. I grabbed my coat and purse, then ran out the door, stopping at the bottom of the piazza as I watched the freezing rain give way to small snowflakes that lazily glided their way between the streetlamps before settling on the ground below.

"It's not melting," Jayne said. "That's not good."

"At least it's not heavy. Maybe that means it'll stop."

She glanced at me, but I just shrugged before heading toward her car. "We have to take yours—mine's been blocked in by the caterer's van."

Jayne drove like an old woman, leaning close to her steering wheel as if that might help her see better.

"It's not even sticking to your windshield, Jayne, so you can definitely drive faster. Or I'll get out and walk and meet you there."

She pushed her foot just a little harder, creeping up to twenty miles per hour. If it hadn't been so cold out, I would have made good on my threat and hopped out.

I tapped my foot from cold and anticipation as I waited for her to unlock her front door, doing my best not to push her out of my way as I ran to the dining room. Jayne flicked on the wall switch to light up the chandelier, and we stood in the doorway looking at the table with awe.

"It's exactly how I thought it would look," I said. "When I said it reminded me of one of those puzzle squares. It's still a bunch of random designs, but look at how they all connect to each other."

"So this was intentional," Jayne said. "Whoever designed this wanted it to look haphazard."

I nodded. "Jack thinks it must have all been designed by Carrollton Vanderhorst, Lawrence's father. He fought alongside George Washington in the French and Indian War and Washington himself called him his 'great strategist.' He designed the cemetery and must have left clues as to where the treasure was hidden."

"But who was he hiding it from? Was he the patriot, since he was friends with Washington? And what about Lawrence and Eliza? What side were they working on?"

I began walking around the dining room table. "I'm not sure—and I don't know if we'll ever find out the whole story. But I think Lawrence was in love with Eliza, but Eliza was in love with Alexander, the British soldier." I told her about Greco being dressed in his reenactor's uniform, and the kiss he'd received when he'd slipped on the peacock signet ring. "Mother said the owner of the ring was a woman, and I'm fairly confident that was Eliza."

"And she wore the brooch, remember? She must have known what it was." Jayne was silent for a moment, thinking. "So—she was the spy," Jayne said slowly. "And she and the British soldier had a thing. Maybe that's why he ended up buried in the mausoleum, too."

"Maybe, because Carrollton would have been the one to decide that. And the interment of the soldier. Even with his patriot beliefs, he must have known that Eliza would want to be buried with her beloved."

"And Lawrence, too. Or maybe he felt that Lawrence belonged there because he was Carrollton's son."

I leaned over the table, mesmerized by swirls and lines. "Jolly told me something interesting. That when she sensed the man following Jack—the man from the cistern holding the brooch, who I suspect is Lawrence—she sensed his heart was deeply wounded."

Jayne nodded. "I imagine if his fiancée was in love with another man, that would hurt. And that she was betraying him by being a spy for the other side would be a double betrayal."

I nodded. "Which is why I don't think she killed herself. That's why she keeps repeating the word *lies*. She wants people to know the truth."

"But what is the truth? That Lawrence killed her?"

I shrugged. "He's the spirit with the evil vibes, remember? The one who spoke through our mother saying that traitors deserve to die and rot in hell. I mean, there's a possibility that Alexander killed Eliza when he found out that she was using information she got from him to pass on to the patriots, but that's not the feeling I get from him at all."

Jayne nodded. "I agree. But whether Alexander was aware of what was going on and either helping Eliza or turned the other way is something lost to history."

I continued to walk around the table, studying the completed puzzle, occasionally reaching over to make an alignment of edges straighter. I slid my finger around the lip of the table, thinking out loud. "Since Eliza and Alexander died before Lawrence, it's entirely possible that he killed them both."

I stopped walking, feeling Jayne's wide-eyed gaze on me. "And that brings us back to the question of who killed Lawrence."

"I suspect someone on the American side—maybe they thought he had the rubies."

"Or maybe they *knew* he had the rubies. Eliza had the brooch. Remember the door on the hidden compartment in her jewelry cabinet, how it had been ripped off its hinges as if in a hurry. Or in anger. And only the brooch was found in the cistern, discarded with the garbage. The one scenario that makes sense is that Lawrence found out about the jewels and somehow found out where she'd hidden them. Maybe he killed her out of anger, or revenge."

"Or a broken heart," Jayne added.

"And then he was killed trying to make his escape, and the rubies were saved. By whom, I don't know for sure. Everything's conjecture at this point. All I do know for sure is that Eliza didn't kill herself, and she wants the record to be set straight."

I returned to studying the maze, the lines and curves simple, like in an artist's original sketch before it's filled in with color. I could almost hear Jack speaking in my head about Carrollton Vanderhorst. *So he figures a cunning way to hide the jewels and uses clues to lead the way just in case he dies before he can find out what to do with the rubies.* A top and bottom of the puzzle were clearly identified now, the top two corners curved in opposite directions, like an arch. Just like the arch over the gate leading into the cemetery.

I jerked my head up, almost laughing at Carrollton Vanderhorst's cleverness. "Jayne, I really need to talk with Anthony."

Jayne looked down at her phone, then began dialing. She waited a moment before ending the call. "It went straight to voice mail."

I looked around the dining room, then walked quickly out to the foyer, toward the stairs. "Where's his room?"

"Melanie, that would be an invasion of privacy. . . ."

I didn't stop. "This is your house, Jayne, and he is a guest. I'm looking for something specific—a couple of drawings I gave him earlier. They belong to me, so technically I'm only trying to recover my property."

"Fine," she said, walking past me down the hall. She stopped outside one of the bedroom doors and tapped. "Anthony?" After waiting a respectful moment, she pushed the door open and waited for me on the threshold.

The room was elegantly appointed with the furnishings of the late owner, Button Pinckney, Jayne's aunt. The bed was neatly made and the draperies open. The only thing missing was any sign of occupancy. "Didn't he bring a suitcase or anything?"

"Sure, but I don't know what was in it. I assumed it was full of clothes. I haven't been in here, Melanie, if that's what you're implying."

I rolled my eyes. "Did he bring a laptop or printer or anything so he could work while he was here?"

She nodded, her gaze traveling around the room. "He had both—I know that because I saw the laptop a few times and could hear the printer from this room." She walked to the closet and opened it. "Empty," she said, her voice hollow. "No printer, laptop. Or clothes. Maybe he just decided he'd already overstayed his welcome and, with the puzzle finished, figured it was time to head home."

"Maybe," I said. "Let me try to reach him again." I dialed his number, but the call went straight to voice mail. "Maybe his battery died. Doesn't matter—we'll see him when we get back to my house."

Avoiding her gaze, I knelt on the floor and lifted the bed skirt, then moved around the room, opening every drawer, finally stopping at the trash can tucked next to the chest of drawers. I eagerly plucked up the can and poured the balled-up papers out on top of the bedspread.

"What are these?" Jayne asked.

"These are multiple copies of the same thing—Anthony was just trying to get them all to be the same size." I opened a ball of paper and smoothed it on the bed, then began opening another, starting two different piles. "One is the copy of the drawing Joseph Longo made from a paper he found on Robert Vanderhorst's desk back in the twenties. The other is a page from the Vanderhorst family archives at the Charleston Museum—the ones Marc tried to throw out and Anthony found. And the third . . ." I held up a black-and-white copy on my phone.

"Is the little panel from the mausoleum door," Jayne finished, her eyes widening in understanding. She reached for one of the balled-up papers and began flattening it. "So these three pictures belong together and are some kind of clue?"

I nodded quickly, adding another paper to one of the piles. "The old cemetery fence was brick and was destroyed when the old mausoleum was rebuilt. Anyway, Samuel Vanderhorst designed the new wrought-iron fence and gates, as well as the mausoleum door. But the two gates were destroyed or lost around the time of Hurricane Hugo, so all that remains of them are these drawings."

"Oh, my gosh," Jayne said as she moved more quickly. "So if we get these all to fit together, they should show us something," she said excitedly.

"That's my theory, anyway," I said, my own excitement at having someone who understood the way I thought almost masking the unexpected twinge of annoyance that the person was Jayne.

When we'd divvied up all the wrinkled pages into their own piles, I spread them out into fans and began to sort through them, comparing those that seemed to match up best with ones from the other two. Catching on to what I was doing, Jayne pulled one from the third pile and held it up to the two I held. "I think this one works."

I nodded my thanks and took it, then held the three of them together up toward the light. "These aren't exact—I imagine Anthony would have the ones that are—but they will work."

I ran out of the room and toward the stairs. "Where are you going?" Jayne called from right behind me.

I didn't answer but led her to the dining room table. "Hold these." I shoved the three pages into her hand, then pulled out a dining room chair to stand on. Holding my phone as high as it would go over the puzzle, I took a photo. "You have a printer, right?"

Before she'd finished nodding, I'd e-mailed the photo to her. "Go pull the photo up in the scrapbooking software you're always talking about, and make it fit in an eight-by-eight square so it matches the other three. And please make it black-and-white. While you're doing that, I'm going to try Anthony again. Failing that, I'll call Mother to see if she's at the house yet and if she's seen Anthony."

She was already running up the stairs by the time I'd finished speaking. I used the initials, S.V., to orient each picture, then pulled out my phone again. When Jayne returned fifteen minutes later, I shook my head in answer to her unasked question, then took the page she handed to me. "Perfect," I said, smiling at her. I placed the picture of the completed puzzle behind the other three sheets and then, after a shared look of anticipation with Jayne, held them up to the light as I remembered Anthony had done.

I wasn't sure who gasped louder, but I was suddenly very glad that someone was with me to share my discovery. With the three pictures held together, four distinct dark circles were clearly visible from the layering of the lines of each page. And each dark circle was now projected onto the puzzle made from the bricks.

"I'll go get a marker," Jayne said. She raced out of the room, and returned quickly with a black Sharpie.

"Good thinking." I continued to hold the pages up to the light while Jayne marked the back side of the last page with black marker. When she was done, I lowered them to the table and slid out the last page, using the marker to darken the spots that had bled through to the front of the puzzle page.

"It's a map of the cemetery, isn't it?" Jayne asked.

I nodded. "And I'd bet a fortune in rubies that these four spots show us where Lafayette's treasures were buried."

The hall clock chimed and our giddy smiles quickly turned to expressions of panic. "We've got to go," I said.

"But I haven't changed my dress yet."

"No time. We need to find Anthony. I'm hoping he'll be at the house by the time we get there."

"And if he's not?" Jayne asked.

"Then we've got a problem."

CHAPTER 33

The flurries had stopped by the time we left Jayne's house and headed back to Tradd Street, but when I checked the weather app on my phone, it looked like the break was temporary, the chance of frozen precipitation going from five percent to one hundred percent by two in the morning.

Jayne squeezed into the driveway behind the catering van, promising to move her car when they were ready to leave, unwilling to park blocks away and walk back in the cold. Nola had texted earlier to let us know that Cooper had brought sand to scatter on the walkway and steps, which I'd have to make sure Jack knew about so he'd stop scowling so much in the young man's direction.

The front door opened as we walked quickly down the piazza, and I held back a shout of surprise when I saw Anthony wearing a dinner jacket and holding two coat hangers. "Ladies," he said with a wide smile. "So glad to see you. We were wondering if you would get here before the guests."

"We've been calling you and texting," Jayne said, turning around so he could help her with her coat. "We noticed that you've moved out—weren't you going to tell me?"

"Sorry—I should have given you a heads-up. I figured I had imposed enough on you and that I needed to get back to my house. That's when I dropped my phone down your stairs this afternoon and it shattered. First thing tomorrow, snow allowing, I'm heading to the Apple store on King Street. I'm so sorry for making you worry—I didn't think to borrow someone's phone to let you know since I knew I'd see you here."

He placed her coat on a hanger, then reached to help me take off mine, pausing slightly when he noticed our dresses but making no comment. "Well," I said, "I'm glad you're here. We need to get to Gallen Hall—can you take me as soon as the dinner is over?"

His eyebrows shot up. "Why?"

I looked at him, surprised. "You didn't figure out the map?"

He shook his head. "What map? Of Gallen Hall?"

"No—the cemetery. I think there's something—" The doorbell rang, cutting me off. He sent it an annoyed look but didn't move to answer it.

I gave him a small shove on his back. "Guests are arriving, and I'd rather we speak in private. We'll talk later."

He looked as if he might argue, but then smiled as he opened the door to allow in a couple I'd seen at another Ashley Hall event. Several other couples followed, including a group of teachers from the school, and it quickly grew loud and crowded as guests began filling the foyer. Nola joined Anthony to help hang up the coats on the rented racks placed in Jack's study, even though I was pretty sure I hadn't assigned her that job on her spreadsheet.

They were kept busy hanging coats for half an hour as people trailed in at different times, most of them having hesitated leaving the appetizer houses until assured the snow would stop. Servers dressed in Revolutionary War–era clothing walked around with tankards of syllabub (made from Sophie's authentic recipe) to keep the party atmosphere going while we waited for everyone to arrive before we were seated.

I was eager to find time to speak with Anthony, but I had to play hostess and give guests the tour of the Christmas trees and discuss how I'd made the centerpieces and wreaths.

"Are these real?" The mother of one of Nola's classmates leaned over to study the oranges in the large bowl on the foyer table that Greco had been kind enough to zhush for me.

"Yes," I said. "All of the fruit in every decoration is real."

She put her hand to the side of her mouth to whisper conspiratorially, "You know, they sell fake ones now that look as good as the real ones, and they last a lot longer."

I kept the smile on my face, considering for a moment calling Sophie and asking the woman to repeat what she'd just said. "Yes, well, I've heard that, too, but we wanted this to be a more authentic experience for the attendees."

The woman moved on as I was approached by an older couple who remembered Nevin Vanderhorst and said they were happy to see the house dressed up for the holidays again. "You've done such a lovely job, my dear," the wife said, her green eyes matching her beautiful emerald earrings. "It certainly has the feeling of being a home again." She took my hand and patted it. "I'm sure Nevin and his mother would be thrilled to know what you've done."

"I'm pretty sure they know," I said, not meaning to say it out loud.

They both looked a little startled as the woman dropped my hand. "Yes, well, I just wanted to let you know that this house finally has the warmth of a home."

"Thank you," I said, feeling my chest puff with love and pride for this house that I'd never wanted to own and that I still had doubts about. But she was right. It was *home* for my family and for me. It was something worth fighting for.

As they walked away, they paused by the centerpiece bowl and I overheard the gentleman say, "I don't believe I've ever seen cloves placed so precisely on oranges in all of my years. . . ."

I hid my smile as I turned toward the front door, watching it open with the last of the arrivals. I knew that Veronica and Michael had been assigned to dinner at my house, so I wasn't surprised to see them, but I was quite certain that Rebecca and Marc weren't on my list. Especially because I'd ensured their names appeared on the dinner list at another house.

"Cousin!" Rebecca squealed as Anthony helped her with her coat. I said hello to Veronica and Michael before they headed into the room to greet Alston and Cooper's parents. I looked in dismay at Rebecca's green velvet dress, thankfully adorned with pink shoes and matching handbag so she, Jayne, and I wouldn't look like triplets. I'd already rethought my whole dressing-the-twins-alike mode in the three seconds it had taken to register that Rebecca was wearing the same dress as Jayne and me.

She hugged both of us before standing back and taking in our dresses. Despite her outward cheeriness, her eyes were slightly puffy and her peaches-and-cream complexion was sprinkled with small, angry bumps along her cheeks. Either pregnancy didn't suit her or her marriage didn't.

"Great minds think alike, right? And I hope you don't mind, but I changed house assignments with another couple so I could come here."

She looked so sad and pathetic that I had to smile. "Sure." I glanced behind her. "Is Marc with you?" I asked, resisting the impulse to cross my fingers behind my back.

Rebecca stuck out her chin. "No. He said he had important 'business' to take care of." She swallowed heavily. "It doesn't matter. I'm here to have fun with my family." She waved to my mother across the room, then smiled shakily at Jayne and me.

"I'm sorry," Anthony said, putting an arm around Rebecca's shoulders. "My brother's a jerk. He has been my whole life. Why don't you sit at our table so you won't have to sit next to strangers?" He looked at me. "Is that all right with you?"

Before I could say no or that I'd spent three whole days and two spreadsheets on planning the seating arrangements, he was headed to the front parlor, where I'd placed Anthony and Jayne at a table with two teachers from Ashley Hall, and I tried not to wince as I noticed him dragging an extra chair to his table. Rebecca leaned close to me. "I hope you were able to use the drawing I gave you."

"I was, actually. It was very helpful."

Jayne widened her eyes at me.

"Thank you," I added.

"So, what was it?" Rebecca asked.

I hesitated, not forgetting that she was Marc's wife. But I owed her.

I couldn't have figured anything out without the one critical piece of information she'd given me. And, as she and my mother kept reminding me, she was family. "It's part of a map."

"A map?"

Jayne nodded. "Yes. Melanie figured it all out. The brick puzzle Anthony was working on is the actual cemetery at Gallen Hall, and the two drawings along with a photo Melanie took of the mausoleum gate are part of the same map."

Rebecca actually giggled. "Wow. Marc couldn't have figured that one out in a million years." She sobered quickly. "You won't tell him I said that, right?"

I rolled my eyes. "I have no intention of speaking with your husband ever again, so the answer is no."

She tilted her head to the side. "Never say never. Marc and Anthony will swear up and down that they hate each other, but Marc said he wants his brother to be godfather to our baby."

"Really?" Jayne and I said together.

We were interrupted by our mother approaching, looking elegant and regal in a dark violet silk chiffon dress and matching velvet pumps. "Mellie, darling, I think it's time for everyone to be seated."

With a quick glance at Rebecca, I moved away to find Nola to give her permission to ring the dinner bell; then Cooper appeared by her side to escort her to one of the smaller tables. She hadn't complained about being seated at one of the "children's tables," as she called them, when I told her I'd saved a seat at her table for anyone she cared to invite.

I helped guests find their place cards and take their seats, and I finally headed into the dining room to take my place at the head of the table just as the caterers began serving the soup course. I remembered my manners, taking turns to speak with diners on either side of me, happily answering questions regarding my connection to Ashley Hall, the house, my job, and whether I was wearing a uniform of some sort, which was why there were three of us all dressed alike. I smiled and ate and talked, all the while aware of something niggling at the back of my mind, as tiny and destructive as a termite.

Keenly aware of the time, I listened for the chiming of the grandfather clock in the parlor. As soon as the last guest left, I'd ask Anthony to take me to Gallen Hall. I was already envisioning dumping the rubies in Jack's hands, and then him kissing me, his anger at me easily pushed aside by his gratitude.

Dessert was served at different houses, so there wasn't much lingering after the guests had finished eating. I might have been too enthusiastic about pulling out people's chairs, removing plates, and bringing coats into the foyer in my haste for them to leave, but it had started flurrying again and I could hear an imaginary clock ticking in my head.

Despite a few stragglers wandering around the foyer chatting and examining the decorations, I went in search of Anthony to make sure he was ready to go as soon as the last guest departed. I found Jayne saying good-bye to Veronica and Michael at the front door.

Her smile faded when she saw me approach. "Where's Anthony?"

"I was coming to ask you the same thing. Wasn't he with you at dinner?"

"Yes, but right after the main course was served, he excused himself, saying that you'd asked him to come find you before the meal was over because you needed him for something."

I shook my head slowly. "No. I never said that." Our eyes met as a sick feeling, as viscous and dark as octopus ink, flooded my insides.

"He must be here somewhere," Jayne said, an unmistakable note of panic in her voice. "I must have misunderstood."

"I'm sure you're right," I said, although I had no such certainty. Together we looked in all of the downstairs rooms including the kitchen and powder room, and even searched the back garden. We found our parents kissing under the mistletoe strung across the threshold of Jack's office. I coughed loudly as we approached, and they, mercifully, pulled away from each other. "Has either of you seen Anthony?"

My father nodded. "I was headed to the bathroom and saw him leave out the back door about forty-five minutes ago. I assumed you'd sent him on some errand."

"No. I didn't." I met Jayne's gaze. Without a word she ran toward the front door and threw it open, leaving it ajar as she raced down the piazza to the front walk. I met her at the front door on her return, her eyes wide and glazed.

"His car's not here." She looked at me. "His car's not *here*," she repeated, as if to convince herself.

I grabbed her hand and pulled her inside, closing the door behind us. "This isn't good, is it?" she asked.

"No," I said. "It's not."

Our parents appeared with Rebecca, all three bundled for the weather. "We're going to take Rebecca with us, if that's all right. It was a lovely event," Mother said, and kissed me on the cheek.

I tried to act relaxed, as if my world hadn't suddenly been shaken like a snow globe. We said our good-byes and I watched them leave. Then I put my face close to Jayne's. "Did you talk about the map at dinner?"

She shook her head. "No," she said. "I didn't." A loud, choking sob erupted from her throat. "But . . ."

"But what?"

"But Rebecca did. She mentioned how you'd figured out everything with her help. I didn't stop her because it was Anthony. I didn't think I needed to. But she didn't say anything about how the three drawings and the brick puzzle have to be used together because she doesn't know about it. That's a good thing, right?"

"Oh, my gosh. Oh, my *gosh*." I squeezed my head between my hands as if that would somehow eradicate all the stupidity that apparently lived there. I remembered the niggling feeling at the back of my head that had started when Rebecca mentioned that Marc wanted Anthony to be the godfather to their baby. "Marc and Anthony—they're just pretending. They're not estranged."

"But why . . ." Jayne stopped, her eyes widening, her breath coming in short, hollow puffs. "They set us up." Her face lost color as the implications settled on her. "Everything Anthony said to us was a lie. He used us. All of us."

I nodded, thinking of snippets of all the conversations I'd had with

Anthony, all the information that I'd shared that he'd told Marc. Beneath the shame and humiliation, I felt the rolling burn of anger. "I have no doubt that they're both at Gallen Hall now."

"But they don't know everything, right? They still need to figure out how you have to put them all together."

"They will, though." I closed my eyes, allowing the dismal dread of failure to swallow me. And somewhere, in the black darkness, I heard my grandmother's voice. *Jack.* I couldn't fail him now, not when he needed me the most. I opened my eyes, a renewed sense of determination flooding my veins. "We can't let them beat us. We just can't."

"But how—"

"Give me your car keys. The caterer is blocking me in and I don't have time to waste to ask them to move."

"Where are you going?"

"To Gallen Hall. To the cemetery. I've got to get those rubies before Marc finds them."

"But what if you run into Marc and Anthony?" Jayne asked, her eyes wide.

"I don't know," I said somberly. "I can only hope that they're still trying to figure out what to do with the map. Or that they're waiting until morning. And if not, then I'll think about that when I have to."

Jayne shook her head. "I'm going with you," she said, already marching toward the door. "So at least it's two against two if it comes to that."

"Absolutely not. You need to stay here. If I need help, I'll call you. Besides, it wouldn't do for both of us to get into trouble without backup. And I don't want anyone else knowing yet—they'll just try to stop me and then I'll be too late."

I could tell her resistance was weakening. "But what should I tell Jack?"

"You don't need to tell him anything. Let him sleep. I'll let him know when I bring home the rubies." I offered a hopeful smile that she didn't return.

"Melanie, I can't let you go alone. We're stronger together, remember?"

"I won't be alone. Eliza is there, and she's on our side. I now understand why she pushed Anthony down the stairs."

"And wrecked his car?"

I shook my head. "No. Now that I know that Marc and Anthony are cut from the same cloth, I wouldn't be surprised if he wrecked it himself to get our sympathy."

"But Lawrence is there, too, Melanie. Remember what happened at the mausoleum."

My arm hurt at the memory, but I couldn't let fear hold me back. There was just too much at stake. "Give me your keys, Jayne. Please. We're running out of time."

With a heavy sigh, she went to the makeshift coatrack and pulled her purse from a hanger. "For the record, I don't agree with what you're doing. I think this would be one of your decisions that Jack would call rash and un-thought-out. Just let me tell him—"

"No. He needs his rest. Let him sleep. I'll tell him everything when I get back."

"If you get back." She dropped her keys in my outstretched hand.

"What do you mean, *if*? It's not like Marc and Anthony are going to kill me or anything."

Her eyes widened. "I used to think Anthony wouldn't be capable of anything like that. Until tonight." She swallowed, and I thought for a moment she might actually cry. "Apparently, I'm not a very good judge of character."

Before I knew what I was doing, I'd put my arms around her for a quick hug. She looked as surprised as I felt. "Well," I said, "if it makes you feel any better, neither am I. At least this way we have a chance to beat them at their own game." I turned toward the demilune chest in the hallway and opened the doors to pull out a heavy pair of sweatpants and waterproof ankle boots. "I slip these on to take the dogs out," I offered in explanation. "They'll keep me warm and dry." I sent a paranoid glance toward the stairs, afraid that I'd see Jack and he'd tell me not to go. "I'll put these on in the car."

"Here, then," she said, diving into her coat pockets and pulling out a pair of thick gloves. "These are waterproof and fleece lined." I gratefully accepted them, knowing they'd be a lot warmer than my leather gloves. "And this." She placed a thick knit hat over my head, pulling it below my ears and tucking in my hair. "But it doesn't mean I'm agreeing that you should be doing this."

"I know. And if anybody asks, I'll let them know that you tried to stop me."

"I'll remember that." Jayne stepped forward to tuck my scarf into the collar of my coat. "I have a phone charger in the car, so plug in your phone so it'll have a full charge by the time you get to Gallen Hall. I want you to call me when you get there, and I'll want you to check in every fifteen minutes with a text. And if you don't, I'm calling Thomas."

"Really, Jayne, I don't—"

"That's the deal. Either agree or I'm going to tell Jack right now."

"Fine," I said, moving toward the door, making sure no one else was in the foyer to see me leave.

"Dad's shed is unlocked," Jayne said. "You'll want a shovel and a flashlight."

"Right," I said, embarrassed that I probably wouldn't have thought about either until I was almost at the cemetery. I pulled open the door and saw Greco's hurricane lanterns flickering brightly as white flakes blew across the piazza, dancing around the glass like fairies.

"My car has front-wheel drive," Jayne offered. "But if there's anything more than half an inch, you won't get any traction. Just remember to keep your phone charged."

I nodded, walking toward the door at the end of the piazza, afraid to look back just in case I changed my mind.

"I love you, Melanie. I'm glad you're my sister."

I just nodded as I let myself through the piazza door, unable to speak because of the sudden lump in my throat.

CHAPTER 34

Fat snowflakes were falling by the time I pulled onto the Ashley River Bridge. Only a few other drivers braved the roads, tempting fate and the potential closing of the bridges. I tried not to think about how I would get back with closed bridges and icy roads. Charleston hadn't had a significant snowfall since 1989, so, except for the northern transplants, not many of us knew how to drive in snow.

My hands hurt from clutching the steering wheel too tightly. I flexed my fingers, trying to make the blood flow back into the tips. I didn't dare take my eyes off the road to check on the status of my phone charge, but I'd plugged it in just as Jayne had instructed. Remembering her concern brought me a small comfort, making me feel less alone on my mission, the cord charging my phone like a lifeline.

I found the road to Gallen Hall after missing it the first time because of the snow. My father's gardening tools shifted in the trunk, clanking loudly as I slowly drove over the uneven dirt road, straining to see through the falling snowflakes. In addition to a battery-powered camping light I'd found in the shed, I'd brought a shovel, a spade, and a pick. I'd grabbed the latter at the last second, realizing that the ground would be rock-hard from the cold. I refused to consider that I might not be strong enough to swing the pick with enough force to even break the surface. Failure wasn't an option, not after I'd come this far. I thought of Jack and how much finding these rubies would mean for him both emotionally and professionally. I recognized, too, that I wanted Jack back—the charming, smart, and capable husband and father I loved. With renewed determination, I straightened my shoulders, then turned Jayne's car into the deep, dark woods, where the trees seemed to swallow me as I drew closer to the house.

When I neared the edge of the woods, I stopped the car and switched off my headlights so I wouldn't alert anyone who might be in the house. My plan was to slip into the cemetery without being seen, do what needed to be done, then head back home before the snowfall got heavy enough to close the roads. It had seemed like a clear plan when I'd left the house, and only now that it was too late could I spot the giant leaps of faith it would take to successfully execute it. I glanced at my phone, knowing one call from me for help would be all it would take. But I had to try. And if I failed, then I'd call.

I peered down the dark road, the snow reflecting the ambient light from the sky like some celestial flashlight, making it easier to see. With a sigh, I reached over to the floor of the passenger seat and grabbed Jayne's umbrella. Bracing myself against the cold and snow, I jumped out of the car and began walking through the thin coating of snow, stopping before I reached the horseshoe of the front drive in an attempt to remain unseen.

With an exhalation of relief, I saw no lights on in the house, nor did I pick out the shapes of a car or cars on the front drive. Either Anthony and Marc had stayed in town, not wanting to risk the weather, or they hadn't yet figured out the final clue.

I felt lighter as I made my way back to the car. I flipped on the headlights, then drove past the house toward the cemetery, stopping in front of the main gate, the lights from the car shining through the black bars and reflecting off the fat snowflakes. I put the car in park, leaving the headlights and wipers on before reaching under the seat for the drawings and the map that Jayne had placed there when we'd left her house.

I pushed the seat back and placed the map on the steering wheel to orient myself to where the four black Sharpie marks indicated the spots in the cemetery. I looked up at the gate and the adjacent fence sections, then back to the map, realizing that the edges of the drawings corresponded to the iron gate designs that edged the cemetery.

Like the red lights on the floor of a plane that led a passenger to the emergency exit door, the fence designs served the same purpose, instructing the treasure hunter how deep into the cemetery one needed to go before bearing left or right to each dot on the map. It was brilliant, really, and I turned my head to share it with Jack, too late remembering that I was alone.

I remembered Yvonne telling us that no burials had taken place in the cemetery since Eliza, Lawrence, and Alexander had been interred in the mausoleum in 1782. It had never occurred to us to wonder why, even though Gallen Hall had been inhabited for more than two centuries afterward and people had presumably died during that period. The moratorium on burials had been part of Carrollton Vanderhorst's great master clue, and we'd overlooked it completely.

Not wanting to get the paper wet, I pulled out my phone and took a photo of the map with the dots marked, then of the pattern of each section of fence I needed to find. Having the images on my phone meant I could make them bigger, making it easier to see the intricate designs.

I sent a text to Jayne to let her know I'd arrived, that there was no sign of Marc or Anthony, and that I was about to head into the cemetery. I made no mention of the fat blobs of snow now splattering quietly onto my windshield. I hit SEND, then slid the phone into my coat pocket. I'd deal with that later. Somehow. I popped the trunk, pulled Jayne's hat lower over my ears, then exited the car.

The smell of gunpowder permeated the air, the jangling of a horse harness ringing out in the quiet of falling snow. I quickly retrieved the camping light from the trunk, knowing with certainty that I wasn't alone. I held it aloft, turning around in a circle, seeing no one, dead or alive, but registering the scent of horses and leather now mingling with that of gunpowder.

"Eliza?" I called out, more because I needed to hear the sound of a human voice than because I expected to hear her answer. But she was there. I felt her presence, warm and comforting, as if she knew that I wanted to expose the truth about her death. And maybe even to let the world know that she'd been a patriot and had stayed true to her cause despite her heart calling her in another direction.

Using the camping light to see the way, I walked through the unlocked front gate, pulling out my phone to access the map and guide me to where the first spot was indicated. A dark shadow emerged from behind an ancient obelisk at the rear of the cemetery. I jerked the light up, trying to find out who—or what—it was. The blood rushed through my ears, my breath frosty puffs blowing out in quick succession. I stayed perfectly still for a long moment, my gaze trained on the spot, but nothing moved.

The sound of iron clanging made me jump. I swung the light toward the mausoleum, realizing it must have been the door swinging shut, briefly wondering why it had been open. The sound of whispering voices came from behind and in front of me, the snow seeming to blur the words, making it impossible to tell what was being said.

My feet crunched over the frozen grass and a thin layer of snow. I was careful to avoid the sunken spots where Sophie had warned me the oldest wooden caskets, some piled in as many as three or four layers, had disintegrated under the ground, making the earth above the concave spots treacherous to walk on. I shivered at the thought of slipping beneath the surface and being buried alive, out here alone where no one could hear me scream. At least no one who could help me.

I shone the light at the fence, studying the pattern on each panel and comparing it with the picture on the phone. The snow was falling faster now, and I had to continually wipe it off my screen. I had reached the halfway point in the fence when I matched the pattern to the edge of the brick puzzle, telling me that it was time to turn right and head into the middle of the cemetery.

The whispers, louder now, had the cadence of a taunt, or a threat. I stopped to listen, recognizing one word among the others, nearly smothered by the falling snow. *Traitors.* I swallowed down the fear and uncertainty. I wasn't by nature a brave person, but at that moment I had no other choice.

I walked around a slight indentation in the ground, then nearly ran into a headstone. I glanced down at my map to make sure I was at the right spot, then shone my light on the slate face of the headstone. The words were worn by the elements but still legible. Leaning closer, I read the name: HERA. I put the light closer, trying to find a last name or dates, but there was nothing. I squatted to see the bottom, scraping snow off to make sure I hadn't missed anything. I sat back, staring at a carving that would be easily missed by the casual observer.

It was of a peacock feather, long and slender, the eye clearly marked at its end. If I hadn't been so cold and afraid, I might have appreciated the cleverness of it all. I remembered Anthony mentioning that Eliza buried her favorite peacocks in the cemetery, and seeing about a dozen stones with only first names on them on my previous visit. Until the Civil War, when the last one had been eaten, the family had apparently continued to bury the birds here, either intentionally or inadvertently helping to hide the four gravesites I was sure were indicated on the map.

Encouraged by my success, I dug the heel of my boot into the ground in front of the stone, stirring up dead grass and dirt so I could find it again without using the map, assuming the snow stopped soon. Looking at my map again, my frozen fingers nearly dropping my phone twice as I remembered to text Jayne that I was okay, I found the other three graves, all with female Greek mythological names. I marked them with the heel of my boot as I'd done the first one, inordinately proud of myself.

I wanted to sink down onto the ground and cry with relief. But I knew I couldn't or I'd risk hypothermia. I needed to keep going. Jack needed me to keep going, no matter how many times in my head I could hear him telling me not to think I could solve all of our problems by myself. But I was here, and I had figured out where Lafayette's treasure was buried. I needed to take care of this now, or risk our losing to Marc Longo one more time.

First, I needed to sit in the car with the heater blasting to defrost myself. I knew I probably had a candy bar somewhere in my purse to give me a burst of energy I would definitely need. Then I'd grab the pick from the trunk and figure out what I was supposed to do with it.

I was so focused on getting to the car that it took me a moment to become aware of movement from the direction of the mausoleum. A violent shiver went through me that had nothing to do with the snow pelting my face and freezing my toes as I recalled my arm being pulled through the gate by an unseen hand.

A bright spotlight flipped on, blinding me, but not before I'd had the chance to register who the two figures were standing behind it.

"Thank you, Melanie. Such a help, as always." Marc Longo moved forward to stand in front of me. "You must be freezing."

I clenched my teeth to keep them from chattering, and looked behind his shoulder to see Anthony. He wasn't cowering, exactly, but he seemed to want to hide behind his brother.

"I hope you're ashamed of yourself," I shouted at him, although the effect was muted by my stiff jaw.

"For helping his brother?" Marc offered. "He did the right thing. As you did, helping us find the treasure. For a brief moment, I thought Anthony and I should take the time to figure it out ourselves, and then I realized we didn't need to bother. You're such a worker bee, Melanie— we knew you'd be on it. We parked our cars out back and waited in the warm house for you to do all the work." He feigned a concerned expression. "We left hot chocolate on the stove for you, if you'd like it. And there's a fire going in the kitchen with a chair in front of it waiting for you."

I frowned. "What? And leave the treasure out here for you to find?"

Marc threw back his head and laughed. He held a can out toward me. "I've brought spray paint to mark the four headstones, so when it warms up in a few days and the ground has thawed a bit, we can go in at our leisure and dig up Lafayette's treasure. Except this time we'll remember to lock the gate against intruders and have someone standing guard."

It occurred to me then that he didn't know what the treasure was. And that it didn't matter to him. All he cared about was winning and crushing Jack and getting what he wanted. If he came into possession of a fortune, too, even better.

"But I found it." I sounded like a child on a playground, but I couldn't think of a better way to say it.

"Yes, you did. But you found it on Anthony's property. According to South Carolina law, it legally belongs to him. Sure, you could probably take us to court, but the process would be long and expensive and you and I both know that you can't afford it. Who knows what the stress might do to Jack? And because you're family, I'm not going to charge you with trespassing. This time."

An icy wind blew through the cemetery, slapping me in the face and forming small tornadoes of snow around us. I saw Anthony glance at them uneasily, and it occurred to me that the funnels might not be part of the natural world. The distinct clang of a horse harness made Marc spin around, taking the light with him. I blinked in the darkness, aware of the sparkle of a gold brooch against a dark form. And behind that was the man from the cistern photo—Lawrence, with the dark hollows for eyes, his white stockings bright against the night. And right before Marc's light blinded me again, I saw the bloody hole in his white shirt.

I was shaking with anger and cold and fear. I had lost everything, and I had no one to blame but myself. I had once loved my aloneness, my independence, which meant I didn't have to rely on anyone but myself. Even with the expansion of my family in the last years, I'd still seen myself as a separate entity—out of either habit or stubbornness, I didn't know, and it didn't matter anymore. Whatever the reason, it had been my undoing.

"But I found it," I repeated, incapable of expressing every emotion that was running through me. I cringed at how toddlerlike I sounded and was oddly relieved that it was so cold that my watery eyes disguised the fact that angry tears were streaming down my face.

"Like I said," Marc responded calmly, "it doesn't matter. Gallen Hall

Plantation belongs to Anthony, and anything found on his property belongs to him."

"Not exactly," a voice called from the front gate.

"Jack?" I said, relief battling with horror in my voice.

Marc jerked around, shining his light in Jack's direction, illuminating three figures walking toward us.

"Jayne?" Anthony stepped forward, then stopped, as if realizing that she might not be happy to see him.

I squinted through the dark and the falling snow, recognizing the tall form of Detective Thomas Riley, my knees almost weak with relief that I was no longer alone.

Marc barked out a laugh. "Wrong again, Jack. Gallen Hall belongs to Anthony. Therefore, whatever is found here belongs to him." He nodded in Thomas's direction. "I'm glad you brought the police with you to help enforce the law. Although I'm hoping reasonable heads will prevail so we won't have to reduce ourselves to using force."

Jack now stood in the circle of light but didn't come stand next to me. He didn't look at me, either, and I told myself it was so he could stare Marc down. Keeping his voice low, he said, "You're right. Gallen Hall does belong to Anthony. But the cemetery doesn't. When Gallen Hall was sold all those years ago, the cemetery wasn't part of the deal. It was still owned by Vanderhorst descendants, until Nevin Vanderhorst willed it to Melanie. Which means that what is found in this cemetery belongs to her."

We all stared at Jack in stunned silence, until Marc struggled to find his voice. "You're lying."

"He's not," Jayne said. "After Melanie left tonight, I realized too late that Anthony might lay claim to the treasure and I wanted to know the legal implications." She shot a quick glance of apology in my direction. "So I told Jack everything, and he called Yvonne from the archives. She has access to several databases on her home computer and was able to look up the property deed to trace ownership. The cemetery wasn't included in any sale, remaining the property of the Vanderhorst family until Melanie inherited Nevin Vanderhorst's estate. She e-mailed me a copy, if you'd like to see it."

"This is ridiculous," Marc said, moving toward Jack just as Thomas took a step in Marc's direction. He fumbled with his words for a moment before a grin lifted his mouth. "You're still trespassing. To get to the cemetery you had to pass through private property and park your cars on land belonging to Anthony." He faced Thomas. "I want you to arrest these four people for trespassing."

"So much for family," I mumbled.

"So you'll have time to remove whatever is buried under those markers?" Jack said. "I think not."

Marc turned to Anthony. "Tell them, Anthony. Tell them that you want them off of your property now."

"Don't you dare," Jayne shouted, approaching Anthony with a raised hand. He didn't even bother to block her slap.

"Detective, that's physical assault," Marc shouted. "We are pressing charges and want her arrested."

"No." Anthony stepped away from where Marc was facing off with Jack. "We're not pressing charges. I deserved that."

He began to walk away, brushing roughly against his brother and making Marc stumble.

"Hey, what's your problem?" Marc said, rushing after Anthony and grabbing him by the shoulders. "You said it was easier than taking candy from a baby, remember?"

Anthony tried to pull back, but Marc wouldn't let go. He tilted his head as he stared at his younger brother. "You didn't sleep with her, did you? I told you not to complicate things."

Anthony drew his fist back for a punch, but before he could swing, Marc flew backward, propelled by an unseen force and thrown twenty feet before landing flat on his back with a grunt.

Thomas was the only one to move, rushing over to Marc. Instead of taking the offered hand to help him up, Marc twisted in the opposite direction, pulling himself to stand and angrily dusting the snow from the sleeves of his jacket. "What the—"

Before he could finish the sentence, he was knocked down again, then dragged through the snow by his feet toward the mausoleum. He clawed at the ground, trying to find purchase, his face showing his terror. Jayne and I both moved forward to help, but whatever was pulling him was too strong and fast. Before we reached him, the mausoleum had swallowed him, his head bumping like a rubber ball against the brick steps, the gate slamming in our faces. We wrapped our fingers around the bars and shook them, but the gate remained unyielding.

"Marc!" Anthony shouted as he and Thomas ran up behind us. Thomas had grabbed Marc's light, and he shone it inside, moving from one crypt to another, then back, looking for Marc.

"Marc!" Thomas shouted. Slowly, he trained the light on the top of Lawrence's crypt and paused. The lid had been slid back unevenly, a corner of it hanging over the edge, the opening big enough for a man to fit through.

"Is there another entrance to this?" Thomas asked.

I half listened to Anthony's answer as I became aware of two black shadows in front of Lawrence's crypt. As Jayne and I watched, the shadows took on human forms. I told my feet to back away, to start running as fast as they could in the opposite direction, but I was frozen, forced to stay and watch whatever was about to unfold. Lying prone, the red spot on his cravat larger now, was the man I recognized as Lawrence, and standing over him was an older man with graying hair pulled back in a ponytail and wearing a heavy cape. He turned to look at me, his cape billowing open and revealing a pistol in his hand. His eyes were piercing, asking me for something I couldn't understand.

"Forgiveness," Jayne whispered from beside me.

I nodded, because I knew that was the word I'd heard inside my head. It was the reason I wasn't afraid. I understood that I wasn't meant to be. And when I looked down at the prone figure of Lawrence, I understood something else, too.

"It's his father," Jayne whispered. "It was Carrollton Vanderhorst who killed him. He didn't feel as if he had a choice."

I nodded, knowing she was right. "Neither did Lawrence." I closed my eyes, trying to hear the voices in my head, to decipher the words that sounded as if they were out of order, nodding when I finally understood. "He felt betrayed by Eliza for being a spy and for loving another man, so he killed them both." I looked at the spirit of the old man, his face a mask of old grief. "Tell Lawrence you forgive him for what he did," I whispered. "So he can forgive you, too."

A soft rumbling vibrated the earth beneath us and I heard Anthony swear behind me.

"It's okay," Jayne said. "Their souls are being released."

The ground trembled one more time as lightning flashed through the sky above us, showering us with the smell of burnt ions and filling the mausoleum with a bright, bluish white light. When it had faded, the mausoleum was empty, the only sounds a low moaning from the direction of the opened crypt and the click of the gate latch as the door slowly began swinging open.

Anthony pushed it fully open and entered, Thomas and Jayne close behind. I felt a soft tug on my arm and turned around, thinking it was Jack, but no one was there. "Eliza?"

A firm push propelled me away from the mausoleum. I grabbed my phone and turned on the flashlight, unsure what had happened to my camping light. "Jack?" I called out. I spun around with my light, looking for him. I'd begun heading toward the front gate when a hard tug on my arm propelled me in the opposite direction.

I had taken only three steps before I saw it was Eliza, and where she was directing me. One of the soft dips that I had just navigated around during my gravestone search was now a gaping hole, a blemish on the pristine white ground.

"Jack!" I screamed. I ran to the edge of the hole and stared down at the mix of dark soil and snow, Rebecca's dream of Jack being buried alive playing like a movie reel in my head. "Jack!" I screamed again.

Jayne came from behind and knelt next to me. "There," she shouted, pointing to something pale and still near the bottom of the six-foot hole. "He's there."

I might have screamed again, the sight of Jack's closed eyes and pale face at the bottom of a grave too surreal to accept.

"I'll get help," Jayne said, moving to stand.

While she ran to get Thomas, I lowered myself into the pit, no longer feeling the cold or the fear of the last few hours. I didn't think about how I would get out of the pit or even whether it was done collapsing. I had no idea how many coffins had been buried here, or how deep. I didn't care. If something happened to Jack, nothing else would ever matter again.

His body was completely covered up to his nose with the dirt and snow. I carefully crawled over, taking care to distribute my weight evenly, until my fingers could reach his face and begin brushing the dirt off his chin and mouth. "Jack, it's Mellie. Don't talk—I've got to get the dirt off your face first. Just nod that you can hear me."

He didn't move or respond in any way, his face as still and colorless as the moon as he lay at the bottom of the grave, just as Rebecca had seen in her dreams.

Kiss him. I wasn't sure if the words had been spoken aloud, but I looked up at the edge of the collapsed grave and saw the British soldier standing next to Eliza, his arm around her. *Kiss him.*

I pinched Jack's nose closed and pressed my mouth against his and blew a deep breath. When nothing happened, I did it again, harder this time, imagining his lungs expanding with the air of my breath. He gasped, his eyes blinking open as he took a breath on his own, his eyelids fluttering until he caught sight of me.

"Oh, Jack. You're going to be okay. I'm here. It's Mellie. I found the rubies!" His eyes focused on me and I smiled. "I love you, Jack."

His eyes looked behind me to where Anthony and Thomas had replaced Eliza and Alexander and were peering at us from the top of the grave. Then Jack's eyes shifted back to me, and there was no warmth or light in them. "Go. To. Hell."

CHAPTER 35

The rest of the night was mostly a blur—the fire and rescue sirens, the ambulance, the trip to the hospital with Thomas and Jayne in the detective's four-wheel-drive truck. I remembered Jack turning his head away from me as they loaded him into the back of the ambulance and strapped him lying down into a bench seat, and I remembered the shock of seeing Marc as they slid his gurney in next to Jack. I didn't recognize him at first, and not because of the large, swollen bruise on the side of his face. It was because of his hair—his thick, dark brown hair had gone completely white, incongruous with his black eyebrows and unlined face. He asked me to call Rebecca, and I did, and that was the last coherent memory I had.

When I awoke the following morning, I was at my mother's house. I vaguely recalled her picking me up at the hospital and telling me that Jack was fine except for some bruising and a sprained ankle. They'd wanted to keep him overnight for observation, and even though I'd been prepared to wait and bring him home the next morning, he'd refused to see me and had requested someone else—anyone else—to drive him. I'd been too stunned to cry and allowed my mother to lead me from the hospital, as Jayne and Thomas had offered to stay and chauffeur Jack when he was discharged.

I sat up in my old bedroom, feeling disoriented, as if I'd been standing on a moving sidewalk that had suddenly stopped. I recalled Jack's hurtful words and could feel nothing but shame, knowing I'd deserved them. I needed my babies, needed to see them and hold them and talk with Nola and confirm we were all going to be all right. That Jack would forgive me. I threw off the covers and pulled on the green velvet dress I'd worn to the party the night before, then ran downstairs in search of my mother.

She was just putting down her cell phone when I walked into the kitchen. She was dressed and perfectly made-up, but her gaze didn't falter as she took in my unbrushed hair and wrinkled dress. "That was Amelia. She said the twins have been perfect angels and she's happy to keep them a little longer if you need her to. She already asked Nola to bring over more supplies just in case your answer was yes."

I opened my mouth to say something, but all that came out was a loud sob that quickly become a torrent of tears I couldn't stop. She came over to me and enveloped me in a warm and sweetly scented embrace, bringing back old memories of when I was a little girl. The girl I'd been before she'd left me behind.

My mother brought me into the parlor and sat me down on the couch, where I continued to sob for five minutes, until I had no more tears left. She waited a moment before pulling back and lifting my chin with her fingers.

"So, what are you going to do, Mellie?"

"You know?" I sniffled.

She nodded. "When Jayne called me to tell me you were all at the hospital, she filled me in on what happened." She kept all judgment from her voice, making me so grateful that I cried a fresh torrent of tears.

When I was done, I wiped my eyes with the back of my hand, recalling what she'd just said. This wasn't how I'd anticipated the conversation going. I'd envisioned her commiserating with me, telling me that even though things hadn't turned out as planned, I'd been smart and resourceful and everything had worked out all right in the end. And then I'd sit and listen while she told me what I needed to do next. When she didn't speak, I asked, "So, what should I do now?"

"You've really hurt Jack, Mellie. And your marriage. The damage might even be irreparable."

I stood abruptly. "Why are you saying this? I thought you would be on my side."

"I *am* on your side. That's why I'm saying this. Because someone has to. You deliberately kept Jack in the dark so you, for reasons I've yet to determine, could solve a mystery and keep the glory all for yourself. Even though you'd promised Jack you wouldn't. You lied to him, Mellie, and now you expect him to applaud your cleverness. That's not how a good marriage works. I thought you'd already learned that, but apparently I was wrong."

I felt the strong impulse to find a disconnected phone and call my grandmother.

"She'd tell you the same thing." My mother looked at me with knowing eyes. "No, I can't read minds, but I know how you think. And finding someone to agree with you is not how you mature. Sometimes you remind me of a moth at a porch light, thinking that if it hits the light one more time it will get a different result. I'd like to think you're smarter than that."

I sat back down on the couch, deflated. "So what do I do?"

"What do you think you should do?"

She raised her brows as my eyes met hers. "Apologize?"

"That would be a good start. It won't be enough, but it's a start."

My heart jerked and skidded. "What do you mean, it won't be enough?"

"You've apologized before, remember? And made promises. But neither seemed to be important enough to you. You have to find a way to really mean it, and to make sure he knows it. Just realize that it won't happen overnight. Assuming he can forgive you." She took my hand. "Mellie, I know I'm partly why you are the way you are. I abandoned you, leaving you to be raised by your alcoholic father. To survive your childhood you decided to rely only on yourself. And I'm so proud of you, of how you've succeeded despite everything. I think your resistance to change is because you've never wanted to forget how far you've come since you were that lonely little girl. Or that you've done it all by yourself." She squeezed my hand. "But just because you might rely on someone else doesn't negate any of where you've been or what you are. You need to learn to accept that."

I shook my head. "I'm *not* resisting change. I want to change—I'm ready for it. I just need to let Jack know." I stood up again. "I'll go over there right now."

My mother let go of my hands with a sigh. I marched to the door and yanked it open. "Oh." The street was indistinguishable from the curbs or sidewalks under the white layer of snow, the points at the tops of the iron fencing less menacing with their caps of white.

Mother came from behind me and shut the door. "May I suggest a shower and hair brushing first? There are new toothbrushes and toothpaste in the linen closet in your bathroom, and you can use my makeup. I'll leave an outfit on your bed—something in a bright and cheerful color—and your snow boots are on the back porch steps and your coat is in the hall closet. Carry your heels so you can put them on when you go talk to Jack. Men do love high heels."

"And you think that will work?"

She shook her head. "No. But it can't hurt."

I frowned. "Maybe I should walk barefoot through the snow to let him know how sorry I am."

"It might be worth a try," Mother said, embracing me. Holding me at arm's length, she added, "Jack loves you so much, Mellie. And you love him, too. And you've got those two precious babies and Nola, who need you two to make this work. Love is a great foundation, but there has to be trust, too. Sadly, trust is a lot harder to maintain than love. You're going to have to work very, very hard to regain his trust." She stepped back, eyeing me up and down. "The only thing I know for sure is that looking like a hot mess isn't a good way to start. And it will give you time to think about what you want to say. You know how badly things can go when you act and speak rashly."

I hurried away up the stairs before I began to sob again.

The winter wonderland I crossed on my walk home was something out of a storybook. Amelia texted me a photograph of the twins bundled up like Eskimos sitting in the snow next to a snowman with stick arms and a carrot nose and what looked like Oreo cookie eyes. The picture made me want to cry, so I slipped my phone back in my pocket and continued to trudge down the street.

The temperature had already begun to climb with the rising of the sun in a cloudless blue sky. The sound of dripping gutters and tree branches tittered along both sides of the street like happy birdsong. Children and adults alike were outside using anything they could find for sleds—including flattened cardboard boxes and inner tubes—spending most of their time looking for something that resembled a hill to slide down. I returned smiles and waves, but my heart felt as frozen as the snow beneath my boots.

My house on Tradd Street was oddly quiet when I opened the front door, only the sounds of the Sunday church bells from St. Michael's echoing throughout the vacant rooms. Someone—probably my dad— had moved the furniture back into position, the temporary tables and chairs already folded and stacked in the dining room to be picked up the following day by the rental company.

The house had the sad, empty air of finality, the laughter and chatter of so many people ushered outside leaving behind only silence. Even the wandering spirits that lived there were suddenly absent, either exhausted from all the activity of the party, or worried about what was going to happen next. Or maybe that was just me.

"Jack?" I called, slipping out of my boots and putting on my heels.

I heard movement from upstairs, but no one responded.

"Jack?" I called again, climbing the stairs quickly. I stood at the top, aware of the lightness in the air, as if it had just been cleansed.

I peered into Nola's room and spotted the jewelry cabinet, all the drawers and the top neatly closed. I thought of the hidden compartment and imagined Eliza bending forward and hiding the brooch with the four disguised rubies. I remembered examining it with Sophie, how she'd said the hinges were broken because the door had been ripped off as if by an impatient hand. I pictured Lawrence threatening Eliza to tell him where the rubies were, or spying on her to discover where they'd been hidden. He'd killed her regardless, making it look like suicide. And his own father had killed him as punishment or to get the rubies back; we'd never know. But they had made their peace with each other in the mausoleum, and Eliza and Alexander were gone, too, together finally for all eternity. Since they'd helped me find Jack, I'd no longer felt their presence. It felt good to know we'd helped one another, a connection through time that I was lucky enough to experience. I'd never thought of it that way before, and I felt my chest expand as I considered the implications.

I paused on the threshold, the white world outside bathing the walls in bright reflected light from the snow, and took a deep breath. It was as if the world was agreeing that it was time for a new start. A commitment to a new way of being. Feeling emboldened, I headed down the hallway to the bedroom I shared with Jack.

The door was slightly ajar, and I pushed it open, expecting to find Jack in bed with tissues in a wastebasket next to him. Instead, the bed had been made, and a suitcase was opened on top of it with several of Jack's sweaters, shirts, socks, and underclothes already packed neatly inside.

"Jack?" I called again, my voice thready.

He emerged from the bathroom carrying his dopp kit, limping on his wrapped ankle. He didn't even glance in my direction as he walked past me toward his suitcase.

"What are you doing?"

"I'm packing." He moved a few shirts around to make room for the dopp kit, then closed the case, the sound from the zipper horrifyingly final.

"Packing? But why? You're sick and you're hurt. You should be in bed."

"I will be. My parents' rental apartment on State Street is vacant and they're letting me use it."

The breath rushed from my lungs and I had to grab the bedpost to stay upright. "But . . . but you don't need to leave. I came to apologize. To tell you I know I was wrong, that I shouldn't have left on my own last night and without telling you what was going on. It was stupid and rash, and I did it anyway." I looked up at him imploringly. "But I've learned my lesson. I won't ever break your trust again. I've changed. I really have. Last night taught me that I have people in my life who love me and who I can rely on. I don't have to go it alone."

As if I hadn't spoken, he picked up his suitcase and walked out to the hallway and then down the stairs. I rushed after him. "Jack, stop. Please. I said I was sorry."

He stopped and looked back at me, his face devoid of all emotion except anger. "It's too little, too late. I'll let you know when I'd like to see JJ and Sarah so we can work out a visiting arrangement."

"A visiting arrangement? How long are you planning to be gone?"

He shook his head. "I have no idea. I need time away from you to think."

"To think? About what? I love you, and I said I'm sorry. I've changed—please give me a chance to show it."

"I've given you more chances than I can count. I just can't live this way anymore. I love you, but it's not enough. Not when I can't trust you."

He took his coat from the closet and put it on. I wanted to throw myself at him, cling to his lapels and force him to stay, regardless of how degrading that would be. I was already hollowed out, scraped clean, with only my empty shell remaining. I had no pride or shame left, just the sickening feeling that I had lost Jack, and I had no one to blame but myself.

"I'll be back this week while you're at work to get the rest of my things." He frowned. "Nola wants to stay here, although she says she's not taking sides. She says she's tired of acting like the only adult around here." His gaze traveled around the foyer as if seeing it for the last time. "How right she is."

He headed to the front door and opened it. I followed him, hoping for one gesture, one look that would tell me there was hope. He stepped over the same threshold he'd carried me over on our wedding day and met my eyes. I held my breath, waiting.

"Good-bye, Mellie." The door closed in my face with a gentle snap.

I stood there without moving, staring at the closed door and listening to the grandfather clock chime every fifteen minutes while the light outside grew dimmer and dimmer as I waited for the worst day of my life to be over.

CHAPTER 36

A week later I sat at Jack's empty desk in his study, attempting to address Christmas cards and trying not to notice that the framed photos of Nola and the twins were gone but the ones of me remained. I wasn't sure what hurt more—that or Jack's empty drawers and closet upstairs in the bedroom we'd shared. I stared at the happy photo of all of us that Rich Kobylt had taken at the Pineapple Fountain, the twins in their mismatched outfits and the dogs wearing nothing at all. And there was Jack, the center of all our lives, his arm casually thrown around me as I looked up at him with a wide smile.

I felt the familiar knot in my throat as I closed a card and shoved it into an envelope. I'd thought about not sending them this year, as if I might be perpetuating a lie. But the little stubbornness I clung to allowed me to believe that Jack would come back. I would give up coffee and doughnuts for life if I could be permitted to hang on to that one bit of stubbornness that made it possible to get out of bed each morning and face a new day.

My phone buzzed and I felt the thrill of anticipation as I looked at the screen to see if it was Jack. Even the short, terse texts regarding his scheduled visits with the twins gave me a lift, as these notifications were proof that he hadn't forgotten my existence. It was the best I could hope for right now.

This text was from Suzy Dorf, reminding me of our chat when she'd asked me to let her interview me about talking with ghosts. She'd offered that in exchange for not telling Rebecca what she'd discovered about the Vanderhorsts and the spy ring. Not that any of that mattered anymore. I wished she'd been in the cemetery the night Marc was dragged into the mausoleum. That might have killed two birds with one stone.

I slid my thumb across the screen to erase the text and pretended I hadn't seen it, promising myself that I would do the grown-up thing and call her back. Just not right now. I hadn't even put the phone back down when something soft struck me in the back of the head. I looked at the floor where the object had fallen and saw Adrienne's red heart-shaped pillow. It had been in my closet on the back of a shelf the last time I'd seen it.

I picked it up and was fingering the ruffled edge when the doorbell rang. My heart skittered, and I almost heard Jack's words in my head about there being no such thing as coincidence. I ran across the foyer to throw open the door, then stood staring at my visitors, forgetting to hide my disappointment that it wasn't Jack bringing back the twins himself instead of using Jayne as our go-between.

Instead Jayne, Veronica, and Rebecca stood on the piazza with bright smiles and what looked like a large doughnut box from Glazed, the sugary smell wafting toward me. When I didn't say anything, Veronica said, "We thought we'd stop by to cheer you up."

I tried to smile, to thank them for their kindness, but I failed miserably as my lips would only tremble. "Unless Jack is in that box, I don't think there's anything you can do to cheer me up right now." I blinked rapidly, embarrassed to find myself on the verge of tears. Again. I thought I'd reached the point of having none left, wishing I could stop so I wouldn't have to keep telling my work associates and clients that I had winter allergies.

"Oh, Melanie," Jayne said, stepping forward and enveloping me in a hug as the others moved past us into the foyer. "We—and the doughnuts—are here to get you through this. And you will get through this."

I sniffled into her shoulder. "But I don't want to get through this. I just want him back."

"Come with us," Veronica said, steering us all into the parlor.

Mrs. Houlihan appeared and greeted everyone, then returned shortly with a tray carrying coffee, cups, and a plate of her Christmas cookies, and placed it in front of me. She patted my shoulder as she left, either in commiseration or as an apology for depriving me all season of her baking confections. I smiled my thanks, although I knew I couldn't eat anything. She'd been tempting me with all my favorite foods, but I could barely find the energy or enthusiasm to do much more than rearrange the food on my plate to make it look like I'd eaten more than a bite or two.

Jayne poured my coffee, heaping in all the sugar and cream that she knew I liked, then filled a plate with a tiramisu doughnut and three of Mrs. Houlihan's cookies.

"Thank you," I said, then took a sip of the coffee and barely tasted it.

Veronica looked at the red pillow I'd placed on the coffee table. "Is that Adrienne's?"

I nodded. "It hit me in the head right before the doorbell rang."

The three of them exchanged glances. "Perfect," Rebecca said. I almost did a double take. She wasn't wearing pink, but a subtle shade of mauve. She caught me looking and said, "I felt the bright pink next to Marc's new white hair was too startling, so I've toned it down a notch. Plus, I think I'll save the brighter shades of pink for after our daughter is born."

"A daughter?" I took another sip of my coffee.

"I had a dream," she said, looking around at the other two women. "Before I was pregnant and got blocked." A small V appeared between her brows. "Around the same time, I had another dream." She paused.

"Go on," Jayne said gently.

Rebecca nodded. "I dreamed that the three of us were at Veronica's house." She swallowed. "Adrienne was there, too, pointing at something around her neck. And there was someone else—someone in the attic. And the house . . ."

"The house was on fire," Veronica finished.

"So we thought . . ." Jayne started.

Rebecca continued. "That it meant we're all supposed to pool our resources and help Veronica find out what happened to Adrienne. To stop the fire, even. You did promise to help her, Melanie." Rebecca gave me the same look I usually reserved for the twins when they didn't eat their vegetables.

"How is this supposed to help me get Jack back?" I sounded as pathetic as I felt.

"Melanie," Jayne said softly. "Helping others is the best way to take our own worries away. And while you're thinking about something else is usually when the solution to your own problems starts untangling in your head. It's a win-win." She smiled at me, and I was ashamed of all the times I'd felt envious of, well, everything about her.

I looked up at the ceiling to stem the new flood of tears before turning back to her. "I'm glad you're my sister, Jayne. I can't tell you how much. And you have my permission to slap me if I ever forget that."

She laughed. "Well, if you could have seen the bruise on Anthony's face, you might change your mind. And, no, I haven't seen him—I have no interest in seeing him ever again—but Rebecca sent me a picture from her phone. I might have missed my calling. Be a prizefighter instead of a nanny."

"Although," Rebecca said, "I think you can call it even now. He hired security for the cemetery until he could find someone to dig up the peacocks' graves. He didn't even try to keep the rubies for himself."

Jayne sniffed. "Because that was the right thing to do. But I still never want to see him again as long as I live."

Veronica pinched a bite from a doughnut, leaving the rest on her plate. "I hope you have those rubies in a secure place, Melanie. Especially after all you've been through to get them."

"They're in a safe-deposit box at our bank until Jack and I decide what we're going to do with them." I'd refused to make any decisions regarding our windfall. I'd wait as long as it took to get Jack back, and then we'd decide together.

Jayne's eyes were warm as she took my hand. "But in the meantime, I want you to think about using your gift. There is so much good we can do. Even after we help Veronica and Adrienne. Thomas has files and files of unsolved cases. And let's not forget that flapper at the Francis Marion Hotel."

Rebecca leaned forward in her chair. "Since my gift is on hiatus for the next six months, I can put all my skills of attracting men to help you win Jack back."

"But . . ." I stopped, thinking about her own marital issues but not wanting to sound rude.

"I know. Marc and I have had our problems. But ever since the . . . incident . . . in the cemetery, he's been quite attentive. He barely leaves my side. I don't know if it's because he's decided he really wants to be with me and embrace impending fatherhood, or if he's just scared witless and doesn't want to be alone. Regardless, I do know a few tricks to keep a man interested and I'm willing to share everything I know with you."

I frowned at her. "What I'd really like you to do is talk Marc out of filming in my house. Then I'll believe he's changed."

Rebecca's large blue eyes watered as she regarded me. "It's not him, Melanie—it's that Harvey person. He won't be talked out of it. And because you and Jack signed the contract, you can't back out. I'm sorry."

I had to blink, feeling my eyes begin to water again.

Veronica turned to me. "You and Jack are the most perfect couple, Melanie. Anybody can see the love you have for each other and your children. This is a rough patch, but all good marriages have them, and they're stronger on the other side because of it. You will work this out—I'm sure of it. And you've got friends and family to help and support you. You know that, right?"

I nodded, unable to speak, as I'd started to cry again. We all ended up in a group hug, sobbing and laughing together, none of us really surprised when the red pillow flew up in the air and landed in Veronica's lap.

EPILOGUE

POST AND COURIER

December 21

by SUZY DORF

Dear Readers,

Many of you have written to thank me for my recent series on hidden treasures in Charleston and the Lowcountry, urging me to continue. I must confess that your enthusiasm alone would encourage me to write more, even if it weren't one of my favorite topics. And while we're talking of topics, please continue to send in your requests for future columns. One never knows what might be discovered by shining a light in a long-darkened corner.

Speaking of long-darkened corners, several of you have asked me about the hullabaloo at the Gallen Hall cemetery the night of the Big Snow. Apparently, much news coverage was dedicated to the five inches of white stuff that covered our city, so that other news was overlooked in the excitement. Some of you inquired as to whether the apparent owner of the land upon which the cemetery sits, and who has been mentioned in this column more than once, might have been involved. Let's just say that this story deserves its own column, with enough room for all the salacious details, of which, I assure you, there are many.

Please keep your eyes trained on this column each Sunday for new revelations and stories centered around our fair city and its citizens, both living and dead. And those in between. I am confident that there will be much material to be discussed in the near future, as a source close to most of the strange goings-on in the Holy City has recently experienced a change of heart that this writer is much excited about.

As for unfinished business related to my previous series on the historic homes in Charleston, please know that the cistern excavation at the former Vanderhorst residence on Tradd Street is still in progress, but an unnamed source has told me that there are more secrets hidden there, and there are bets going on in certain parts of our society on whether the owners of the house will be residing together in the home by the time the last treasure is revealed.

Until next time,
Happy reading

THE
CHRISTMAS SPIRITS
ON TRADD STREET

KAREN WHITE

Questions for Discussion

1. We have seen Melanie grow up in so many ways throughout the series and in this book. Why do you think she allows her insecurity to get the best of her and her relationship with Jack?

2. Family can be wonderful but can also be tricky to deal with. In the case of Marc and Anthony, how do you think two brothers who were raised in the same home can grow up to be such different people?

3. Speaking of family, how would you describe the dynamic between Rebecca and Melanie? What caused their relationship to dissolve and what causes it to grow closer again? Is blood truly thicker than water?

4. Jack loves Melanie for who she is and accepts her faults. Why do you think Jack couldn't tell Melanie the truth about what happened to him, his editor, and his book? Do you think he was bound by the sense that he needed to support his family or to show the same level of independence that Melanie exhibits?

5. Melanie has the ability to see and interact with ghosts. Would you want that ability and would you do what Melanie does to help enable the ghosts to rest in peace? Or would you ignore your ability?

6. Marriage plays a prominent role in the book, and we see many different aspects of it—the good and the rough parts. Did you like seeing both Melanie and Jack's tender moments and their moments of frustration? Could you relate to the ups and downs?

7. Why do you think Melanie feels she has to be the one to solve everyone's problems? Why is she unable to allow herself to accept help from others, including from her parents and Jack?

8. In the next (and final) book in the series, where do you expect to find the characters—especially Melanie and Jack?

Read on for an excerpt from
Karen White's next novel,

THE LAST NIGHT IN LONDON

Available in spring 2021 from Berkley

The cool, clear night shuddered, then moaned as the fluctuating drone of hundreds of engines eclipsed the silence. A wave of planes like angry hornets slipped through the darkened sky over a city already wearing black in preparation for the inevitable mourning.

She tasted dust and burnt embers in the back of her throat as she hurried through a crowd of stragglers running toward a shelter. A man grabbed her arm, as if to correct her movement, but an explosion nearby made him release his hold and hurry after the crowd. She shifted the valise she cradled in her arms, the pressure on her chest making it difficult to breathe. Fatigue and pain battered her body, both eagerly welcomed, as they disguised the bruise of overwhelming grief. She staggered forward, the blood dripping unchecked from her leg and forehead, the acrid stench of explosives mixed with the sharp smell of death.

Gingerly, she moved through the darkened high street so familiar in the daylight but foreign to her now. The night sky blossomed with fire and scarlet light as the loud bark of the antiaircraft guns answered the banshee wails of the warning sirens. Pressing herself against a wall, as if she could hide from the noise and the sounds and the terror, she closed her eyes. *Moonlight Sonata.* Someone, she couldn't remember who, in an underground club perhaps, had whispered that that was what he called the music of the nightly bombings. She'd thought then it had been a beautiful sentiment, that it was a wonderful way to make something good out of something so terrible. But she'd been younger then. More willing to accept that the world still held on to its beauty when everything lay charred and smoldering, with roofless structures like starving baby birds, mouths open to a useless sky.

Another incendiary bomb fell nearby. Another fireball lurched upward. Another building, another home, another life destroyed as the haphazard finger of fortune pointed with random carelessness. The sidewalk rumbled beneath her, causing her to stumble into the street, almost losing hold of her precious bundle. The shrill whistle of an air raid warden rang out, the sound padded into near oblivion by the thunder of the engines above them. The baby lay still as she ran, the partially closed top of the valise protecting him from the ashes that drifted from burning buildings.

She ducked into a doorway to catch her breath, oddly grateful to the fires for lighting her way. Fairly certain she was on Mac Farren Place, she flattened herself against a recessed door, imagining she could hear approaching footsteps coming for her. She needed to keep running until she reached her destination. She wasn't sure what she'd do after that, but she'd think about it then.

Another wave of planes slithered overhead, the rumble of their engines echoing in her bones. She was tempted to collapse on the doorstep and remain there until dawn or death, whichever came first. But she couldn't. She felt the heft of the valise in her arms again, a small movement within it reminding her of why she couldn't give up.

She stood, planting her feet wide for balance and for the false sense of strength it seemed to give her. As the world vibrated beneath her, she clung to that tenuous spark of will that wouldn't allow her to stop. It pushed her out onto the street again to begin moving as the roar of the next approaching wave of planes galloped behind her.

She hid in another doorway as the planes flew overhead, letting go of their bombs as they neared Oxford Street. Her shoulders and arms ached from carrying the valise. How could such a small thing seem to weigh so much? But she couldn't stop. Not now. Not after everything that had happened. One more loss would be insurmountable, the largest and final hole in her cup of luck.

Her ears rang from the cacophony of destruction raining down around her, the coppery tang of blood filling her mouth from biting her lip to keep it from trembling. A stray bomb could explode on top of her and her precious cargo regardless of its intended target, the erratic hands of fate never quite sure where to land.

Avoiding wardens and anyone else who would veer her off course, she continued to hurry forward until she reached Davies Street and the square of beautiful Georgian terrace houses now sheathed in black, the windows darkened like sleeping eyes. She knew the house, had been inside it even. Knew that the basement was being used as a private bomb shelter, one complete with electricity and stocked with food and soft mattresses and blankets. But that was not why she was there. She wouldn't be staying.

The flashing white undersides of an air warden's gloves beckoned two women dressed as if they'd just been dragged from a party; they stumbled toward him as he guided them to a public shelter. Holding the valise closer, she pressed herself against the wrought iron fence of the house, ducking her face to hide its paleness. When the three disappeared, she moved cautiously along the fence, then unlatched the gate. Carefully taking the steps down to the lower level, she turned the doorknob, not thinking until she did so of what she'd do if it was locked.

The door opened to an unoccupied room, filled only with mattresses and cushions piled against the windows and walls, the flickering firelight from outside showing her a closed door across the room. Memorizing her path, she shut the door behind her, enveloping herself in complete darkness. Soft murmuring voices came from behind the door opposite as she approached. She stopped in front of it and raised her hand to knock, then paused to mouth an old prayer she remembered from childhood to a God she no longer thought listened. "Amen," she whispered to the dark when she was finished, then brought her knuckles down sharply against the wood.

The voices stopped, and she held her breath as footsteps approached.

"Hello?" A woman's voice, clear and refined. English.

Her knees almost buckled with relief. "It's me. Please open the door."

The door was jerked open, allowing her to see inside the small room with the tidy cots around the perimeter, a small crystal lamp sparkling from the polished surface of a round table with cabriole legs. If she hadn't been so exhausted, she might have laughed at the absurdity of crystal and fine furniture in such a place, at such a time, when the world above was being smothered with ashes and blood. The person she'd been might have been amused. But she wasn't that person anymore.

The woman looked out into the darkened street as if expecting to see two other people seeking refuge.

"I'm alone. There's no one else."

A look of understanding and grief crossed the woman's face before she nodded briefly and straightened her shoulders. "You're hurt," the woman said, her fine skin glowing like alabaster in the lamplight. Reaching out manicured hands with scarlet nails, she said, "Come in. Quickly. We have a doctor."

She shook her head. "I can't. I have to go." For the first time, she relaxed her hold on the valise. Setting it down, she picked up the baby, his soft body stirring sleepily in her arms. Pressing her lips against the smooth forehead, she smelled deeply, the stench of the torn night erased by the sweet scent of new life. She lifted her head, then handed him over before she could change her mind and be the ruin of them all.

The woman's pale eyes widened with surprise, then understanding, as she accepted the child, pressing him against her chest, an unasked question dancing in the air between them.

"I've got to go back. He . . ." Her arm gestered aimlessly. "It might not be too late. . . ." Despair escaped from her chest and filled her mouth.

"But you can't leave. Not now. There's a raid. . . ."

"I have to. There's no one else." A sob caught in her throat. "I have to try." Her eyes moved to the squirming bundle, but she dragged them away.

The woman hadn't reacted to the news except for a quick intake of breath. With studied composure, she said, "But you're hurt. Surely you can wait five more minutes."

"No." She shook her head. "I've already stayed too long." She took a step back to emphasize her words. "I think they might be looking for me."

"All the more reason you should stay here. We can keep you safe. We can help you get the proper papers. . . ."

As if the woman hadn't spoken, she said, "You'll take care of the baby?"

"Of course. But—"

"Good."

The woman looked so lovely standing there, with the light prisms sparkling against the wall behind her as she held the baby. She'd done the right thing, coming here. "Be safe," the woman said. "But this won't be good-bye. We'll see each other again, when this is all over."

"I hope so," she said, allowing her eyes to rest on the pale moon of the baby's cheek for just a flicker. She took another step backward. "When this is all over." She turned and let herself out of the second door and back into the wounded night.

She passed through the gate and hurried toward the street corner and paused, getting her bearings, knowing only that she had to keep running. Just for a moment, she allowed herself to close her eyes, to see the baby's face again one last time.

A high, keening shriek split the air around her, jerking open her eyes. Her chest heaved from the percussion of the bomb hitting the building across the street, bricks and glass and plaster being thrown into the air like the discarded toys of a petulant child. Something hard struck her in the back between her shoulder blades, throwing her against the pavement, knocking her to her hands and knees. The stray thought of how she'd never be able to repair the damage to her clothing trickled across her brain as she watched the debris falling in slow motion around her, a lit piece of floral wallpaper drifting down and extinguishing itself on the sidewalk.

She struggled to stand, pain radiating like fever, the bleeding scrapes on her palms and forehead merely an afterthought. Her right leg buckled under her, her knee bending in a way it wasn't intended to. *No, no, no. Not now. Not like this.* Sucking in her breath, she began to crawl back to the shelter, a fading glimmer of self-preservation driving her forward, defeat nipping at her heels.

Darkness danced behind her eyes, seductively calling to her. She fought it as she pulled herself up on the gate, reaching for the latch, forcing herself to stay conscious as she felt for the release. Propelling herself forward with her elbows, she tumbled down the steps, her body landing against the door with a thump, her face turned toward the sky in silent supplication. For a brief moment she imagined she was walking in sand, the sound of a distant ocean teasing the air. *Home.* It was there, as it always had been, just beyond her reach.

Please. The word echoed inside her head, but her lips remained mute as the darkness overcame her and the sky above screamed with a thousand unanswered prayers.

Author photo by Marchet Butler

Karen White is the *New York Times* bestselling author of more than twenty novels, including the Tradd Street series, *Dreams of Falling*, *The Night the Lights Went Out*, *Flight Patterns*, *The Sound of Glass*, *A Long Time Gone*, and *The Time Between*. She is the coauthor of *The Forgotten Room* and *The Glass Ocean* with *New York Times* bestselling authors Beatriz Williams and Lauren Willig. She grew up in London but now lives with her husband and two dogs near Atlanta, Georgia.

Karen-White.com
KarenWhiteAuthor
KarenWhiteWrite
KarenWhiteWrite